MAGNIFICENT PRAISE FOR MANDA SCOTT'S
BOUDICA NOVELS

BOUDICA: DREAMING THE BULL

"Readers will be swept away to the blood-drenched lands of Britannia and the scheming city of Rome. Battle scenes are full of action, and readers who skip the military strategies will miss the most telling moments of characters and story. Suggest this thrilling historical novel, with its sympathetic characters and suspenseful plot, to fans of Arthurian fantasy and romantic historical fiction." —*Booklist* (starred review)

"Finely and lyrically written . . . A deeply emotional and affecting work."
—*Publishers Weekly*

"One of the boldest of recent adventures in historical fiction . . . [a] richly textured, robustly plotted yarn . . . Scott celebrates the mystic matriarchy of the British tribes with lush lyricism and story-weaving panache. . . . Strong, sophisticated fare." —*Independent* (UK)

"The best of the current crop of novels about Rome, its empire and its victims . . . Scott is almost as good on the authoritarian, rational piety of the best of the Roman invaders as she is on the wild, intense spirituality of her Druids and women warriors. . . . Scott has an intense visual sense [and] passion." —*Independent Magazine* (UK)

"Many authors attempt historical novels, but few succeed as admirably as Manda Scott. . . . In *Dreaming the Bull*, she is at the top of her form. . . . Reminiscent of the classical historical recreations of Robert Graves, Mary Renault, or Rosemary Sutcliff, *Dreaming the Bull* combines the best of history and fiction. . . . Skillful plotting, stirring action and intrigue, penetrating character insights, and vivid observations of the elements, the seasons, the customs, and the motivations of an ancient civilization fighting for its life on both a human and heroic scale." —*Advocate*

BOUDICA: DREAMING THE EAGLE

"A powerful novel about one of the most intriguing and mysterious women in history. Scott has done her research, and the mix of real images and her imagination has created a completely believable world. Her characters are so true to life that they all but jump off the page, and the story is alive with the love, deceit, wisdom and heroics of humanity. Read it and enjoy!" —Jean M. Auel

"The new Mary Renault . . . A truly remarkable story full of wonderful atmosphere . . . Intensely exciting, a tale of passion, courage and heroism against huge odds, which is intensely moving." —*Publishing News*

"A staggeringly imaginative invocation of Britain's secret history. Manda Scott has created a fictional universe all her own, but close enough to our reality for it to both warm and break our hearts. Breathtakingly good, it reveals the best and worst in all of us." —Val McDermid

"What's amazing to me about this tale of Boudica, Britain's legendary female warrior, is the pitch-perfect fluency with which Manda Scott brings it forth. It's not like a contemporary writer crafting historical fiction; it's like an eyewitness recounting real events that she really saw and really participated in. It's even better than that because Ms. Scott's reimagining of this age, when the tribes of Britain clashed with the legions of Rome, includes interior monologues, multiple points of view, dreams, visions, ecstasies, and interlocutions with the dead, all of it utterly convincing and compelling, and made even more astonishing because historical sources for this era are virtually nil. All of this came out of Ms. Scott's heart and head. A stunning feat of the imagination and an absolute must-read for lovers of historical fiction."
—Steven Pressfield, author of *Tides of War* and *Gates of Fire*

"Manda Scott has created a book to stir the hearts and souls."
—Leslie Forbes, bestselling author of *Fish, Blood and Bone*

"A masterpiece of historical fiction, Scott's richly detailed novel brilliantly captures the driven, passionate soul of the Celts. The lyric prose captivates, the characters ensnare. In Scott's talented hands, the legendary Celtic queen Boudica breathes, lives, and absolutely rivets."
—Karen Marie Moning

ALSO BY MANDA SCOTT

HEN'S TEETH
NIGHT MARES
STRONGER THAN DEATH
NO GOOD DEED

BOUDICA: DREAMING THE EAGLE

AND COMING SOON
BOUDICA: DREAMING THE HOUND

BOUDICA:

DREAMING THE BULL

Manda Scott

Delta Trade Paperbacks

BOUDICA: DREAMING THE BULL
A Delta Book

PUBLISHING HISTORY
Delacorte Press hardcover edition published May 2004
Delta trade paperback edition / June 2005

Published by
Bantam Dell
A Division of Random House, Inc.
New York, New York

Book design by Karin Batten

Library of Congress Catalog Card Number: 2003070044

Delta is a registered trademark of Random House, Inc., and the colophon is a
trademark of Random House, Inc.

ISBN 0-385-33774-4

Printed in the United States of America
Published simultaneously in Canada

www.bantamdell.com

BVG   10   9   8   7   6   5   4   3   2   1

FOR KATHRIN

ACKNOWLEDGEMENTS

Heartfelt thanks to H.J.P. "Douglas" Arnold, Roman military historian and astronomer, for his unfailingly cheerful reading of the various drafts of this novel and its predecessor and for his insight, honesty, and accuracy; without him, the writing and research of the Boudican era would have been immeasurably harder and the result far less coherent. As ever, there are places where I chose to ignore his advice, and any inaccuracies of fact or concept are entirely my responsibility. Thanks to Robin and Aggy for input on caves and for general support in the writing. Thanks of an entirely different nature to Debs, Naziema, Carol, and Chloë, who, at various times and in various ways, kept the realities together, and to Tony, for friendship, grounding, and thoughtful sanity. Thanks in perpetuity to my agent, Jane Judd, and especially to my editors on both sides of the Atlantic for their care, insight, and stamina. Finally, thanks to all those who have shared the dream and do so still.

CONTENTS

CHARACTER LIST

THE ECENI

The Eceni: a confederacy of Iron Age tribes inhabiting what is now east Anglia in southeast England. A largely agrarian community, they are famed as horsebreeders and as workers of precious metals. Ferociously anti-Roman.

Airmid of Nemain: Dreamer of the Eceni, later of Mona; friend and companion to Breaca

Bán: Breaca's half-brother; hare-hunter and dreamer of the horse, son to Macha and Eburovic

Breaca: Eceni warrior, dreamer of the serpent-spear; also known as the Boudica, "She Who Brings Victory"

Dubornos: Singer and warrior; childhood companion to Bán and Breaca

Eburovic: Breaca's father; warrior and smith of the Eceni; now dead

Efnís: Dreamer of the northern Eceni

Graine: Breaca's mother; hereditary leader of the Eceni; now dead

Hail: Bán's hound

Macha: Graine's sister; dreamer of the wren, mother to Bán; now dead

Silla: Bán's younger sister by Eburovic out of Macha

ELDERS, DREAMERS, AND WARRIORS OF MONA (ANGLESEY)

Mona, known today as Anglesey, is the sacred island where selected dreamers and warriors from all tribes (including Eceni, Caledonii, Cornovii, Brigantes, Silures, and Votadini) are sent for training under the foremost dreamers in a tradition going back centuries, if not millennia. The dreamers' training takes up to twelve years, warriors' somewhat less. Once trained, the apprentices return to their tribes to bring the teaching to their people.

Ardacos: A warrior of the Caledonii; former lover to Breaca

Gwyddhien: A warrior of the Silures; lover to Airmid

Luain mac Calma: A singer, healer, and dreamer of the elder council of Mona, originally from Hibernia (Ireland)

THE TRINOVANTES

The Trinovantes were originally led by Cunobelin, Hound of the Sun, war leader both of this tribe and the Catuvellauni. He was a warrior and diplomat and held the sworn oath of more warriors than any other leader south of the Brigantes. He controlled the rich ports of the Thames and thus controlled a large part of the trade with Rome. He kept a difficult balance, maintaining diplomatic relationships with Rome while not offending the anti-Roman tribes, particularly his northern neighbours, the Eceni. Of Cunobelin's three sons, only Amminios (cf) was loyal to Rome.

Amminios: Second son of Cunobelin; born to a Gaulish woman; a friend to Rome; now dead

Caradoc: The third son of Cunobelin; born to Ellin, war leader of the Ordovices; lover to Breaca; father to Cygfa and Cunomar. Caradoc is the only warrior ever to have passed the warrior's test of three separate tribes; coleader of the western resistance against Rome

Cunobelin: Of the line of Cassivellaunos; known as the Sun Hound: leader of the Trinovantes and the Catuvellauni; now dead

Mandubracios: Legendary traitor, a Trinovantian who betrayed Cassivellaunos to the legions of Julius Caesar during the first Roman invasion

Togodubnos: The eldest of Cunobelin's sons; born to a woman of the royal line of the Trinovantes and hereditary heir to that tribe; a diplomat, his instincts were to tread the same path as his father, that of appeasement of both sides; now dead

Other Key Individuals: Various Tribes

Cunomar: Son of Breaca and Caradoc

Cwmfen: A warrior of the Ordovices, mother of Caradoc's first child, Cygfa

Cygfa: Daughter of Caradoc and Cwmfen; half-sister to Cunomar

Gunovic: Trader and traveling smith; also a warrior and horse racer; later becomes a member of the Eceni

Iccius: Belgic slave-boy killed in an accident while enslaved by Amminios; friend and soul mate to Bán

FURTHER TRIBES

The Brigantes: Northern tribe based in the area that is now the north and east of England, either side of the Pennines; led by Cartimandua, ally to Rome

The Cantiaci: Based in Kent, focus of one wave of the Roman landings

The Catuvellauni: United with the Trinovantes under Cunobelin's leadership

The Dobunni: Southern tribe, south of the Thames, led by Beduoc, uncertain allies of the eastern confederacy

The Ordovices: The Ordovices occupied the land that is currently north Wales and that led to the sacred isle of Mona. Of all the tribes, they were bound closest to the dreamers. After his mother's death, Caradoc was accepted as their leader.

The Silures: Southern neighbours to the Ordovices, once their sworn enemies but united in alliance against Rome

THE ROMANS

The events described in *Dreaming the Bull* and *Dreaming the Eagle* span the reigns of three Roman emperors: Tiberius, Gaius (Caligula), and Claudius. Tiberius had no interest in expansion of the Empire and made no effort towards invasion. Caligula instigated the buildup to the invasion of Britannia but was assassinated before he could complete his task. Claudius oversaw the final act of invasion and the subsequent destruction of the Iron Age tribes.

Julius Valerius: Officer in the auxiliary cavalry, originally with the Ala Quinta Gallorum, later the Ala Prima Thracum

Quintus Valerius Corvus: Prefect of the Ala Quinta Gallorum

Longinus Sdapeze: Officer with the Ala Prima Thracum

Publius Ostorius Scapula: Second Governor of Britannia, AD 47–51

Marcus Ostorius Scapula: His son

Aulus Didius Gallus: Third Governor of Britannia, AD 52–57

Quintus Veranius: Fourth Governor of Britannia, AD 57–58

Marullus: Centurion with the Twentieth Legion, later with the Praetorian Guard in Rome

Umbricius: Actuary with the Ala Quinta Gallorum

Sabinius: Standard bearer with the Ala Quinta Gallorum

Gaudinius: Armourer with the Ala Quintal Gallorum

Emperor Tiberius Claudius Drusus Caesar: Emperor of Rome

Agrippina the Younger: His niece, also his fourth wife, mother to Nero

Germanicus, a.k.a. Britannicus: Son of Claudius by Messalina, his third wife

Lucius Domitius Ahenobarbus, a.k.a. Nero: Son of Aggrippina the Younger and Gnaeus Domitius Ahenobarbus

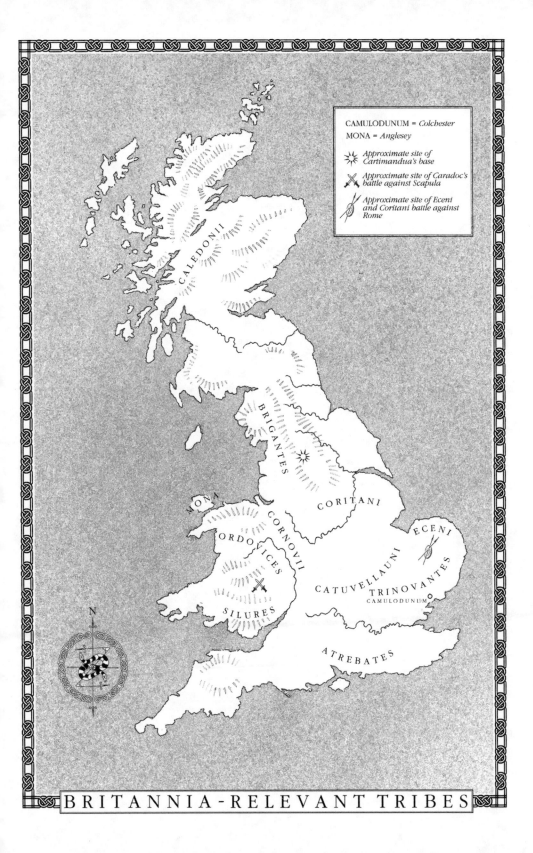

CAMULODUNUM = *Colchester*

MONA = *Anglesey*

※ *Approximate site of Cartimandua's base*

✕ *Approximate site of Caradoc's battle against Scapula*

⚹ *Approximate site of Eceni and Coritani battle against Rome*

CALEDONII

BRIGANTES

MONA

ORDOVICES

CORNOVII

CORITANI

ECENI

CATUVELLAUNI

TRINOVANTES

CAMULODUNUM

SILURES

ATREBATES

N

BRITANNIA-RELEVANT TRIBES

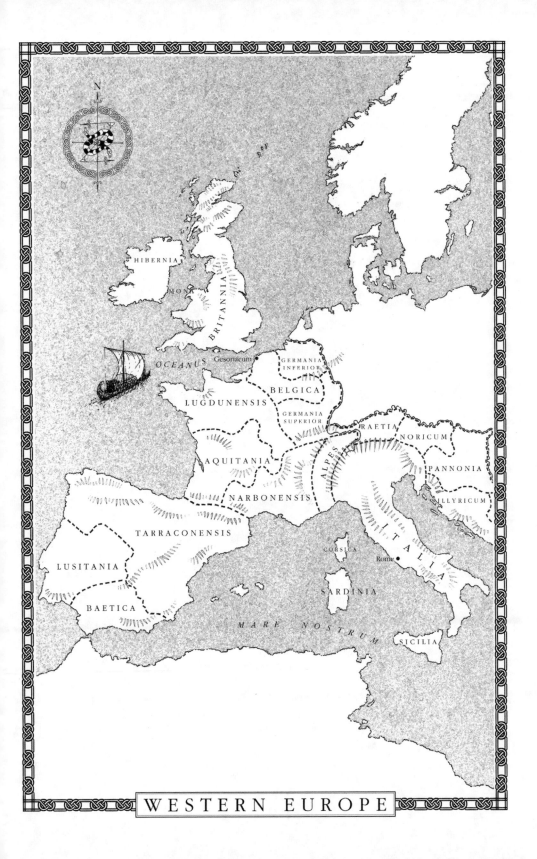

WESTERN EUROPE

PROLOGUE

Listen to me. I am Luain mac Calma, once of Hibernia, now elder of Mona, adviser to the Boudica, Bringer of Victory, and I am here to teach you the history of your people. Here tonight, by this fire, you will learn what has come before. This is who you were; if we win now, this is who you could be again.

In the beginning, the gods ruled the land and the ancestor-people lived in their care. Briga, the three-fold mother, held them through birth and death, and Nemain, her daughter, who shows her face each night in the moon, gave succour between these two journeys. Belin, the sun, warmed them, and Manannan of the seas gave them fish. The ancestors saw that this island of Mona was sacred to all the gods, and for untold generations warriors, dreamers, and singers from the tribes have come to sit here in this greathouse and learn.

With time, the tribes grew, each with its own strengths. Rome, too, was growing; her traders sought hides, horses and hounds, tin and lead, jewellery and corn, and they found them here in abundance.

It was greed for corn, for silver, and for our people as slaves that brought Julius Caesar to our shores. He came twice, and each time the dreamers of our ancestors called on Manannan to send a storm to wreck his ships and drown his men. The first time Caesar barely escaped with his life. A year later, returning, he fought a small battle against the heroes of the east, at the end of which they agreed to talk with him rather than spill more blood. He offered them trading treaties and monopolies on the wines and enamels from Gaul and Belgica, and those who saw their future in trade, and saw no threat from Rome, agreed.

We lived in peace for nearly one hundred years. In that time, a single man came to rule over the tribes on either side of the great river: Cunobelin, the Hound of the Sun, dealt skilfully with Rome. While the Caesars Augustus and Tiberius marched their legions out over Gaul and the Germanies, Cunobelin sent envoys promising peace and trade, but not so much of either that he offended the tribes who hated Rome and who might otherwise have come to view him openly as an enemy.

While Cunobelin lived, there was peace. There were many among our elders and grandmother-councils who watched the Roman subjugation of Gaul and feared that we would be next. Amongst those were the Eceni, the Boudica's people. Their lands bordered those of the Sun Hound, and although they were not at war with him, they refused to trade in anything Roman, nor would they sell to Rome their horses, hides, or hunting hounds, which were the best the world has ever seen.

The Eceni were in conflict with the Coritani, and it was in killing a Coritani spearman that Breaca, who became the Boudica, won her first kill-feather. She was twelve years old and still a child, but the warrior showed in her clearly. Breaca's half-brother, Bán, was younger, but his head was cooler and his heart perhaps more open. The gods loved Bán and sent him dreams of a power unknown since the time of the ancestors. Breaca loved him as any sister loves a brother.

In Cunobelin's lands, life was not peaceful; the Sun Hound set his own three sons against one another, thinking to teach them by constant competition. Togodubnos was eldest and could hold his own. Amminios, the middle son, thrived in the constant conflict, but Caradoc, the youngest and the most ardent warrior, loathed his father and escaped to be with his mother's brother, a seaman.

The gods, who know these things better than we, caused Caradoc's ship to be wrecked on the eastern shores, and the lad was washed up, half-drowned, at Breaca's feet. Thus began one of the greatest alliances in our history, although it took them years to come together, and without war it might never have happened.

With Caradoc was shipwrecked a Roman, Corvus, who came to know the Eceni and care for them. In the spring after the shipwreck, Breaca and her warriors escorted Caradoc and this Corvus south to the lands of the Sun Hound. They were well received and treated with honour, but for Bán, who fell into a game of Warrior's Dance with Amminios and beat him. Above all else, Amminios hated to lose, and it was this that spurred him to mount an attack on the returning Eceni.

They fought a battle at the Place of the Heron's Foot, and many were slain. The greatest loss was the boy, Bán, against whom Amminios held his grudge. Breaca saw her brother slain and his body taken by Amminios, and although the dreamers have searched all the pathways to the other world, none has yet found his soul that it might be returned to the gods.

Four years ago two things happened to change the peace of the tribes: Cunobelin died, leaving his sons to fight amongst themselves, and across the ocean, a new emperor came to power in Rome. Claudius was weak and had a need to prove to the Senate and the people that he had the skills of Julius Caesar, whom they still revered. He sent four legions and four wings of cavalry against us. Forty thousand men and their horses, servants, engineers, and doctors took ship for Britannia.

The battle of the invasion lasted two days and will be told for ever round the fires. A thousand heroes lost their lives on the first day, for the death of ten times that many Romans. Late in the evening, when we were winning, Togodubnos and Caradoc found themselves trapped, unable to advance or retreat. Their deaths were certain until Breaca led a charge that smashed the Roman lines and freed those caught within. It was then that she earned the name by which we know her: Boudica, Bringer of Victory.

Togodubnos was wounded and died that night, but his brother Caradoc took up leadership of his warriors and, with Breaca, prepared to fight the next day. They would have fought without rest until all were dead or we had victory, but the gods deemed it otherwise, sending an entire legion across the river in the early morning so that there was no time to make a stand against them.

We dreamers called a mist, and the gods demanded that Breaca and Caradoc lead the warriors and children to safety—without them, you would not be alive and Rome would rule unhampered. They did not wish to leave the field of battle, but Macha, who had been mother to Bán and was more than a mother to Breaca, demanded it. Macha herself stayed to hold the fog, and it lifted only with her dying, at the very end, when all of our people had escaped.

And so we live now with the results of that. Rome marched north and captured Cunobelin's dun. They call it Camulodunum and have built a fortress there of a size to numb the mind. Breaca and Caradoc fled west and now, with the support of Mona and the dreamers, hold the western lands, killing all Rome sends against us. The time is right for our victory. The old governor who led the invasion will be recalled shortly. Replacing him is Scapula, a general renowned for his savagery. But between one and the other, is a space of time when the Roman legions in Britannia are leaderless, and we will hit them then, when they are weakest, and perhaps drive them back into the sea.

One thing more: I have spoken of Breaca's brother Bán and his death at the hands of Amminios, brother to Caradoc. I have travelled in Gaul, and I am coming to believe that Bán did not die but was taken into slavery by Amminios. Later, escaping, he joined the cavalry, serving under Corvus, the Roman officer who had been shipwrecked in Eceni lands and was his friend. A man of Bán's description, showing knowledge of our people and great skill with horses, fought in the invasion battles and serves now with the cavalry at Camulodunum.

If this man is Bán, if he did join the enemy cavalry, it can only be because he believed that Amminios had slain Breaca and all his family. Left thus alone, he might easily have considered that he had nothing left to live for. He must know otherwise now—the Boudica is renowned from the west coast to the east and in all ways she is unmistakable.

Nevertheless, this man has not come to us asking help and forgiveness. I believe his true commitment to Rome and all it stands for was made after the second day of the invasion battle, when he found his mother's body burning on a funeral pyre. If he holds himself responsible for her death, then it may be that he fears himself beyond redemption, for ever cut off from his gods, his people, and his closest family.

If I am right, this is a man to watch and fear. The boy that I knew was a dreamer to match the power of his mother and a warrior almost to match his sister; if Bán has lost his connection with the gods and the love of his family, then he will be damaged beyond all knowing. Damaged men are ever the most dangerous, to themselves and others. We stand against them at our peril.

I do not believe the gods would cast out one of their own, however appalling his crimes, and I am seeking ways to find Bán and to speak with him. If I am to do so, it is imperative that Breaca, Airmid, and Caradoc continue to believe him dead.

You, here, are in the greathouse under the care of the gods. I swear you now to secrecy; only on my death or that of Bán can you speak freely and then only to Airmid, who will know what to do. For now, you may sleep, and dream, and know that the gods take care of you.

SECTION I

AUTUMN–WINTER A.D. 47

CHAPTER 1

He had been branded once before, long ago, when his name was not Julius Valerius. Then Bán had fought the men who held him down, and it had been done badly so that the wound had festered and he had nearly died. Now, kneeling tied and blindfolded in the claustrophobic dark of a wine cellar, beneath a house that was less than three years old and with the snuffed wicks of the candles sending rank smoke into the dark, he yearned for the touch of the iron. When the masked centurion wiped the wine down the line of his breastbone and pressed his thumb in the centre to mark the spot, he leaned forward to meet the pain.

He had forgotten how bad it would be. The shock was blinding. Fire, and something worse than fire, wrapped his heart, closing tight, like a fist. It wrenched at his breath in a way that wounds taken in battle had never done. He forced himself to silence but need not have done; the noise of one man was lost in the echoing chant of forty male voices. The stench of burned flesh drowned in a flood of sweet smoke as someone threw a fistful of incense onto the brazier.

Later he wondered at the expense of that: frankincense cost more than its own weight in gold. At the time, he only knew that, however briefly, the pain of the fire consumed the other, greater pain of his soul, and it was for this that he had come to the god. As to a lake on a hot day, he threw himself into it, riding the heat that spread from his chest until it drew him out of himself and he watched his body from a place apart, one with the fire and yet separate. At its height, when the bearable became unbearable, someone standing behind stripped the blindfold from his eyes and cut the cords at his wrists, and someone else lit the seven lamps before the sun-disc so that, in deepest darkness and blinding pain, the god's light offered solace.

He would have liked to accept the offer, to fall into the waiting, welcoming arms of the deity, to know peace and certain salvation. The men branded on either side of him did exactly that. From his left, he felt the shudder of flesh that matched exactly the moment of surrender when a horse first accepts the bridle. From his right, he heard a whimpered exhalation, as of a man at the climax of love. For these and the others beyond them, divine joy engulfed all pain, erasing its threat for ever.

It was what he had been promised and what he had craved. In an agony that was more of the heart than the body, he cried aloud in the void of his soul for the voice of the god: he was not answered. Too soon the iron was gone, leaving only the ache of scorched flesh and a curl of smoke that rose to join the taint of those who had been branded with him.

The centurion stepped back, swinging the reddening iron. The double curve of the raven blurred and steadied and lit the space between them. Hidden eyes regarded Valerius from behind the god's mask.

"Know now that you are my sons under the Sun, the last for whom I will be Father and special for ever because of it. I will leave this province soon, with the governor, travelling with him to Rome to accept such postings as the emperor chooses to bestow. I will be a centurion of the second cohort of the Praetorian Guard. Should you come to Rome, make yourselves known to me. The new governor will arrive with next month's first auspicious tide. With him will come new officers to replace those who are leaving and new recruits to replace those we have lost. Meantime the welfare of this province, the honour of our emperor and of the legions, is in your hands and those of your brothers under the god.

"You are his now, first and foremost. Before the legions, before all other gods, you belong to Mithras to death and beyond. He is a just god; ask and he will give you strength; weaken and he will destroy you. By the brand will you know and care for one another, and if the god grant that we meet again, I will know you by it also."

They were seven in the row, naked as infants, newly marked and newly named. Not one spoke. On the far side of the room, a man's voice set up the chant of the newborn. It was joined by others and others and, last, by the new initiates until the full weight of forty-nine voices surged onto the walls and fell inwards, deafeningly. As the sound faded, a single lamp was lit beneath the image of the god. The centurion turned and saluted. Behind him the others did likewise. From his place above the candle on the northern wall, smiling Mithras, capped and caped, caught his bull and drew his blade along its throat.

CHAPTER 2

Only the children sleep on the night before battle and sometimes not even them. On the night before the Roman governor of Britannia took ship and left for ever the land he had conquered, two thousand warriors and half as many dreamers gathered awake on a hillside, less than a morning's ride from the most westerly of the frontier forts. Singly and in groups, as their gods and their courage dictated, they prepared themselves for war on a scale not seen since the legions' invasion four years before.

Breaca nic Graine, once of the Eceni and now of Mona, sat alone at the edge of a mountain pool. She breathed on a pebble cupped in the palm of her hand and sent it skipping over the water.

"For luck."

The stone bounced five times, shattering the moon's reflection. Shards of broken light scattered into darkness and were lost. The river ran on unheard, the music of its passing drowned beneath the stutter of bear claws played on hollow skulls nearby. The light of a thousand restless campfires gilded the water's edge, and smoke hazed the air above it. Only by the river was there solitude and darkness and the peace to ask favours of the gods.

"For courage."

The second pebble clipped the edge of the moon and was lost. On the unseen slopes behind, the skull drums reached a crescendo. A woman's voice called to the gods in the language of the northern ancestors. Other voices answered, grunting, and the un-rhythm of the drums changed. It was not good to listen too closely to that; over the years, more than one soul had been lost in the mesh of woven bone-sounds and had never found its way home.

"For Briga's care in battle."

The third stone, more accurate than those before it, bounced nine times and sank into the moon's heart, carrying the prayer directly to the gods without the intermediary of the river. If a warrior wanted to believe in omens, it was a good one. Breaca, known as the Boudica, sat as the moon settled again and was whole, a crisp half-circle of silver lying still on a bed of moving black.

Stooping, she picked up a fourth stone. It was wider and flatter than the others and bounced smoothly on her palm. She breathed a different prayer into it, one for which tradition did not supply the words.

"For Caradoc and for Cunomar, for their joy and their peace if I am taken in battle. Briga, mother of war, of childbirth, and of dying, take care of them for me."

It was not a new prayer; in the three and a half years since her son was born, she had spoken it countless times in the silence of her mind in those moments before the first clash of combat when everything and everyone she loved must be put aside and forgotten. Breaca had learned early that a warrior who wished to live rode into battle with an empty mind lest the distraction of a rising memory should slow her sword arm or the lift of her shield. The difference now, in the rushing dark by the river, with the chaos of preparation held temporarily at bay, was that she had spoken for the first time aloud and had felt the prayer clearly heard. She was beside water, which was Nemain's, and on the eve of battle, which was Briga's, and the gods were alive and walking on the mountainside, called in by the scores of dreamers whose ceremonies lit the night sky.

After nearly four years of despair, she could feel the promise of freedom just within reach if only bone and blood and sinew could be pushed hard enough and far enough to make it happen. With the gods' help, she believed it could.

Knowing a hope greater than any she had felt since the invasion, the Boudica drew back her arm to throw her stone.

"Mama?"

"Cunomar!" She turned too fast. The pebble skittered over the water and was lost. A child stood on the river bank above her, tousled from sleep and stumbling uncertainly in the dark.

She reached up and lifted her son by the waist, bringing him down to the water's edge where he could stand safely. He was the living scion of her heart, her beacon in the dark, the one source of life that had pushed her to fight at the times when all hope seemed pointless. It hurt even to have him this close to battle. Holding him tight, she could feel the trip of his pulse. She kissed the top of his head and said, "My warrior, you should be sleeping, why are you not?"

Blearily, he rubbed a small fist in his eye. "The drums woke me. Ardacos is calling the she-bears to help him. He's going to fight the Romans. Can I watch the ceremony?"

Cunomar was not quite four years old and had only recently begun to grasp the enormity of war. Ardacos was his latest hero, second only to his father and mother in the pantheon of his gods. The small, savage Caledonian was the stuff of childhood idolatry. Ardacos led the band of warriors dedicated to the she-bear; they fought always on foot and largely naked and surpassed all others in the stalking and hunting of the enemy by night. The skull-drums were his, and the chanting that accompanied them.

Breaca smoothed a hand through the silk of her son's hair. She said, "We're all going to fight the Romans, but no, I think the ceremony is sacred and not for our eyes unless they call us in. When you are older, if the she-bear so grants, you can join with Ardacos in his ceremonies."

The boy's face flushed in the fire-glow, suddenly awake. "The she-bear will grant it," he said. "She must. I'll join Ardacos, and together we will drive the legions into the outer ocean."

He spoke with the conviction of one who has not yet known defeat, nor even considered it possible. Breaca had not the heart to disappoint him. She lifted him back up onto the bank again, smiling. "Then your father and I will be glad to save you some Romans to fight. But in the morning we must kill the ones in the fort beyond the next mountain, and before that, Ardacos and two of his warriors must make the land safe for us. It may be he has need of me in a part of his ceremony. If I go to him, you must go to bed first. Will you do that?"

"Can I sit on the grey battle-mare before you go to kill the legions?"

"Yes, if you're good. See, your father's here. He'll hold you while I go to Ardacos."

"How did you know—?" The child's face was awash with awe. Already he believed his mother partway to divinity; for her to predict the appearance of his father out of the maelstrom of the night was only another step to godhood.

Breaca smiled. "I heard his footsteps," she said. "There's nothing magical in that." It was true; more than Cunomar, more than any other living being, she knew the tread of this one step. In the chaos of battle, in the silence of a winter night, she could hear Caradoc walk and know where he was.

Now he waited at the top of the bank. With the firelight behind, his face was invisible and only his hair was lit. Spun gold flickered around his head so that he looked as might Camul, the war god, on the eve of battle, or Belin, who daily rode the mounts of the sun. It was a night to sustain such fancies, and the gods would not be offended.

In the voice of men, Caradoc said, "Breaca? The she-bears have called your name. Are you ready?"

"I think so. If you will take care of your son, we can find out." She passed Cunomar up to the waiting arms and hoisted herself up by the hazel roots. "Briga gives me luck and her care should the luck fail. It appears I may have to find my own courage."

The fourth stone was forgotten, deliberately so. There was no way to predict what the gods might make of it. Breaca could not imagine them exacting retribution from a child for his mother's failure to cast a stone truly. Her own fate was unknowable, but then it was always so; any warrior who had lived through more than one battle knew that life was a gift of the gods and could be withdrawn at any moment. Caradoc's life was too precious to contemplate. If she allowed herself to imagine him dead, or even sorely injured, she would never be able to ride into battle at all.

Caradoc grasped her forearm and pulled her the last half-length up the bank. Close, he was a man again, his face lined by lack of sleep and the weight of leadership. He hugged her lightly. "The she-bears believe you have courage to spare. Tonight would not be a good time to disillusion them."

Breaca grimaced. "I know. To them I am god-filled and can never die. You and I know the truth, that I am as human and fearful as any other on the field. Courage is too fickle to be held fast from one day to the next. Like sweeping the moon in a fishing net, the water sifts through and the light stays as it was. Each time I ride into battle I believe it will be the last."

She should not have said that. Caradoc looked at her closely; the fourth stone was not fully forgotten, and he could read her as well as she could him. He asked, "Does the coming battle feel bad to you?"

"No more than it ever does. And it doesn't matter. We have enough in Mona's council who know what to do if one of us dies. Even if half of us die, the war will continue without us."

"But I wouldn't want to continue without you." He kissed her, a brief press of dry lips on her cheek, and then quickly, to cover what had been said, "And if Ardacos can do as we need, fewer may die."

"We can hope so. Take care of Cunomar; I can find the she-bears on my own."

Away from the river, the hillside was alive with warriors painting themselves and each other, weaving their warriors' braids and fixing at their temples the kill-feathers that gave notice to the gods of the numbers of enemy already slain.

Ardacos's she-bears formed a circle on the western slope of the mountain, sheltered by late-berried thorns. As Breaca drew close, the night came alive with the clatter of bear claws played on bone-white skulls, and it was hard to hear anything beyond the soft, insistent absence of rhythm. The sound was a river that washed into the mind and soul and carried them to places Breaca had never been, or wished to go. Older than the ancestors, it spoke directly to the gods, promising them blood in return for victory and demanding courage and something greater than courage as its price.

Knowing exactly the limits of her own courage, Breaca nic Graine, known throughout the tribes as the Boudica, Bringer of Victory, stepped forward into the firelight.

The men and women of the she-bear made a circle around her. In daylight, she could have named each one. They were her friends, her closest comrades, warriors for whom she would die in battle and who would, without pause or question, die for her in return. Lit by the leaping flames, those who circled her were barely human, and she could not see Ardacos at all.

"Warriors of the she-bear, we have need of you."

"Ask." The voice was a bear's, carried on a wave of drumming. "The bear lives to serve, but only one whose heart is great enough to know the risk may ask."

"The gods will test my heart as they test yours." The words, like the rhythms, were the ancestors', old beyond imagining. Pitching her voice above the rattling claws, she said, "We who fight battles in daylight ask the aid of those who hunt men by night. There is a task for which no others are suited. There is danger beyond that which any others can face. There is need of one who can track and one who can hunt and one who can kill and leave not a single one of the enemy alive. Can you do this? Will you do it?"

The dance throbbed. The drums tugged at her soul. Waves of passion, of regret, of love and loss and pity scored her heart. Fighting for outward calm, she said again, "Warriors of the she-bear. Can you do this? Will you do it?"

A single bear-robed figure shuffled forward. It could have been man or woman, both or neither. In a voice Breaca had never known, it said, "We can. We will. We do."

"Thank you. May Nemain light your way, may Briga aid your fighting and the bear guard the honour of your dying. I am grateful—truly."

The last sentence was hers alone, not given by the generations before. Breaca stepped sideways, leaving open the place before the fire.

On a soft, husking cough, the skull-drumming stopped. The circle opened and disgorged into its centre a decurion of the Roman cavalry and two of his auxiliaries. As if under Roman orders, the three marched to stand before the fire.

The officer stood a little ahead of his men and was more richly dressed. His cloak was a deep liver-red, striped at the hem in white, and his chain-mail shirt caught the moonlight and made of it stars. His helmet gave him a little extra height but did not bring him close to the stature of the two warrior-auxiliaries who flanked him, each a hand's length taller. Beneath their helmets the face of each was painted in white lime; circles around the eyes and knife-straight lines beneath each cheek made them other than human. All three smelled, overpoweringly, of bear grease, stoat's urine, and woad.

They made a line before the fire. Each bowed a little and gave something of himself, or herself—at least one of the disguised warriors was a woman—to the flames. The offerings flashed as they burned, giving off the greens and blues of powdered copper and the whiff of scorched hair. When the fire was quiet, all three turned and lifted their cavalry cloaks so it might be seen by their peers that, beneath the chain mail of their disguise, they were naked and that the grey woad that was their protection under the gods coated all of their skin. A small incision on the left forearm of each bled a little into the night, black against the silvering grey. The skull-drums chattered a final time in recognition, approval, and support. When they stopped, a measure of magic departed the night.

It was hard to move, as if the earth had become less solid awhile, and returning, the pressure of it bruised the soles of the feet. Breaca moved further away, giving room before the fire to the drummers and dancers; they had further to return and would feel the strangeness more strongly. The enemy decurion followed her.

"Am I Roman?" The man tipped his head slightly, and by that, by his voice, and by his lack of height, Breaca knew him. She smiled.

"Ardacos, no, no one could imagine you Roman. But by the time the enemy are close enough to realize it, they will be dead."

She laid her palm on the hilt of his sword, the only part of him another could touch without desecration until he had killed his foes or died in the attempt. "You know that if it were possible, I would go in your stead."

"And you know that there are some places where the Boudica excels and others where the she-bear is all that will suffice."

Behind the skull paint, Ardacos's eyes were bright as the stoat's that was his dream. He had been her lover for a while between Airmid and Caradoc; he knew her as well as any man, knew the weaknesses, real and imagined, that she took pains to hide from the greater mass of warriors.

He said, "I couldn't lead the warriors down the hill tomorrow if their lives and mine depended on it. I couldn't stand with my back to the sunrise and speak to them with the voice of Briga so that they believe themselves touched by the gods and fit to defeat any number of legions. I couldn't dream of riding alongside Caradoc in battle, weaving the wildfire so that the weak and the wounded find new heart and can fight where before they thought themselves dead." Less soberly, he said, "The gods give to each of us different gifts. I could not be the Boudica, but also I do not wish it. You should not wish yourself a she-bear. Be grateful you don't spend your life with the stink of bear-grease in your nostrils."

She wrinkled her nose. "Do you think I don't?"

"No. You think you don't, and I know you don't know the first part of it." He grinned, showing white teeth. He, too, was forbidden to touch anyone but those with whom the night's oaths had been spoken until at least the first of the enemy was dead. Deliberately, he kept his hands folded across his sword belt. "We must go while the night is still with us. The Romans are soft, and they drink wine in the darkness to give themselves courage." More formally he said, "Be of good heart. We cannot fail."

"And if you do, the bear will take you."

"Of course. It is the promise we make. But it is made gladly." He turned, sending his cloak spinning. "Wait by the fire. We will return not long after dawn."

CHAPTER 3

The air stank of woad and bear grease and thus of conflict. For a child conceived in battle and born into war, it was the familiar smell of childhood, as common as the scent of roasting hare, if less pleasant. Cunomar, son of the two greatest warriors his world had ever seen, clung to the mane of his mother's grey battle-mare and tried, surreptitiously, to breathe through his mouth. His mother's arms kept him safe on the horse's neck in that place, ahead of the saddle, where brave children rode if they were good and did not ask too many questions of those preparing for war.

It was hard to be good. The night had been alive with a shimmering danger, and few of the adults had time for a child. Only Ardacos had said good things, but then he had needed to begin his ceremony, and when he had finished, the man who emerged was somebody else.

Cunomar liked Ardacos. One of the child's earliest memories was of the small, dark-skinned warrior with the creased face bending over him in firelight, signing with his fingers the words of protection before lifting him and carrying him away to hide in the dark of a river valley, where they lay together under the hanging boughs of a hazel tree with running water at their feet and boulders on either side for protection. Cunomar remembered little else but that the night had been unusually long and rain had fallen through most of it, masking the sounds of fighting so that he could not tell how close the enemy had come, or how sorely the wards had been tested.

Ardacos had been the real protection, greater than the wards. He had crouched next to Cunomar through the night with his battle knife drawn; together they had listened to the sounds of killing. When dawn came, the little man had walked soft-footed into the rain and returned with the newly severed head of an enemy soldier, to prove it was safe to come out. It was then Cunomar had decided that when he was older, he would be a warrior like Ardacos and would fight under the mark of the she-bear, coating himself in bear-grease and woad that the enemies' eyes might not see him, nor their blades bite.

In the year since, Cunomar had learned to recognize the distinctive patter of claws on a skull that called the warriors of the she-bear to the start of their ceremony. He had watched exactly how the little man mixed white lime with river clay and used it to make his hair stand up on his head so that he seemed taller and more fierce, and how he painted rings round his eyes and lines on his cheeks in the shape of a skull to warn his foes of impending death. The result was terrifying, and Cunomar was not surprised that the enemy fell dead before the warriors of the she-bear. The only surprise was that they kept coming back and had not yet learned to return whence they came and leave for ever the land that was not theirs.

They would do so soon, everything and everyone said so. The promise had been heard daily through the summer in the quiet talk of warriors preparing for war and in the certainty of the dreamers, only now the woad said it in a way that could not be ignored. After a while, when the stench of it seemed less overpowering, Cunomar realized the extra sharpness was of the stoat, which was Ardacos's dream, and that the bear-warrior had mixed it in to make him stronger.

Even without that, Cunomar would have known that this battle was going to be greater than the ones that had marked the high points of his life so far. Alive with a gilded pride, he had heard his mother speak to all those gathered on the hillside. As a cold dawn sharpened the air and Nemain, the moon, lowered into her bed in the mountains, Breaca had stood on the back of her mare and addressed the massed ranks of warriors and dreamers, naming them all Boudegae, Bringers of Victory, and swearing before them that she would fight for as long as it took to rid the land of the invader.

She had seemed truly like a goddess then; the mist had parted, and the first slanting rays of the sun had lit her from behind, melding her with the battle-mare so that two became one, a thing greater than either apart. The light had burnished her hair, making copper of the flaming bronze, casting in relief the warrior's braid at the side and the single silver feather woven within it that marked the scores of the enemy who had died at her hand. The serpent-spear on her shield had glistened wetly red, as if freshly painted with Roman blood, and the grey cloak of Mona had lifted behind her in the wind. At the end, she had raised her blade high, promising victory, and there was not one among those gathered who doubted they could achieve it.

They had not cheered for her because the enemy was too close and might be alerted, but Cunomar had seen the flash of a thousand weapons raised in salute. He had ached with pride, but this time, perhaps because he was older and understood more, he felt the knifing pang of a new fear that had nothing to do with the possibility of his mother's death or even the closeness of war but was rooted instead in the awful possibility—even the probability—that the fighting might be over before he was old enough to join it.

Watching the warriors begin to disperse, he had prayed silently to Nemain and to Briga, her mother, and to the soul of the she-bear that the war into which he had been born might not end before he was of an age to carry a weapon and win honour for himself and his parents.

Cunomar pushed himself back against his mother's chest until the links of her mail shirt pressed cold on his neck and he felt the shivered thrill of danger. Grinning, he looked around to see who he might share it with. Airmid, the tall, dark-haired dreamer who held half of his mother's heart, stood on a rock to their left, but she was lost in the world of the dream, her face still and her eyes fixed on a horizon that only she could see. Efnís, a dreamer of the Eceni, and Luain mac Calma, the elder dreamer who journeyed often to Hibernia and Gaul, were near her, but both were similarly preoccupied. Each was too distant and too intimidating to share a child's morning joy.

More promisingly, a few paces to the right was Cygfa, his half-sister, who sat astride the neck of the great chestnut horse that had once belonged to an officer in the enemy cavalry and was now their father's warmount. Caradoc himself was turned away, speaking to a woman who stood on his sword side, but his shield arm held his daughter to his chest, loosely, because she was eight years old and could manage the horse well enough on her own, but distinctly, so that everyone could see that Caradoc, war leader of three tribes, honoured his daughter in the time before battle.

Cygfa wore a torc in woven gold around her neck, a gift from a chieftain of the Durotriges who was one of his parents' allies, but it was the stolen legionary dagger in its enamelled silver scabbard dangling at her hip that Cunomar coveted most. Turning, she saw him and grinned. He scowled back dramatically. He had recently begun to understand that his sister was more than twice his age and would therefore become a warrior before him, but he could not accept at all that she should carry the spoils of victory when he could not. Forgetting what good children did, he raised his head and wriggled round to tug at the front of his mother's cloak.

"Mama, when the enemy are all slain, can I have a——?"

Her fingers tightened on his shoulder, and for a joyful moment he thought she had heard him and was about to promise that the sword of the enemy general would be his when she returned. Then he looked up into her face and followed the line of her gaze down into the valley to the place where the parting mist gave up a figure, and then another, both coated in iron-grey woad-grease with lime stiffening their hair and painted in white rings round their eyes. They carried something heavy between them and left it at the bottom of the hill. The smaller of the two ran forward alone.

Cunomar let go of his mother's cloak and pointed. "Ardacos," he said distinctly. "He has killed the enemy."

"We can pray so."

Ardacos was one of his mother's closest friends. Cunomar knew that she feared for the bear-man and tried not to show it. Breaca spoke to the battle-mare, and they walked a few steps down the slope. The mare was old, but she came alive when the woad spiked the air. She walked forward lightly, as if ready to run. At a rocky outcrop, screened by a straggle of rowan and hawthorn, they stopped. Ardacos loped up the slope towards them.

"It is done." Breathless, the little man gave the salute of the warrior first to Cunomar and then to his mother. The lined skin of his face was smoothly stiff beneath the white clay paint, but his eyes were fired with exultation and only a small measure of pain. In answer to Breaca's unspoken question, he said, "There were eight of them, all thick with wine and afraid of the night. Only one fought well. We lost Mab, but the beacon is ours."

"And the others? Do we have the whole chain?" Cunomar heard a tension in his mother's voice that made his stomach lurch and left his mouth dry.

Ardacos said, "We do. The dreamers and the gods were good: the mist cleared for us when we needed it. We raised a torch and saw it returned with a second to show that the chain is whole. We have every beacon from here to the coast. When the governor's ship leaves harbour, we will know of it. However good a general his successor might be, he will still sail in to find the country ablaze and his armies in flight, and it is Roman work that will have made it possible. We will turn every one of their weapons against them, as we turn their horses, their armour, and their blades." The little man grinned, cracking the ring of paint round his mouth. "To this end, I have a gift for the warrior-in-making."

He meant Cunomar. The boy's heart surged. Ardacos signalled behind him, and the second warrior ran up towards them. Even before she reached the top of the slope, Cunomar could see what she brought. He thought he might weep with joy and wondered if that would be a good thing to do on the eve of battle. Before he could decide, Ardacos had knelt before his mother's grey mare and held out a legionary sword in both hands. Formally, using the cadences of a singer, or an elder in council, he said, "For Cunomar, son of Breaca and Caradoc, cousin and namesake to Cunomar of the fires, who gave his life that we might live, I bring the weapon of the bravest of this night's enemies."

Stripped of its sheath, the blade lay naked across Ardacos's palms, a thing of silver smeared stickily black. Cunomar felt his mother's hands on his waist, and then he was swung down to the ground and she was standing behind him, one hand on his shoulder.

Before she could prompt him, the child drew himself up and, following the conventions he had heard in the summer councils, said, "Cunomar, son of the Boudica and of Caradoc, warrior of Three Tribes, thanks Ardacos of the Caledonii, warrior of the she-bear and of the honour guard of Mona, for his great gift and pledges . . ."

He ran out of words. He had no idea what he pledged; the weapon held all his attention. It was smaller than his mother's war sword, and he was sure he could lift it. With both hands, he grasped the hilt and pulled. The blade slid off Ardacos's open palms and fell, point down, to pierce the turf between the warrior's feet. Cunomar's pride fell with it, turning to shame and fear of failure and the ill omen of a warrior-to-be who could not raise his own sword. Tears welled in him and spilled over, and he took a breath to howl his disappointment.

"No. Look. There is no harm done. See, we can lift it together." His mother's arms encircled him, stemming the grief. "It's an enemy sword, and Mab's blood is still on it. We must clean it and dedicate it to the gods, and then we'll put it away and keep it safe until you're a warrior and can wield it in battle."

That was not what he wanted. Cygfa had her knife and could wear it openly; he wanted the same, or better. He felt his lower lip quiver, and the tears massed again on his lids, like water behind a dam. His mother ruffled her fingers through his hair and went on as if she had never meant to stop. "But before that, you can try one swing, to get the feel of it. See—I'll hold it, you can make the stroke."

With one hand, she lifted the blade, making it light as straw, and with the other, she pressed his own small fist in before hers, and he found that he could make the backhanded killing stroke in the way he had seen Cygfa do when their father first began to teach her, and then, because it was a Roman blade, he followed it with a lunge forward as the enemy were said to do, killing empty air that had every Roman in the world at the end of it.

His mother laughed breathlessly. "That's good. See? The blade knows its rightful owner and—" She stopped, and this time he did not have to look up to see why, because he had seen the thing before her and it was his own small gasp that had made her look with him to the horizon, where a beacon fire blossomed like a second sun. Cunomar knew in the depths of his soul that it signalled the beginning of the war to end all wars and that he would not be old enough to wield his new blade before the fighting ended.

The world changed dizzyingly fast. Breaca stood, suddenly, taking the Roman blade out of reach, and her son did not protest. He heard her call out a name, and a cry rose up around him, the keening of the grey falcon that was the sign of the Silures in whose land they lived and fought, and of Gwyddhien who led the right wing of the honour guard. The sound multiplied as her warriors joined it, and the mountain rang as with a multitude of hunting birds, ready for the kill. The child's world darkened as men and women in uncountable numbers mounted their horses and raised their shields, blocking out the sun.

Cunomar turned, seeking his mother, and found she was crouching beside him again, snapping her fingers and whistling into the long shadows beneath the hawthorn trees where the war-hounds lay awaiting battle.

Three hounds emerged. The grey-white bitch was first, who had been called Cygfa until Cunomar's half-sister was born, when the hound's name had been changed to Swan's Neck and then to just Neck. She was foremost among his mother's brood bitches and had given birth to Stone, the tall young hound who came out next and who would run beside the grey battle-mare and help the warriors to defeat the enemy. But it was three-legged Hail for whom his mother waited, for whom she would always wait, sire to Stone and uncounted others. The great white-spotted war-hound had once belonged to Breaca's brother Bán and, because of that, was now and for ever the most beloved of the Boudica's beasts.

The singers told more tales of Bán, lost brother to the Boudica, than of any other hero, living or dead. For one who had died before he ever sat his long-nights, the litany of Bán's achievements was dauntingly long. Hare-hunter, horse-dreamer, and healer, he had been born with power such as had not been seen since the time of the ancestors. His first battle had shown him also to be a warrior; as a child not yet come to manhood, he had, they said, fought and killed at least twenty of the enemy before he was tricked into carelessness and slain. The tragedy was made worse by the fact that it had been Amminios, brother to Caradoc, who had betrayed the boy-hero and slain him. The singers played heavily on that; it would have been far less of a tale if the traitor had been an unknown warrior from another land.

They sang of the hero's hound, Hail, in the same tones and often in the same songs as they did of Bán, telling of the beast's outstanding courage in battle and his prowess in the hunt. From when he was too young to fully understand the words, Cunomar had listened to his mother's voice singing him to sleep, so that he dreamed through the nights of a god-touched boy who killed with the ease of a man and of his three-legged war-hound who belonged now to the Boudica and had claimed for ever a large part of her soul.

Cunomar had tried to love Hail as his mother did but had not succeeded. In the spring, when a dog whelp had been born with the same white ear and spattering of white spots on its coat as its sire, Cunomar had hoped that perhaps his mother's affections might shift so that the new hound would displace the old, but it had not been so. The whelp had been named Rain because there could only ever be one Hail, and although Breaca had cherished it and spent too much of her time in training it, Hail was still the one who ran at her side on the morning of battle, and it was Hail before whom she crouched now, in whose pelt her fingers dug deep so that her nose was level with his nose and to whom she spoke as if the hound were a warrior and could understand.

The hound grumbled deep in its throat, and when the Boudica let go, it sighed and turned to make its stilted way to Cunomar's side. Hail was too big, that was part of the trouble. The great head loomed over the child's so that the boy had to look up into its eyes. He thought it regarded him with disdain, measuring him against those who had given their lives in battle and finding him not of their stature.

With an effort, Cunomar dragged his gaze away. Breaca had come to crouch before him as she had before the hound with her face close to his, smiling. He reached out and hugged her, burying his face in the crook of her neck, breathing her in to the depths of his chest. He thought she should have smelled differently today, of battle and resolution, but she smelled as she always did, of sheep's wool and horse-sweat and a little of hound-spittle where Hail had licked her face and she had not wiped it away, and over all of those, she smelled of herself: his mother who would never change.

Cunomar's hair was corn-gold like his father's. She smoothed it, tucking it behind his ears. Her lips pressed into his crown, and he knew she was speaking but not what she said; the words were Eceni and too difficult for a boy raised on Mona amongst the dialects of the west. He ached for knowing she must go when he so badly wanted her to stay and be *his* Boudica, to blaze with the wildfire just for him.

Instead she smiled the secret smile that she kept for her son and his father and said, "My warrior-to-be, I'm sorry, I have to leave you. The beacon fire says the enemy governor has sailed away, and we must destroy his legions before another comes to take his place. I've asked Hail to take care of you while I'm gone, but really he's old and he needs you to take care of him. Will you do that for me?"

He would do anything for her, she knew that. Reaching up, he touched the silver feather that dangled in her hair. It was beautiful, each part of it perfect, so that Cunomar could imagine the smith had taken the wing feather of a crow and dipped it in silver, running gold in bands round the quill to number the hundreds she had killed. He wanted his mother to kill another thousand Romans so that she could have more feathers, but the words were too complicated, so instead he smiled for her and said, "I will guard Hail, I swear it, his blood for my blood, his life for mine," as he had heard the warriors do.

It was the right thing to say. She clasped his head in both hands and kissed his forehead, then rose swiftly, speaking again in Eceni. A shadow fell across the ground before him, and Cunomar turned to find Dubornos at his side, the tall gaunt singer with sparse red hair who was one of his mother's oldest allies.

Cunomar was not afraid of Dubornos, but he did not understand him. In a world where the wearing of wealth was an open honouring of the gods, the singer bore no gold or silver adornment but only a narrow band of fox-pelt on his upper arm to mark his dream. Moreover he carried about him a grief that drained him of humour, and he spoke rarely and always with great gravity, as now, when he reached down and took Cunomar's hand as if he were a small child and said, "Warrior-to-be, I have pledged to stay and take care of the younger children. Will you help me with that?"

Anyone could tell that he found it uncomfortable to speak so and would have preferred to take care of the children himself. Still, it was not done for a warrior to turn down a request for help before battle. Cunomar withdrew his hand as politely as he could and touched the skinning knife at his belt. "I will help," he said, "their life for mine," and he saw his mother clasp Dubornos's shoulder and heard her soft word of thanks and knew it was what she had wanted.

There were eight children, of whom Cunomar was the second youngest. With Dubornos's help, they scrambled up the mountain to take their place in a high eyrie, behind a rocky escarpment that gave them a view down to the river and across to the enemy fort that squatted on the opposite side of the valley.

Cygfa joined them presently, her face tear-streaked from her parting with their father. His sister may have been going to be a warrior sooner than he, but in Cunomar's opinion, she did not know how to part properly with the warriors before battle. She spoke briefly with Dubornos, and then the two of them came to lie with Cunomar, one on either side. They watched as the mass of horses threaded their way down the mountain and the warriors of the she-bear, who went into battle on foot wherever possible, ran down the slopes, grey as boulders with the woad-grease, and were swallowed by the mist.

For a while, stillness held the valley. Trumpets sounded distantly from the fort. The Romans, too, had seen the beacon, but there was no knowing what they made of it. Certainly they were not likely to believe that the beacon hill had been taken and their fort was under attack. The gods or the dreamers, or both, kept the mist thick round the river and sent layers of it rising on the warm morning air, concealing the movements of warriors. Looking carefully, Cunomar could see the glint of a mail shirt or a spear-tip, but the harnesses and helmets of the warriors were well wrapped to keep them quiet and unseen for the longest possible time.

The boy's attention drifted. He was watching Hail, who was, in turn, watching a spider string a web across the heather, when Cygfa nudged his elbow and hissed. He raised his eyes in time to see his mother and father lead the charging warriors up through the mist.

For the rest of his life, Cunomar remembered that battle as if he had taken part in it, flying as one of Briga's crows in the air above his mother, guarding her and marking the enemy for death. He heard the drum of the hooves and the war-cries of the warriors and knew the point when they gave way to the screams of the wounded. He smelled the blood and the horse-sweat and the curdling acid of spilled guts and the first threads of smoke as the men and women of the she-bear carried brush and burning brands up the steep turf ramparts of the fort and set fire to the wooden palisade on top. He saw from up high the moment when the commander of the enemy forces chose to order his men out of the gates to fight in the open where the fires might not catch them, and he knew, with a jubilation that lifted him cheering to his feet, that this was what his mother had planned and prayed for. He saw the brief hiatus in the fighting as the warriors withdrew to let the bulk of the enemy sweep out of the gateway and then the crash as of a breaking wave as they surged back in again, annihilating the foe. Through it all, his mother and father killed at the fore, copper hair and corn-gold making two beacons for the warriors to follow. At no point did it occur to him that his mother might die, or be injured. She was the Boudica. She lived to kill the enemy, and Cunomar, her son—her only child—would do the same when his time came.

CHAPTER 4

On the eastern side of the country, far from the chaos of war, Julius Valerius, second in command of the third troop, the Fifth Gaulish Cavalry, stationed in perpetuity at Camulodunum, woke to numbing cold. It gnawed into his dreams, which were bad, and made them worse until he woke. He pulled his cloak tighter and rolled over to lie on his side. It was too dark to see. Stretching a hand to the wall, he felt a slither of ice on the rough plaster where the breath and sweat of four men had frozen. His fingers were stiff. He blew on them and tucked them under his armpit, swearing aloud as the blood returned. The brand was the only warm part of him; a raven's silhouette of fire still burned in the centre of his chest a full month after the iron had first seared his soul.

He pressed his thumb to the scar, tracing the outline in the fragile, healing skin. The flesh beneath was not hot, but a perpetual flame burned in the cavity of his chest as a reminder of the night in the cellar. The god might not have visited him, but it was the god's mark that kept the bad dreams from becoming disabling nightmares, or so he chose to believe. Lying in the dark, he would have liked to believe, as his fellow acolytes clearly did, that the brand gave him courage, that it made him one with Sol Invictus, that it joined him to an elite that those outside envied but did not fully comprehend. The last part of that might have been true—those who gave themselves to Mithras might possibly become subject to the warped envy of those excluded from the god's grace—but he could not believe the rest.

On a good day, Valerius could persuade himself that he had never desired unity with the sun and his obvious failure to attain it in the god's ceremony was of no moment. This morning, with the new governor installed and the threat of an eastern war increasing, he would dearly have liked to feel a measure of blind, uncomplicated courage, or simply to feel warm.

He rose, stamping life into his feet and his feet into his boots. The water in the washbowl was thickly iced. He broke it with rigid fingers and splashed the sleep from his eyes. He shared the room with three other junior officers of his troop: Sabinius the standard-bearer, Umbricius the actuary, and Gaudinius the armourer. All three turned and mumbled restlessly in their sleep but did not wake. Valerius was the only one of the four known for his early rising.

Beyond the doorway, the corridor lining the barracks block was more still than usual and lacked the customary draughts, as if, a full year after its construction, someone had finally found and blocked all the gaps in the brickwork. The night-time lamps had burned out long since, and the space was darkly empty. Valerius stood awhile, feeling the stillness. Asleep, night was his enemy; awake, it became his friend. It had taken him a long time to acknowledge it, but recently he had begun to realize how much he enjoyed the anonymity of the dark.

In a while, brushing his fingertips along the walls, he made his way to the outer door. The night was not like other nights. The crunch of his feet on the corridor's gravel was muffled, folding in on itself and dying away too soon, and the air smelled clean and sharp so that, when he breathed in deeply, grains of ice formed in the hairs of his nose, and when he let the breath out, it made white fog round his head.

Because it was dark and he was concentrating on finding his way without stumbling and was not keeping his mind in check, a twenty-year-old memory rose from nowhere, of a night just like this, with a three-quarter moon hanging low over winter oaks, of himself as a small child, wrapped safe in the folds of his mother's winter cloak, standing at the borderlands between the wild wood and the horse paddocks, with exactly the same feel of ice crystals forming and melting in his nose. Walking the length of a barracks corridor, he heard his mother's voice whisper in his ear, showing him the hare that lived on the moon's surface and was the god's messenger to her people. He'd screwed up his eyes, staring hard until he saw the outline of the beast sitting side-on to the world. When he found it, his mother's hands enfolded his and raised them, explaining how to make the salute the dreamers made to the moon so that he would always be able to ask help of that god when he was in need. In the world of the legionary barracks, his arm rose to shoulder height before it hit the wall.

It was an unforgivable lapse. Cursing aloud, Valerius spun backwards and jammed his shoulders hard against an upright oak beam. Urgently, pressing the back of his head on solid wood and his thumb on his brand, he called up the images of Mithras that had been shown him over these last two months: the youth in cap and cape emerging fully formed from solid rock, the corn of his fertility, the serpent and the hound that drank on the bull's spilled blood. In the stretches of time between heartbeats, Valerius built his god layer by layer in the air before him, manifesting by will-power alone the bull, most worthy of all opponents, to dance and struggle with its captor until the knife stabbed into its throat and a fountain of blood wept onto the earth.

The images worked, as they always did, slowly and imperfectly. Sweating, Valerius spoke the prayers to Sol Invictus aloud in his mind until they overwhelmed everything else. The power of the god had kept his mother from his dreams since the branding, and it banished her now from his waking inattention, destroying every memory, down to the soft husk of her voice in his ears.

Her voice lasted longest, and he had to chant openly not to let her words slide snake-like into his head and heart. He had once believed his mother dead, with his father and sister, and had sworn allegiance to Rome on the strength of it. Later, standing beside her newly slain body on the invasion battlefield, he had watched her soul cross to the otherworld and had tried to follow. His mother had forbidden it, cursing him with continued life. Before Mithras's intervention, her ghost had returned to him nightly, standing in judgement of his deeds, taunting him with the many different pasts and futures that could have been his had he not chosen to fight for Rome: Valerius the dreamer, Valerius the warrior, Valerius, friend and lover of dreamers and warriors, night-walker, hound-caller, hare-dreamer, hero of battles. Most often she brought bright, vivid images of his sister, who, alone of all his family, was still alive. Word came daily of the resistance in the west and her part in it.

If his mother, who was dead, despised him, Valerius had no difficulty imagining the undiluted loathing with which his sister would view the man he had become. There were moments in the darkest nights when Valerius wished her dead and himself free of the consequences of her continued life—and hated himself for wishing so. More than anyone or anything else, it was to escape the living reality of the Boudica that Julius Valerius had first offered himself to the Infinite Sun.

Valerius continued to chant, not trusting silent prayer alone to keep the phantoms at bay. When he was calmer and could see only Mithras and the bull in the worlds beyond the one around him, he levered himself care-fully away from the oak upright and continued to feel his way down the corridor. At the far end he found the door and pushed it open.

Outside, there was snow. He had known there would be from the cold, but the depth of it surprised him. It came to his knees, with a crisp skin on top that crackled under his weight.

If he had slept without dreams and woken free of memories, the beauty of the night would have left him silent with awe. The vast area of the fortress and the land around it had been brought together under a bear's pelt of unmarked snow so that Roman land and native land were one. Above, the sky had emptied itself and the clouds had gone, leaving the god's arc purest black. A million scattered stars reflected snow light so that, even without the moon, he could see clearly the outlines of the bar-racks stretching in all directions. On the eastern horizon a finger's breadth of not-black presaged the dawn. For an ordinary man in ordinary times, it would have been a night to find a hound and go hunting, to take a spear with a good blade and seek out the wry-tusked yearling boar that had evaded the best of the legions' trackers all through the summer, a night to fire the blood and pump the heart and remember what it was to live.

Were Valerius younger and still in love, he might have done exactly that, deaf to the responsibilities of rank. Youth and passion had protected him once from the realities of life, but he was no longer in thrall to either of these things, and his promotion to duplicarius was a recent one, long sought and much cherished. Now he ignored both the beauty and the po-tential for joy in the world around him and looked instead for the many and varied chances of disaster.

He did not have to seek far. The pipes leading to the latrines had frozen; he found that almost immediately. He used them anyway, know-ing that what he deposited would sit and stink until the flow of water could be restored. He was not the first; someone else had risen early and had the same need. They, too, had come after the last fall of snow. A pair of boots had left clear prints, and Valerius followed them for a while un-til the two paths separated: the boots to go left, to the eastern gate and the annexe beyond, which housed the latest wing of cavalry to arrive from Rome; Valerius to go right, to the horse lines, where his duty lay.

The lights at the stables had not gone out overnight; two men would have been flogged had they done so. By their pooled light, he could see that the mounts of his own command were quiet and none of the stable roofs had collapsed under the snow's added weight. That had been his greatest fear, and he was grateful not to find it realized. He took a fistful of corn from the feed room and walked down the line, doling it out sparingly. At the end, separated by a gap from the other mounts, stood an oddly marked pied horse, all black with streaks of white running down from poll, withers, and croup, as if the night sky had been laid on its hide and then the gods had splashed it with milk, or shards of ice.

This one horse did not lean out and lip at his palm for the corn as all the others had done but plunged forward, straining over the door to snatch with bared teeth at the edge of Valerius's cloak. He knocked its head away with the balled edge of his fist, and it came back faster a second time, head snaking and ears laid flat with the whites showing round its eyes and its teeth agape.

He was already sliding sideways between the oncoming teeth and the door when a voice said, "He is as evil as they say, then?"

Valerius had believed himself entirely alone. The shock of finding it otherwise stopped him just long enough for the horse's bared teeth to meet the flesh of his shoulder, stunningly. He fell as if struck by a lump hammer.

It would have been hard to say who was the more shocked. The horse jerked back, flinging its head high. It spun in the box, crashing against the walls so that the whole line became restless. The stranger was calmer but more aware of his fault.

"I'm sorry. I should have waited before I spoke. They told me his name is Crow, which means death, and I thought it a wine-fuelled jest. Clearly I was mistaken. Are you hurt?"

"No. I always fall at my mount's feet first thing in the morning. My physician recommends it. Thank you."

Valerius took the offered hand and pulled himself upright. His shoulder boiled as if filled with liquid lead. Many years ago he had taken a sword wound in exactly that place, and the flesh bruised more easily than elsewhere. He rolled his arm a little, feeling if the bones had broken and, hearing no grating, nor feeling any, chose for the moment to ignore it and deal with the more pressing matters of the foreigner—he must be a foreigner; not a single member of the garrison would have been so carelessly familiar—and the pied horse.

In the world of Valerius's priorities, horses always came before men. He lifted the catch on the door and slid inside. The Crow, whose name did indeed mean death, turned to kick as he entered the box, which was a good sign that the horse was not as shocked as it had looked. Sliding past, Valerius grabbed for a hank of mane near the top of its neck, then crooked his arm under its throat and across the bridge of its nose as a makeshift halter. Between them it was a signal that the man had won and the beast could accept his gift of corn with its pride intact. It did so, and he walked it to the door, easing out before it could strike again.

"Thank you. I believe he—" He was speaking to empty air and so stopped. The foreigner was further down the line, leaning over a box door talking to the chestnut mare inside. He was a man of Valerius's own age, old enough to have been a warrior amongst his own people and then to have trained with the cavalry and risen up from the rank of trooper, but not so old that he had seen many battles. He was half a head shorter than Valerius, which still left him taller than most Romans. In the light of the stable lamps, his hair took on the russet brown of a stag at the rut, and it hung thickly to his shoulders without the plaiting or adornment that would have been usual in a Gaul. He wore horseman's boots, not *caligae*, which meant he was cavalry, not infantry, and the trail of prints from one stable to the other matched exactly the trail Valerius had tracked from the latrines. Valerius set himself a small and silent wager as to the man's rank and nationality.

Seeing him coming, the foreigner turned from his preoccupation with the chestnut mare in the box. Without saluting, he asked, "Is your shoulder damaged?"

No one ranked lower than duplicarius would have spoken with such easy familiarity; anyone higher would have demanded some kind of acknowledgement. The foreigner's rank, then, was equivalent to the master of horse; first part of the wager won.

Valerius said, "No. At least, not badly. The Crow has spent the past eight years trying to bite me, and that was the first time he's ever succeeded. I was afraid he might feel he had reached the zenith of his life and should lie down and give himself to the god. He seems well, however, for which I am duly grateful. Without a horse to fight, what would a man do in the long days of the governor's peace?"

It was a test, of sorts, and was recognized as such. The foreigner's mouth twitched in the beginnings of a smile. "Polish his armour, perhaps? And await the call to war?" The answer was a safe one, saying all that was needed. Neither was about to compromise himself before the other in a way that could be considered treasonous, but each hated equally the tedium and inactivity of life in the fortress.

Valerius walked on to the next stable block in which the horses of the second troop were housed. They were not strictly his responsibility, but he did not fully trust the one who should have cared for them, the one who was clearly still asleep, unaware that it had snowed through the night. He reached the first box and gave the last of his corn to a roan gelding who liked him.

He was halfway down the line when the foreign horse-master caught him up. The second half of the wager remained outstanding. It was part of Valerius's pact with himself that he could not ask any question outright. He said, "You are with the cavalry unit that came over with the new governor—yes? The one camped in the annexe alongside the bath-house. Are your horses settling in after the sea crossing and the ride here?"

The foreigner shrugged, loosely. "They're settled and resting, although they weary of the cold, as I do. In Thrace it snows, but the air is not so wet, and the cold does not eat so at one's bones. And we were told it would not snow here for a month."

In Thrace? Hah. Thracian! It had been an unsettling night, but the day was proving better. Valerius had won a brief skirmish against the Crow, or at least had not lost; had unequivocally won the wager he had set himself, and the god had kept his horses from ruin in the snow. Feeling better than he had since waking, Valerius said, "It doesn't usually snow this early. This is unfortunate."

"Or perhaps fortunate? The gods have sent it as a gift to the new governor. The natives will be as cold as we and will not press their rebellion."

They were walking together, with an ease of long familiarity. Without thinking, Valerius said, "If it is a gift, then it has been requested of their gods by the dreamers and granted by them as evidence of good will. Have you ever been in a native roundhouse?"

"Not such as you have here."

"No, well, you will have to believe me when I say that we may have brought them civilization in the form of freezing barracks with four men to an unheated room, but the natives will have slept the night in a roundhouse the height of ten men, with forty families within, and a fire that was banked high and gave heat all night. They will have slept with their hounds at their backs and their lovers close, and they will not have needed to wrap up in their cloaks, or even to wear a second tunic, to have slept well and woken rested. They will have risen this morning to warmth and food and the companionship of their families, and if they choose not to read the signs sent by their gods the night before, they won't know it has snowed except by the smell of the air and only then as they lift the door-flap. I wouldn't say this is a gift from Roman gods, and it will certainly not quench the fires of rebellion."

He stopped, biting his tongue. The Thracian stared at him thoughtfully. Another man might have asked how a junior officer in the Gaulish auxiliary had come to be so familiar with the interior of a native round-house in winter, or at least would have asked the questions that confirmed the rumours or denied them. This man rubbed the side of his nose a moment and said only, "I have heard that you lived for a while amongst the Eceni. Is it true that their women lead the warriors into battle?"

The charge from the west was led by a woman. The name they are calling is Boudica, she who brings victory. The voice was Valerius's own, younger and still mercifully unaware.

His mother, coming later, knew everything and judged him for it. *Her mark is the serpent-spear, painted in living blood on Mona's grey. Once it was red on Eceni blue. Yours could have matched it, the horse or the hare painted on blue. You could have been dreamer to her warrior. With you at her side, she would have been . . .*

"No."

For the second time that morning, Valerius turned his back on the foreigner and walked away. In front of him, the *principia* dwarfed the buildings around it. Only the governor's house came close in grandeur to the great quadrangle of the legion's assembly hall, and at that moment Valerius was not concerned with the governor's peace and comfort. He had responsibilities due his rank. In the honouring of them was his best, possibly his only, defence.

Speaking over his shoulder, he said, "We should finish our inspection of the stables and then check the *principia*. Did the tavern rumour-mongers tell you also that the roof caved in last winter under the weight of the snow and was not rebuilt until after mid-summer? Our recently departed governor, may the god grant him long life, wished to display to the natives the full splendour of Rome. There are tiles under that snow so bright they would make your eyes water if you had to stare at them under a full sun."

The Thracian laughed, a little late, as if his mind were elsewhere. "And the beams are made of straw that they do not take the weight?"

"No. The beams are made of green oak, which is what you get if you build a fortress in a newly conquered territory and have to use whatever materials are to hand. The first architect built on Roman lines, believing that the beams must be slender to look good. The second learned from his predecessor's mistakes. The new ones are twice the size of the old, but this snow is twice as thick. It should be swept from the roof without delay. I can see to that, or find someone who can. If your horses and your men are well and you can spare the time, it might be good if you sought out the water engineer. The baths are the child of his heart, and if he finds the pipes are malfunctioning, he may, like the horse, decide it is time to lie down and give himself up to the god. His name is Lucius Bassianus, an Iberian—you will have heard of him?"

The foreigner was leaning against the wall of the last stable in line, with his thumb in his belt, and he was studying Valerius as a man might study a newly bought colt. He was manifestly unconcerned by the fate of the *principia* or the latrines. "I'm sorry," he said, shaking his head. "I haven't, but then I have been here less than two days, and those who tell tales are concerned with bigger minds than a water engineer and the sewers he builds. The most talkative, or perhaps the most vengeful, speak of a newly made duplicarius of the Fifth Gallorum with a pied horse that is evil incarnate and of his once-friend, the prefect Corvus, who was once a captive of the natives."

The tilt of his head left the way for a question and its ready answer. Any normal man would want to know what others said of him when his back was turned. In return, such a man would offer more information than the rumour-mongers could provide.

Valerius had a good idea what was said of him and had no desire to hear the embellishments spewed from late-night wine. He said, "Did they tell you that we have a governor who rode into his province expecting the rich pickings of conquest and found himself instead in the midst of an unfinished war that could take him ten years and as many legions to win?"

The Thracian conceded defeat with a good grace. "No," he said. "For the hard truth, I come to my elders and betters. In the minds of those I drink with, talk of war is a waste of breath when we could be talking of love and loss and the passions that arouse us. The word of the governor was all of his son, who is senior tribune with the Second Legion, stationed in the far south-west. The lad, they say, had barely settled into his new lodgings when he was sent back to attend the governor's war council with word that the legion is beset by natives and the legate dare not leave his post."

"Which, of course, has much to do with love and loss and the passions of arousal."

The Thracian grinned. "It might do. I am told that the governor's son is tall and very beautiful, with jet black hair and eyes like a doe, and the legate has really sent him east to keep him safe from the centurions of the Second who have been in post too long and are tiring of the other ranks." He evaluated the effect of this and then, only a little more gravely, said, "But of course those of us of more senior rank know that he will have been sent because he can be relied upon to impress on his father the severity of the threat posed by the hostile tribes that besiege his legion."

"And those of us of more senior rank can imagine that if the young man succeeds, we might well find ourselves riding west to support that legion in battle."

"Would we mind that?"

Valerius said, "The Gauls would be delighted. They are ready for action. I don't know about the Thracians. Can you ride your horses in knee-deep snow?"

The Thracian blinked slowly. With a childlike gravity, he said, "Of course, but we would not choose to do so unless forced. In Thrace a man's horse is his brother. We would never make him lame to prove a point."

Valerius laughed. It was a long time since he had been bested in conversation, and longer still since he had laughed aloud and meant it. Better than anything else, it cleared the last vestiges of the dreams from the night. He said, "If you drink in the sewer taverns long enough, you'll find that the men of the Quinta Gallorum prefer to ride mares because they can pass urine at a full gallop without needing to slow or to stop, and that to a Gaul a man's mount is far closer than his brother."

The smile that met Valerius's was brilliant. "But you're not a Gaul?"

"I am not."

They walked on in peaceful silence to the junction with the *via principalis*. The snow was thicker here. Drifts piled deeply against the side of the nearest tribune's house, made citrus by the light of a late-tended lamp. The frozen crust was thicker here, too. Almost, they could walk on it without sinking through.

The Thracian said, "I will find the engineer Bassianus and tell him that the pipes leading to the latrines are frozen and also some of those feeding the bath-house. I looked in before I came up here, and at least half are not flowing as they were last night. In the course of my search, is there anywhere I might come across real cooked food?"

He asked his question casually, which must have taken some effort. Every fortress had somewhere among its guard posts a reliable source of decent, safe, hot food that could be begged or bought on a cold night. For a trooper or a legionary newly arrived, the knowledge of who cooked it and where was one of those many small details that transformed fortress life from the barely endurable to something more pleasant. The secret was not always freely given, however, or even readily bought.

At another time, or with another man, Valerius might well have feigned ignorance or simply refused to answer. Instead, pointing to his right, he said, "Try the south tower of the east gate. They keep alight a brazier, and I have never known them not to have meat. At worst, on poor days, it isn't spiced."

Grinning, the Thracian clapped him on the arm. "But today will not be a poor day. Will you join me?"

With all that had just passed, Valerius might have considered it, but he had seen a lamp lit in the doorway of a house further down the *via principalis* and had a need to find out what it meant. "With regret, no," he said. "There is still the matter of the snow on the roof of the *principia*. I should report now, while there is still time to act."

"Then I will go alone." The Thracian saluted. "It has been a pleasure to know you."

"And you." They had parted and taken ten paces before Valerius turned back. "You didn't tell me your name."

"Sdapeze, Longinus Sdapeze, armourer and horse-master of the Ala Prima Thracum." The man's smile was open and friendly. He had pale eyes, almost yellow, like a hawk's. "We will ride out together one day soon when the snow will not make the horses lame, and you will see that a Thracian mount can match any colt bred in Gaul, however bad its temper."

The man was lost in the gloom before Valerius turned his mind to what had been said and found that this last, which had sounded like a request, had in fact been a challenge and an offer, and that, nodding, he had accepted both.

CHAPTER 5

If he had been faithful to the requirements of rank order, Valerius would have reported the facts of the snow and the frozen latrines to his immediate superior, the decurion Regulus. If, instead, he had followed the imperatives of his god, he would have sought out the centurion of the third cohort of the Twentieth Legion, who was his new Father under the Sun, replacing Marullus, who had gone to join the Praetorian Guard in Rome. He did neither of these, but followed the light of a single lamp south down the main arterial road of the fortress. As he walked, he tracked a single set of footprints in the snow, passing in the same direction.

Quintus Valerius Corvus, prefect of the Ala Quinta Gallorum, occupied one of the smaller tribunical houses located near the southern end of the *via principalis,* on the opposite side to the great covered quadrangle of the *principia.* The prefect had given Valerius the name he now bore and, for five good years, a reason to live. There had been a time, before the building of the tribunes' quarters was complete, when it had seemed likely that Valerius would be granted his own room within Corvus's lodgings. Indeed, in the chaos of building, when men throughout the fortress lived in half-finished accommodations, sleeping amongst piles of bricks with wet plaster on the walls and the smell of whitewash in the air, Valerius had known which room it would be even if he had not yet slept there.

Then the embers of passion had still warmed Valerius's heart, and the impossible pressures of his life had not begun to take their full toll. He had been of junior rank and liked by his peers. The unstable patronage of the then-emperor Caligula and his own relationship with Corvus, which could so easily have soured his standing with the other men, had instead elevated him to the rank of mascot within the troop. He had found honour fighting the hostile Germanic tribes on the Rhine, and in his twisted half-mastery of the Crow-horse, he had proved himself a horseman worthy of the rank Corvus had bestowed on him.

To the cavalry, horsemanship and fighting prowess were intimately entwined, and in a wing drawn almost exclusively from the ranks of conquered Gauls, Valerius had been one of the very few to have seen real combat before he had enrolled. His peers invented stories of the dark-haired tribal boy who had ridden his mad horse to freedom and then, eschewing all offers to return to his homeland, had joined the legions to fight for Rome. Rumours grew around him and Corvus, further tangling their joint past until it was said that the Roman prefect had been captured by barbarian tribes as he spied for the emperor in Britannia and that Valerius had conspired to free him, waiting on the shore until Corvus could sail back alone to find him. The wilder tales said that together they had fought the dreamers to wrest Valerius back to civilization, calling down the power of Roman gods to best those of the natives. No one thought to ask why a boy raised in the freedom of the native tribes should prefer the discipline of the Rhine legions, beset by river-mist and the constant threat of hostile attack, nor later, fighting the dreamers and the fog they called down on a battlefield, did anybody question the ability of one man to fight against them and win.

The truth was both less and more unlikely, and it waited for Valerius in the waking dreams of his nights, when fear of his mother kept sleep at bay. Then he lay in the dormitory listening to the sleeping breath of men he did not love, and it was hard not to compare the cold and isolated damp with the comfort of a crowded roundhouse and the close, uncomplicated warmth of a hound, or the unexpected joy of intimacy with Corvus, which had opened the world and made life possible again.

The paths to the past, once travelled, were not easy to avoid. Valerius had found by experience that half a night could be lost staring into darkness trying to decide if the gossip was half right and the spark with Corvus had truly been there in the six months when the young Roman officer had, indeed, been a captive of the tribes and a boy with a passing knowledge of Gaulish had become his confidant and friend. It was too long ago ever to be sure, and the memories, when they came, had an otherworldly sense to them, as if they were tales of another man's life, told so often as to gain a credence of their own. Only some things came back in full, and those most often in daylight, cripplingly: the sudden knifing images of love and its aftermath; the flash of a blue cloak and the smile above it; the sheer exhilarating power of a red Thessalian mare, racing a

man on a dun colt; the flash of sun-struck bronze as a line of Trinovantian horsemen raised their shields and the Eceni, schooled by a Roman,
came against them. All these could sweep through without warning, leaving Valerius ragged, irritable, and looking for someone or something to
shout at.

With adequate sleep and no dreams, he could manage the worst excesses of his anger, but the constant presence of his mother and the judge-
ments she brought had eroded his equanimity. The first few months after
the invasion had been chaotic, and everyone had lived on short tempers
and little sleep. The warmer, longer days of spring had restored most
men's humour; it was only Valerius who continued to vent his rage at whoever was within reach. The men came to like him less and fear him more,
and although this was almost certainly what had earned him the promotion, it had not restored peace to his soul.

It was Corvus, ultimately, who bore the worst and deserved it least,
and it had been at Valerius's own request that his room in Corvus's house
had been given over to other use and he had been billeted instead with the
other junior officers of his troop. He had believed at the time that it was
a temporary necessity and that he was acting to protect both himself and
a man for whom, at the very least, he still had utmost respect from his own
unpredictable, unforgivable, uncontrollable, and ever-increasing lapses in
temper. Even now, two years later, he continued to believe he might one
day go back.

He had visited only twice after the house had been built, both times in the
first month after his change of billet. On each occasion a lamp lit in the
doorway had been a signal that Corvus was alone and would welcome
company. It seemed likely it did so still. It was possible that the lamp had
been lit tonight for Valerius and that, if he chose to, he could enter unan-
nounced and follow the familiar line of sheltered candles to the private
apartments. He did not so choose.

Corvus's household was always first to wake and deal with the events
of the night. The snow had been shovelled away from the doorways and a
broad corridor dug out into the *via principalis*, easing the route for the
passers-by. It was a helpful gesture that also effectively removed the possibility that anyone could follow the trail of a single set of boot prints
from the several that passed down the roadway to this particular entrance.

Frozen gravel crunched underfoot as Valerius walked to the door. A
bronze bowl stood to one side, a small mallet above it. He struck the one

softly with the other and waited as the sound embrazened the night. Everything around him was white. Even the walls of this place were washed with simple lime, leaving it pure, like the snow, clearly set apart from the tiled and painted glory of the legionary tribunes' houses set on either side.

The gong was answered, as Valerius had known it would be, by Mazoias, the Babylonian. The head of Corvus's household was a white-haired old man with a crooked shoulder. In his cups, Mazoias claimed kinship with princes of Babylon and the royal house of Persia. Sober, he was a slave whom Corvus had bought at a market in Iberia and subsequently freed, who chose to continue in place because a life spent in service to Corvus was better than any other he could envisage. The old man recognized Valerius. His gnarled features froze midway through their message of welcome, and the door, which had been opening, began to close.

Valerius put his foot in the jamb. "I think not. I have a message for the prefect. Tell him the snow is an arm's length thick on the roof of the *principia* and it will take more men than I can order to clear it. If he wishes the governor to make his first public address to his legions in safety and warmth, he will order out at least one full troop of men. Tell him also that the pipes to the main latrines are frozen. I have sent a man to find Bassianus, but the prefect may wish—"

Each man has his own scent. It may lessen a little when he is warm and oiled from the baths, or running freely with other men's blood in battle, but it never departs entirely. After a night wrapped in sheepskin against the cold, it is as strong as it will ever become, unless that night has been spent in company, in which case it is stronger. Corvus, Valerius thought, had spent this night alone, but perhaps not that part since waking. No amount of work or responsibility or prayer to the god could protect him completely from the impact of that. He drew his foot from the door-jamb, fixed his gaze on the wall opposite, and saluted.

Corvus said, "Thank you, Mazoias. I will speak with the officer."

There was a brief clash of wills, the outcome of which was never in doubt. With a glance that promised eternal damnation if his master was left out of sorts, the old man withdrew.

They were alone. Neither spoke. Snow sucked at the silence, softening it. The lamp nearest the doorway was of clay with a Capricorn painted in rough glaze on the bowl. It had never burned cleanly and did not do so now. Out of habit, and for something to do, Corvus reached up and altered the lie of the wick. A spiral of smoke rose to stain the ceiling, and the light glowed more strongly after, so that more of each of them could be seen. Corvus had not been awake long; his brown hair was still damp from a hurried morning wash and not adequately combed. In truth, it was never adequately combed. The back was cut properly short, but the flick of life at the front swooped in an unruly curve across his forehead and mirrored the arc of his brows. It said all one needed to know of the man and his attitude to authority. The scars and the weather-browned skin told the same tale. Only his eyes could tell more, did he choose, but they were hidden in shadow. His words fell out of the same shaded space.

"What do I call you now?" Their last argument, the most damaging, had been over Corvus's use of the old name, now abandoned. They had never resolved it.

Valerius said, "I am Julius Valerius in the records, as you know. My men call me duplicarius, or master of horse. Both are acceptable."

"Good. I'll try to remember. How is he?"

"Who?"

"Your man-killing horse. The one of whom you are master."

There was a thread of humour in the voice. Caught off guard, Valerius replied in kind. "He's well. You'd be proud of him. He managed to bite me this morning. The shock nearly killed us both."

Distantly, he was aware that his shoulder ached, but the pain was not yet fully part of him. Like the brand, he yearned for it to come home, as if pain were something real in which he could hide. Experimentally, he rolled his arm back and winced. He had forgotten in whose company he stood. Corvus had reached a hand for his cloak and turned the neck of it back before either of them remembered that he no longer had leave—and then remembered also that he was a prefect and could do anything he chose with the cloak and person of a junior officer. Valerius swayed back at his touch and came upright again, parade-ground stiff.

Corvus hissed through his teeth and snatched his hand away. "I'm sorry."

"No harm." Valerius believed it. The cloak may have been turned back, but the fit of his tunic covered his shoulder. He did not find until later that the spreading bruise had crept up his neck, turning the flesh blue-black from shoulder to ear and from collarbone to scapula, and that a great butterfly's wing of it showed clearly in the light from the lamp. Longinus Sdapeze must have seen it, too, but had the sense not to comment.

Corvus stared ahead, saying nothing. Rarely were they so formal in each other's company. It damaged them both and destroyed what they had been.

Pulling his cloak straight, Valerius said, "I'm sorry, I was distracted. One of the Thracian cavalrymen came with news that the pipes to the bath-house are frozen. Longinus Sdapeze. He's astute. He thinks of problems before they occur."

Men like that were few enough. On the Rhine, Valerius and Corvus had vied with each other to find them, to single them out and train with them, to set them apart from the greater mass of unthinking brutality that was the legion and its auxiliaries. They had not concerned themselves with the other ways by which men set themselves apart.

As if following the thought, Corvus said, "I heard you are given to the bull-slayer. That you have taken the raven."

It was not a secret. Everybody knew the names of the initiates. The secrecy lay in the nature of the tests and the oaths required of the acolytes; in this was the god's ultimate strength. Only with Corvus did the fact of one man's vows mean so much more.

Stiffly, Valerius said, "I believed it would be constructive in the development of my career."

Corvus raised one brow. "I'm sure it will be."

They waited. A thin northern wind coursed down the *via principalis.* Shouted orders rode on the back of it. Enough men had woken for others to realize the danger posed by the snow. The part of Valerius that genuinely was concerned with the future of his career saw the urgency of his message diminish, and with it the credit for raising the alarm.

Corvus ran his tongue round his teeth. After a moment he stepped back, holding the door open. "Would you come in? I have sent word to the decurions to have the fifth and sixth troops clear the roofs of the main buildings of the *principia.* The fourth will see to the *praetoria*, although it is furnished with hypocausts and I suspect the governor's household will have burned the fires throughout the last several nights to banish the cold. It would not surprise me to see the tiles shine free of snow and steaming when the sun rises."

"Rank will have its privilege," said Valerius drily.

"Indeed. Which is why I think you should meet the governor's son. He is inside, and I have left him alone too long. We were discussing the uprising in the west. Will you join us?"

CHAPTER 6

Corvus's morning visitor waited, as was proper, in the prefect's office. It was a spare, sparse room to be dignified with such a title. The walls were whitewashed and without adornment. The plaster was finer than in the barracks and the place lacked the clutter of the legionary lodgings, but otherwise there was little to choose between this room and the one in which Valerius had awakened before dawn. This one was bigger, that was all, and there were lamps at every available point in case the prefect should require to read something while standing in the farthest corner. In addition to those, it was favoured with the added advantage of a table and two chairs, one of them occupied by a man who stood as the door opened.

"Corvus? Who was— Ah, we have a visitor. An auxiliary. Can I guess who this is?"

"Probably, but I'll introduce you anyway. Valerius, come in. Don't stand in the doorway, you'll let in the cold."

And so he had to enter, into the presence of the smiling youth with the perfectly black hair and the eyes of a doe who almost certainly did know exactly who Valerius was and what he had been and did not find his presence uncomfortable. Indeed, it seemed likely that this particular youth had never had reason to feel uncomfortable at any time since the day of his smooth, sedate birth into the splendour and riches of Rome.

Longinus Sdapeze, a Thracian tribesman with only a passing veneer of civilization, had remarked on the beauty of the governor's son. The Thracian had not remarked on the sheen of good breeding the young man carried and the quiet assurance that went with exceptional wealth and the certainty of a senatorial future. He had not mentioned, either, that the lad was twenty and that the vigour of youth shone from him as if from a newly backed racehorse so that, even if one loathed him on instinct, it was impossible to look elsewhere.

In a fortress full of hardened legionaries, Valerius was not used to feeling old or, given his own height, small. In the presence of the governor's son, he felt both, and for that alone he would have left if propriety and his pride had allowed it. Neither did, and so he stood just inside the door and was formally introduced.

"Tribune, this is Julius Valerius, duplicarius of the third troop under my command—the officer of whom we were speaking earlier. Valerius, this is Marcus Ostorius Scapula, tribune in the Second Legion. His legate has sent him here with news of the worsening situation in the west."

The hair prickled on Valerius's neck . . . *of whom we were speaking earlier.* The voice of quiet irony that filled his mind in times of personal crisis noted that at least part of Longinus Sdapeze's rumour was true; the tribune had been sent to appeal to his father for aid. That did not make the rest of it false. *They say the legate has really sent him to keep him safe from the centurions who have been in post too long and are tiring of the other ranks.* One could wonder if the governor would consider a prefect a better match than a centurion for his son.

Mazoias had reappeared, bringing a third chair and well-watered wine. He fussed around the corners lighting more lamps, as if the room had a sudden need to be brighter. The governor's son was happy to stand under the glare of more lights; he was used to being stared at. Crossing his arms on his chest, he said, "We were discussing the most recent Siluran uprising and the likely impact on the client tribes around the fortress. The prefect tells me you may have a useful insight into their likely response should the governor choose to have them forcibly disarmed."

What?

One does not gape at a governor's son even if his father has just proposed an act of monstrous insanity before which a junior officer's personal concerns are rendered so trivial as to be meaningless.

Valerius found a wall behind him and leaned against it. With great care he said, "The governor is very new to the province—he has been here less than one full day. He arrives at a time of great disquiet, and it is certain that the Silures and their allies have timed their uprising to coincide with his predecessor's departure so that—"

"We know that. The war chief Caradoc plans his strategies as if Caesar himself were advising him. What we do not know is what the eastern tribes will do if we confiscate their weapons. I understand that you have some experience of life amongst the natives and may therefore be in a unique position to tell us."

Too many betrayals crowded Valerius's brain. From the far side of the room, Corvus said, "Tribune, that's unfair. Valerius is a duplicarius and only newly that. Were he a full decurion, he would not feel able to answer honestly now that you have told him the plan is the governor's. Even I would only say this in private, but you have to believe me that the tribes will fight for their weapons as hard as any Roman would, possibly more so. Valerius would tell you the same if he had leave."

"Then I give him leave. Duplicarius, I put you on notice that the discussion taking place in this room is private, and I caution you not to repeat any part of it beyond these walls or in other company. Do I have your oath that this is so?"

Valerius nodded. "You do." What else could he say? He had seen men at sword-point given more freedom to move.

"Good, then I am similarly bound. I may give my father my advice based on your information and that of the prefect, but I will not reveal its source. Therefore you are free to answer as you believe. In fact, I command you to do so. What will the tribes do if we require them to give up their weapons?"

A man's career could fall on such as this. When it is all that he has left, such a thing matters a great deal. Valerius took a steadying breath. Letting it out, he said, "If you disarm them, without question they will rebel."

"Why?"

Images jostled for space in the crowded morass of his mind, none of them Roman, none of them suitable for a governor's son. Selecting the few he could readily present to tutored Latin sensibilities, Valerius said, "To the tribes, a warrior's blade is a living thing, as precious as a hound or a well-trained battle-mount, not simply because of its worth as a weapon but because it carries the dream of the one who wields it, the essence of the true self that only the gods know. In the sword resides the quality of the warrior's courage, the honour, the pride, the humanity, the generosity of spirit—or lack of it. If it is a blade of the ancestors, passed down from father to daughter, from mother to son, then it carries also the ancestors'—"

"Stop. 'From father to daughter, from mother to son'?"

They were not doe-eyes. The governor's son was a pitiless black-eyed falcon, and his eyes promised swift death to all who scuttled under their gaze. Quietly he said, "A centurion of the Second Legion has been demoted to the ranks, and twelve of his men flogged, for stating in reports and under questioning that a woman led the greater mass of the Siluran warriors in their attack on the westernmost fort and that other women fought at her side. I questioned the men myself, and they would not change their accounts. The governor believes this to be the fantasy of defeated minds. Was he right?"

Longinus had asked much the same question, but he could safely be ignored, where a governor's son could not. *Her mark is the serpent-spear, painted in living blood . . . Yours could have been the horse, or the hare . . .*

Valerius would not—could not—look at Corvus. A name burned the air between them and was not to be spoken under any circumstances. In a voice that strained for normality and fell so very short, he said, "The governor is always right."

He heard the silence crack.

"So he was wrong."

Marcus Ostorius Scapula paced the length of the room. With his face to the far wall and his hands locked behind him, he said, "You were explaining why the eastern tribes will rebel if disarmed. If I understand you aright, they value their weapons as amongst their most prized possessions, and if we were to confiscate these blades—if we were, say, to have a smith break them on an anvil in full sight of their people—we would cause them great pain as well as diminish their capacity to rebel. Am I correct?"

"You would as well crucify their children."

"It may come to that."

The young man turned. He was not, after all, entirely without pity, one could read it on his face, but he was the son of the man who had taken command of a province expecting at least a winter's peace and had first to achieve it. Sitting, Marcus Ostorius leaned forward, placed his elbows on his knees, and made of his fingers a steep-sided tent that tapped a slow rhythm on his lips.

"You will know that there has been insurrection in the lands north of here in the last half month. Two forts have been destroyed by the Eceni, and a unit of the Twentieth was forced to seek refuge here in the fortress. The governor has two choices. He can order the decimation of the two cohorts that fled in the face of the enemy as punishment for their cowardice, or he can subjugate the tribes as punishment for the uprising and as a means to prevent its repeat. Which of these would you advise him to choose?"

Valerius did gape then. Even Corvus shifted in his chair. With exaggerated deference the prefect said, "Decimation, tribune? Is the governor truly considering this?" Scapula's reputation, ferocious as it was, had not extended that far.

Scapula's only son smiled tightly. "He is. It may be he needs to do both, but I think not. Decimation hasn't been practised since the time of the Republic. To order it now would send a message to the four legions of Britannia that they had better fear my father more than the tribes who would attack them. The sad truth is that both the tribunes and the legates who have command now are new to their posts; it is not certain the men would obey an order to beat to death one in ten of their comrades. It isn't something we would wish to test in current circumstances. The only alternative is to subdue the local tribes without delay. We cannot fight a war in the west if there is a risk that the east will rise at our back. Camulodunum must be made secure."

Camulodunum. He named it Camul's dun, home to the war god of the Trinovantes, not Cunobelin's dun, as it had been before. All of the Romans had done so since they first arrived, as if told this was its name. No one living had considered it expedient to tell them otherwise.

Valerius did not correct him now. The perpetual knot in his gut was shifting and changing, coming alive with a flaring admixture of fear and anticipation. Whispers of raw terror traced lines up his spine and with them a spark that blazed bright as the god's light and promised the blessed oblivion of battle. He had seen too little of that, these last four years.

Thoughtfully, he asked, "You have two thousand veterans in Camulodunum who have been promised land when they retire. Whose land will they be given to farm?"

Marcus Ostorius answered, "The Trinovantes'. Once the colony is formed, this place becomes an extension of Rome, at which point the natives will no longer have any legal claim to any of their land."

He said it as if the facts were obvious, which they were not.

Stiffly—later, one could think unwillingly—Corvus said, "Valerius . . . in Rome only citizens may own land. Only one of the Trinovantes has been made a citizen, and he will retain his steading. The rest of the population automatically forfeits all land rights. It may be that the new governor will choose to recompense the families for their loss, but he is not required to do so."

The rumours had said as much, but sane men did not believe them. Gripping his hands together to keep them still, Valerius said, "In that case, you have no choice but to disarm the tribes immediately, to crush them completely using utmost force. Those who have half a mind to rebel will do so, but if you make examples of them, harshly, the rest may subside. They will loathe us for it, but they loathe us anyway. We have more to lose than their opinion of us."

He was no longer obeying orders but the dictates of his body. The rising hairs on his neck and the sweeping heat and cold in his belly and the clash of weapons and the far-off cries of the wounded were both a memory and a premonition. He did not know the ways in which his face changed as he spoke, but he felt the stir in the air, and when he finally removed his gaze from the blank wall on which the battles had been fought and lost, he found that it drifted, without his will, to Corvus's face. The concern he read there surprised him. Still, it was Marcus Ostorius, the governor's son, who spoke. His voice was quiet, as it might be were he speaking in the presence of one who slept and must not be wakened.

"Why must we crush them so completely, Valerius?"

"Because in taking their land, you are taking their livelihood. They can live without weapons, they know that even if their pride won't let them admit it, but they can't live without the means to eat. If the Twentieth departs and the Trinovantes are still in possession of their weapons when the veterans begin to take their fields, their cattle, their grain, then you will have no colony by the end of winter, and the war here in the east will make the one happening now in the west look like a petty skirmish. If the veterans are to have any hope of survival, you must confiscate all of the natives' weapons, punishing everyone who resists, or you must kill them all down to the last child at the breast. Those are your only choices."

CHAPTER 7

"It is in my mind that a people faced with death or slavery as their only choices are not readily going to relinquish war."

Longinus said it, five days later, standing on the rotting ice of the river. The Thracian's horses, who were indeed his brothers but no more than that, had drunk from holes chipped at the water's edge and were pawing holes in the snow to graze. The mounts of Valerius's troop mingled with them as they had done since the afternoon of their first meeting.

With their charges safe, the two horse-masters had sought a wager that was hard enough to make a satisfying win while still being within the bounds of possibility and, at a stretch, of personal safety. The treacherous melting ice had provided the answer. Each man was halfway to winning, or losing, when Longinus brought up the topic of the governor's speech.

It was a diversionary tactic, designed to throw Valerius off his count, and the Thracian took care to check the length of the river in both directions before he spoke. Longinus might have been rash, even ridiculously prone to personal risk, but he was not stupid.

The governor had not ordered decimation, but three men had been flogged for sedition, and none had questioned the wisdom of Scapula's tactics in the west as explicitly as Longinus. Still, the mutterings continued. The disarming of the eastern tribes had been accepted readily by the ranks; they were safer if the barbarians around the fortress were stripped of their weapons. The governor's inaugural speech, given in the freezing hall of the *praetoria*, had made them far more restless. Scapula was not a man to take his orders lightly. He had been instructed to make the west safe, and he had determined that the best way to do so was to extinguish the entire tribe of the Silures. Nothing of such severity had been practised in the province since the invasion, nor even threatened. It was all too easy to imagine the response of the western warriors when faced with the reality of a governor who had sworn to kill every man, woman, and child of their tribes.

Longinus rocked on the ice and spread his arms for balance. "You know them," he said. "Will the Silures let us kill their men and enslave their women and children as he has promised?"

Valerius said, "If they do, it will be the first time in the history of their people. Only the Ordovices are more savage, and if they are united with the Silures, nothing we can do will stop them. And then as soon as word gets out of the governor's threat, the other tribes who might have been unsure of Rome's enmity will believe the dreamers who tell them we come to destroy them all."

This, too, was subversion, but no worse than what had gone before, and it did not put Valerius off his counting. He leaned on a many-pronged hazel stump that had been cut long and left as a tethering post. With one hand he tapped the rhythm of his heartbeat on the nearest stump. Out on the river Longinus did the same, although his beat was noticeably faster. The Thracian stood rock-steady on the chalky ice with his feet planted squarely on either side of a crack the width of his fist. He had bet that the ice would hold his weight for the count of fifty heartbeats. In accepting, Valerius had not thought to specify whose heart should define the counting. He still believed he would win.

Longinus said, "So what you are saying is that the governor has given the dreamers a gift and done nothing to ... that's it ... forty-nine ... fifty ... Now!"

He leaped a spear's length forward onto the bank. Where his right foot had been, an ice plate no thicker than a man's thumb tilted sideways into sluggish water. He looked up, grinning his triumph. "The falcon-headed dagger is mine, I believe?"

The knife was small, of a length to fit in the palm of the hand and not be seen. A small Horus adorned the end of it, subtly carved, with tiny beads of jet as its eyes. It had been a gift from Corvus in their days on the Rhine, when the invasion of Britannia had been a fiction, a joke men shared at Caligula's expense. Once it had mattered to Valerius that he keep the blade. Now he reversed it so that the handle faced the Thracian and then spun it high with an added twist so that to catch it unharmed was, in itself, an achievement.

Smiling, Longinus reached out and snatched the thing from the air. If he knew that Valerius Corvus, prefect of the Quinta Gallorum, took the falcon-god as his personal emblem, he did not remark upon it. Sitting on the hard-packed snow, he said, "When the governor first made his speech, I had hopes that the western tribes might never come to hear of it. Since then, however, I have been drinking in the sewer taverns that you recommended. The word in the bottom of the wine cups is that the enemy dreamers can send their spirits as white birds to fly on the wind and that a single word, carelessly spoken, will be carried back to those who guide them. Is it true?"

The horses moved out in larger circles to graze. One of them disturbed a winter hare that neither men nor horses had known was there until she started up and ran for safety, a white rag windblown over snow. On the far bank of the river, a dog-fox stalked prey too small to be seen. A buzzard flew, mewling, across the god's arc of unblemished blue. Each, in its own way, journeyed west, towards Mona.

The fox pounced, delicately lethal. Valerius heard the small squeal of a vole dying. He lay back in the hard-packed snow and watched the buzzard ride the wind. If he had the knack, and if gods other than Mithras had not forbidden it, he could see how it would be possible to slough off his body and mount the sky to fly as that one flew. If he pressed a thumb to the scar of the god's brand and felt again the pain and the way it had spun him out of himself into darkness, then it was not so hard to take the separate parts of his soul and let one out, as if on a thread, to rise up into the greying blue of the sky, to feel the buffeting wind press his body and give lift to his wings, to look down on a small herd of horses, feeding in snow, and the two men beside them, one lying vacant-eyed, the other bending over him in anxious solicitude.

"Valerius?" A hand passed in front of his eyes, breaking the thread too fast and too hard. Longinus's face loomed too close, his breath sour with last night's wine. "Julius Valerius? Did you hear me? I was asking if their dreamers could listen to men's thoughts and carry word to their people. Will they take word of Scapula's threats back to the warriors?"

The man's eyes were too concerned, and far too close. Valerius remembered, thickly, why he preferred to water the horses alone. He stood, brushing snow from his legs, making a distance between himself and the Thracian, and whistled the pied horse. It came promptly; better than anything else alive, it knew precisely that quality of Valerius's temper and that precise line that, when crossed, made it unwise to refuse an order. The beast would take its revenge later; this was understood.

Riding back, Longinus kept his distance. He had awaited a reply and, when none came, had mounted and turned his horse to follow without further comment. They were within reach of the gates when Valerius reined in his horse.

Without turning, he said, "The dreamers may be able to do as you say. I don't know; I have never seen it. But even if they can't, soldiers talk, and a nervous man passes on the threats of the strength he perceives behind him. The first time they face each other across a barricade, some stripling of the Second still in swaddling will shout it at the warriors who are about to take his life, and if just one of them understands Latin and lives beyond the battle, the rest will know the full measure of the governor's threat."

Longinus smiled lopsidedly. "Then we had best hope they speak no Latin."

"Caradoc speaks it, who leads them. And the dreamers. If they send their spirits anywhere with word of what they hear, it's to their fellow dreamers who live among the tribes. Before full winter every warrior in every one of the western tribes will know that Scapula intends to eradicate all memory of the Silures. It will not improve the peace."

Two days later the Twentieth Legion, newly replenished and missing only a single cohort left behind in Camulodunum to guard the governor, marched west through melting snow to the aid of the Second Augusta. They took with them food and firewood, weapons and armour, horses, mules, and men, to replace those lost in the fighting. In the flurry of their leaving and its protracted preparation, the men of the two cavalry wings remaining in the fortress were given their orders, which were to systematically disarm the local tribes. The manoeuvre was to be prosecuted with force but not violence, as if the one could readily be separated from the other. Particular care was to be taken, however, at the steading of an elder of the Trinovantes who was a personal friend of the Emperor Claudius, who had, for his part, granted the man Roman citizenship. The same elder had volunteered to make available a smith who would destroy the weapons of his countrymen. For such local knowledge the elder was paid handsomely by the new governor. What the tribes thought of him, Valerius could only guess.

"His name is Heffydd. He was one of their priests who served the old king Cunobelin and did not care much for the man's sons. He took control of the dun in the chaos after the invasion and ordered the people to welcome Claudius when he rode in on his elephants at the head of his legions. He saved the first governor the inconvenience of a siege and spared

the emperor the risk of injury. He was made a citizen by Claudius himself. We are to treat him with due respect."

It was Regulus, the troop's decurion, who spoke. He had the air of a
man who talks to fill the silence and the silence was winning. Those
around him nodded or smiled, according to rank, and said nothing; a
good soldier does not chatter on his way to war.

Valerius rode in the second pair beside Umbricius, his troop's actuary,
one of the three men with whom he shared a billet. The man was pleasant enough company and did not make conversation for the sake of it,
which made it possible to shut out the day. The Crow-horse stretched its
legs and listened to what was asked of it. Somewhere amongst the hoofbeats of the dozen nearest horses, Valerius could hear one striding short
and put some effort into locating both the beast and the lame limb by
sound alone. Almost, he could have forgotten where they were going and
why, but Regulus, ever wary of silence, would not let him.

"The Trinovante steading is over the rise, in the lee of the dyke.
There's a fort this side of it, abandoned now. Claudius ordered it built
when it seemed the elder's family might be the subject of reprisals by the
natives. The Batavians manned the place before their quarters were ready
within the fortress. I don't know which would be worse—being vilified as
a collaborator by your own people or left under the protection of Civilis
and his homicidal tribesmen."

An officer of the Thracians laughed dutifully. Behind him the men of
the Quinta Gallorum maintained a studied silence. Regulus was Roman
and had only the barest understanding of what it was to be a people occupied by force. His troop, almost to a man, were Gauls whose recent ancestors had fought against Rome and whose tribal elders still told tales of
the great heroes and their tragic subjugation. From childhood they had
been able to name those families whose members had aided the enemy
and profited by it. They knew exactly which of Regulus's options would
be worse.

The two troops rode past the skeleton of the abandoned fort, now
stripped of all wood, and down a long, shallow slope to the farmstead beyond. The place was bounded by a ditch and a dyke but no stockade.
Miraculously, trees still grew around it; by the emperor's express order,
they had been spared the axes of the legion. Valerius had forgotten what
it was to ride through woodland under the gaze of winter crows with
snow scattered like salt on black branches and dying leaves spinning light
in the wind. He touched his brand and made the sign of the raven as the
birds launched upwards, cawing. Seeing it, Regulus raised a brow but said

nothing. Soon after his arrival in Camulodunum, he had made known his wish to serve the god, and it seemed likely that, come spring and the next initiation, he would do so. Until then he was as ignorant of the god's ways as any other man.

Within the ring of trees, fat, long-horned cattle grazed in pasture better than that reserved for the cavalry mounts near the fortress. A red-and-white-patched bull raised his head as the line of horses approached. He snuffed the air for danger to his herd and, seeing none, returned to the hawthorn hedge on which he had been grazing, lashing a long tongue round surviving fragments of green. At the fortress, the beef had long since been killed and salted for winter. Here there was good grass, and the neatness of the surrounding fields promised fodder for winter. This was not yet the country of people ground down by punitive taxes or the privations of war.

The steading itself sat atop a small rise. A wide track led up the slope to a gap in the turf bank. Within, smoke rose from the fires of four roundhouses and a number of smaller huts. In the spaces between, workshops, log sheds, and granaries stood closed to the snow. Somewhere out of sight a tethered hound set up a frantic baying and was joined by others, all at different pitches, so that the noise upset the horses and destroyed the mellow mood of the men.

"Gods take them, they're doing that deliberately." Regulus turned in his saddle. "Where are their warriors? We should have seen them by now."

It was the question Valerius had just asked of himself and the god. He said, "I don't know. But they know we're coming and why. There may be warriors even amongst the homestead of a collaborator who would rather die than surrender their weapons. We should perhaps assume they're prepared to fight, in which case we could go in fast and break for the battle line at the top of the hill. It will let them see we are ready to engage if it comes to that."

"Good." Regulus signalled Sabinius, the standard-bearer, who rode at his left hand. "Give us a full gallop forward, and then break at the top of the hill. Bring us as close to the gates as you can."

It was what the cavalry had trained for. In two columns, horses and men who had practised manoeuvres to the point of tedium and beyond through a summer of no action readied themselves for a brief burst of controlled speed. Regulus said, *"Now!"* and the standards stabbed the sky and sixty-four horses broke from a walk to a gallop, keeping in pairs. The eyes of their riders remained fixed on their standards, waiting for the order to change. Valerius, whose mind was torn too many ways, heard at last that the lame horse was the chestnut gelding with a white blaze ridden by the decurion of Longinus's troop. That was unfortunate. The man was a superior officer and could not be reprimanded, and Valerius would have liked, just then, to shout at someone. Deprived of the opportunity, he held the Crow-horse to a steady gallop, and man and beast fought each other for the chance to run all the way up the long slope to the steading.

In one moment the gateway was empty; in the next Gaius Claudius Heffydd, by gift of the emperor citizen of Rome, filled the space from edge to edge, made broad by the billowing of his cloak in the wind. Heffydd was not a young man; his hair was entirely white, kept in place by a thong of twisted birch bark at the brow. In the whole of the east, he was the only man openly to wear the mark of the dreamers, now forbidden. That in itself set him apart from his peers. His cloak was the yellow of gorse flowers, and the reflection of it leaked like melted butter on the remnants of snow at his feet. He bore a spear with a blade such as one might use for hunting boar and a battle-sword hung from one shoulder.

Sabinius was as good a standard-bearer as any in the province. At the right moment, without any additional command from either Regulus or Valerius, he raised his standard high. Two troops of cavalry, acting as one man, spread sideways and halted, precisely in line. The Gauls, Valerius thought, were that fraction sharper than the Thracians. A part of him rejoiced.

The echo of hooves hushed to nothing. In the pause while no decisions were made or orders given, Heffydd stepped forward and stooped to lay both of his weapons in a cross on the ground before Regulus's horse. Behind him the hidden hounds reached a frantic climax and held it. Of the hundred or more warriors reputed to be in the steading, there was still no sign.

The two decurions, Roman and Thracian, dismounted together and walked forward to meet the dreamer. Valerius sat rigidly still at Regulus's right-hand side and fixed his gaze on the half-white left ear of the pied horse. He was close to Heffydd and did not wish to be. In the morass of regret and recrimination that infected his mind, his hatred of the Trinovantes burned as an unsullied flame.

His mother never taunted him with memories of Cunobelin or his people; she had no need. Long before he had sworn allegiance to Rome, Valerius had sworn the death of the three sons of Cunobelin and as many of their tribe as he could send with them. Two parts of that oath were fulfilled: Amminios had died in Gaul, and Togodubnos had been mortally wounded in the first day of the invasion battle. Only Caradoc was left alive, the unmatched warrior who had offered Valerius friendship and then betrayed him.

News of Caradoc, last surviving son of Cunobelin, came daily from the west, with word of his part in the resistance. When the messengers had presented themselves to the governor and been dismissed, Valerius bought them drinks and a meal worth a month's pay and drained them dry of details, the better to know his enemy. On the good nights, the ones when his mother did not visit, Valerius dreamed the many deaths of Caradoc and his own part in each. When he prayed to the god, most often he prayed that at least one of these dreams be granted.

Heffydd was not Caradoc, but he wore a yellow cloak and was within close reach, which made him a good substitute. The pity of it was that the auxiliaries had been ordered not to kill a single native without due cause. The governor, in his briefing to the officers, had been explicit.

"Use all necessary force, but do not start the war afresh. Don't enter their homes unless they give cause. If any one of them resists, make of him an example the rest will never forget, but do not wipe them out." Scapula had stared specifically at Valerius as he said, "Remember, I want a docile tribe of farmers who will grow grain and make profit to pay off their loans to the emperor, not heaps of charred bone on the funeral pyres. These people are the tax revenue that pays the legions, and dead men pay no taxes. If you kill too many of them, you'll see it reflected in your pay."

Scapula had smiled then, and the effect was not nearly as becoming as in his son, but he was governor, second only to the emperor within the province, and every man present had laughed.

Dead men pay no taxes. Valerius eased forward in the saddle and ran a hand down the pied horse's neck. It was important to remember, for it and him, that they should remain calm.

Heffydd waited above his surrendered weapons. The gesture was an empty one. As the sole Roman citizen among the Trinovantes, his own weapons were not forfeit, and he must have known it. He was, therefore, sending a message either to his still-hidden warriors or to the troops who came to disarm them. If the latter, Valerius could not imagine what that message might be.

Regulus did not appear to be seeking an explanation. Dismounting, he lifted both blades, examined them, exclaimed at their workmanship, and returned both to the emperor's friend. Valerius, who had been granted his citizenship by a different emperor and knew exactly its worth, chose to look elsewhere—and froze as a flagging of yellow cloaks caught his eye.

Warriors. They had moved forward silently from behind each of the roundhouses, a good hundred of them, all on horseback, all armed for battle with their circular bull's-hide shields loose on their shoulders and their spears at their backs and their great ancestral long swords naked in their hands.

"Father of All Light, they *are* going to fight us." Valerius breathed it like a prayer, thanks for his wish fulfilled. His sword-grip came clammily to his hand, loose in its oiled sheath. The Crow-horse quivered once, all over, and then stood rock-still beneath him, like a hound on point. To Sabinius, he said, "Be ready to signal the—"

"My lord, no." Heffydd was at his bridle, too close, too fast, to both horse and rider. Valerius could smell rosemary on his hair and wormwood on his breath. Underneath both he smelled age and corruption. The dreamer's eyes were yellowed and cloudy. Valerius fought to avoid meeting their gaze.

The old man said, "We do not come to fight you. Our warriors offer no offence. They merely wish to honour the general in the surrender of their weapons. I have shown the way, and they will follow."

Regulus was not, and never would be, a general, and he was too old to respond to flattery. From behind the old man's back, he gave a flat hand signal to Valerius. Aloud he said, "Duplicarius, it seems they wish to surrender their weapons with some formality. We should allow them to do so, provided it offers no threat. You will take the men as we agreed and see to the disarming. Be courteous while they offer us no discourtesy. I will remain with the priest and take his hospitality."

The hand signal said, more privately, *And he is our hostage for their good behaviour.*

Valerius nodded crisply.

Beside him Sabinius raised a brow. "Do I signal the dismount?"

"Not while the bastards are still mounted." Valerius spun the pied horse out of line. Raising his voice to reach the most distant of the men, he said, "Re-form the columns until we're through the gates, then break sideways again for a battle line. Keep it sharp and don't move above a trot. The first one who touches his weapon without leave will regret it."

Sabinius still awaited his signal. Valerius raised his arm and led his men through the gap in the encircling rampart to face the waiting warriors. There, because he had to, he stopped.

He had expected many things, but not a spectacle such as he saw now. He had forgotten, completely, the splendour of the tribes when they chose to display their wealth. The Gauls and the Thracians of the two cavalry troops sported their tribal brooches, and some wore short-sleeved mail expressly to display the enamelled armbands beneath. Such things were allowed by their commanders provided they did not interfere with the men's safety, nor become a focus for factions and in-fighting. To Roman eyes, and those who had spent too long in Roman company, they looked gaudy and not a little barbarian. Here, matched against the dazzling splendour of the Trinovantes, they looked simply impoverished.

The tribes might have lost a two-day battle, and with it a war, but they had not yet lost their pride, nor had they been required to melt down their armbands or torcs to cast into coins for the payment of taxes; they wore their wealth and their heritage on their arms with manifest pride. Their horses, too, were sleekly fit on a summer's good grazing and polished to outshine their gold. At least half were better bred than the mounts of the cavalry. As Sabinius signalled the halt, Valerius saw finally that the warriors wore their hair braided on the left side, and woven into each strand were black crow feathers with fine bands of gold wire encircling the quills. Raw joy floated from his chest to his head, dizzyingly.

"They're wearing their kill-feathers," he said.

"What?"

"The feathers in their hair signify a kill. The colour of the band tells you who died and how. A gold band signifies one or more legionaries; the width defines the exact number. They are letting us know that they fought against us in the invasion."

"Then they need to know that they will never fight again." Umbricius, the actuary, was on his left. The man had a wound in the groin from a native warrior that had left him uncertainly potent, and he both feared them and ached for revenge.

Valerius motioned him forward. "You and Sabinius dismount and leave your horses here. As we agreed, mark a place where the weapons are to be left. We'll call the smith to break them later; first, we need to see how they plan to hand them over." An idea was growing inside him of what he would do in the same circumstances, knowing what the warriors must know. The threat of it left a taste like raw iron in his mouth. He swallowed, drily, and waited.

The two officers marked out the rectangle five paces by ten as had already been agreed. Before they completed it, a single rider walked his horse forward from the centre of the warriors' line. The man was huge, bigger than any of the auxiliaries, with the red-gold hair of his people and the bearing of an emperor. He wore the brilliant yellow cloak of the Trinovantes as his birthright, and his blade was bright with the honing of generations. He balanced it flat across his palms and then, in a breathtaking display of horsemanship, pushed his horse to a full gallop and executed a perfect circle around the rectangle just marked out. At the end, he halted, dismounted, and knelt before Umbricius.

"Jupiter, father of all the gods, I don't believe this." Sabinius had been a chieftain's son of the Parisi before he was ever a standard-bearer for the Quinta Gallorum. His eyes were wide and bright. "If he places that sword at Umbricius's feet, the boy'll gut him with it."

Valerius smiled tightly. "Not unless he wants to spend the next two days watching his skin being flayed from his body he won't."

For a long time after he joined the legions, Valerius had not understood the true value of discipline. Here and now it came home to him, perfectly. Umbricius the Gaul, humiliated beyond all endurance, would undoubtedly have done his best to kill the red-haired giant who knelt at his feet in an exact parody of Vercingetorix's surrender to Caesar in the time of his grandfathers—and would have died for it. Umbricius the trained auxiliary, in testament to a dozen floggings and an uncounted number of nights' fatigues, remained standing at perfect attention while the giant surrendered his spear and his battle-knife, either one of which would have killed the Gaul before he could raise the sword. Smiling, the red-haired warrior stepped back.

Amongst the ranks of the auxiliaries, men who had not been breathing breathed. Valerius found his hands sticky and refrained from wiping them on his thighs; he, too, could hold his discipline.

Longinus was beside him, dependably solemn. Looking down to adjust his horse's harness, he murmured, "There are over a hundred of them. We can't let them all do that."

"We don't have to. See? The others are dismounting. They've made their point and they know it. There isn't a Gaul in the entire wing who hasn't been reminded of how his ancestors were conquered by the army for which he now fights. The first Thracian who taunts him with it will have his skull crushed and his balls ripped off. Make sure your men know that."

"I think they do. Look at them."

Valerius turned. Along the lines of horsemen, the air was crisp with the threat of violence. Not a single Thracian auxiliary smiled.

Valerius turned to the men of his own command. Now that the time for action had come, he found he could immerse himself in that and not think ahead. To Sabinius, he said, "Signal the dismount. Break into fours, one to hold the mounts, the three others to take weapons. Split the natives into groups. Don't let them bunch. Take their weapons but leave their shields. Only if they rebel will they forfeit those as well."

It was what they had planned, if not exactly how they had planned it. The men worked, as they slept, in groups of four. They spread out along the line of warriors and divided them into groups, herding them back towards the roundhouse and workshops. A handful of children came to take the natives' horses, and it was clear that this, too, had been planned. The warriors simply knelt now and placed their weapons at the auxiliaries' feet. It was not the exact mimicry of Vercingetorix's surrender that the red giant had enacted, but a close enough shadow. Moreover, by retaining their shields, the warriors held on to a sense of security. It was not good, but it was the governor's command.

The troopers were efficient, as their training required. They were still outnumbered but not at such a disadvantage as they had been. They could call on five hundred more horses and as many legionaries as needed, and both sides knew it; in this lay their true strength. Alone of his command, Valerius remained mounted and back from the groups in a place where he could keep watch over all of them. The first of his fears had been realized. The rest might yet be.

He knew the worst when he saw the remaining children return. A small crowd gathered to the left of one of the roundhouses. They were boys and girls in equal numbers, dressed alike in their gorse-yellow cloaks, all brooched and banded, all too young to wear kill-feathers but old enough to have been at the invasion battle, if not fighting, then carrying water or holding the horses or mending broken weapons behind the lines. They were of that age, coming up to their warrior's tests, when insecurity plays against bravado and both overwhelm reason.

Gaudinius, the troop's armourer, had stooped to take up a blade when a tall, skinny, dark-haired girl advanced on him. Hatred splintered clear in her eyes, leaked from the sheen on her skin. The notches of ancient use showed clearly on the surrendered blade, honed down through the generations but never ground away. Like a warrior's scars, they were a constant source of pride; to lose them at any age was unbearable; to lose them within sight of the long-nights, and adulthood, was something to kill for, whatever the cost. Valerius saw the rock in the girl's hand, raised to strike.

"Not now, damn you." He had been holding the reins of his company's horses. He threw them to Umbricius, who was near. "Hold them. Be ready to mount."

The pied horse was already moving. Valerius pushed forward, and the crowd, as a mass, edged back. There were more of them now; men and women who were not warriors had joined the throng, watching in silent accusation. The girl thought she could still throw her stone, even having been seen. Valerius leaned down and caught her arm before she could raise it high enough. A tall, lean woman with the same black hair was already at her other side. In formal Trinovantian, Valerius said, "They have orders to make examples of the troublemakers. If your daughter wishes to die, she might choose a way that will not cause her family also to suffer."

He had not been sure he could remember the language until the need came. They stared at him, mother, child, and the crowd behind, disbelieving their ears. The girl tipped her head back. In the same tongue, Valerius said, "If she spits, I will have her flogged. She will not survive it."

The woman wore eight kill-feathers, all broadly banded in gold, and had just laid the blade of her ancestors at the feet of the enemy with all the dignity she could muster. She could, it seemed, control her daughter as well as she controlled herself and that without words. The crowd parted and let them through, and when Valerius looked round, the other children, too, had gone. He drew his horse back and circled it to where his men waited. Stooping, he retrieved the reins from Umbricius, who stared at him. "Why did you do that?"

Valerius had acted on instinct and surprised himself. *She reminded me of someone I once knew.* Aloud, he said, "She's a child. If we had flogged her, she'd die."

"So? A child doesn't pay taxes. Myself, I think she is exactly what the governor had in mind when he—"

He stopped. Valerius said nothing. Umbricius had crossed him only once and would not forget it. Frustrated, the man said, "So who do we take as an example when every one of the bastards kneels at our feet and gives us what we ask?"

Valerius smiled grimly. "Be patient. There will be one. They won't all give up that easily."

He believed it, although it was still not clear who amongst the Trinovantes might be prepared to take a risk. The tension increased after the children dispersed, but the desperate theatre continued, as if each warrior had been schooled to the part. In a while, when the pile of gathered weapons had reached knee height, Valerius ordered the smith to bring his forging block into the open and break the blades.

Big, broad, and red-headed, the smith was the exceptional horseman who had first laid his weapons at Umbricius's feet. He had seemed the most likely to rebel, but even when ordered to break what his ancestors had made, he did not do so. Sabinius, who had once been armourer to the troop and understood the value of what was being destroyed, said, "He would make a good auxiliary, could we persuade him to fight for us."

Valerius said, "His grandsons maybe, or those who come after. This one will never be anything but an enemy."

Enemy or not, the giant was a methodical man. He broke each blade exactly in half, laying the hilts with their decorated pommels to one side and the blade-tips to the other. It was not fast work. A blade that has seen the wars of five generations, that has been tempered in the blood of a hundred enemy warriors, does not break easily. Some had to be heated before they would break, and that took time. The harshness of burning metal caught at the throat and stung the eyes. The auxiliaries coughed and wiped their faces and continued with the work. Only the natives remained dry-eyed.

The change came at the final roundhouse. A young warrior with startling corn-gold hair knelt and laid his sword at the feet of Gaudinius, the armourer. It was a good blade; the weld-patterns woven in the metal stood out proudly from nights of polishing, and the hilt was tightly bound in copper wire, but the pommel was plain, lacking enamel, and while the warrior wore four gold-banded kill-feathers, the blade itself bore no notches to show it had been used in battle.

Valerius was already behind Gaudinius when the warrior rocked back on his heels, and it was to Valerius that the youth's eyes rose. They held a defiance, a guarded question, and perhaps, in their depths, a plea. Word had passed, then, that Valerius spoke their language. What had not passed with it, because it was not known, was the depth of his loathing for their people and the identity of the man who had spawned it.

The moment of decision was not without turmoil; Valerius still believed in the laws of honour and maintained an abiding respect for personal dignity. Had the warrior's hair been other than gold, had his nose been less distinctive, had his eyes not been that particular iron-grey so that one could less readily imagine Caradoc's smile beneath them and Caradoc's soul within, what followed might have been different. They were not. The Crow-horse pushed between the man and the crowd.

"Stop."

Gaudinius had stooped to pick up the sword. He froze and then stood, empty-handed.

Valerius said, "He's giving you a false weapon. This is not the blade of his ancestors."

He said it in Latin, as was required, and then repeated it in Trinovantian. The scuffle had been noted. Already Longinus was at the pied horse's shoulder. Others ran to assist, forming a defensive knot. Valerius registered their presence as he would register the arrival of reinforcements in battle—distantly and without taking his attention from the enemy who would kill him. His gaze was locked entirely with that of the young corn-haired warrior who had just tried to save the blade of his ancestors.

The youth was a good actor; he could control his face but not his eyes. Anger followed shock and was followed in turn by a brief, swamping despair. Valerius knew that feeling intimately, the desolation of the soul when what one has most feared becomes reality. He knew also where it led. He was ready long in advance for the moment when the warrior took refuge in action.

The blade lying flat on the beaten earth was not the one with which the corn-haired man had grown to adulthood, not the one with which he had killed so often in battle, but it was good and he had used it enough to have the feel for its weight and swing. Certainly it was enough to kill a young officer who had lost his battle-sharpness. Gaudinius died where he stood, spraying blood from his opened throat. A Thracian auxiliary would have been next if Longinus had not slammed into the man's shoulder, hurling him sideways so that the killing blow cut only the flesh of his upper arm.

The warrior backed against the wall of the roundhouse and was joined by two others, and yes, finally, as had been clear all along, the red-headed smith was one of them. Valerius felt a moment's exhilaration, tainted with an unexpected sorrow that one with such dignity should choose to die in such a manner, and then the Crow-horse, following a barely articulate thought, rose above the gathering melee and drove a smashing forefoot down in a blow not even a giant could resist. The beast relied on his rider to block the weapon that would slice open its guts, and Valerius did so, wielding a cavalry sword that was the best Rome could offer and did not come close to the quality of the blades that it met.

Yet it was enough, and the sparks flew high over the thatched roof of the roundhouse, and Regulus was yelling, "Don't kill them all. I want one to hang," and then, too soon, it was over, with the corn-haired warrior alive and the smith and a woman dead, but not one with dark hair and an unruly daughter, for which, surprisingly, Valerius found he was grateful.

The governor had wanted an example, and he was given it. They flogged the corn-haired warrior before they hanged him, and it seemed likely he would have died of the one if they had waited too long for the other. A half-troop of auxiliaries took a pole from the wood store and balanced it on two uprights between the harness hut and the granary and raised the man until only the tips of his toes touched the ground. In the time that he took dying, which was not short, Regulus divided the auxiliaries into three groups and sent them out: one to guard the natives, one to collect and burn their shields—now forfeit, on the governor's orders—and the third to search each of the roundhouses and huts for other weapons.

Sabinius said, "One of the roundhouses belongs to the priest. He's a citizen."

Regulus spat. "And one of his warriors murdered my armourer. If he resists, hang him alongside his man."

All pretence of civilization, of dignity and courtesy, was gone. The search was brutal and effective. For each weapon already surrendered, they found spear-heads, battle-knives, or full blades hidden in the thatch, under the beds, in the small, secret places in the corners.

Valerius, who knew better than most where to look, took Sabinius and Umbricius and searched the granary and the harness hut, where he found a cache of spears bound up in leather hidden beneath a stack of stiff unworked hides. Out in the open, the auxiliaries broke the hafts and threw them on the fire made of the shields. The spear-heads were added to the bundles of broken blades to be taken away by the auxiliaries when they left.

One place remained untouched, a small hut on the western edge of the enclosure. Half a dozen hounds bayed from behind the black mare's hide that blocked the doorway, but that was not the reason the men were reluctant to enter. On the lintel, the marks of Nemain and Briga were clear: a crescent moon hung above the sinuous waves of a river, a wren circled above a foaling mare. Newly carved and dyed in red, a she-wolf stalked a skinny goat, a ram, and a bull.

It may not have been widely known that the Quinta Gallorum took the Capricorn as its emblem, nor the Prima Thracum Aries, but anyone who had watched the governor's arrival closely and seen the display of standards could have deduced it. Very few outside the legions should have known the significance of the bull, but the troops standing outside the hut knew exactly what it meant, both for themselves and for the ones who had cut and painted the image. Half a dozen gathered a spear's length from the doorway, making the sign to ward off evil. None would go inside.

Valerius stood closer, listening to the hounds within. His brand ached. Sabinius joined him. He was braver than most. "We should take some of the women and make them go in ahead of us," he said.

"No. It is safer if we go in alone."

Sabinius stared at him. "We?"

Valerius smiled, a thing he had not done in days. "No, just me. Bring me a lit torch, and then wait at the fires. If I don't come out soon, burn the place without coming in. Whatever's inside will be destroyed in the flames."

"Including you."

"Yes. You can come in and look for me if you want, but I wouldn't advise it. No one will blame you if you don't."

Sometime in the day he had remembered the words of Trinovantian that were used to calm hounds. He spoke them now. By the time Sabinius returned with the torch, the beasts within were almost silent. In the steading was an equal hush. Feeling the eyes of every woman in the tribe burn into his back, Valerius pushed back the mare's hide and entered.

It was not a big hut. The hounds were tethered on either side of the door. They strained against their collars, whining hoarsely, choking themselves in their need to reach him. Speaking softly, he loosed them one by one, ruffling his hands through the coarse hair of their necks, and they gathered about him, testing the smells of blood, hate, and fear. They were bigger than any hound of the legions and had been kept fit. If the day had gone differently, he might have been able to trade for one. Now the natives would cut the throat of any hound he asked for rather than let him take it.

"Go now." He said it in their own tongue, opening the door-flap, and the beasts spilled out in a joyful rush, not knowing that the world to which they returned had changed beyond all recognition.

With the hounds gone, the place seemed bigger. The torch burned feebly, as if lacking air. Within moments it went out. Valerius could have left the flap open for more light but did not. A fire was lit on the western wall. Thin smoke rose to the roof and passed out through a baffled hole. The flame gave light enough. Searching along the junction of wall and floor near the door, he found a knife honed to razor sharpness and put it to one side. Instinct, and three nights' dreams, told him there was more than that to be found.

"You should ask my leave, dreamer, before you take my blade."

He nearly killed her. His sword sliced through smoke and a brief, curling flame and stopped only because his mind caught up with his body and a single word of what he had just heard made no sense. Keeping his guard, he relit the torch to give himself light and saw, hunched on the far side of the fire in the darkest corner, a woman older than any he had seen outside in the steading. Her face was the creased bark of the oldest oak, her hair had thinned almost to baldness, leaving white strands trailing from a pink scalp. Her eyes were oddly clear where he would have expected cloudedness. She was a true grandmother, and there had been none like her amongst the gathered crowd. He should have noticed that and had not. He cursed his inattention.

The old woman watched him with the sharp regard of a hunting bird, a thrush seeking beetles in dung. Unbelievably, she smiled. "Welcome, dreamer. I have waited since dawn. You are not in the hurry I had thought."

That word again, and a tone that came straight from his childhood. *Your mark could have been the horse. Or the hare* ... The skin on Valerius's neck crept. "I am not a dreamer," he said.

"Are you not so? Your mother would be sad to hear it."

"My mother?" The sword quivered in his hand, a thing alive. With effort he restrained it. "My mother is dead."

"As is her son in soul, it seems, if not in body." The old woman grinned at his discomfort. "Why are you here?"

"To gather weapons. Rome would have peace. This is a means to achieve it."

"If by peace you mean subjugation, yes." She cocked her head. "So, if you will not answer clearly, I will ask it another way. Why do you gather weapons for Rome who was born to fight against it?"

He swayed on his feet. In the darkness was the echo of the god's silence of the wine-cellar crypt. In a voice below the threshold of hearing, his mother spoke the litany of his nightmares. *You are forsaken. The gods condemn you to life.*

Hoarsely, he said, "I have no choice."

"Ha! There speaks a man of the bull." She was laying fine, dry twigs on the fire. Small flames danced in the rolling shadows. Smoke rose to Valerius's nostrils. An old, forgotten part of him coded its separate strands: hawthorn, rowan, yew. He sneezed on something harsher than any of those and was confused until it came again and he recognized the bitterness of singed hair. No grandmother burned animal hair without evoking the strength it offered.

"What are you doing?" he asked.

"See for yourself."

She passed him a handful of twigs from the pile at her side. He used the light to seek out those bound with hair. Unwinding one, he found what he already knew would be there: curled hairs in red and white taken from the poll of a red-and-white-patched bull. He dropped them all on the fire. Thick smoke fanned up to fill his head. In the density of it, he heard many women's voices, laughing, and the bellow of a bullock at castration. The bones of his skeleton crept from his flesh. He tasted death and a fear that battle had never brought him. Again, more desperately, he said, "I have no choice. I had none in the time of battles, and I have none now."

"You are wrong. There is always choice, and no oath is binding but we make it so." Her voice was clear and louder than the rushing in his ears. She waved her hands through the dense air. "See, I offer another choice clearly now. Turn round. There is a cloak behind you. Take it and put it on."

He had not seen the cloak. The folds hung softly, of finest wool. Lifting it towards the firelight, he found it was blue, the colour of the sky after rain, with a border worked in russet. His sister had worn a cloak of exactly that colour the last time he had fought at her side. She wore the grey of Mona now, and despised him. The gorge rose in his throat. In his hollow heart, his mother said a second time, *You are forsaken.*

With shaking hands, he returned the cloak to its peg. Like a child, he said, "I can't wear this. If I walked out with it on, they would hang me."

The grandmother mocked him. "There are other choices, dreamer. You can wear it openly or in your heart. Either way you would find the welcome you crave."

"I crave nothing."

"Liar." She was standing now, a small thing, barely up to the god's brand on his chest. Her voice carried the power of centuries. No man could withstand it. "All your life you have craved but one thing—a true belonging to your people and your gods. I offer it now, a gift freely given. Leave here now, knowing it possible, or know yourself by your own hand for ever cursed."

"No."

The one thing the god had taught him was how not to hear the voice of deity. In the darkness of the crypt, that voice had not been directed solely at him. Here, in the bitter blackness of a place his mere presence defiled, he was the single point on which it focused, resounding in his soul. The brand on his chest burned as if new, holding him captive in his body. His mother's voice was silent, withdrawing even that support. He put his hands over his ears and blocked out the gods, the crackle of the fire, the voice of an old woman, weaving him to a death beyond which was only desolation.

"No." It came the second time through tight teeth, robbed of conviction. The bull-smoke wreathed his head, holding him as ivy holds oak. Tendrils invaded his mind, eating at his sense of self. The old woman loomed over him, crooning in the tones of an elder grandmother, of *the* elder grandmother. "Take it, child. It is your birthright. The man who made it was a dreamer before he was a warrior. It will sing for you." She was not speaking only of the cloak. Something greater than bull-hair burned on the fire.

"*No!*"

In her desperation, in her flagrant use of power, was the strength he needed. Thrusting her away, he kicked the fire apart, scattering hair and hide and burning embers across the floor until the smoke billowed thick and clean. It caught straw and flared up. By the new light he saw that, where the heart of the fire had been, the earth was not packed flat but was friable, as if newly dug.

He looked up at the grandmother, his eyes squeezed against the smoke. Suspicion filled him where before had been only resistance. "What are you protecting?"

"Nothing of yours."

"Of course not. None of this is mine, is it? None of it has been about me." The truth, so obvious once revealed, destroyed the last shreds of his pride. "I should have known you would only call on your gods to protect your own, not to seduce an enemy." Resentment needled him into action where fear had not. He used her skinning knife to push aside more of the fire. The earth beneath was not as newly turned as he might have thought, but lines clearly showed where a hole had been dug. If he had to guess, he would have said it had been done four years before, at the time of the invasion, when an emperor came to Cunobelin's dun and was welcomed by the treachery of an elder—a man who might have betrayed his gods and his people but would never enter this one place from which he had always been forbidden. Valerius, who believed he had lost the last of his scruples, stabbed into the centre of the hearth and heard the knife hit iron.

"Leave it! What harm it has done you is past. Leave it and go!"

The old woman was clawing at his arm, her fingers bird-boned to go with her bright, sharp eyes. He grasped both of her wrists in one hand and held her at arm's length. With his other hand, he unearthed the linen-wrapped blade the fire had hidden. It was longer and broader than any that had yet been broken on the smith's anvil. When he grasped the hilt, the power of it raked like lightning up his arm, close to the threshold of bearing. The pain was cleansing, as the brand had been.

Speaking through it, Valerius said, "You offered me a choice that was no choice. My path was set long ago, and not one step of it has been of my choosing. I take now what life I can and make the best of it, the very best. If there is a curse, then it came in childhood at Caradoc's hand. I cannot escape it." It hurt even to speak the man's name aloud. He gave it as an offering to the dark and did not know why he did so.

She said, "It was not Caradoc who branded you or killed your soul-friend. Was the brother's death not vengeance enough?"

One other living man in all the world knew how Caradoc's brother had died, and he was not of the tribes. Swallowing, Valerius said, "Amminios did not pretend friendship and then betray it."

Scathing, she said, "And so you take vengeance against those whom you do not know, in order better to attack the one whom you can never reach?"

The blade lay across his knees, liquid in the firelight. The hilt was bronze, of the oldest design, and the pommel bore the mark of the Sun Hound, carved in the time of his great-grandfather. In a wash of recognition that assuaged all the hurt, he knew exactly whose blade it was and why they had valued it so highly, risking everything on its protection. Joy, or something close to it, enwreathed him. His blood ran thin in his veins, leaping at his temples. He said, "I take no vengeance. I carry out the orders of those who command me. That is enough."

"Then let it be enough. You are cursed, Julius Valerius, creature of the bull-slayer, servant of Rome, cursed in the names of the gods you have forsaken to live barren and empty, to know neither true fear nor love, neither joy nor human companionship, but only the dull reflection of these; to kill without care, to hold the dying without grief, to find no satisfaction in the pure moments of your hate, to live only to carry out the orders of those who command you, and to dream at night of what you have lost. The gods know you deserve it. They alone will know if it can end."

She was shrill in her anger, old-woman-voiced, no longer the mouthpiece of the gods, but Valerius held the blade of Cassivellaunos, ancestor to Cunobelin, forerunner in lineage and in heart to the man he most hated of all those still living. He could have asked for no greater gift. The joy had run out of him, leaving him clear as a blown reed.

He cocked his head as the grandmother had done. "Do you wish to die by this blade, or another?" he asked.

She spat at him. Gobbets of phlegm sat proud on his cheeks. At his feet, embers of the swept fire smoked in the straw. Flames devoured it.

Valerius had control of himself now, had no need of further vengeance. Reasonably, he said, "If you walk out, they will hang you for fear of who you are and what you might do. If I leave you in here, they will let this place burn and you will die by the fire. If either of those is your choice, I will honour it. I am offering you a cleaner death."

"Fool." She whispered now. He could barely see her through the smoke. "Do you as you wish. I am already dead."

It was not true, although he made it so, using the blade of Cassivellaunos, who had once surrendered to Caesar, laying another man's blade at his feet. The grandmother died without resistance or sound. He laid her on her left side on a bed of straw with her head towards the west. "Go to your gods. Tell them I serve another now and am content." He believed it. He had rarely felt so calm. The flames were eating her feet when he left.

Outside it had begun to snow again, the gift of one god or the other to cover the destruction. The body of the gold-haired warrior had been cut down and laid on the pile of the burning shields; fragments of greasy smoke fluttered up past falling flakes. A warrior among the women saw the man leave the hut and what he carried and raised a cry that was keener and carried more pain than the ululation for the dead. In a cacophony of women's voices, Valerius walked forward and offered the blade to Regulus.

"This belonged to Cassivellaunos, ancestor to Caradoc, who leads the uprising in the west. They have kept this blade in the hope that the last living son of Cunobelin would return and lead them to freedom. Longinus Sdapeze is both armourer and master of horse for his troop. His father was a smith. He will be able to break it. I thought you might like to see it happen."

CHAPTER 8

The snow continued, fitfully. Beneath its shroud, the disarming of the tribes progressed. Troops rode out fresh each morning and returned each evening smoke-stained and bloody. Word of the events of that first day spread amongst the natives and the men alike, and all pretence at courtesy vanished. Roundhouses were stripped and searched. Within three days, the second of the women's places had burned to the ground, and the hidden weapons had been raked from the ashes as puddles of waxen iron.

Soon the killings began. In one steading, where armed warriors had been waiting for the auxiliaries and killed three before the troops retreated and called in aid, every adult male was hanged. The women were spared; to hang them would have been to acknowledge their status as warriors, and if Scapula was not ready to do that, then neither were his subordinates. News of the savagery of the reprisals spread but did not stop others from rebelling. In places where fear constrained the adults, the children staged their own revolts, hurling rocks and sticks at the auxiliaries. Always it was the youths near to their warrior's tests who broke first, those who had grown in a free land, who had dreamed from infanthood of becoming heroes and wielding the blades of their ancestors and could not bear to watch both hopes and blades destroyed. Orders had been given that children were not to be harmed, but the line was fine and both sides knew that it was only a matter of time.

In the middle of the month, after a fifth trooper had died to a grief-stricken warrior, Scapula ordered that the executed natives should be denied their burial rites and their bodies hung instead outside the steadings as a warning. Neither he nor any of the officers specified the height at which they should be suspended, and the auxiliaries, acting in haste, did not hoist them high, so that, by the old moon, wolves from the forest migrated into the pastures, seeking easy meat. Soon places that had been safe became unsafe, and four men of every troop spent each night protecting the horse paddocks where the remounts grazed. The troops grew impatient and edgy. Roundhouses began to burn as well as the women's places. Smoke rose to the sullen sky and gathered there. Breathing became a chore.

Valerius's rank exempted him from night watch on the paddocks, but it did not free him from responsibility, nor smooth his sleep. On his return from the raid on Heffydd's farmstead, with the grandmother's curse loud in his ears, he had returned alone to the consecrated cellar beneath the centurion's house in Camulodunum and had spent the hours of darkness alone in prayer. It had not been a quiet night, and at no time had he felt the true breath of the god, but he had believed afterwards that he had been heard. At the very least, Mithras kept the many and multiplying dead from invading Valerius's dreams. Mithras's powers did not extend, apparently, to keeping at bay the recurring faces of the living: of a dark-haired girl with a rock in her hand; of her mother, pulling her back; of the endless storming sea of women staring their accusations and their hatred.

Nor could it remove the constant flicker in his arm, as of lightning, that had come from Cassivellaunos's sword. The grandmother had been right in that much: the blade had sung to him, and what was left of his soul sang back its regret that the song had been broken and would never return. Each night, lying awake, he remembered the grandmother's curse and did not know if he should welcome the death-within-life that it promised or fight against it. Either way, by the end of the month, when the killing was at its height, he was too short on sleep to care.

He took to walking the perimeter of the horse paddocks alone, armed only with his belt knife. It became his offering and his open challenge to the god. *I am here, poorly armed and vulnerable. Protect me if you can.*

He walked as if blindfolded. Distant fires flared scarlet on the horizon. If he looked at them, they left a cast in his eyes so that the night around seemed darker after. The sentries' torches offered unreliable light, prone to moving just when one needed them most, or simply to burning out. In the absolute dark, Valerius came intimately to know the shadows of the hedgerow and the shapes of standing horses, and he could name each one by its outline seen against the grass, without moonlight or starlight, simply black on black. Thus, even on the night of the old moon, a month after the first disarming, when the clouds pressed down on the earth, bleeding grey mist over the red blur of the shield-fires, he knew that the shadow in the third paddock was not that of the Thracian decurion's second mount alone, but that a man stood beside it.

Drawing his knife, he crouched in the lee of the hedge. The horse was a narrow-boned chestnut gelding; not a mount he would have chosen, but reliable in its way, and it knew him. He pursed his lips and made a hushing noise, like the soft sliding of snow. The beast turned its head and shuffled forwards, too idle to raise a trot. The man-shadow walked at its side, one hand gripping the mane, pacing its footfalls to that of the beast.

Just beyond killing range, it spoke. "If you kill me, the first *turma* of the Prima Thracum loses its master of horse. Do you want that?"

"Longinus Sdapeze." Valerius stood up slowly. The knife stayed in his hand. "Why are you here?"

"Tonight I prefer the company of horses to that of men." The man took a step sideways, and the outline of the gelding divided and became two. Like Valerius, the Thracian chose to walk unarmed and unarmoured. In the dark, still beyond reach of the knife, he saluted, a thing he rarely did these days.

Too formally, he said, "I did not come to disturb your travels. There are paddocks enough for both of us. We need only walk in opposite directions."

"Thank you. In a moment." Valerius sheathed his knife. It was a plain one, drawn from the armoury. The hilt was of elm and the pommel of unadorned iron printed with the Capricorn. He had not yet grown used to the feel of it. He kept the heel of his hand on the hilt and rubbed his thumb over the wood. "I heard your decurion hanged a pregnant girl today. Is it true?"

"Yes. I'm amazed only that you heard of it. Amongst all the carnage, I would not have thought the death of one more would reach the ears of Valerius. Unless, like the native dreamers, he knows everything?"

Longinus sounded sour and weary, and angry with himself as much as others. Valerius stepped beyond the shadow of the hedge and walked down, as the other must, towards the gap in the hedge where a man could squeeze through but not a horse. As they met, he said, "I know only what men tell me—that your troop entered northern Eceni territory and met—or created—resistance; that of the thirty-two men who rode out, only eight came back alive and that you were one of them." Valerius had not asked that, but the man who gave him the information had found it necessary to tell him so repeatedly, as if he might care. "I know that the decurion who gave the order for the execution was one of the first killed, and that you were injured, but not fatally. I wonder, in all of this . . . carnage, that you mourn a dead girl."

"Do you? Then you know nothing of Thracian honour. She was fifteen, maybe sixteen, not long into womanhood. She had the warrior's braids, but no kill-feathers. They had killed her lover whose child she carried, and she stood over his body as a hound protects the one it loves. It took three men to overwhelm her, and one of those died. The decurion ordered her hanged with the warriors. She was pregnant, Valerius, and it made no difference."

The first woman, the first child. A barrier broken. If Valerius were not so hellishly tired, either or both of these might matter more. "Was it that that sparked the violence?"

"Yes. The people would not stand and see her die. Were she mine, I would have killed for her, also." Longinus spat. "Romans! They think women and children are fit sacrifices in war and anything less than crucifixion smacks of leniency. And they call us barbarians."

You would as well crucify their children.

It may come to that.

The night was thick with fog and frost and unspent dreams. Valerius stared into nothing and waited for anger, or regret, or an understanding of the pain, for the reality of Eceni deaths to overwhelm him. Nothing came but weariness and visions of worse to come. In a while, thinking not of himself, he asked, "Have you daughters?"

"No." It was said sharply, as if it were an insult to ask. "I have no children. But I have sisters and a younger cousin who was born when I left to join the legions. She would be eight years old now. For any one of them, I would have fought as the Eceni did today, had I their courage. I doubt that I do. They were unarmed; we had taken their swords and broken them, destroyed their spears, burned their shields. They fought us with rocks and brands from the fire, and when there was nothing else, they clawed at our faces with their bare hands. And they killed us. If we had not got to our horses and run, the eight of us would not still be alive."

Longinus rubbed his arm. Rumour reported a burn wound that had cost him an evening in the hospital awaiting treatment. He smelled lightly of goose-grease, which would seem to confirm it.

"According to the decurion, Prasutagos, their leader, was supposed to have sworn fealty to Claudius and been made client-king for it. We were told the man was the glove into which Scapula inserted his hand and that, at the governor's request, he would deliver his people without conflict. I think the 'king' forgot to tell his warriors."

The king. Never in their history had the Eceni accepted the rule of a king, and Prasutagos was not made of kingly stuff. In races, on foot or on horse, he had always come second. In boar-hunts he was behind the hounds, and his spear was always lodged in the chest of a dying beast, never the first one to strike. In war . . . it was impossible to remember how Prasutagos had been in war. He might have acquitted himself well once, but he had lost an arm in doing so, and if the governor were to be believed, the defect left him sour and weak-willed and easily bought by wine and gold. It was hard to imagine Eceni pride taking orders from such a man as that.

"It may be the king instructed his warriors and they chose not to listen," Valerius said. "The Eceni have never taken orders from just one individual. Their grandmothers rule their councils, and the dreamers rule the grandmothers. It would be a mistake to expect too much of 'Tagos merely because he bows to Rome. He may have gold enough to buy those who care for it, but that doesn't mean they will listen to him if their dreamers or their own instincts tell them otherwise."

"Their instincts run to war now, and I don't blame them."

As if each had decided it alone, they walked together down towards the river. Valerius said, "Do you regret your place in this?"

Longinus's face was a blur in the dark. "I would rather be on this side than the other, but yes, I would rather be in the west where they have open, honest warfare than in this mess of pretended peace."

"We are on the verge of open war here as well. It may be that it has already started. Listen." Valerius had heard the noise when they left the field but not been sure of its source. Closer to the river, he heard it clearly: the sound of a horse pushed to its limits, stumbling in the dark over snow-hidden ground. "What would make a man ride that hard at night?"

Longinus said, "He's under attack?"

"Or his post is. There is a fort in the territory of the northern Eceni. I will bet you a decent salve for your arm against the return of my falcon-headed dagger that the Eceni have risen, that the fort is a heap of burning beams, and that we are sent north to stamp out the rebellion." Valerius turned to Longinus. In a world of many fears, his worst was now realized. As with many things, it was not as bad as he had thought it might be. The grandmother's curse had dulled the edge of his fear. To that extent, it was good. Smiling, he said, "Unless you have already lost the dagger to someone else and can't give it back?"

Five days later, in the lime-washed peace of the hospital, the falcon-headed dagger was returned to him. Valerius sat on the edge of Longinus's bed, turning it over in his hands. The blade was broken near the tip, leaving a jagged end. The god Horus had taken a dent in the back of the head, loosening one of his eyes.

"It's your fault. Your mad bloody horse trod on it." Longinus smiled with the half of his face that was not a fulgent, greening bruise. Pain showed in the creases beside his eyes.

Valerius slid the blade back into its sheath. He was exhausted beyond anything he could ever remember. Not even the two days' battle of the invasion had left him this worn. He said, "Next time I'll remember to stop and pick up the dagger before the man."

"And leave me to your barbarians with their witch-carvings?"

"No. I would have taken a hammer to your head before I left you to that."

"Thank you."

They made a joke of it to cover their fear, but each knew the other was serious. Valerius had killed two men with his lump hammer, neither soon enough. Having been reminded, it was impossible to think of anything else.

Longinus said, "Did you know the first one was there when you rode up the column?"

"Of course not. How could I? I just knew we were walking into an ambush. I wanted to say something to Corvus before the governor's bloody infantry got us all killed."

It was not strictly speaking Scapula's infantry, but that of Marcus Ostorius, his son, and in that young man's pride, and his presence, lay the fault for a great many deaths and grievous injuries.

The problem had been one of protocol. Scapula had ordered his son, the tribune of the Legio Secunda Augusta, to remain in the east while the reinforcements marched west to the aid of his legion. It was his right and any father's duty to protect his son from the ravages of the western war, but the boy chafed in the harness, desperate to fight, and anyone with half an eye could see it. When the officers had met to determine their response to the uprising among the Eceni, Marcus Ostorius had first offered to lead the full cohort of the Twentieth Legion on a forced march into the native strongholds. It is not easy to gainsay a tribune, still less a governor's son who lays his pride so openly on the table. The discussions that followed had been unusually diplomatic. In the end it had been unanimously agreed that Marcus Ostorius would take two centuries of the legion to assail the Eceni, leaving the remainder to guard the fortress against the possibility of an uprising among the Trinovantes. The two wings of cavalry, one thousand men in all, had been detailed as "escort" for his one hundred and sixty legionaries.

Thus had the disaster unfolded. The cavalry had been forced to ride at the pace of marching men, and so a journey that had taken a terrified rider less than half the night took the returning units nearly two days. It was dawn on the second day when they reached the smoking skeleton of the fort that had been attacked. Roman deaths must not go unmarked, and so Marcus Ostorius had ordered that they burn the remains to the ground in honour of those who had given their lives in its defence. In the heart of enemy territory, a thousand battle-ready men had spent a morning gathering firewood, jumping at shadows and untoward noises, until an entire tent-party of eight legionaries had been injured by their own comrades in a mistaken confrontation and had to be sent back to the fortress under the care of a half-dozen troopers. With their numbers thus reduced, those left had piled the wood around the base of the fort and lit it. The blaze of their labours threw flames to the tops of the highest trees and did nothing to make them feel safer.

Loyal Trinovantian scouts had been sent out when the fort was first found, and two of five returned to the pyre with news of Eceni warriors massing to the north-west. The track along which they guided the troops that afternoon was no more than two horses wide and led into thicker forest than any they had so far passed. Mounted again, the cavalry rode in battle formation with their swords unsheathed and their shields ready on their arms, but at walking pace so as not to outrun the infantry who accompanied them. A man could have grown tired of waiting if he stood in one place for the length of time it took the entire column to pass. A different man could see it as a gift from his gods in the planning of an ambush.

Valerius rode at the rear of his troop with Sabinius at his side. It was Corvus's battle-plan, and both wings adhered to it: the second in command of each troop rode last in the column so that, if the snake were to have its head cut off in ambush, the tail could yet turn and bare its fangs at the enemy, led by an officer with some experience of command. Valerius had no experience of command in combat, but he had three years' practice at giving orders and had listened often enough to Corvus's descriptions of battles past to trust his own judgement. His judgement now told him that he was riding into an ambush and that nothing he could do would stop it.

To Sabinius, Valerius said, "If we are attacked from the sides, get off your horse and put your back to mine. Keep your horse on your shield side as protection and be ready to mount and ride south for safety if I am killed. Someone should survive to get word to the governor; it may as well be you."

"You have thought of this already?"

"Before we ever left the fort."

Soon after, a command from the tribune halted the column, and Valerius was called to the front. He smelled the blood and the voided urine as he cantered to the head of the line, a common enough smell in the past month, but not here where the disarming had not yet begun. The sound of retching and the acidity of vomit reached him as he approached the first ranks.

The leading officers were gathered at the margins of a small clearing, in the centre of which an ancient yew spread boughs over black loam; neither snow nor sun penetrated here. Dismounting, Valerius noticed first that Corvus had used his dagger, that its hilt and his right arm were stickily black. With the care of habit, he noted that Corvus had not been sick but was close to it; that he had not wanted to call on Valerius but had been forced to by circumstances or the order of the tribune; and that already he regretted it.

Only after that did Valerius look beyond to see what the milling horses had hidden. The body of a naked man hung suspended by one heel from a bough. It turned slowly, back and forth, spun by a nonexistent wind. Flaps of skin had been flayed from the back and hung down like wings. At the front, black blood had flowed down from the mutilated groin to drip onto the earth beneath. The throat had been cut some time after the genitals, and all that was left of the man's blood had flooded out onto the hungry loam. It was impossible to see the face.

"One of the Trinovantes?" Valerius asked.

"Who else?" Corvus's lips were a pale, straight line. "There are markings carved on the chest. The upper one is the running horse of the Eceni—the same as the one we saw on the walls of the burned fort. The others are new. We have not seen them now or during the invasion. It may help us if you could identify them."

The clearing was very still; in this place the gods themselves held their breaths. The one god was not present, this was not his domain. Feeling his absence, Valerius walked up to the body. The man's testes had been severed and stuffed into the jaws, the just punishment for a man who aids his enemies. Crouching, he found that the eyes had been gouged out and placed on the forest floor so that one watched forward and one backward. That, too, was just under tribal law; the man had been a scout, he had sold his eyes to Rome, and they had been given back to the gods. Both were submerged beneath the tide of fresh blood that had spilled from the scout's severed throat. Touching it, Valerius found his fingers slid wetly on his thumb; here there was no sign of clotting. The chill on his neck became a stave of ice. Unwilling, he turned to Corvus, who had recently used his knife.

"This is freshly spilled. Was he still alive when you found him?"

"Yes."

"God." Always before, the men had been dead before the cuts were made. Even in the invasion, when the anger of the tribes was at its height, the throats had been cut, or the men had died in combat, and the mutilations had been visited on them afterwards. The gods demanded just penance, but they had never previously required a man to suffer for it as this one had. The Trinovantian scout had been gone half the morning, but his body hung less than a thousand paces from the burning fort. None of his wounds was fatal. Had the auxiliaries taken a different path, he could have hung there, living, for the rest of the day and into the night.

Valerius pressed a shuddering hand to his eyes and waited until his guts settled. "They're learning from us," he said. "A slow death spreads fear to those who have seen it happen."

Only by the change in the quality of the silence did he know he had spoken aloud.

Corvus said, "The marks carved on his chest are not the serpent-spear. We need to know what we face."

"And meanwhile half of the Eceni nation is surrounding this clearing with intent to hang us all by our heels." Marcus Ostorius was nervous and let it show, which did nothing to stiffen the courage of his troops. "We need to move quickly while we have daylight, and there is a chance we can ride out of this accursed forest. Read the markings and be done with it. We should not be here."

Valerius had already seen them. The understanding of what they meant had churned at his guts before the rest. With his eyes on Corvus, he said, "The mark beneath the horse is a fox. See, here . . . this single line flows from the nose to the tail, and here . . . above the nose are the two ears and beneath it the forepaws. Its position below the running horse means it is the personal mark of whoever's leading the warriors."

"And who is that? Who has the fox as their dreaming?"

"I don't know." That was not entirely true. A memory teased at the back of his mind but would not come forward. Aware of Corvus's impatience, Valerius shook his head. "We'll find out soon enough. If the fox is carved here with the horse of the Eceni, it will be worn clearly in battle. When we come upon the warriors—if we ever see any of them before they kill us—this man will be easily seen."

"Or this woman," said the tribune sourly.

Their eyes met. Valerius nodded. "Indeed."

Marcus Ostorius turned on his heel and mounted. The troops moved out in battle order, each man ready to kill and be killed. The deepening woods were god-filled, and the gods were not those of Rome or its allies. In the ranks, prayers were offered to Jupiter, god of the legions, and to Cernunnos, antlered forest-god of the Gauls. The Thracians called on their own gods in their own language. Valerius and those like him touched their brands and renewed their oaths to Mithras, bull-slayer and protector of his own.

By order of Marcus Ostorius, Valerius rode now in front with the officers, the faster to read any marks the natives had left. He passed beneath trees whose branches sang to him in ancient ancestral tongues. His skin felt newly flayed, so that every sound brushed against it. When Corvus, riding close by, asked, "What was the third sign?" he jumped.

"The one beneath the fox? I'm not certain. It was hard to read—the man struggled as they cut it, and the lines were not clear."

Corvus had never allowed him evasion and did not do so now. "It seemed to me it was a bird," he said. "A hawk."

"It may well have been. The question is which hawk? I think . . . I am very much afraid that it was the red kite."

"And if it was?"

"Then the warriors of the Coritani and those of the Eceni have put aside the enmity of seven generations and are united against us." Valerius forced himself to smile and knew the effort was seen. "Be happy. The tribune desires a conflict to match the one he is missing in the west. If we are fighting the warriors of these two tribes combined, he will have it."

They rode apart after that and did not speak. The remaining two lost scouts were found along the way, one hanging like the first, the second pegged out, facedown in a marsh with a stone keeping his head free of the water and the dream-marks cut on his back. Valerius killed them both, swinging his spiked lump hammer at the skull, between the eyes and a little above, as he would have done for a horse with colic. The deaths were swift and merciful. Both came half a day too late.

The three bodies had been left at intervals along a clear route, as a hunter might leave hunks of meat for a bear, luring it into a trap, and Valerius had not been surprised when, shortly after the pegged man, spears had begun to fly from the forest. If he had planned an ambush, he would have done it there, where the path was narrowed to a single horse's breadth and the auxiliaries were trapped with dank, sucking marsh to one side and dense forest to the other, the trees too tightly spaced for mounts or men to penetrate.

The infantry, being slower, caught the brunt of the spears; it had been clear from the start that they would. They linked their square-edged shields edge to edge and crouched behind the wall they made, but the spears arced high and fell down from above, and the wall broke in places, leaving gaps for other spears, and men died like sheep at slaughter.

For the first few moments of the attack, the cavalry circled uselessly at the edges, losing horses and men as fast as the infantry. They could not penetrate the trees; nor could they protect the crouching legionaries. At Marcus Ostorius's express command, both wings pushed their horses to a gallop and fled. The spears herded them like deer towards the open space at the end of the track. The infantry, led by centurions who had no wish to see men die for the sake of it, picked up their shields and ran after them. A little over one hundred men survived to reach the clearing.

Bursting out of the forest at the head of his troop, Valerius found himself in a stretch of more-open land, thinly scattered with oak and elm. To his right, the marsh made a firm boundary as solid as rock. Thick forest swept up to the left. In front, blocking the broad space between marsh and forest, a barrier of cut oak trunks had been erected, high enough to shield men to their shoulders and three hundred paces long. Behind that the massed warriors of two tribes waited. At a conservative estimate, rapidly made, they numbered at least three thousand. Flashes of colour from cloaks, armbands, and weapons showed others in uncountable numbers packed in the forest to the left and hedging the marsh to the right. There were equal numbers of Coritani amongst the Eceni, confirming the worst.

The auxiliaries should have fought on horseback. For the rest of his life, Valerius believed that if they had not dismounted, they could have won, or at least lost fewer men, but Marcus Ostorius was an infantry officer at heart, and he had his surviving half-century of infantry still to protect and bring home alive. Thus the tribune had signalled the dismount, and disbelieving, men who had trained since childhood to fight on horseback found themselves foot soldiers at the last.

Marcus Ostorius had read books on strategy, had spent hours in educated argument with the peers of his youth dissecting Scipio's actions against Hannibal and Octavian's against Marcus Antonius. Faced by an enemy in overwhelming numbers stationed behind an unbreachable barrier and lacking the necessary equipment for a siege, he divided his men into two wings while he himself planned to assault the centre with the surviving men of his two centuries.

The Eceni laughed. Valerius heard them from his place at Regulus's side on the left wing of the supposed assault. As the auxiliaries turned towards the forest at their flank, the insults rang off the trees as if the waiting crows had learned the tongues of men. Some of it was in Latin; most was not. Of all those on the Roman side, only Valerius and Corvus could possibly understand the full measure of their enemy's derision and perhaps share it. Corvus led his men twenty paces to Valerius's left and twice refused to meet his eye; he would die loyal to his superior officer, however insane the command.

It was entirely insane. The Quinta Gallorum drew their swords early and used blades designed for slashing skin and flesh to hack instead through beech fronds and entangling bramble. From the start it was clear that, deeper in, the shields would become caught on undergrowth and would have to be tugged free or pushed forward to force a space, leaving the man behind exposed to the thrust of an Eceni spear.

Longinus's wing had the harder task: that of negotiating a mere of unknown depth to come in from the right against warriors who could see them coming and pick them off at will. Marcus Ostorius Scapula, true to his heritage, set himself at the head of his remaining hundred legionaries. He had them raise their shields over their heads that they might resist thrown rocks and spears, and then he led them, like some glorious ancient general, in charge after charge against a solid oak barrier and three thousand waiting spears.

Valerius saw flashes of the carnage at the barrier later in the ghastly, annihilating fight that followed. Not even in the first fruitless battles of the invasion had he seen so many men die for so little effect. In the hateful lucidity of killing, it came to him slowly that this was what the bird-eyed grandmother had meant. *You are cursed . . . to live barren and empty, to know neither true fear nor love, neither joy nor human companionship . . . to kill without care . . .* Throughout the battles of his past, terror and the need to live had spurred him, and afterwards he had salved his conscience with the excuse that he fought to survive. Now, in his first true battle under the care of Mithras, he had no conscience to salve. He fought hand to hand with men and women whose faces haunted his dreams and whose voices, pitched for battle, had been the thrill and yearning of his youth, and he felt nothing. He crossed swords with warriors who fought not only for their honour and freedom but for vengeance against an unspeakable wrong, and he felt their anger course over him while his own lay dormant. He saw Regulus step into a trap set by four waiting warriors who hacked the decurion's head from his shoulders, and he felt neither satisfaction nor sorrow nor fear that he himself risked the same death with each forward step.

The remnants of the Quinta Gallorum—less than three-quarters of the wing—broke through the trees not long after Regulus's death. The line of the enemy fell back. More auxiliaries ran in from the forest and were joined by wet-legged Thracians sweeping in unopposed from the marsh. The space behind the barrier, which had been filled with mixed warriors of the Coritani and the Eceni, was suddenly a place of polished mail and helmets, of coloured plumes and white shield discs. It felt like a victory, and men who had felt their lives lost saw them won again. Swords clashed on shield hubs in exultant celebration, and Marcus Ostorius's name was raised as a chant that spilled over the departing warriors as a wave spills over flotsam on a beach.

From nowhere and for no good reason, Valerius remembered a childhood tale of a fish-trap set by a bear where spawning salmon had been lured up into the pool behind a beaver's dam from which the water was then diverted, leaving the fish as easy pickings for the beast. It had been intended as a tale for infants to teach them hunting, but it applied no less to adults at war. In his god-cursed clarity, Valerius saw the flashing scales of legionary armour swirling in bloody spirals over the barrier—and then the tide of the warriors returning to smash a small, poorly led force caught with its back against solid wood with no means of escape. Already the foremost warriors had turned and were engaging the closest auxiliaries.

"It's a trap!" Valerius shouted it to Corvus, who fought close by; he had never let him out of his sight. "Get back to the tribune! Tell him we've swum into their trap."

The warriors were engaging in ever greater numbers. Hard-pressed simply to live, Corvus laughed. "So find us a way to swim out at the other end. There's no going back."

There was no going forward, either, until Valerius saw the mark of the fox. It was not painted on the shield of a warrior, as he had expected, but drawn instead in red ochre on the brow of a singer above an encircling thong of horse-hide that marked one of highest rank. The man wore a simple band of fox-pelt around his upper arm but was otherwise free of ornament. In a field of warriors who rode to war in a panoply of enamelled gold, decked with kill-feathers and all possible marks of dream and rank, this one was remarkable for his austerity. Nevertheless, he had command of the warriors and the flow of battle. He stood apart from the fighting on a small rise, and a knot of blue-cloaked warriors gathered close, both guarding him and waiting to relay his orders to their peers. A small wind arose around him, lifting his thin red hair, and he turned a little, showing his profile.

"*Dubornos!*"

The name had been itching half-formed at Valerius's mind since they'd found the scout hanging in the forest with the fox cut on his chest. He hissed it to himself now and saw the man's head come up as if he had called it aloud. The god did enter Valerius then, despite the curse. He felt not blind courage or the passion of battle, but a mote of undiluted joy, a spark in the endless night, a gift of certainty that this one man, alone of all the Eceni, he could kill without fear that this one spirit would return to haunt his sleep.

Raising his blade, he screamed, "Here! The fox is here! Kill him, and we break the trap!" and charged.

He should have died. In the red haze of battle, fighting up a hill, he faced alone a wall of blue cloaks, interspersed with the green-striped Coritani, but then Umbricius and Sabinius were on either side, fighting with him. Aeternus, a young Helvetian, joined them, and his cousin, who had been wounded and was quickly slain. They fought together as four and were joined by Longinus, who brought others from the Thracian wing, and the god smiled and they formed a line with their big oval shields locked at the edges and their swords hacking through the gaps exactly as they had practised in the months of probation before they were admitted to the cavalry, and like this they could survive, could fight to win, could press forward over the bodies of dead and dying warriors to reach—nothing.

In their unity they had won the rise, but the fox-dreamer had not stayed to meet them. Down the gentle slope on the far side were set sharpened stakes, pointing upwards to deter men and horses alike, and the warriors had retreated beyond them, taking their singers. Beyond the fen was forest into which none but warriors could safely, or sanely, pass.

Valerius turned. Behind them the fighting still raged at the oak barrier. The trap had been sprung, sending the warriors back to flood against the struggling legionaries and their unmounted auxiliary allies. Marcus Ostorius was there, a few paces forward from the barrier, but going no further. Close by, Corvus fought to reach him. Blue- and green-cloaked warriors encircled them. It did not seem likely that either man could live.

Valerius killed a woman warrior with coppery hair and looked past her to find Longinus Sdapeze on his shield side. The man was whole, but for a bruise on his forehead where a head blow had slammed his helmet onto his brow. Grinning ferociously, he said, "Two can lay traps like this. We could come in at them from the back and finish it. There are enough of us, almost." He raised his arm and howled in Thracian. A dozen more men of his wing ran to join him.

Valerius shook his head. "No. Count them—there are less than half of the Eceni down there. Do you think the fox and his warriors have fled? I don't. The moment we are fully engaged, when it would be death to turn our backs, they will come in again, and we will be caught between two forces and crushed."

"Then what do we do?"

"We get to the mounts and fight on horseback as we should have done at the start. It's our only hope."

Longinus laughed. "It may be your hope, but not ours. Not all of us ride man-killers. My mare is good, but she'd never come in here." He raised his hand, palm out, in the cavalryman's salute. "You get the horses. They'll follow you and your pied brute. I'll take whoever will follow me and see if we can't reach the tribune. The governor won't thank us if we don't at least return to him the body of his son."

Valerius grinned and returned the salute. "Make sure the golden boy's face isn't marked when they kill him. You have to be certain the body's still pleasing to look at."

Neither of them expected to live. In war men will do things that later are manifest madness but feel them sane at the time. There were no warriors between the salmon-trap and the woods where the horses stood. Valerius threw his shield to a Thracian auxiliary, whose need of it was greater than his, and ran.

The cavalry mounts had been left in the care of a dozen Gauls, who were dead. The horses themselves had not been touched; the Eceni valued good mounts above anything else living besides their children and would not harm mounts who could bring good blood to their herds. No warriors waited near them, seeing no need. The horses were battle-trained; they stood by the bodies of the last men to command them and would continue to do so unless summoned by a voice they knew. Valerius's voice was known. He found himself alone in the open space between trees and marsh and saw the Crow-horse raise its head to look at him. Retching from the run, with the iron taste of blood in his spit, he put his fingers to his mouth and whistled.

As Longinus had said they would, the herd followed their leader. The Crow-horse came at the gallop, and the surviving remains of two wings of horses followed behind. They might have stopped if he had asked it of them, but he could not be sure and, in any case, Valerius had his pride. The grandmother's curse had not robbed him of that. The mount by an armed and armoured man of a running horse was a feat celebrated by cavalry and warriors alike, and all of them, however preoccupied with death and survival, had heard the churning roll of massed horses at the gallop. In full view of his god, his enemies, and those who might have been his friends, Julius Valerius, duplicarius of the third troop of the Ala Quinta Gallorum, servant of Mithras and of the emperor, executed a near-perfect cavalry mount on a running horse ahead of a herd that would have crushed him to pulp if he had failed and fallen beneath them. Afterwards he thought it would have looked better if he had not thrown away his shield.

Only Longinus knew what he planned to do. The Thracian screamed himself hoarse clearing men back from the barrier. To do that, they had either to press forward, making space, or to duck out sideways into mere or forest. Men did all three, and many of them died. Those who survived watched their duplicarius face his pied horse at a jump that reached the height of its stifle with no clear view beyond and saw the horse gather itself and leap. Three dozen of the closest horses in the herd followed him, before the bulk of them balked at the height of the barrier and turned away.

Valerius, riding high over the battle in what should have been a crowning moment, tasted the dust and ashes of failure and knew once again that his god had abandoned him. Seeking solace in the approval of men, he saw the moment when Longinus was struck on the arm by the backswing of a Coritani blade. He shouted, and the one man left whole on the battlefield who recognized his voice heard him and turned; and so Corvus, who had fought his way through to his tribune and gained a clear space around him, was struck from behind by a spear and then a blade.

It was then that Valerius, howling Eceni war-cries, gave up all pretence of being a man and let the unbridled savagery of the Crow-horse run wild. Man and horse killed together, endlessly. At least one of them enjoyed it.

In the cool, well-lit hospital, insulated from the aftermath of battle, Valerius said calmly, "Did you know they have awarded Marcus Ostorius the oak-wreath for saving the life of a fellow citizen?"

It was the highest order of personal valour any man could win. Longinus's eyes stretched wide. "Who did he save? Not one of the legionaries—they were all dead. And I'm not a citizen, so I don't count. Corvus then? The tribune saved Corvus? I thought I saw him go down."

"You did. He took a sword cut to the back just before you ran into the Coritani shield boss that knocked you out. When the horses pushed the Eceni back, Marcus Ostorius carried him out beyond the barrier, and we brought him back on a litter. You would have got the same, but you were delirious and wouldn't get down from my horse."

Longinus grinned. It creased the bruised half of his face, and the cost showed. "I wasn't going to give up the only chance in my life to ride him, even if you were holding me crossways in front of the saddle." He shook his head, at himself or at the memory, and stopped smiling. He reached out for Valerius's hand and gripped it. His palm was clammy and cold. In a while, when it was warmer, he said, "Why are you here and not with him?"

He asked it too casually; they knew each other too well for that not to be seen. Valerius thought a moment and gave him the truth. "The tribune has forbidden him visitors. In any case, I don't think Corvus wants—"

He looked down. Longinus had pressed the falcon-headed dagger back into his palm. Shaking his head as if to one of slow wits, the Thracian said, "Go and see him. If nothing else, he needs to know what you did. Tell Theophilus you are necessary to his recovery. He'll support you, and a tribune can't overrule a physician in the practise of his craft."

CHAPTER 9

Valerius waited for a long time in the corridor outside the door. The hospital was arranged in concentric squares around a main courtyard; the windows of the most secluded rooms faced inwards, away from the cacophony of the fortress. The walls were lime-washed with the insignia of the legions and wings; the Capricorn, the Boar, the Pegasus, painted in subdued colours at intervals along their length. The air smelled cleanly of cut sage and rosemary: the sweet undertones of festering flesh were confined to the areas around the few rooms where men were clearly dying.

Valerius stood outside a door on which the Eye of Horus had been newly painted in blue and breathed in air spiked with lemon balm and a light peppery incense and the smell of a man he would know with his eyes closed.

He had tried twice to enter but neither time with any conviction. It was, he knew, his own failure of nerve more than Marcus Ostorius's orders that had prompted the doctor to turn him back. In the few days since the battle, Valerius had found he could dissect his own motives as cleanly and with as little passion as he judged others. Standing on the wrong side of a closed door, he knew that he did not want to see the extent of Corvus's injuries, to find if a body that had once revelled in its battle-scarred wholeness was crippled beyond repair, as had seemed likely when they brought him out over the barrier. Deeper than that, Valerius was afraid that a different, less material door that had always been open had finally been closed. If so, it had closed before the battle, and nothing that had happened since would open it.

The first sign of that closing had come in the chaos of arming men as they gathered to depart for the Eceni fort. Men and horses had milled in semi-organized chaos in the annexe where the army gathered before departure. Valerius had been ordering the horses of his troop when Corvus called him to his side.

They had ridden knee to knee, a little away from the wing. Corvus rode his remount, a red roan mare with all four legs white to mid-pastern and striped hooves. She was finely bred and outclassed most of the rest of the wing, but she was not the horse who had borne him through the invasion battles and should have borne him through this; that was a bay mare of Pannonian descent, and Corvus had loaned her, possibly given her—who can ask for a loan back from a governor's son?—to Marcus Ostorius.

Valerius noted it with raised brows. To another man, the gesture could have meant anything. To Corvus, it asked questions and answered them all in one movement. "If he is to fight the Eceni and live, he needs a decent horse."

Valerius smiled tightly. "The Ala Quinta Gallorum has some excellent horses. You did not have to give him yours."

"You would rather I gave him your pied man-killer?"

"The governor would hang you for attempted murder did you even suggest it."

"So instead he has mine, which will not kill him and may, instead, keep him alive."

"And does he know that his horse is his nursemaid as well as his prefect?"

He had always been able to read Corvus's moods. This time, as ever before, he sensed the change before he saw it. As never before, the understanding came as a blow to the chest that knocked his heart from its rhythm.

Anger burned in the prefect's eyes. With quiet force, he said, "If you say that again or anything like it, I will have you flogged and demoted to the ranks. Do you understand me?"

In eight years, however they might have fought, Corvus had not used his rank as a weapon. Feeling the skin tighten to parchment on his skull, Valerius said, "Perfectly."

You will know neither love nor joy . . . The curse had not debarred him from feeling the withdrawal of love, nor from mourning its loss. He had imagined it a thing for ever, as certain as the rising and setting of the moon, something solid he could rail against in safety and return to later, when the rage had burned out. Shock left him hollow and weightless. He fought to listen, to mark Corvus's words and their meanings, inner and outer.

Corvus said, "Good. Then listen and consider your answer carefully. As you may know, the client-king Prasutagos now lays claim to rulership of the Eceni. He does so through a woman named Silla, who professes the royal line. She has borne her 'king' two stillborn sons and may yet present him with a living child to act as his successor."

He paused, waiting for a response. None came. The world of fortress gossip had long since brought Valerius news of 'Tagos's kingship, but not the reason for his elevation. Men raised in a world of men had thought wine and gold enough to buy status. Valerius, raised differently, should have seen the truth but had not. In his mind, Silla was too young to take any man; she was three years old and sharing his bed, clinging like a limpet for warmth because, even in the height of summer, she could not bear the aloneness of lying apart. She was six, lying on the turf outside a forge, watching her father make a sword that would one day bear the serpent-spear on its pommel. She had no interest in swords, and so instead she watched a late wasp land on a leaf and tried to grasp it. Her brother brought her the crushed comfrey leaves to take the ache out of the sting. She was eight, kneeling in mud with her arms tight round the neck of a hound, holding the beast back so that he would not run after the riders on their way to Cunobelin's dun. Her voice reached out across years, high and childlike: *Don't be gone more than a month. He'll stop eating and die without you.* Her dress was the green of old oak leaves just before the turn. It had a border of bright saffron yellow along the hem. The memory of it stayed as an afterglow in Valerius's mind.

He had been gone a lifetime. The hound might well have stopped eating and died. Silla had borne two sons to 'Tagos, and both were dead. Her daughters, if she had any, would not be counted by Rome.

Corvus was speaking again. ". . . which means we will pass through his lands on our way to the fort, and the king will undoubtedly wish to offer us hospitality. It seems to me that you may wish not to meet this man or any of his near kin. If this is the case, there may be reasons you would be required to remain at the fortress. There is still time to find a temporary replacement as second in command of the third troop."

"You could have me flogged, you mean, and I would have to stay behind?"

Valerius had meant it as a joke, of sorts, a means to break through the formality. Corvus nodded, as if the possibility were real. "If you like, although I had considered something more certain. Were you to be flogged now, I suspect the governor would still require you to ride out at noon."

"I'm sure he would. I'm grateful, but if the prefect permits, I would prefer to ride with a whole skin."

"But you are certain you wish to ride?"

"I am."

They had reached the south gates of the fortress. Valerius turned the Crow-horse away. He was tired, suddenly, of word games. In the past, they had not been necessary. In the future, perhaps they would not be possible, replaced by the distant formalities of rank. It was not a concept he wished to consider in depth. He said, "It was a good thought and I am genuinely grateful, but there is no need. 'Tagos may know you when you meet. He will not recognize me."

Corvus caught at his bridle. Alone of all other men, he could handle the Crow-horse without risking his arm. Baldly, he said, "And if the warriors we fight bear the mark of the serpent-spear on their shields, or if they are led by the red-headed woman whose mark it is, what then?"

The wind whistled between them, raising the hairs on their arms. In four years, neither of them had mentioned the existence of the serpent-spear or of the woman whose mark it was. That Corvus did so now marked either his desperation or the utter diminution of his care.

Against a rising panic, Valerius said, "The warrior who bears the serpent-spear is not here. You heard the tribune. She's in the west, leading the uprising with Caradoc."

Corvus shook his head. "That was over a month ago. Marcus Ostorius has ridden across the land since then, and Breaca has had time to do so also. If I were your sister, I would be raising resistance in the east. If she and Caradoc take us on two fronts, they can beat us."

Valerius felt his worlds collide, as they had not done since before the invasion. He closed his eyes and sought his god, who did not come. The brand lay cold on his chest. A grandmother cursed him, laughing.

I had no choice. I have none now.

Fool.

Thickly, he said, "I will do as you will do and for the same reasons. I am committed to the legions; I have taken the oath before the emperor and another before the god. Whoever we meet, however we meet them, I will follow orders and I will fight."

"And if you are ordered to crucify their children?"

The pied horse flung up its head, and the bridle was ripped from Corvus's hand. Biting hard on his own lip, Julius Valerius, duplicarius of the third troop of the Ala Quinta Gallorum, saluted his prefect with rigid precision. "Then I will follow your lead, in that as in everything."

It had been a parting of the worst kind, and nothing that had happened since had improved it. They had, indeed, spent a night under Prasutagos's care, and the client-king had not known either of them. In truth, there had been little risk that he would; the conversation had been of other, deeper things. More, it had marked the ending of something neither had believed would ever end.

Valerius stood now in the hospital corridor outside a room that smelled of lemon balm and knew that he did not have the courage to open the door.

"The hero of the battle. You didn't tell me that last time. I wondered how long before you came back again."

Valerius spun on his heel. Theophilus, the lean and long-nosed doctor, leaned against a wall behind him. Once he had ministered to an emperor, but then the emperor had changed and it was no longer politic for members of the old court to remain in Rome. He had fled to Germany and found a home amongst the legions on the Rhine, travelling with them to the new province of Britannia as part of the invading army. Since then he had become sole medic to an entire fortress, alternately tending to men sick with fever and those wounded in combat. It was hard to tell if he was happier when men came back injured from battle or whole.

He regarded Valerius from under white brows. Like the dreamers of the tribes, Theophilus knew the secrets of a man's heart.

Valerius said, "I was leaving. I would not disturb him."

"No, but perhaps he would disturb you." Theophilus never spoke without need and always with words beneath the words. A new caduceus in gold glittered at his breast: a gift from the governor. Beneath it his old one, carved in applewood, hung from a leather thong. He touched this one with his thumb in the same way Valerius touched his brand. "The tribune is with him. Did you know?"

"I guessed. Even were he not, it is not my place to visit. I will leave and—"

"No. Don't go." The door swung back. The scent of citrus oils flooded out, and the stale blood beneath. Marcus Ostorius Scapula, resplendent in white and scarlet, stood on the threshold. If they had made him emperor and dressed him in purple, he could not have looked more regal. He turned the full weight of his black gaze on Valerius and smiled beautifully. "Duplicarius, come in. The prefect would be happy to see you."

It was an order, disguised as an offer, and could not be denied, however much one might wish so to do. Inside, the room was quiet, the breathing of the man on the bed so shallow as barely to disturb the air. Corvus lay flat, white as the linen. Part of his scalp had been shaved, the better to treat the wound on his head. His chest was bound round with bandages. His right arm lay limply on the sheets, waiting for something with more will than he currently possessed to move it.

The door closed, and the tribune was on the inside. The duplicarius was not to be left alone with his prefect. Valerius stood to attention at the foot of the bed. Corvus's gaze swept over him and came back, too complex to read. He fought openly for composure and found it; against what pain could not be known.

"Julius Valerius . . ." Words cost him breath, and breath, clearly, was pain. Valerius settled himself to patience.

The governor's son was less patient. He said, "You will know that the weather has improved and a ship has docked south of the fortress. It brings a message from the emperor commending the governor's actions and supporting an increase in the scale of warfare in the west. It will return with a despatch detailing the peaceful disarming of the loyal eastern tribes and the suppression of a revolt among the Eceni and their allies, the Coritani, with mention of the ferocity with which they fought and the extraordinary courage and discipline of our men in defeating them. It will be the last ship to travel the seas this winter. By spring the fresh reports must show a winter's work. The prefect and I were discussing—"

The suppression of a revolt . . . Valerius laughed harshly. The sound rang loud in the quiet room. Corvus's eyes were black with pain. They fixed on his.

Ignoring their plea, Valerius said, "Forget the spring reports. By the end of winter, we will have been overwhelmed. Those warriors of the Eceni and Coritani who survived the 'suppression' are even now celebrating with the fox-singer on the success of his salmon-trap. They will not sleep in their roundhouses filling their bellies just because there is snow on the ground."

"Duplicarius, you go too—"

"No. He has the right. We gave him leave to speak his mind once before. It's fair he does so now as long as he is aware that his words are for this room only and would be considered seditious were they to be repeated in other company."

Marcus Ostorius was no longer smiling. He was twenty years old and could order any manner of punishment of a junior officer of the auxiliary wings, and it would be carried out without question. His tone and his bearing said he could do so; possibly he had already done so in other circumstances. He stood at the open window, staring into the courtyard. Slanting sun slid across his face, leaving him in shadow. Outside, a late cockerel reminded them day had long since dawned.

"Tell me." He spoke without turning. "If you were the governor and you needed urgently to ensure that the united tribes were disunited, or at least did not press their advantage, would you consider pressing reprisals against them that are more severe than those already imposed?"

You would as well crucify their children.

"It is the only hope." Valerius had thought of little else since his escape from the salmon-trap. "We could have talked with the elder council, perhaps, after the fort burned and before the battle, but not now. If your father wishes to remain governor of a province still under Roman rule, he will have to single out at least one village and destroy it. There is no other way."

"You had somewhere in mind?"

"The first village that sparked the revolt: those who attacked the Thracian troop. If you hang the entire population and make as many of the nearby Eceni as you can find come to watch, they will spread word to the rest. Let it be known through them and through Prasutagos that for every legionary or auxiliary who dies henceforth, an entire family, picked at random, will die. They have raised the stakes with their killing of the scouts and their ambush. The governor must raise them so high, so fast, that the people themselves will not allow the dreamers to continue their war."

Marcus Ostorius frowned. "Is it the dreamers' war? I thought the one with the fox-mark was one of their bards."

"He was, although he bore the arms of a warrior and I saw him fight. Even so, the singers and the dreamers are as one. The warriors follow their command, not the other way round. The dreamers are set against us now, and they have the warriors behind them. Our hope of survival rests in our willingness to do more harm to them than they can do to us. If we can't, then we should take the next ship back to Rome."

"It is easy to say." Marcus Ostorius turned abruptly from the window. "But you are asking the men to kill women and children without the scent of battle to give them heart. Would you do it?"

Valerius looked at Corvus. "If my decurion ordered me to. Or my prefect."

Marcus Ostorius closed his eyes briefly. Opening them, he said, "Regulus is dead. You have no decurion. Replacements must be found for him and for all those others who died. At least some of the promotions will be made on the basis of exceptional valour and the leading of men. If you were to be promoted to decurion, say, of the second troop of the Thracians, third in command of the wing, would you lead them in service of the governor, whatever the order?"

Valerius's world swam. All of his adult life—all of his life that now mattered—he had served under Corvus, prefect of the Quinta Gallorum. He had been part of his troop almost since it was first formed. If he had few friends, he had men at whose sides he had fought in battle, whose lives he had saved, whom he trusted to save him, men he knew as intimately as brothers. All but two of these were Gauls. Longinus and the Thracians fought under a Roman prefect who had ordered the hanging of a pregnant girl, a prefect who, above all else, was not Corvus.

In Valerius's mind, his own voice said, *I believed it would be constructive in the development of my career.* Corvus, breathing easily, laughed as he replied, *I'm sure it will be.* Neither of them had imagined that the development of his career would require him to leave the wing that was his home and the man who led it. Neither of them had wanted it to, until now.

In the hospital, in a quiet room, he needed badly to sit.

From the bed, Corvus said, "Marcus . . . ?" and the tribune raised a lazy brow and, smiling, said, "Of course. I'll be outside when you need me."

The door closed, and they were alone, a newly made decurion and the man who was no longer his prefect.

A bench had been placed next to the bed. Valerius sat on it without asking leave, then stood, remembering his place, and sat again at Corvus's nod.

Silence held him. What does one say? *I saw you die, and if my world had not already ended, it would have done so then. But I am unable any longer to feel either rage or grief or love, but can only mourn their loss. It is the curse of the gods and the one god cannot lift it. Can you forgive me? Can we be as we were, knowing I cannot feel?*

No point. His answer stood in the felt presence of the tribune on the far side of the door and the single informal name spoken as a quiet request: *Marcus?* Very few beyond close family would have been granted the right to call the governor's son by his first name.

Reaching forward, Valerius lifted Corvus's limp right hand and felt a tremor of intended movement. In his mind, he could see how it would heal, given time. That much was good.

In a while, when he had more control of himself, he looked past the hand to the face beyond it. What had once been an open book was closed beyond any power of his to open.

"Why?" he asked.

He did not mean the promotion, but it was easier for Corvus to answer as if he did. He said, "Your actions on the battlefield were seen and reported to the governor. Both the attack on the dreamer and the fetching of the horses were acts of outstanding courage and an example to all the ranks. These things cannot be put in the despatch—nothing can be seen to outweigh the tribune's actions—but they can be rewarded." Corvus's gaze became more keenly focused. "I didn't know you could command an entire troop of horses by voice alone."

"I didn't. They followed the Crow. All I had to do was point them at the barrier where the warriors were thickest and the auxiliaries least and trust they would jump over. The Eceni will not kill a riderless horse. They don't have it in them."

"But riderless horses will kill the Eceni?"

"Only if they feel themselves attacked. It's in their training."

"And a horse, which has no conscience, will act by its training. For a man to do so takes more courage." Corvus's voice had roughened, losing the brittle bite. Reaching out with his good left hand, he asked, "What did it cost you?" Almost, his face was as it had been.

I knew you were behind the barrier and that you would die. I would have made you proud of me, this one last time. The curse has not destroyed my pride, or yours. It was my gift to you, freely given, and your black-eyed tribune has stolen it.

Valerius shook his head. "Nothing." He let go of the hand he was holding and drew himself back. Where Corvus had just recently hidden, he, too, took refuge. "Why must I join the Thracians when I have served these last nine years with the Gauls?"

The brittleness returned, and the layers of rank between them. Corvus said, "The second troop has need of a decurion. It's an obvious promotion for you, a clear demonstration that your actions were seen and valued. You are a good example. If we are to survive the winter, we will need men to show initiative when it counts, and clear courage."

"Regulus also died. I could remain with the Gauls." *I would still serve under you. Please let me?*

"No. This is best. The decision is the governor's, but I believe he will take advice from the tribune."

And doubtless from the prefect whose life his son has so valiantly saved.

Valerius could have said that last aloud, but his courage was not so great, and he found that, after all, he did not wish to be flogged and demoted to the ranks for the sake of gaining the last word. He let go of the hand he had been holding and smoothed down the bed linen. "I should go," he said. "The tribune waits outside and should not be made to stand for longer than necessary. I wish you good health and a swift recovery."

He was by the door when Corvus spoke.

"Valerius?"

"Yes?" He turned too fast. He had not passed beyond hope.

"Longinus Sdapeze will be made duplicarius of the second troop, serving directly under you. Theophilus swears he will be fit to ride by the end of winter. He's a good man. If you take care of each other, we might all come out of this alive."

SECTION II

SUMMER–EARLY AUTUMN A.D. 51

CHAPTER 10

The child was born on Mona, in late summer, when the fighting was at its height.

Mona was safe. The governor, Scapula, remained intent on subduing the Silures. His pride would not let him stop, nor his oath to the emperor, nearly four years old and not yet fulfilled. He had not yet turned his attention on the dreamers and their island; or more likely, he had not yet gained the military mastery that would allow him to strike that far north and west. Every spring for four consecutive years, the Second Legion had held the very southern tip of the land against attacks from the Durotriges, while the Twentieth had marched out of their winter encampments and done their best to push their line of forts further west into Siluran territory. In places and at times, they had succeeded. As often, they had failed.

The mountains of the west had become a constant battleground. Corn was planted and harvested now only by the very young, the old, and the infirm: all those who could not hold a weapon in war. Horses were bred in favour of cattle to replace the many lost in the fighting. Game became scarce. In those places where Rome gained ascendancy, the legions hunted to extinction all that lived within easy reach of their forts. Their indiscriminate felling of the forests to supply timber and firewood ensured that those beasts that had fled would not return. In the occupied lands of the east and south, grain, which had once been freely owned by those who worked to plant and harvest it, became the property instead of tax collectors or of the Roman veterans who owned the land but ordered others to farm it. Starvation stalked the months of winter in ways it had never done before the invasion.

On Mona alone life continued as close to normal as was possible with the legions less than two days' ride away beyond the straits and the mountains. Dreamers and singers still took apprentices from amongst those tribes who chose to send them. Those not under the Roman yoke sent more than they had ever done, feeling a greater need to be close to the gods. Those who lived under the shadow of the legions sent few and in great secrecy, and each one came knowing that if their calling was discovered, their family, at best, would hang.

In the same spirit and with the same fears, girls and boys nearing adulthood who showed the spirit and potential for war journeyed west to pass the rites of the long-nights in safety and afterwards, if their acts and their dreams showed them worthy, to train at the warriors' school. The luxury of ten years' tuition was denied them; many went into battle after their first year, but some few older ones remained on the island to hold the core of the school together.

Breaca, who as god-chosen Warrior of Mona should have been teaching the future generations the skills of battle, spent the greater part of every summer fighting the enemy with those of her own generation who had survived this far. That much was different from how things used to be. Venutios, her predecessor, had left the island only once in the twelve years of his tenure as Warrior. In the changed new world of constant war, she was the Boudica, and her place was in the front line of the attacks on the forts, or the ambushes of supply trains, or the encircling of auxiliary troops lost in the mountains. Her presence brought heart to the warriors and fear to the enemy. For the eight years since the invasion, she had received the blessing and instruction of the gods, relayed through the dreamers, who sat in almost continuous council, monitoring reports from the occupied lands. War was her life, and in so far as anyone could be in a land under threat, she was content.

It was her body that betrayed her, and the timing of the gods in sending a child when it was least needed. There had been nearly seven childless years since the birth of her son Cunomar. She had thought herself barren and had not taken the infusions that would have kept her so in the lull after the fighting. When, in late winter, the fact of the pregnancy had become clear, she had panicked and sought out Airmid, dreamer, healer, and heart's-friend, to ask her help in its unmaking.

Airmid had smiled, which was a gift in itself. Unlike the warriors, she had not enjoyed a winter's respite from the strains of battle. Since Scapula's slaughter of innocents in the Eceni lands, the dreamers had sought the destruction of the governor by any means the gods might provide, and winter was their time to discover what that means might be.

Breaca had walked alone to one of the stone circles scattered through-out the island: vast rocks quarried elsewhere and erected by the ancestors to form a focus for their dreaming in the days when the whole land had dreamed. It had been snowing, and the ground was sparsely white. The circle stood alone in the valley between two low hills. Stunted, wind-driven oaks leaned to the east; snow powdered their limbs and fell as grey dust in the evening light. A huddle of heavily pregnant ewes found forage in the lee of the circle.

Airmid stood near the westernmost stone, facing the rising moon. Nemain, god of night and water, showed her face more distinctly here in the west than she had ever done when they were children in the eastern lands of the Eceni. Even now, with night not yet on them, one could see clearly on her surface the hare that had brought the first dream to the peo-ple and had acted as messenger ever since. In the god's light, Airmid be-came a dream creature in her own right. Already tall, the linear shadows cast by the stones on either side made her taller. White snow made her hair a falling of night, bound back by the birch-bark thong at her brow. A necklace of silvered frog bones glimmered softly at her throat, the only outward sign of her dream. Her eyes were a gateway to the true dreaming, the messages of the gods, sent to guide the people.

Breaca leaned against the north stone, waiting for the woman she knew to return and inhabit the living flesh. Her hands linked on the small mound of her belly, seeking the pulse of life within. In her head, she formed the words of apology to a half-made soul that it must leave early, with its life's promise unfulfilled. Her daughter stirred under her touch. In the gods' space of the circle, she took form. A young woman, coming near to her long-nights, stood in the gap between two stones that had just now been empty. She was not the daughter Breaca would have imagined; a child of two parents so tall was not expected to be so slender and slight, nor her hair so richly dark, the colour of ox-blood, when her father was corn-gold and her mother the burnished red of a fox in winter. She stood in the drifting snow, and her eyes alone were recognizably Caradoc's, iron-grey and clear, with an honesty that did not allow for doubt and a depth of love that carved the soul.

The girl turned, seeking guidance. Her eyes met those of her mother. The fire of recognition leapt between them, to be replaced, too fast, by surprise, then fear, then something intangible that went beyond either: understanding and surmise and love buried in grief. Only at the last did she smile, and the sight of it cut through the weight of the present and became a channel to a past that had been too long buried.

"Who does she remind you of?"

Breaca found her eyes closed and opened them. The dream-child was gone. Airmid stood where it had been, her face still alive with the presence of the god. "You thought of someone then," she said. "Who was it?"

Words were hard. It was best, suddenly, to speak without thinking. Breaca said, "Graine. That is, my mother. And her sister, Macha, the wren-dreamer. She was both."

"Then you have two names that would be good. You will know which one is best when she is born."

There was no question, then, of unmaking the child. Breaca said, "She was a dreamer. I saw the thong at her brow." A dreamer bred from two warriors was not unheard of, simply unusual. She did not mention the other things she had seen, the battle-stained tunic and the weapons of war that were not the tools of a dreamer and were, in any case, forbidden a girl approaching her long-nights.

Airmid, if she knew of them, chose not to comment. Nodding, she smiled a dreamer's smile of unspoken mysteries. "She will be," she said. "Not 'she was.' Remember that always: your daughter is the future, not the past."

Winter leaked into spring. Snow melted to muddy water and filled the rivers cascading down the mountainsides. Hawthorn blossom hung white and was shed, to be trampled underfoot in the rush towards spring and the onset of fighting. Leaves unfurled on the trees, and the first shoots of barley broke through winter earth. Lambs were born and were followed by foals, stilt-legged in the fields. The seas opened to traffic, and the ferry began to make its daily way across the narrow straits from Mona to the mainland, taking dreamers out into the wider land and, occasionally, bringing war-leaders back for council, or warriors to be healed of their wounds.

The child who was the future, not the past, grew steadily in her mother's womb so that, by the third month of fighting, Breaca was no longer fit to ride into battle. In disgust she took the ferry to Mona that she might not become a burden to Caradoc, who commanded the western tribes alone in her absence, nor to Ardacos and Gwyddhien, who between them led the trained warriors of Mona. She would have stayed simply to be close to the fighting and take part in the strategies and the talk after battle, but in the previous year the legions had made a practise of sending a troop or two of their auxiliaries round the perimeter of any fighting to capture alive the families of those warriors engaged in the battle. They had hanged some outside the gates of their forts and sold others into slavery, but Scapula had long made it known that the capture alive of the Boudica or Caradoc or any of their kin was a matter of highest priority and that their fate, in Rome, would not be the swift death of a battlefield hanging. It would have taken more warriors than could be spared to guarantee Breaca's safety, and that in itself would have alerted Scapula to her presence. Thus the Boudica left her warriors to find victory alone and the fighting continued unchecked without her.

She was in council when the birth pains began, in the greathouse of the elders of Mona. Built by the ancestors and maintained by each passing generation, it was large enough to enable every dreamer, singer, and warrior on Mona to fit into it standing and not feel crowded. The walls were of stone, cut and dressed by the lost generations in a time so far back that the oldest tales did not record it. The vast roof beams were of oak taller than any that grew on the island; the ancestors had floated them in from the far northern coast. The dream-mark of each successive Elder and Warrior was carved in the wood, spiralling up into the smoke-dense heights. Stag and snake, horse and salmon, beaver, fox, eagle, toad: each one came to life when the fires were lit and the people gathered. Breaca's own mark of the serpent-spear writhed alongside the bear that was the dream of Maroc, the elder dreamer, and beneath the leaping salmon of Venutios, the man who had been her predecessor as Warrior and now led half of the Brigantes, the vast northern tribe whose aid could be the straw that tipped the balance in the battle against Rome.

Venutios was there; the council had been called on his arrival, meeting swiftly so that he stood now before the fire in the greathouse of the elders in his travelling cloak, explaining as frankly as possible the nature of the conflict in Brigante lands between his own followers and those loyal to Cartimandua, with whom he jointly ruled. Cartimandua had borne him a daughter, but that did not mean she shared his hatred of Rome, or his lifelong care for Mona and the dreamers. Above all she loathed Caradoc and had stated publicly that she would support no venture of which he was a part. More than anything else, that hatred strengthened her ties to Scapula and Rome.

Venutios was not a man of great height, and the conflicting

responsibilities of stewardship weighed him down, but he carried himself with the pride of one who had been Warrior, and his voice was respected and heard. Firelight danced on his face as he spoke, flattering the care of years.

"A civil war amongst the Brigantes will be of no help to anyone," he said. "Cartimandua has spies everywhere. I can raise warriors in secret, but the numbers must be small—a few from each settlement, meeting as if for hunting. If we muster in thousands, she will hear of it and betray us to the enemy. If Rome were distant, this would not be an undue hardship, but the Fourteenth Legion is already camped on our borders. To be certain of defeating them, I would have to raise ten thousand, and I cannot do that. With less, we are always at risk of attack before ever we reach the battleground."

Speaking for the council, Breaca asked, "How many warriors can you safely bring without its being known?"

"A thousand. Maybe two."

"More than that." A young straw-haired warrior of the Brigantes spoke up from his place on the other side of the fire. Standing to be better heard, he said, "It may be that the war-bands of the Selgovae would join us from the north. They are not numerous, but Cartimandua has no spies amongst them. That would give us another thousand."

It went against protocol for any to speak out of turn, but the youth, Vellocatus, was cousin's cousin to Venutios and had supported him from the moment the elders of the Brigantes had called the Warrior back from Mona. His point was heard and accepted.

In her head, Breaca mapped out the numbers and position of the legions and the tribes as the last reports had placed them, adding in Venutios's promised warriors.

"That may be enough," she said. "We are five months into the fighting, and the legions are faring badly. Scapula has sworn to come west, but even so, his men are losing morale. With three thousand, we could—"

She stopped, biting down on her lip. The sporadic clenching of her womb, which had been mellow and bearable, became suddenly neither of those things. She stared fixedly at the fire until it passed. Nobody spoke. Of those dreamers and elders present, many were women who had borne children of their own. The men, for the most part, had aided as many births as she had fought battles.

In the temporary relief after, she said rapidly, "I must go. Get word to Caradoc of the three thousand. He will know how best to use them. With that many, fresh and well armed, we can crush Scapula before he has time to call for reinforcements. Tell him—" A sharp wave spiked and died. "Tell Caradoc to use the salmon-trap again. It worked for Dubornos in the east. It will do so again here." She took her leave after that, swiftly. Hail ran at her heel.

That had been the late afternoon. By the long insect-ridden dusk, the pains were so close that she could count the intervals in breaths and the length of each spasm in heartbeats. It was thirty breaths and ten beats when Airmid came to join her.

"You should walk."

"I've been walking since I got here. I've walked enough for now."

She was in the same stone circle in which she had had the first vision of who her daughter could be. It was not a common choice of delivery place. Summer births on Mona frequently took place in the open, but most of the women chose the forest or the river bank and were guarded at need against wild beasts. The circle stood on a piece of open moorland, and if it lacked shelter, the risks of attack were slight. In the circle, Breaca had Hail for protection. The three-legged hound was still one of Mona's better hunters; neither beast nor invading army would reach her while he lived. He lay in the lengthening shadows at the edge of the circle and padded at her side when she walked the perimeter. Her blade and shield hung from one of the westerly stones, more to give strength to the child than to provide protection for the mother. More useful were the two stakes, already driven into the turf a shoulder width apart in the centre of the circle, ready for her to brace against at the last heaving. She was a while away from needing them. The next wave took her, shuddering. She pressed her forehead to stone and counted: twelve beats now.

Airmid came to stand behind her. A cool hand wrapped her belly, feeling the muscles tense beneath. Breaca felt the frown but couldn't see it. In a soft, clear voice, the dreamer asked, "Is there pain?"

"A little. When the pressure is highest." Breaca turned round and put her back to the stone. The cold on her shoulders helped her think. "Has Venutios gone to raise his war-band?"

"Soon. He'll wait until nightfall to take the ferry. Vellocatus has gone ahead to seek aid of the Selgovae; he is not so widely known and so can travel more safely. If it can be done, they will bring us the three thousand. You are not to think of it now." Hail was beside her, leaning his weight against her thigh. On the other side, Airmid took her arm. "Come with me. We'll go round the circle again and then I'll light a fire. We can douse it later, when the babe comes. This one should be born only into moonlight. Nemain will shed light on her own."

The sun rested on the horizon, hurling ever deeper reds into the darkening blue. Insects in their thousands reached the height of their feeding. Airmid lit a fire and laid pine needles on it to make smoke to keep them off. Later, when that was not enough, she brought from her belt-pouch a stoppered flask and smeared the infusion it contained on herself, Breaca, and Hail. The smell was of stewed fungal plates, as familiar a scent of summer as cut hay and mare's milk. Long ago, in their joint childhood, Breaca had planned a gift of the same for Airmid but had been forestalled. She wanted to say so, but a cramp came on her that lasted a full sixty heartbeats, and she was gasping for breath by the end.

"Keep walking."

"I can't. She's here, I can feel her."

"Then come and kneel at the stakes and let me see where you're at."

The stakes were of ash wood, planed smooth, with the sharp end driven an arm's length into the ground and a spear's height left above it. Caradoc had made them in spring before the fighting started, had spent two full days painting them that he might be with her in spirit if he could not be in fact. The eagle and the serpent-spear, his mark and hers, ran in chains along the lengths of each with the war hammer of the Ordovices and the running horse of the Eceni at either end.

Horse hides rolled with the hair outwards made a bench between them, so that when Breaca knelt, leaning forward to grasp each stake and resting her arms on the hides, she made the shape of a foaling mare. From the times of the ancestors, the Eceni had given birth in this way. It made for vigorous children and, in a strong dam, ensured a fast, clean delivery.

Another wave came and passed, and then another, stronger now so that she could not breathe through them. Airmid spoke from behind her.

"That's good. The birth-sac is here."

Strong fingers probed. Something broke within her, and water gushed hotly. The salt-sweet of birthing fluid spiked the air. Breaca said, "She doesn't feel like Cunomar."

"She's a different person. Wait for the next wave, and put your strength behind it."

She did so, repeatedly, in pain and without success. Over time the insects withdrew, and the fire dulled to embers. Hail fell asleep and dreamed, twitching. The sky became a purpled bruise spreading wider until the sun gave the lighting of the world over to Nemain, the moon, who rose almost full above the top edges of the standing stones. In the centre of the circle, under the god's light, Airmid of Nemain struggled to bring her successor into life.

"Breaca, she's coming backwards. It will be harder than Cunomar and may take longer. If you can hold on and not press, I'll see if I can turn her. Can you do that?"

"I can try."

A battlefield was so much easier. There, at least, she could do more than simply breathe and let the imperatives of her body clash within. She held her breath while Airmid slid a bloodied hand alongside the child, and when she had to breathe, she did so in sucked gasps that did not spark the next wave of spasms. The noise of it brought Hail to her side. Laying his head on the horse-hide bench next to her arms, he crooned gently, his old eyes worried. She had no breath left to reassure him; the pressure of waiting took everything she had. In the end, she could hold no longer, and the pain this time left her sobbing.

"Drink this. Drink it, Breaca. You must. We have to turn her or bring her backwards. Drink. It will help."

Airmid, who had been behind, was at her head. The world swam, nauseatingly. She felt a cup pressed to her lips and drank. The infusion was bitter, and she did not recognize the taste. The hand that held her was jellied with blood and slime; her own.

Rarely, she had seen mares when the foal would not come. Macha, who had managed the births in the Eceni village of her childhood, had two responses. In those cases where the mare was everything, she had taken a blade in her cupped hand and, sliding it into the womb, had cut the living foal to pieces, that it might be pulled out and leave the mare intact. In those cases where the foal was the end of a long waiting, the result of many planned matings on whom a dynasty depended, or the dam was clearly dying, she had taken a spiked lump hammer to the mare's head, killing it cleanly before cutting it open to drag the foal, living, from the womb.

Raggedly, after the next wave, Breaca said, "Use the hammer. Don't kill the child."

"Don't say it. We will have both of you alive." That was the great joy with Airmid, one never had to explain. Equally, the dreamer could not hide the concern in her voice as she might have done from another birthing mother; knowing it, she did not try. Instead, she said, "I need Efnís to help. Or Luain mac Calma. Can you wait with Hail while I find one of them?" and left, because there had never been a doubt of the answer.

Pain drew her thin and compressed her again. In the midst of it were three voices and then hands on her shoulders, raising her higher. A voice rich with the accents of the northern Eceni said, "Breaca, we need you to stand. Can you do that for us? Don't let go of the stakes, just stand upright between them so the babe points down. Hail will stay with you. I'll move the mare's hide out of the way."

Another, with the faintest touch of Hibernia, said, not to her, "This one is Nemain's child and will come only for her light. I'll get a bowl with water, and we will give her the reflection. She will come more willingly for that. Can you keep her steady for that long?"

Time took hold of the answer and spun it out in a web of meaningless syllables, in the centre of which, like a waiting hunter, was a cracked and tearing pain. It ended, blindingly, in a wash of silver that faded into night.

Graine, daughter of Breaca, granddaughter of Graine, first-born daughter of the royal line of the Eceni, came into life in the care of the land's three most powerful dreamers, slipping bloody between their hands towards a bowl of tarnished moonlight. Her mother remained conscious for the birth and for long enough to walk back to the hut set apart for newly delivered women, but fell into sleep shortly afterwards, her new daughter naked at her breast. She woke once a while later and was helped out to the appointed place to pass clotted blood and mucus and the turgid mass of the afterbirth and returned to feed her child and sleep again. The infant was redly bald and bruised where the birth had squeezed her tight, and her unfocussed infant gaze was the blue of the sky after rain. In her mother's eyes, she was perfect.

CHAPTER 11

"She's ugly. Will she always be ugly? I don't want a sister that's ugly."

The voice was high and peevish, made loud by hurt and fear. It broke into dreams of a future in which the children came safely to their long-nights and wore newly woven tunics, free from the blood and dust of battle. Breaca turned her head to the side. Noon sun pierced the loose thatch of the hut in which she lay, casting knife-edge shadows across the floor. Her son, thus transected, stood halfway between the door and her bed. Behind him Airmid grimaced an apology and left.

"Cunomar." Breaca stretched a hand to him. Graine, who had been feeding, rocked slack-jawed from her breast.

"Look, she can't even suck properly. How will she eat when we are away, fighting the legions?"

"She's sleeping, beloved. She can suck strongly when she wants to." He was seven years old and had been supplanted. He was not consoled. The space between them grew desolate. She said, "Heart-of-life, will you come to me? I could get up, but it feels like a long way from here."

She used the Eceni, which he had been learning, and addressed him as she did his father. Like a shy horse, Cunomar came forward to her outstretched hand, eyeing askance the new unwanted thing that had arrived to shake his world. Breaca tried to remember how she had felt when Bán was born, or later Silla, and failed. Life had been different then, a sibling always a thing to cherish. He reached her bed and stroked her hair as it fell back from her brow, his touchstone for safety.

"Hail's here." He offered the hound's presence as a gift, and she knew its cost. "I stayed with him through the morning like Airmid asked. He wanted to come back to you sooner, but I wouldn't let him. He's waiting outside now. Should I call him in?"

"In a while, when I've had time alone with you." She made herself smile against a sudden uncertainty. She was not alone with her son and never would be. She had forgotten how it would be, how it had been with Cunomar; until his birth, she had not known it was possible to hold so small a thing so dear. Until that moment, she had not known the terrifying, glorious truth that the part of her heart not already given to others had just split afresh in two, and one part was newly installed in a separate body.

Graine woke, searching muzzily for the nipple. Cunomar tentatively touched a foot and watched its languid withdrawal.

"She's very small."

"Yes, but like a foal, she will grow big."

"Not as big as me."

"No, I don't think so. You will always be bigger." He was his father in all but temperament and the colour of his eyes; he would have his father's height. "Cunomar—" She made herself be serious. "The legions are not yet defeated. If your father and the gods work well, it may be that they will be defeated this year." She saw his sudden panic, swiftly hidden, and worked not to show it. "Even if so, there will be more battles beyond it; the tribes south of the sea-river would welcome the legions back, and they would have to be defeated."

"So the fighting could go on for years?" The thought cheered him visibly.

"It could. And if your father and I are in it, then we could be killed, you know that."

"Yes." His eyes were entirely his own, an acorn brown fading to amber. Neither parent and none of the grandparents had shared those. Now they stretched wide as he stopped thinking of himself and thought of the possibility of his parents' death in battle. Solemnly he said, "We would sing of you for generations." He had heard it at some fireside more than once.

"That would be kind, but I would ask a further favour of you." She watched him brighten, then saw suspicion creep at the margins. Before it could take hold, she said, "If we are both killed, your sister will be your closest living kin. I believe one day she will be a great dreamer, possibly of a power to match Airmid, or Luain mac Calma, but only if she grows safe to her long-nights and beyond. She mustn't know the power she has; it would change her growing. You must swear to me on the lives of the ancestors that you will never tell her without my permission. Will you do that?"

In her own way, Breaca could make magic, if only with her son. The new sister was to be a dreamer, not a warrior, and so was not a threat. Moreover, he would be warrior to a dreamer, as his mother was to Airmid. His feelings for Airmid were complex, but at the bedrock lay awe and a profound respect. For Luain mac Calma, he felt the fear of a child who has seen a man call lightning from the sky and believes him half a god.

His eyes were luminous, truly amber. The oath with which he swore was long and bound him absolutely in sickness, health, and all manner of inebriation not to breathe a word to his sister of her possible future. He stumbled only on the child's name, which was unfamiliar.

"Graine. It's Graine, after my mother. Good. So then, if your father and I are killed, Graine will need someone to protect her. I could ask one of the other warriors, but it would best be her brother, who will care for her always. In the beginning, she can know that you protect her as a brother. Only later we can tell her that you will be warrior to her dreamer. Would you pledge that for me, here, on the serpent-blade?"

His smile reflected the sun. He may have loved her and feared Luain mac Calma, but he regarded his mother's blade with the far more prosaic worship of a would-be warrior for the weapon that will one day be his own.

It hung from a hook above the sleeping place, always to hand. She let him reach it down and lay it, sheathed, on the hides at her side. Carefully, she drew a hand's length free so the mackerel stripes of the weld-patterns shimmered in the light. Even so little brought forth its history: the months of making by her father with her spit and his sweat melded into the metal and the score upon score of lives taken after. Cunomar gasped a child's breath of ecstasy. Breaca, who was more hardened to the sight, felt its song weakly in the old scar on her palm that was the relic of her first kill and warned her always of battle.

This oath was more formal. For generations a warrior had pledged the protection of a certain dreamer with words laid down in the times of the ancestors. Breaca was speaking the phrases for him to follow when a shadow crossed the doorway. She counted five legs and wondered that Hail should be so reticent. It was not like the hound to stay silent when someone approached, unless that one could prevent him from barking a warning—or he knew such a warning to be unnecessary. A light breeze brought her the scents of horse sweat and man sweat and the iron-blood of battle, and she chose not to believe it. The day was good; to hope and have that hope dashed would destroy it.

"... guard her life with mine, to the ends of the earth and the four winds."

Cunomar pronounced the final phrases with the care of one handling the newborn. The strength of the oath and its binding altered his face, showing for the first time who he could be when grown. Breaca watched him with half an eye. Behind him the five-legged shadow stepped into the doorway and divided: two legs and three. Cunomar heard his mother's indrawn breath and turned, his face alight.

"You're here!"

The young could squeal it as the grown could not. Cunomar threw himself into his father's arms, breathlessly relaying muddled and misunderstood facts of the birth. Thus far the magic had worked. In the presence of Caradoc, who was most certainly a god on earth, the child was no longer the supplanted favourite but a sworn protector, charged with eternal care of his ward.

Caradoc held his son to his chest and let him ramble. His eyes asked the necessary questions of Breaca, his heart's ease, and had them answered. In Eceni, too fast for Cunomar to follow, he said, "Airmid has told me the details of the birth but no more. I gather we have the gods and dreamers to thank that you are both alive. Is she as you dreamed?"

"I believe so. In twelve years we will know."

Hail came to Breaca, laying his vast grizzled head on her shoulder, his eyes on the child. He had licked her clean and already taken her care to heart. Graine tipped her head to the new scent and stared at him vacantly. Then with a little help, she looked up at her father.

Because she was watching, Breaca saw the moment when Caradoc changed, when the tensions and strains of war fell away, when he let go of the war-leader and became simply the father, in first company of his daughter. It was a sight as precious as any she had seen or could hope to see. Caradoc had one daughter, Cygfa, by a different mother. Breaca had not been sure, until she saw it, that a second would mean as much.

She ought not have doubted him; in that moment of meeting, he was a youth again, shipwrecked and washed up on a headland, hovering in the space between life and death with his heart freely visible for all to see. She had fallen in love with him then and did so again now.

Kneeling at the bedside, he reached forward a tentative finger, knuckle bent, to stroke his daughter's face. "She is you," he said. "The most beautiful woman alive."

"I don't think so." Breaca grinned, an unexpected, welcome sensation. "She's Graine if she's anyone, with Macha's heart and power, although she doesn't look like either of them until she smiles. And she has your eyes. You can't see them in her yet, but they'll be clear when she's grown. Grey eyes and dark red hair, the colour of ox-blood."

Caradoc lifted his gaze from his daughter. His smile was a well-spring of infinite courage. "She's you inside," he said. "In her soul. I can see that already." Leaning forward, he kissed her. His lips were dry and salty from the sea wind and rasped against hers. His breath joined her breath. His world enfolded hers, and she was afloat in the sea he held.

Breaca lay in summer shade and knew her life perfect. Graine squirmed and shifted to the other breast, rocking her. Cresting the tide of it, Caradoc came to sit at her side, Cunomar on his knee. He was stained with the dust of travel and the old blood of killing and the unkind spray of the straits. His skin, which had once been fair and smooth as a girl's, was weathered to oak boarding and scarred on both sides of his face. His hair, bright as polished gold after a summer's sun, was uncombed and was marked at the brow by the line of a helmet, or cap. He had travelled, then, in some haste and with his hair covered as partial disguise. Since the invasion neither he nor the Boudica had worn a helmet in battle. Their hair was their best banner and gathering mark for the warriors. His eyes were a little bloodshot, as they became when he lacked sleep. His hand lifted hers, and Breaca felt the calluses of the sword hilt match the smoother, less ridged lines of her own. In three months, she had softened. She imagined the work it would take to reach battle fitness again and winced. Her mind turned back to war.

"Venutios," she said. "He can bring his Brigantes and a thousand Selgovae—"

"I know." He hooked his fingers under hers and kissed the backs of her knuckles, lightly. "And we have a place to set the salmon-trap. It's all in hand. This once you can let the battle slide you by. If it goes well, the dreamers will have their greatest wish fulfilled by the moon's wane or a little after."

The dreamers had only one wish that great. Sunlight died inside her. "Scapula's here?" she asked.

"Not yet, but soon. He's marching west with fresh recruits to bring the western legions back up to strength. Word is that he will go first to the fortress of the Twentieth and then come north with all of that legion and three cohorts of the Second. When he gets here, we will be ready to fight."

"But he'll drive west, to the heart of the Silures' land. We need him further north if Venutios's war-band is to join us."

"I know. It's been seen to. The legate of the Twentieth has good reason to believe we are massing against him in the north. Scapula will come to us where when we want him."

. . . *has good reason to believe.* Horror brushed her spine. In the past, warriors of outstanding courage had "defected" to the legions. Not one of them had escaped with their lives, and most, if the spies were correct, had died slowly under Roman blades and irons, skin peeled back, eyes gouged and flesh burned to tear the truth of their hearts from their mouths. The only word Scapula would believe now would be that of a wounded man or woman captured alive on the battlefield, who would live long enough to spread the lie, but not so long that the truth could follow. It was a sacrifice greater than any she wished to imagine, and it came to her suddenly that she did not know who had made it. At any other time, she would have known as friends each of those who had prepared themselves to be taken, would have spent time with them before the battle and prayed for them afterwards, sitting by fire or water with Airmid, or Efnís, or Luain mac Calma, until they were sure the soul had crossed to Briga and was free.

She could have asked for a name or names but did not. The question came to the front of her teeth and stopped there, held by Graine, who squirmed, wide-eyed and helpless, on her breast so that, once again, Breaca fell into the vast, incoherent space where her own unbounded love met unbounded terror for the life and welfare of her daughter and the knowledge that, for the rest of her life, she would want to protect this child and keep her free from all harm, and that ultimately she could not.

It was not a time to sink into the horror of another's pain. She took Caradoc's hand and held it. Together they each cupped their daughter's back and felt her smallness shift and mumble beneath their touch. Briga was mother of life as well as death; one could believe with all one's heart that a new child and the hope she brought was prayer enough for her protection.

In a while, when Breaca could think more clearly and look ahead at where another part of her heart would ride alone into danger, she asked, "Where will you set the trap?"

Caradoc was a war leader, and he loved her. He could imagine a little of the frustrations of the one left at home. He gave her what she needed with the crisp exactitude of a council summary. "It's already half-set at the River of the Lame Hind. There is only one route the legion could take out of the fortress. It crosses the river at the lower fording place. Gwyddhien and Ardacos are there now, building a barrier in the cleft between the mountains. We will hold them at the river awhile and then fall back to the barrier and then let them flow over it and on into the valley beyond. The far end is already blocked by a rock-fall so that no legion can get beyond it. We will hit them from the sides. If Venutios can bring his two thousand Brigantes, even without the war-bands of the Selgovae, he can take them from behind, and we will crush them to pulp. If he fails, we will kill as many as we may and then leave them. There are forests on either side, and behind that no Roman will dare to enter."

"Can you win?"

"I don't know." He had always been honest with her. "It's one battle of many, and it depends on a lot of things over which we have no control. We may not win, but we won't lose."

It was a good plan, marred only by one thing. She had thought of it in the midst of birthing, when the pains were at their height. "What will you do if Scapula recognizes the salmon-trap from the battle in the Eceni lands? He may not take it."

He smoothed a hand through her hair and ran his fingers over her scalp. She pushed against the flat of his palm like a hound seeking a caress. His shoulder leaned into hers as Hail's did, a steady presence, for ever hers. The slow surety of his smile soaked into her bones.

"I think he'll take it. The gods are on our side. Half the legion will be raw recruits, with poor discipline. If they see us in retreat, they'll follow and Scapula won't want to stop them. In any case, he didn't see the first salmon-trap. He will have heard of it, but that was four years ago, and a hundred battles have passed since then. There's no reason to think he'll remember the detail of that one above the rest. The only one who was there and will remember is the decurion who rides the pied horse. He broke the barrier; there is no chance he will forget. Our only hope is that he will not come this far west."

"Or that he dies early." A sourness filled her mouth. More even than Scapula, the shadow of that man's reputation dulled the morning. Word of the atrocities amongst the Trinovantes had spread west like slow poison, and the trails of his dead wailed in her sleep on the nights when the battles did not take all of her dreams. She said, "Airmid could find the decurion for you now. She has felt enough of the death he has wrought. A knife in the dark could kill him. The gods know that one does not deserve a death in battle."

She had not meant it as an oath, but there was more power in her one spoken breath than in all of Cunomar's careful recitation, swearing the protection of his sister. The gods listened and heard, and somewhere, in other worlds, was an echo. Moths panicked in her chest. The somnolence of motherhood broke and became the urgency of combat. Breaca lay flat on the bed and stared at the thatch and, for a while, forgot that she had ever become a mother.

Caradoc brought her back, slowly, with the stroke of his fingers on the nape of her neck. Still, the joy of the morning had gone and could not be recovered. Drily, she asked, "When will it happen, the trap against Scapula?"

"Within the month. Scapula is marching west already."

"Then you must leave soon?"

"Not that soon." His smile was the making and breaking of her heart. "The legions are marching slowly, and he will go south first. I think we have ten days to repair the weapons and heal the wounded. Most of the others have returned to their hearths to help with the harvest. I've never been very good at cutting barley. I had thought to have at least that much time in peace with my family."

He kissed her a third time, and she found that it was not, after all, too late to recover the joy in the morning.

CHAPTER 12

"We ride to take Caratacus, to kill him or to capture him, to wipe out his mountain rebels and bring peace to the west."

Scapula said it in the great hall of the *praetorium* at Camulodunum, speaking to five thousand newly trained infantry and two wings of horsemen on the morning before they marched west. The new recruits repeated it, chanting in marching rhythm with the verbs made scurrilous and Scapula as much their target as the man they marched to kill. The cavalry spoke it to their horses, quietly, as a prayer and a protection; they had ridden against enemy horsemen and knew their mettle.

Julius Valerius, decurion of the first troop, the First Thracian Cavalry, second in command of the entire wing and thereby acting leader of the half-wing currently on campaign, heard it repeated over and over in the rhythm of the Crow-horse's feet and felt the promise of ultimate vengeance fill him as a gift from his god, made greater by the absence of the ghosts and the nightmares. Always they fled in the face of action, even when that action was against women and children in a three-hut steading. In the face of real war, they were gone so far it was possible to imagine they might never have been. He slept well and ate well and drank for pleasure, not for need. Longinus Sdapeze, recovered from his war-wounds and promoted to standard-bearer of the troop, rode with him. The man was intelligent and thoughtful and understood better than anyone living the mercurial swing of Valerius's moods.

We ride to kill Caratacus. Caradoc. To kill him. To kill . . .

As far as it could be, his life was perfect.

———

The rain began on the third day out of Camulodunum. Without a following wind, it fell thinly from a patchy sky, a warm, steady drizzle that saturated hide and hair and leather and wool, that made slick the tracks worn to ruts by the tread of the several thousand new recruits who had marched this route over the past eight years to die for Rome in the wild mountains of the west.

Sadly, the clouds did not cover the waning moon, which hung palely on the western horizon. The Thracians considered it ill luck and cited the rain as proof that they were right. Valerius rode his pied horse at a walk through the mud and listened to the mutterings of his men as they grew in conviction and coherence. A horse drew up on his left-hand side.

"Someone should tell the governor—"

"No."

"You don't know what I was about to say." Longinus contrived to sound aggrieved, which was a significant achievement given that it was less than a month since an accident in the practise arena had seen him take a shield-rim across the throat and he had not been able to speak for several days, nor even, in the first night, to breathe.

Valerius grinned acidly. "I know exactly what you were about to say. You want me to inform the emperor's representative in this province that his army should wait in the night-camp until the moon sets—which will be halfway to noon—or turn back to Camulodunum and delay his advance until the rising of the new moon, at which time the lady's light will grant certain victory in war and love to all men, although why anyone should want Caradoc to have the same luck as us is beyond me. I tell you what—" He turned in his saddle. "You tell the governor. I bet you my horse against yours that you'll be less than three words into the first sentence before he hears your voice and has you dismissed from the ranks and sent home. If he's having a really bad day, he'll send the rest of us back as your escort."

Valerius had gone to some lengths to keep the extent of the Thracian's injuries from his superiors. In certain quarters, it was believed that a man who could not shout his orders across a battlefield was a liability to himself and his troop. Valerius did not believe it, but he did not want anyone to have an excuse to exclude Longinus from the battle plans. In the uncertain politics of the fortress, there was a very real likelihood that the entire wing would have been left behind to keep him company.

Longinus knew the reality as well as anyone. He shook his head. "I don't want your horse. It's simply that, as your standard-bearer, I don't want to see you dead sooner than you have to be." The Thracian's cavalry cloak fell in sodden folds to his horse's rump, and his rain-darkened hair straggled from beneath his helmet, but even in the rain he had the stare of a hawk. It was the sharpness of his eyes that set him apart from his compatriots, giving light as they did to the sharpness of his mind.

Valerius had a great respect for the sharpness of Longinus's mind. "Why should I be dead? Is it the moon or is there something else?"

"I don't know. I can't see the way you can. I know only that something is coming that is worse than battle. When I know what it is, I'll tell you. In the meantime, I think you should take your horse and ride it somewhere hard and fast. You're as cramped in as he is, and it's upsetting the men. They're afraid you'll take it out on them when we get to the fortress."

"I'll take it out on them before that if I can find something for them to do. Tell them. It'll give them something else to worry about that isn't the moon."

"I don't have to. They all have ears. They heard."

"Good."

The mountains remained in the distance and the marching men passed through gentler land, just past harvest. The wars of east and west had not touched the centre of the province, and even in the rain the fecundity of this place was clear. On either side of the track, men and women of the Catuvellauni cut beans in long, straight-sided fields. Elsewhere ewes and lambs grazed, guarded by youths with throwing sticks. In larger paddocks, young weaned bulls fought one another haphazardly or watched from the shelter of aged beech and oak that the axe had not yet sought out. Buzzards circled high over fields where corn stood in shining sheaves, and scruffy children with sapling hounds hunted the rats that made their nests within.

The children were the only ones to respond to the column of armed men passing through their land. In the beginning, as the first centuries of the first cohort passed them by, they had run to the field edges to stare. The boldest among them skipped alongside, offering the men water or pocketfuls of malted barley or twists of smoked meat in return for a coin or a carving. Later, as the morning grew old and the armoured ribbon did not cease, they grew bored and returned to the rats, who gave more sport more consistently. Only when the cavalry passed did they turn once again to stare at the horses and nudge one another and lay uncollectable wagers as to which was fastest or would make the best brood mare.

Valerius came last of the last, the snake's second head, guarding the rear. He felt the children's eyes on the pied horse as they came within sight and heard the change in tenor of the whispers and knew, with a familiar, unnameable mix of resentment and defiance, that he was recognized here as readily as he was in the east, and if here, then it would be the same in the west. The pied horse felt the tension of his hands through the reins and set its jaw against the bit. If he chose, Valerius could lose himself in fighting it.

"They will be waiting for you, the spear-carriers of the mountains, if we ever see the field of battle."

Longinus rode a mare that should have been almost as well known as Valerius's mount but, being chestnut and blandly marked, was not.

"Is that the source of your bad feeling—that they will know me?"

"It should be; they will have their dreamers mark you and set the spear-throwers on you from the start, but no, it's something more than that. I'll tell you when I know. In the meantime, there's a river ahead that's flowing fast enough to make the swimming hard. If you want something for the men to do, that might provide it."

Longinus had always thought like an officer. Valerius grinned. "If I make them ford it, they'll think it was my idea."

"Would they be wrong?"

"No. Would you care to bet that Axeto loses hold of his horse before he reaches the far side?"

"Hardly—that's a certainty. But I'll lay you the first flagon of wine tonight that he's mounted again before the last of the others is on land and that he doesn't lose his sword to the river-gods this time."

"Done."

Valerius commanded the eight troops who made the left half of the wing. Of those the first seven were strung out ahead along the sides of the marching column; only his own troop rode with him at the rear, his fangs in the snake's second head. They were his honour guard and moulded themselves on the pattern of the enemy that was as much the pattern of Thrace. They loved him and hated him, and they had all smelled the river and then seen it, and the order to swim, when it came, was not a surprise.

They were alone in their endeavour. Dry-footed, the infantry crossed the water on one of two bridges built by the engineers of the Twentieth when that legion first marched west. The other half-wing of cavalry, the Quinta Gallorum, assigned to the head of the column, had long since walked their horses across in warmth and comfort; in all likelihood, they were at the fortress already, settled and resting. The early troops of the

Prima Thracum had similarly crossed without incident. Lacking an order from Valerius, their decurions had not made them swim.

The thirty-two men and horses of the first troop, who trained under a decurion who had trained with the Batavians on the Rhine, dismounted, tied their helmets more tightly on their heads, and fixed their swords to their belts with leather thongs tied in a complex loop that might be easily undone even when wet. In fours they took to the water, swearing viciously at the cold and then at the current and then at the cold again as they emerged, four abreast in good order, on the other side. The jeers of the infantry watching from the banks became slowly less derisive.

Longinus and Valerius swam it last, as rear guard, turning a slow circle in the middle of the river because they were officers and must be seen to do more than their men. The water was brownly turbid, and the current swift. It grabbed at armour, limbs, and harness with searching hands. They swam holding their horses and then let them go, to show that they could do that, too. They emerged onto dry land, and the wind, mild as it was, cut through wet wool to the shivering skin below.

Valerius said, "We should have brought wine."

"I did, but not enough for the entire troop. In any case, you owe me a flagon. Axeto didn't lose his sword."

"You'll lose it before we get to the fortress. In the meantime, the horses need to run. Take half the men a mile up ahead and circle back. I'll take the others when you're back."

The rain ceased at some point between the time when the moon set and the sun replaced it low in the rinsed sky above the mountains. Threaded cloud caught fire above the jagged silhouettes of the peaks, spreading from saffron to scarlet to a bruised purple where the rain still hung on the lowest edge of the skyline. The upper layer of cloud was turning from lilac to an uncoloured grey as the last of the cavalry approached the fortress of the Twentieth: the legion's home in the west.

This was not a night-camp built by legionaries of sods and carried staves, nor a frontier post, designed to last only as long as the fighting season, but an unassailable edifice of stone and wood built by the same engineers as those who had first put together the fortress at Camulodunum.

Exactly as at Camulodunum, a lively settlement had grown beyond the oak stockade of this new fortress. Merchants' huts lined the road leading in from the east to the lion-mounted gate of the *porta praetoria*, and others spread back and out from that central trunk. On the margins were living huts and fenced enclosures in which the livestock of the traders grazed and sheltered. At the outermost ring, larger paddocks housed the breeding herds of cattle and their attendant bulls.

Approaching them, Valerius heard before he saw the cluster of men leaning in over the dry stone wall surrounding the most easterly of the fields. Closer, he saw the red hair and armbands of the Gaulish cavalry, all alike in russet tunics with the Capricorn and the Eye of Horus stitched on the left sleeve. Corvus's men, riding at the head of the column, had arrived, settled their horses, taken their orders, paraded for their governor and the legate of the Twentieth, and been dismissed. They had eaten and drunk, and then because they were not required the next day to ride into battle, they had drunk some more, until someone, somewhere, offered a wager that was more enticing than further drink, or perhaps involved further drink and likely some violence and a woman, or a boy or a pliant sheep. The Gauls were not well known for their moderation, or for their ability to stay clear of trouble when drunk.

"This is it." Longinus pushed the chestnut mare alongside Valerius's horse. She shied a little at the noise coming from the field and pushed at the bit. As much as any of their mounts, she knew the smell of war and yearned for it.

"The ill luck you felt?"

"Yes. We should ride by."

They should and they would not—each knew that. Already Valerius had heard the rising nasal whine of Umbricius, the man who had been actuary in the days when they had both served under Corvus in the Gaulish horse. Umbricius hated his old billet-mate and was hated in his turn. The man had soured since the battle against the Eceni, resenting himself and Valerius for surviving when most of their troop had died. On top of that, he had watched Valerius rise in the ranks of the Thracian horse while he himself had remained an actuary. It had been Umbricius who had thrust the shield-edge into Longinus's throat in practise, and it had been as much an attack on Valerius as on the Thracian. The flogging ordered by Valerius afterwards had been every bit as personal.

Umbricius's presence alone would have drawn Valerius in, but over it he had heard the bellow of a bull in pain, and the bull was the god's messenger on earth and could not be ignored. There was a hound, too. It had barked once, with a voice like molten iron poured over gravel. It would be big and male, and Valerius, who would have sworn to any man, Longinus included, that he had not taken note of it, bet himself that it would be brindle, with a white ear. A white *left* ear. In the days before a battle as big as the one that was coming, he could recall his ghosts and not fear them. Like a man afraid of heights who stands on a cliff edge, he did so deliberately, watching the ebb and flow of his own terror, held at bay by the necessities of war. It gave the illusion of control, and he was happy for it.

Longinus had ridden a stride or two ahead. "They're baiting a bull," he said.

"Obviously. The question is what kind of bull, and what are they baiting it with? More important, will it win? If it's going to gore Umbricius, we'll put money on it and leave."

"It's too young to win. He's going to kill it, but not yet." The Thracian spun his horse on its hocks. "Julius, it's a red roan. It's not white. You don't have to be here."

Longinus had been invited to join the ranks of the bull-worshippers and had declined; his Thracian gods could not be supplanted. His knowledge of Mithras came through hearsay, and he had never once asked Valerius for confirmation or refutation of the many rumours. He knew the raven brand intimately, and the other marks that had come later when Valerius had risen above the lowest rank, but he had never once asked their source nor their meaning.

Valerius said, "It doesn't have to be white to be the god's. That's a myth."

A crowd gathered at the gateway. To a man they were Gauls, and Valerius had trained with at least a third of them on the Rhine and fought at their side in the invasion battle. Those who had begun together were loath to part and kept themselves separate from the incomers sent to replace those who had died. Valerius, whom they had once regarded with affection as a luck-bringer, they now saw as a traitor for having moved to other ranks.

He pushed the Crow-horse through the heave of bodies, and men grudged him room. He had reached the gate when a high whine began to sound in his ears, like the hum of swarming drones. A pressure built in his head and on his brand in a way that had not happened before. Feeling attacked, he looked about him for the source. He was in the land of dreamers and had not guarded against it, not knowing how. He saw nothing and no one, and the whine became louder and was clearly only in his head. From the field, the bull wrecked the earth with its horns and then lifted its eyes to meet Valerius's. The whine became a whistle that passed beyond hearing and came back again, and it dawned on him slowly—

stupidly slowly—that this was what he had prayed for these past years and not felt: the genuine presence of his god.

He had no idea what to do. Four years' training in the cellars of Camulodunum had taught him the litanies and the rituals; he could fast and pray and had once acted in the induction of new acolytes. He knew the songs that told of Mithras's birth from untouched rock and of his acts as he walked the earth, but he had no notion of how to act in his presence.

He prayed; he could do nothing else. The bull accepted his prayer and transformed it. Valerius fumbled to hold on to the feel of it.

A man—Umbricius—shouted a challenge, and the moment fell apart, sickeningly. From the west of the field, a young hound yammered, close to hysterics. From the gate, Valerius could see that it was neither broken-coated nor brindle and had no white ear. Its pelt was the smooth blue of newly chipped flint, and its ears were round-tipped like those of the hound carved on the altar on the wall of the Mithraeum beneath the first centurion's house in Camulodunum. The hound on the altar drank the blood of the slain bull. In the field outside the fortress of the Twentieth Legion in the high mountain country of the Cornovii, this hound was trying its utmost to drink the blood of a Gaulish actuary, or at least to spill it.

Umbricius crouched with his back to the gate, a dozen paces into the field. The paddock was a small one, set aside for the best of the young-stock bulls, those too old to be kept in large groups without fighting but not yet old enough to challenge the prime bulls for the right to serve the cows and sire next season's young. A dry stone wall surrounded the perimeter, high as a horse's stifle. Oaks shaded it, with trunks so broad three men could not link arms round them. Wild roses grew in tangles between, dripping waxen hips bright as the spilled blood of the sacrifice.

The gloss on the hide of the young bull facing Umbricius was of a deeper red than the rose hips and was shaded through with white at the shoulders and rump. He was proud, and it was easy to see why he had been singled out to be kept entire, not cut with the rest and salted for winter beef for the legion. His horns swept out and forward, and the tips were clean; the bull, or one who cared for him, had not let them catch hair and leaf-litter and mud about the tips. He bellowed, and his voice was the god's, speaking from the ageless heavens. A man had only to interpret it, and he could ride the world.

Valerius had no idea what it meant.

Longinus, whose gods spoke in voices other than a bull's, was at Valerius's left. He said, "The hound will break free from the boy if Umbricius doesn't get out of there. If it kills an officer of the auxiliary, they'll kill the hound and hang the boy. Umbricius isn't worth that." They had never spoken of hounds and what they might mean in the past history of either man; there had never been the need. It was too late now, but perhaps was still not necessary.

Valerius lifted a hand to shade his eyes from the late sun. A youth held the hound. In looking earlier, Valerius had failed to see that. He was not an exceptional youth in any way; his hair was dark, and he was of middling height and gangling. Nothing linked him to the god except that he was kneeling on his left knee with his arms about the hound.

Something metallic flashed in the air. The bull flinched and bellowed. The hound howled. The boy shouted something in the language of the Cornovii. Alone among the tribes, they worshipped the horned god before the Mother. The boy's eyes met Valerius's and begged for help. Uncounted others had done so in the steadings of the Trinovantes, and he had ignored them, had slain their sisters, had hanged the ones who begged, silently or aloud. Then, the god's breath had not whined in his ears, nor the bull stared him down.

For the god, not for a dark-haired youth and his hound, Valerius pushed the Crow-horse close to the gate and shouted, "Umbricius, leave the bull alone."

The Gaul was twice armed. A short throwing-knife glinted in either hand. He was the son of a fisherman; where other men, given the right knife and the right pacing and enough practise, could throw a knife and sometimes hit a target, Umbricius could throw any knife and place the point to within a finger's width of his aiming place. Three other short, wide blades hung from a belt slung over his shoulder. He was known to carry nine, the number of luck. Of the remaining four, three lay on the turf around the bull. The last one thrown jutted, vibrating, from one massive shoulder. The gloss of the beast's coat hid the blood.

"Umbricius, leave it. That's an order."

Umbricius was only an actuary, albeit on double pay. A decurion of any troop outranked him. The first decurion of another wing ranked so far above him that only a prefect could call back any order he gave. To ignore him was a flogging offence. Umbricius ignored him.

The gate was closed, and there was no room for the pied horse to jump it. Gauls crowded close, and none made any move to support the Thracians. Somewhere far back Valerius's troop had gathered, but they were too few and too far away, and anyway none of them could force a way through to the gate. Valerius and Longinus stood alone within a sea of Gauls. Men had died in similar circumstances, and the threat of decimation had not brought forth the names of their killers. Valerius doubted that either Scapula or Corvus would choose to slaughter ten men in a hundred of their foremost cavalry wing on the eve of a battle against warriors renowned for their use of the horse.

"Get Corvus." Valerius said it without turning, in Thracian. The whine in his ears altered the sound of his voice.

Longinus said, "I'm not leaving you."

"You are. I order it. If you ignore that, I'll have you flogged with the Gaul. Do it."

There was a breath's silence, and room to feel shock and regret and to know that, in this company, it was not possible to take back the words. In Thracian, Valerius said, "Just go. Please."

Longinus saluted rigidly. His chestnut mare backed away from the gate. The Gauls were more willing to let her go than they had been to let her in.

Valerius turned the Crow-horse sideways to the gate. "Umbricius, if I have to come into that field and get you out, you'll regret it more than anything else in your life."

"The bull is mine. The boy insulted me."

Valerius found suddenly that he liked the youth. He pitched his voice to carry. "Why? Did you try to take him and he refused you? Anyone with eyes in their head would refuse you. He should be given half a year's advanced pay and offered a place in the wing for displaying uncommon good sense."

The men about him were Gauls, and he knew them well. In the press of bodies, men sniggered. Umbricius coloured unflatteringly. "I did not—"

"Really? The bull, then? I don't think even gouging its eyes out will make it any more amenable. Face it, you're going to spend tonight alone, and all the nights after this, until one of Caratacus's spears finds the dried goat-turd that is your heart and breaks it open. Now get out of that field. If you go now, while Longinus is away, no one need know that you were lax in following an order."

It was said for the men closest to him because not all of them favoured Umbricius, and Valerius had, after all, brought the horses over the barrier at the salmon-trap and kept them alive. Talking, he had given them time to remember that, and to find that they did not want to hate him. They grinned, and when Valerius slid down from the Crow-horse, they crowded less close. He vaulted the gate neatly and was applauded.

The hound bayed at him. The bull slashed the turf with its horns. Valerius prayed to the god that the beast knew he came to help, not to injure.

His presence changed the balance in the field. Before, Umbricius had had a clear run to the safety of the gate if the bull charged. With Valerius blocking his escape, the Gaul was trapped between two foes, both of whom wanted to kill him—three if he counted the hound.

However much one hated him, one could never say of Umbricius that he lacked courage. He grinned and drew two more knives from his chest belt and began to juggle them flashily. He, too, was applauded. Gauls liked excellence, and if he was not beautiful, Umbricius could create a measure of beauty with his knives.

In the juggling, the Gaul took a single pace back, and where he had stood between Valerius and the bull was now clear space. With his eyes on his knives, he said, "If the bull kills you, will they decimate the natives, do you think?"

"Maybe, after they have hanged you." The bee-whine in Valerius's ears made it difficult to think, more difficult still to remember the exactitudes of a language he had not spoken regularly for half a lifetime and had made some effort in the past two years to forget. He tried, feeling for the words, raising his voice so that it carried over the keening of the flint-pelted hound to the youth who held it. In the dialect of the dreamers that was common throughout the tribes, he said, "Take your hound and leave. I will keep the horned one safe."

He felt the cut of the boy's stare. The Cornovii worshipped the god as stag, not as bull, but they would know of Mithras and perhaps believe that one god or the other would keep the beast safe. Valerius spoke again, remembering more words. "Go now. The hound is in danger if you keep him here. If you care for him, you must take him to safety."

A boy will care for the welfare of his hound when his own pride might require him to remain in danger. Peripherally, Valerius saw the youth clasp his hound closer and speak to it. The urgent keening ceased. The humming in Valerius's ears did not, which was a pity but could not be altered. It had only come once before, and then only briefly, when he had gathered the Crow-horse to ride him over the barrier at the salmon-trap. He had thought then that it signalled his imminent death and that only luck and the god had prevented it. He prayed again for the same luck, or for the god to keep safe his soul if he died. On the western edge of the field, the boy began to move towards the gate, dragging his hound with him.

A knife danced in an arc and sliced across the forehead of the bull. It bellowed and turned towards Valerius, who was closest. Horns as long as a man's arm gouged the turf, flicking black soil to the treetops. Its eyes were dark as walnuts and too soft for true rage. The red roan hide blackened around them smudgily, as if one of the officers' wives had applied paint in haste and the rain had smeared it. Valerius had long enough to see that and for part of him to want Longinus to see it and to share the joke before the eyes dipped and the horns became horizontal and the bull charged. It was not at all too soft for rage.

The world divided and became two; at once impossibly fast and infinitely slow. In each world, Valerius both met his death and avoided it. In the slower, he noted small things: the change in the timbre of the god's voice in his ear, so that it became lower and calmer and was a pleasanter prelude to death; the sudden flurry of crows in the upper branches of the oaks, when he had not realized any birds were watching; the tight jingle of armour as men in repose came suddenly to attention in the unexpected presence of an officer; the sound of Corvus's voice, shouting.

"Bán! In the name of all the gods, get out of there!"

It was the wrong name spoken in the wrong language and with a depth of care he had not heard for four years. Shock spun the two worlds impossibly far apart. Longinus's voice followed and could not heal the rift. "Julius! Move yourself, damn you."

He was already moving. In the faster world, the one in which Valerius's body moved without the care of his heart, a bull sent by Mithras came to kill him with the speed of a galloping horse. Because he had fought daily for years with a horse that moved with the whip of a snake, his body carried him sideways and down and rolled him like a tumbler to come up on his feet beside Umbricius. As in the best of battles, terror fired him, raising him up. He came to his feet with his sword in his hand, and only the presence of Corvus stopped him from burying it in Umbricius. The Gaul saw it and lost the last vestige of colour. Valerius laughed. "Run for the trees. I wager your life against mine that the bull can outrun us both." They were a spear's throw from safety. It was not an impossible distance, only improbable. Umbricius ran. Valerius, still caught in two worlds, did not, but backed away slowly.

The bull reached the gate. If the men crowding outside had been calm with it, or had given the youth time to reach it, the beast might have stopped, but the gathered Gauls were afraid and excited and stabbed at the great head and heaving roan hide with sword-tips and knives, and the god that was not a god turned back into the field and charged again.

The youth was running, dragging his blue-pelted hound with him. He tripped on a tree root and let go of the collar. Caught in a field with two men and a rage-filled bull, the hound saw only that the one man it had come so recently to hate was running and could be hunted.

In the pantheon of the god's beasts, only the hound is faster than the bull. Valerius saw it coming and knew that in this hunt he was not the prey. In the slow world, in which his mind saw clearly, he saw the death of a Gaul and the death after it, inevitably more slowly, of a hound and a dark-haired youth who had knelt as did the god. In the fast world, he stepped sideways and spun hard to his right, and his sword sliced, back-handed, across the throat of the running hound.

The bull was only fractionally slower and did not discriminate between one foe and the other. In the moment of the hound's death, while his slow heart was seeking the words of a death-rite he had not heard spoken in over twenty years, Valerius saw the sky turn from lilac-grey to red-roan and then to black. In that same slow world, the god for whom that death-rite had no meaning took over his body, filling it. Without any will on his part, Valerius pressed himself flat to the turf and rolled sideways along his length, as a child might roll down a snowy slope in winter, for the joy of it.

The god did not fill him with joy, but with splintering light and a unique inexpressible pain that burned across his back on the side opposite the brand. Spurred by the power of hurt, Valerius thrust his hands down and launched up and forwards, and where there had been turf and trees and the calling of crows was a stone wall, over which a god-filled man could vault as easily as he might vault onto a horse before battle. The bull collided with the wall behind him and knocked the top third of it down. The god kept the stones from striking Valerius's head. He lay on his back in longer grass and felt the god leave him, taking his breath with it. Lying very still, unable to breathe, fighting to hold his vision clear when the world came at him in tunnels and was dark, what concerned him most was that he could still not remember the words of the death-rite for the hound.

Longinus reached him first. A hawk's eyes filled the tunnels of light. Ungentle hands grasped his shoulders. A raw voice said, "Breathe, god damn you. Julius, breathe."

A different voice said, no more gently, "He can't. The bull smacked him across the back. If he's lucky, he's winded. If he's not lucky, he's got a back full of broken ribs and he'll never breathe again. Let me look at him."

It was into Corvus's care that he fainted.

CHAPTER 13

They kept him in the cool and the dark for five days. For the first three of those days, in delirium, he grieved over the death of a blue-pelted hound with rounded ears who had not drunk the blood of the bull. In his sleep, he strove endlessly to remember the rite of the battle-dead heard once in childhood and long forgotten. He searched the pathways of the dreams for the one to whom the rite was dedicated and did not find her. He railed against rejection and forgot that that god was not the one to whom he had given his life and dedicated his death. Later, remembering, he hunted the caverns of his soul and the uncertain vessel of his body for the lost light of the god that had so blinded him in the presence of the bull. He did not find that, either.

We ride to kill Caratacus. On the third day, towards evening, he remembered that. The thought levered him up, and he would have risen had not a long arm reached out and pushed him back.

"Not yet, I think. Not unless you want Longinus to lose your salary as well as his own."

"Longinus? What has he— Theophilus? What in the god's name are you doing here?"

Theophilus had been left behind in Camulodunum. The world was not, then, as Valerius remembered it. He collapsed onto the bed and spent the next several moments striving to breathe again through the hammering pain in his back thus created. His heart smashed into his ribs, and the pulse soared in his ears like a high mountain waterfall. Over the noise of it, he could see Theophilus smiling. That was a good sign. Theophilus rarely smiled when death was near.

When he could hear properly, the physician said, "You don't change, do you? I rode relay horses for a day and a half to get to you. Strangely, I had expected you to thank me, or at least to pay attention to what I might have to say."

"Thank you." Valerius could breathe again, if painfully. He pushed himself up on one elbow. "Are you telling me we're not in Camulo-dunum?"

"We are not. We're in the fortress of the Twentieth Legion in the shadow of Caratacus's mountains, guests of the legate and of his eminence the Governor Scapula, who has also, as I understand it, placed a significant quantity of gold on your speedy recovery. More important from your point of view, he holds the army awaiting your presence. That's not the official reason, of course. They say they are waiting until Caratacus has committed himself to a single mountain pass for his trap, but I strongly suspect that the day you can mount your Crow-horse, we will find Caratacus also has committed. You are considered lucky by the men. Even the Gauls will fight better in your presence, however much money they have lost by your being there. No commander will march leaving his luck behind if he can avoid it."

The quality of the light told him it was evening. No longer searching for the god, Valerius mapped out the physical margins of his body and the pain it held. He breathed in deeply and exhaled with vigour. Neither was unbearable, and with some testing, he found that if he did it slowly, the world did not come at him through a tunnel. *We ride to kill Caratacus.* He slid his legs to the side of the bed.

"I can ride now. We should be moving. The longer we wait, the more likely they are to draw other warriors to their cause."

"No. That is, perhaps, yes, you will fight better than you might otherwise have done, but no, you are not yet fit to ride."

"I may be bruised, Theophilus, but I have no broken ribs. I can ride with a bruised back. I won't notice it once the fighting starts, I promise you."

"I'm sure you won't. I never cease to be amazed at the wounds men can bear in battle, but you are not here alone in the legate's private lodgings simply to care for the state of your back."

The physician pulled a stool to the bed. Exhaustion showed in the lines around his eyes and the cracked and reddened skin about his nose. Theophilus always developed a head cold when he had been working too hard. The old caduceus in apple-wood hung from his neck; he had lost the gold one soon after it had been given him. He stroked the rising snakes a moment, thinking, and then stretched to the foot of the bed and brought up a beaker. "Drink this."

"Not if it's poppy. I don't want that."

"And I wouldn't give it to you. Where you have been, poppy would be a hindrance, not a help."

"But this will help?" The infusion smelled of plantain and cow parsley. He drank a little. His tongue shrivelled. It was more bitter by far than the poppy. He remembered something like it from his youth. He had slept for a day and a night then. "What will this do that time and rest will not?"

"It may keep you from talking in your sleep."

"Ah." That had not happened for a very long time. "In Latin?"

"Sometimes. Sometimes in Thracian. Most often not. Some of the time, when you speak Latin, you talk of the god, or to the god. It's not something the men should hear."

"No. Thank you." He may have been considered lucky for his actions with the bull, but an officer who raves to and of his god in his sleep can become its opposite very quickly. An unlucky decurion was a liability who was likely to find himself dead in the thick of battle with no one afterwards able to say who struck the blow.

He drank the rest of the draught, feeling the bitterness drag at his cheeks and his tongue. The after-taste was more of elder and not unpleasant. Slowly the fog in his mind cleared, leaving isolated memories as rocks in a placid sea: Longinus and his raw concern, a boy grieving a slain hound, Corvus.

Corvus, who had called a name in a language both men should have forgotten.

Valerius asked, "Who brought me here, away from the men?"

He had been silent longer than he thought. Theophilus was half-asleep, leaning on one elbow, his eyes fixed elsewhere, his breathing thick through his fuddled sinuses. His head came round slowly, like an owl's, and, owl-like, he blinked. Presently he said, "As I understand it, the prefect of the Gaulish horse gave the order that you be brought here. One assumes that he consulted with the legate and the governor first. Longinus Sdapeze is the one who carried you in, as he is also the one who has sat with you throughout. I think it is safe to say he heard all that you said and not all of it was of the god. Sleep opens you. You speak to those for whom you care most. They are not always the same as those who care most for you. I sent your friend away to sleep when I got here, else he would be here still."

Your friend. At what cost to them both? "I should thank him."

"You should. At the very least, you should accede to the timetable on which he has gambled both your salaries."

"Both our . . . oh, bloody hell. He'll be betting against the Gauls, I suppose? Yes, I thought so. What has he said I will do?"

"The Gauls believe it will be a good half-month before you can ride. Your Thracian friend believes you will be on your horse by the first day of the new moon." The physician dragged a hand down the length of his face. It rearranged his sleeplessness. "You have three days in which to mend. I strongly suggest you petition your god to give you some peace, and between us we can have you fit to fight your nemesis."

It was not Mithras that disturbed Valerius's peace, but his lack. For a further night and a day, he lay on the pillows searching within for the places the god had touched. Sleep came and went, and he spoke less in it, Theophilus said, and more often in Latin or Thracian than in the languages of his youth. In the waking times, he drank and ate what he was given and lay still, feeling dry and hollow and empty with nothing remaining of the high whine in his ear or the scintillating light that had so blinded him in the presence of the bull, but only the dullness of old pain that spread out with the blackened bruise across his back.

He thought of Corvus and, because of that, of Caratacus; love and hate were too easily entwined. Time fragmented, and when it came together, he was on a headland in a storm and two men were washed up by the sea. In his dreaming, it was impossible to tell which was loved and which hated. He wanted to kill both for their separate betrayals and could not. He planned a battle in which the one was killed and the other's life saved by the actions of a decurion on a pied horse and knew that at least one part of that had happened already and the world was no different for it. He tried to think of other things.

When Theophilus came to feed him, he asked, "Did they kill the bull?"

"No. They might have done if you had died, but the legate here is anxious to keep the natives sweet, and you had already slain their hound. In any case—don't look at me like that, I know why you did it—in any case, the first centurion of the Twentieth is branded for the god, and the Mithraists among the men would not have seen it die, not after you had spoken the god's name in its presence and were seen to lay your hand on its brow before you performed the bull-leap to escape it."

"Did I do that?"

"Longinus says not, but the myth that surrounds your life says that you did, and those of us who care for you are not inclined publicly to deny it. The senior tribune of the Twentieth wishes to speak to you on matters concerning the bull and the infinite sun. I have told him you are still with the god. If you are well enough, I could tell him otherwise."

The tribune of the Twentieth was Valerius's current Father under the Sun, the highest rank before the god in the province. Only the governor would have been higher, and the governor was not given to the god. The tribune was grey and dry and had spent altogether too much time in the company of humourless men, so that the life had leached out of him. The staff and a sickle were inked on his wrists as open proclamation of his rank before the god. Valerius should have been honoured by his presence.

"I am honoured," he said.

The tribune had tight grey lips. He pressed them together. "No. You were honoured three days ago by the touch of the god; we merely act to show our recognition of it. I am come to tell you that you are now ranked Lion under the Sun and that the necessary rites have been spoken in your name. When you are well enough, you may offer your own prayers at the altar. Meanwhile know that the god is well pleased with his son."

He was not sure of that. The god, having blinded him, had departed utterly and showed no inclination to return. Without his presence, Valerius's rank and grade within the temple were tokens only, a means to advance a career that had already reached its zenith. He was already foremost decurion of his wing. It had long ago been made clear that he would never be raised to the rank of prefect; that was reserved for equestrians of Roman birth. Unless Valerius wished to leave the cavalry for the legions—which he did not—there was no higher rank he could attain. Somewhere in the jumble of his memories he heard his younger self and then Corvus.

I believed it would be constructive in the development of my career.

I'm sure it will.

He had believed it then, or told himself so. Now he knew only that there were three men permitted to hold the grade of Lion within the temples of the province and that for him to rise to that position now meant that one of them was dead. He wondered, briefly and without interest, which it was who had met his end and how. It was possible he was expected to ask. Certainly the tribune was awaiting something.

Valerius nodded, attempting a measure of grace. "Thank you. If it's possible, I would spend time with the god before we ride to battle. I was told there is a cave here that is the god's, not a cellar. Is it true?"

"It is. The mountain is like a sponge for holes and caves. The god showed one as his own."

"May I go to it? Alone?"

It was not a usual question. The tribune reflected, touching his tattoos. "You may." He gave, in brief, directions as to how it might be found.

Valerius inclined his head. "Once again, I am honoured."

"The god honours us all."

The tribune left. Someone else took his place at the bedside. Expecting Theophilus, Valerius said, "I need to go out. If I walk on my own two feet, will Longinus still hold his bet?"

"I will."

The Thracian stood at the foot of the bed. He was more rested than Theophilus, but not by much. His stag-brown hair had been washed, and he had shaved too close; the skin of his cheeks was unusually pink, and a thread of blood marred his throat. He moved as if he might step forward and then stopped cautiously. He was not usually a cautious man.

Valerius's thoughts were still with the grey tribune. He pulled them back. Between him and the man at the foot of the bed was a gulf that threatened to become unbridgeable. It was harder to smile than he had thought it would be. He made the effort. "I could spend the rest of my life thanking you for bringing me here and apologizing for whatever I said in the worlds beyond sleep. I will do it if you want, but I think you would tire of it quickly."

"I might, but then a life is a long time." The Thracian rubbed the side of his nose. His hands rested lightly on the bed end, the nails pared back to fighting length. He looked down at them and then up again. "Were you thinking to try?"

"Not from this distance." The hesitancy affected them both. Valerius reached out a hand. The relief he felt when it was grasped was greater than he had expected.

It was, after all, only two steps from the end of the bed to its head, not an insurmountable space. Longinus crossed them and stood at his side, still holding his hand. A little light-headed, Valerius said, "I don't break, I think, if touched."

"Do you not? Theophilus seemed to think you might. If he's right, we both lose our salaries."

"Then we had better be careful."

Longinus was not Corvus, but it was, after all, overwhelmingly good to see him. They were careful. Valerius did not break. The night was not exceptional, but it was good.

CHAPTER 14

The god's cave was partway up a mountain steeper than any Valerius had ever climbed. He walked up with Longinus before dawn, in the darkest part of the night. Taking no torch, they found their way by the thin light of the stars and a Thracian facility for navigation in the dark. They climbed the paths slowly, as hunters might, or scouts spying on enemy lines, taking care that they were neither followed nor overlooked.

The penalty for revealing the cave's location had not been made explicit, but a man may die in battle for many reasons, and profaning another man's god is not the least of them. They had discussed it, briefly, in the hospital ward before leaving. Longinus had asked, "Are you sure you want me to come?"

Valerius had paused in dressing. "I am, but if you'd rather not, I don't mind. I don't believe you would offend the god by your presence, only that men will protect what they feel they own."

"No one owns what is the gods'."

"I know."

Neither questioned the other's reason for going; for four years they had fought nothing more taxing than poorly armed men and women, had slaughtered children and pregnant mothers and grandmothers whose best and only weapon was a toothless curse. Faced with their first real battle since the disaster of the Eceni salmon-trap, they were not the only ones from the legions and the auxiliary to seek out a sacred place from which to watch the sunrise. Over the past days, many men had gone out, each to make his peace with his god alone or in the company of the one for whom he cared most. Such a thing was obvious; it was not necessary to speak of it.

They were both battle-fit, and each had grown amongst people for whom moving silently in foreign territory was a skill valued above many others. They climbed through bracken, over rocks, through heather, and across mountain streams, and the best of the enemy's scouts would have been hard-pressed to find them.

The cave mouth was narrow and tall and set back a spear's cast away from a white-water river and the waterfall it became, flowing over the edge of a cliff. In his childhood, Valerius had lived within sight of a waterfall less than the height of a child and had thought it infinitely vast. The contrast here would have been laughable were it not so overwhelming. The crash of the torrent numbed the mind almost as much as the sight. Valerius could readily imagine that, heard from inside, magnified by the echoing walls, the sound might become the voice of the god. New initiates, fuddled by lack of food and water, heads thick with incense, would be astounded when the blindfold was removed that had also covered their ears. The noise would enhance the brightness of the god's light, drawing them further out of themselves as the brand-iron pressed in. He would have liked to be introduced to the god first in a cave. There might have been more chance of meeting him.

There was light now, from the eastern horizon, enough to see the hazel tree that drooped its nuts across the entrance and to pick out the jars of honey and small sheaves of corn that had been left around the cave mouth. A great many men had come in the last few days to offer gifts directly to the god.

Longinus said, "It's darker in there than it is out here. There's no starlight."

"I brought one of Theophilus's dipped-tallow candles. We can light it when we're out of sight."

"You want me to come in?"

"Unless the god tells us otherwise."

A sharp-edged boulder lay across the threshold and had to be climbed to reach the entrance. The mouth was narrower than the width of their shoulders so that, having scrambled across the guardian, they had to turn and edge crab-wise along the first few paces of a long corridor. Presently it angled left and opened, and they could walk straight and then side by side. The floor sloped downwards and the ceiling came to meet it so that they stooped and then crouched and then crawled and then slid, belly down on rough stone, feeling their way forwards in a darkness more absolute than night. It went on longer than any sane man would have wanted. Valerius tried to imagine the grey tribune doing this in the robes of the Father and failed. If the offerings had not been left at the cave's mouth, he might have believed he had the wrong cave.

Behind him Longinus said, "I don't relish going backwards up here if there is no room anywhere to turn round."

"There's room. I can feel air."

He felt air, and then he felt no floor and no ceiling and had no idea how great was the fall ahead of him. He stopped, sweating. Still crawling, Longinus crashed into his heels. Valerius said, "Stop."

"You should light the candle."

Valerius lit the candle. It took him longer than it might have done. His hands did not yet answer fully the commands of his mind, and the pitched tinder was not completely dry. He knelt, nursing the flame, and so was not first to see what was there to be seen.

"Julius, look up." Longinus spoke in Thracian, as he did at night, or in battle, or at moments of strain.

Lifting the flame, Valerius looked. Ten years of responsible leadership and some forewarning of the ways of the god prevented him from dropping it again. With shock-numbed fingers, he held it over his head and stared.

Light came at him from too many directions. In the first moments, it was overwhelming, as the god's light of the cellar should have been but rarely was. With time his eyes picked out detail amidst the blinding gold; he was facing a still lake, the surface of which spun back the candle-light as if it had been laced with oil and fired. In the walls behind and above, in the soaring roof of the cavern, the sodden, dripping rock gave off a rippling wall of light, brighter than stars. If a priest had spent a lifetime implanting diamonds in the rock, it could not have shone more, and yet there were no diamonds, only water, and the fire of the single flame. As Valerius turned, still staring, so the sheen turned with him, flaring as living light.

"Mithras . . ." He breathed the god's name with true reverence. "He could have been born in a cave such as this."

They were too close to the mystery for one not of the god. "I'll wait outside," Longinus said.

Valerius could have argued and did not. He heard the slip of wool on rock and a scuff of boots on the wall of the tunnel, and the Thracian was gone.

Left alone with his god, Valerius was slow to move. The lake spread before him, mirror-still and gilded with fire, and he watched the flowing undulations of his breath as the candle-light spread across it in waves. The dreams of three days still held him, and he saw things in the fire-mirror that he had thought only to see in the dark of his own mind. Caradoc, son of Cunobelin, washed ashore on the Eceni coast, and this time, as he was hauled from the sea, his hair was a pallid red and his face was that of his brother Amminios, and he rose to his feet laughing and drew a sword from the sheath of his own right thigh and, with it, killed the men, women, and children who had come to rescue him, ending with a yellow-haired Belgic slave-boy named Iccius.

Because this was not a new dream, and years of repetition had taught Valerius some measure of control over the outcome, the boy Iccius did not rise from the bloody sand and come to kill him, but instead lay where he was and withered to skin and bone, as did the bodies of the tribal dead when left on the death platforms for their gods. Because, too, he was awake and not sleeping and he knew Amminios to be dead, Valerius bent his mind to the smiling half-ghost in front of him. He painted out the straggled red hair and replaced it with corn-gold, made the amber eyes the colour of clouds, and made less of the nose. Only the smile he could not change, and the affirmation of treachery. In the dreams, the ghosts were voiceless. In the mirrored fire, the voice he loathed most in the world said, *We nearly won. Think how different the world would be if none had emerged alive from the Place of the Heron's Foot.*

"I thought none had."

As you were meant to. Would you have joined the legions if you had known your sister lived?

Valerius was in the place of the god. Here images sent by the god could ask questions that no man, dead or alive, would have dared ask, and he, sworn to the god, must own an answer he would have drunk any amount of wine to avoid.

"No."

So. And you would not have come to Mithras. Is it your loss?

He was in the place of the god. What could he say? "It is not my loss."

Amminios was no longer Amminios, nor even Caradoc. Where he had been, the god knelt on the placid lake with his arms round the neck of the hound. The cape fell about his shoulders, drinking in the fire and giving it out again, brighter. Elsewhere, in other places, a bull gored the earth and a loose-lipped serpent drank blood that was not yet spilled. The god's eyes burned him, and Valerius knew himself seen; each part of him flayed from the rest and spread open before a gaze that encompassed eternities.

"I would rather have known she lived," he said. "Even if I had died trying to reach her, it would have been better."

The youth in the cape ran long fingers down the muzzle of the hound, thoughtfully. He smiled a little. *Honesty becomes you.*

"I would not lie to you."

But only to yourself.

"Sometimes it is necessary."

Perhaps. Do you hate him enough to kill him with your own hand?

"Who?"

Caradoc. The one whose death you dream even in the presence of your god.

"He betrayed me. He betrayed us all. For that I would see him dead, yes, by any means."

Only for that?

"Is it not enough?"

Perhaps. There was a space, in which all possibilities opened and only some of them closed again. *If his death was balanced by your death, so that you died when he died, would you still do it?*

"Yes." The word was said before he had time to think. Thinking, he found it still true.

And if the cost instead was the life of one you love, what then?

He had thought himself beyond panic and was not. "Corvus?"

A god's silence is a frightening thing.

"Longinus?"

Perhaps. Your love binds more than you allow. Think on that before you kill. Or choose not to.

The hound was gone, melted into the mirror. The kneeling god became less and less clear until all that was left was the flicker of a dying flame on water. At the end, his voice came over the dark. *What will fire your life, Valerius, when the flame of vengeance is gone?*

"It is all I have."

The god laughed. It rang off stone and came back again, echoing. A bull bellowed, dying. A voice other than the god's said, *Then find more.*

He could have stood for hours, or days. Falling candle-wax burned his hand; he flinched and the wilting fire-mirror shattered and spat. Molten light spread across the floor and walls of the cavern and settled back to the lake, which was still again, and only barely lit. It came to him, standing still and cold, that the bull that he had seen die three times over had not been white but red roan. He did not understand why that should be so.

A long time ago Theophilus had warned him against spending too long in worlds beyond his own lest it become impossible to return. The physician had been speaking of the nightmares and the waking dreams, but the danger was as real here as anywhere. The pull of the water was that of a lodestone, with his body the iron. Senses other than sight and sound told him that the lake was not shallow. He could walk in and keep walking, and in twenty paces he would have joined the god and would know for himself all possible destinies of those left alive.

"Valerius?" Longinus's voice came through the tunnel, warped by distance and the convoluted rock.

He stepped back from the water's edge. "Soon. I'll be out soon."

He could not leave yet. Turning his back on the lake, he used the poor light of the candle to explore the remainder of the cavern. On the wall opposite the lake, he found the altar, chiselled out of virgin rock, and the place behind it for the nine-fold torches and the incense-burners that would make the ceremonies of initiation more than simply rituals held in the dark. Beyond it, in the wall opposite the tunnel, he found a tall, narrow opening. The interior was blacker than the cavern had been. The air flowed from the larger cavern inwards, pushing him forward. Holding the guttering flame ahead of him, Valerius squeezed himself sideways and stepped into the entrance.

NO.

The word pressed into his ears from the centre of his head. The breath blocked in his chest and clenched tight at his throat. His heart crashed to a halt and restarted. It was not at all the voice of a kneeling youth.

He took a step back and could breathe again. The fall of his feet sounded faint. Step by slow step, he backed away until his heels pressed against the wall through which he had first entered. Sometime before he reached it, the candle went out. The tunnel lay to his left, and he found it after some searching.

Too fast for comfort, too slowly for peace, he crawled and crouched and rose and walked into walls and past them and out into a mountain morning where the air was wet with the spray of white water and a buzzard mewed like a gull.

Longinus was waiting, not far from the entrance. After a while, without moving, he said, "Did you see your own death? Or mine?"

"No."

"Then come with me and sit by the water. Whatever it was, it will pass."

Three days later, on the first day of the new moon, the decurion of the first troop, the First Thracian Cavalry, was seen to be riding his pied horse in the exercise yard. His friend, the standard-bearer of the first troop, collected his winnings and was seen to be exceedingly cheerful. On the following morning, a scout's report was read verbatim to the assembled troops. It described, in detail, the position of the rebel leader Caratacus, the numbers of his warriors, and the reinforcements he might reasonably expect to receive from other tribes.

The governor, Scapula, added afterwards his own assessment of the likely tactics of the enemy, based on his position and strength. At the end, as Theophilus had predicted, he gave the order to move out, with immediate effect.

CHAPTER 15

The harvest in the western mountains and on Mona was gathered more speedily that year than any of the eight that had come before it. At the end, the granaries of the tribes were not full—too few had been present for sowing, and fewer had been spared in the intervening months to weed—but there was sufficient to ensure that none among the people should starve, whatever the outcome of the war. In the days after, children began to gather cob nuts and field fungi and small, bitter crab-apples that would sweeten by spring. The elderly ground woad into powder and mixed it with the juice of pulped bramble-berries for dye and brewed ale that would keep them warm through the winter. Warriors ate and slept and loved and honed their weapons in the company of their children. The dreamers sought the word of the gods. Scouts reported the arrival of Scapula in the fortress of the Twentieth Legion and his departure, several days later, with one and a half legions and two wings of cavalry. Their progress north was monitored and harried lightly from the sides and rear. No one of significance was slain on either side. It was not expected that they would be, yet.

On the fourth night of the new moon, under a black frosted sky, the healed and rested warriors of Mona joined with the massed spears of the Ordovices, Silures, Cornovii, and Durotriges. Those who had fought for freedom these last eight years were joined in their thousands by the young men and women newly come to adulthood who chose war above servitude. In all, they were nearly ten thousand, a number to match two legions.

Against the tribes marched the men most responsible, in the eyes of the gods and of the dreamers, for the death by hanging of two entire Eceni villages, down to and including a three-year-old girl, plus the appalling repression of the Trinovantes that still continued. The forthcoming battle was for retribution as much as it was for freedom.

Following Caradoc's prediction, the River of the Lame Hind formed a boundary between the two armies. Fires burned through the night on the slopes on either side of its widest point. This once there was no need for the tribes to hide their presence or position. As he had done once before, Caradoc had ordered more fires lit than there were warriors, so that the legions, seeing them, might believe they faced overwhelming numbers and lose heart. In the river valley, white water reflected star points of light and the greater orange bloom of flame. A long, narrow defile ran northwest away from the two encampments, the only route out of the valley. Passage through it was blocked by a solid rampart of oak logs and boulders the height of a man and half as much again; the barricade of the salmon-trap, reproduced in larger scale from Dubornos's original. Caradoc had learned a lesson from the reports of the earlier battle; no horses would jump the rampart this time to wreak havoc among the tribes caught behind it.

Both sides settled for the night. The dreamers built their own fire, apart, on a rocky outcrop just below the mountain's peak. A stunted rowan drooped berries by the handful over the vertiginous fall of the slope beneath. On the flat stone at the lip of the outcrop, a vast blaze of beech wood, apple, and hawthorn cracked sparks high into the night.

Two hundred singers and dreamers gathered round it. Never since the invasion had so many of those trained on Mona come together, nor with such focused intent. If it were given them, they would see the death of Scapula before the fire was lit again. Of those with greatest power, whose dialogue with the gods was most direct, only Airmid was missing. Her place was on Mona with the Boudica and the new child. Breaca had not been alone in dreaming Graine as key to the future of the tribes, and the infant's early days were guarded by all the known means. Thus Airmid's absence was accepted, even while she was missed.

Dubornos felt her lack as he would the loss of his shield in battle. He did not work closely with her; months could go by without their exchanging a word, but he knew her presence and absence as surely as he knew light and dark, heat and cold, love and loss. It did not make his part impossible to play, but it made it immeasurably harder.

On the night before a battle that was bigger than any he had seen since the invasion, he stood before the fire with the others with whom he shared the greathouse on Mona; with Maroc the Elder and Luain mac Calma, once of Hibernia, and Efnís, who had been foremost amongst the dreamers of the northern Eceni until the hangings began and it was no longer safe for him to remain there. These three were the greatest: the bear, the heron, the falcon—hunters all, with the insight that gave to their dreaming. At their sides were a hundred others who had lived and trained with them for ten years or more and were accustomed to working together. Joining them for the first time in battle were the dreamers of the western tribes, those men and women who had remained to hold safe the heart of their people in a time of ceaseless war. They came together in groups of like kind, and alliances were formed or re-formed that gave strength to each that was greater than they could dream of when working in the relative isolation of the tribes.

Efnís, dreamer of the Eceni, led the gathering. Alone of them all, he had seen the faces of the three among the enemy whose deaths mattered most to the tribes: the Governor Scapula, the legate of the Twentieth Legion, and the decurion of the Thracian auxiliary who rode the pied horse. So that the others might know them as well as he, he offered his memories to the fire, each bound with the hair of a red mare to sticks of green hawthorn. In the smoke of their burning, others inhaled the essences of the men they hunted, letting them settle in their minds; a flash of a face seen in profile, the particular scent of one man in battle that sets him apart from the rest, the sound of a voice raised in command or lowered in repose, the love of a father for his son and of a man for his shield-mates, the complex loathing of one who kills to cover his own self-hate.

Nothing was clear, but there was enough of each man that, in the chaos of battle, the dreamers might find the loosened souls of those they sought and bring them fear or despair or a slowness of reflex that would give the warriors a chance to land a killing blow. It was the best they could do and it was not perfect, but it had worked in the past, and with the gods' help, it could be made to work again.

When it came to the last of the three, the decurion who rode the pied horse, Dubornos added his own sticks to the fire, similarly bound. He had taken four days to make them, sleeping alone with his memories of a time he would have preferred to forget, sharpening to a focused clarity patterns previously hidden in a fog of grief and anger, and then binding them with his own blood and tears to the green-cut branches of a berried hawthorn.

If there had been a way to do it without remembering, Dubornos would have taken it, whatever the cost. After the burning of the fort, when it had been clear that Scapula was going to send his forces against the Eceni, Dubornos had organized the first salmon-trap and had believed it a success. Men and women of the Eceni and the Coritani had died in their hundreds, but they had sold their lives at an overwhelming price, fighting with a savagery unknown in the history of the tribes to destroy the auxiliaries sent against them. Dubornos had wept at those losses even while his soul exulted at the victory that had sent the handful of remaining enemy back to the fortress bearing the bodies of their fallen officers across their saddles. In the days immediately afterwards, before they had understood the nature and unthinkable extent of Scapula's reprisals, his only disquiet, his single gnawing doubt, had been the frisson of raw hatred he had felt from the junior officer who had seen the danger of the salmon-trap and had later led the horses in over the barricade to save his surviving comrades, riding at the front on a pied horse that killed as savagely as any warrior.

Dubornos had seen the horse long before he took notice of the man. When the auxiliaries had abandoned their mounts and fought on foot, there had seemed a good chance that the beast might be captured and brought into the breeding herds. Later, seeing it ridden, the regret at its loss had been greater. Only afterwards, when the hangings of the villagers began, had the temperaments of both beast and rider become clear. Dubornos's one source of solace in the time of desolation and despair after the atrocities was that he had not instilled such unremitting hatred into Mona's horse herds. In the making of his memory-sticks, he had bound the horse as closely as the rider, merging both into a single entity and marking it as evil.

He leaned forward and placed the last branch in the heart of the blaze. Wizened berries shrivelled and burst. Flames wrapped the skin of his forearm and he felt no heat. The fire consumed the wood and hair, sending his memories to the gods and the waiting dreamers. There were few words that could do justice to the evil he felt from this man, but he gave them as well, to flesh out the picture. *He is tall and lean, and his hair is black. He rides a pied horse that kills as he kills. With his own hands, he killed the children.*

Sighing, two hundred dreamers took in his words and gave them life. The air around the outcrop shivered in the heat. With smoke in their hearts and flame scalding their skins, the dreamers of Mona and the west drew a collective breath and, with it, began to bend their minds to vengeance.

Dawn broke behind them, cold and clear. The dreamers' fire died to glowing ash and the two hundred dispersed, scrambling down the mountainside to find and wake their warriors and give them the gods' good will before battle. Dubornos sought the largest of the warriors' fires and found it at the northerly end of the ridge above the waterfall that marked the broadest point of the river. Here the honour guard of Mona had slept, sharing the fire with Caradoc and his Ordovices.

Men and women were waking, stretching sleep from cramped muscles, rubbing heather dew on their faces or seeking out the small streams that tumbled over the rock-strewn slope. A few slid down through the scrub towards the midden trenches. Others had clearly been awake longer. Ardacos, who led the warriors of the she-bear and was the left arm of the Boudica's honour guard, crouched to one side near a blackthorn thicket with a dozen of his band. They smelled strongly of woad and bear-grease and grey symbols swirled on their naked bodies, the result of half a night's painting. The hafts of their spears were made of white ash, dulled almost to black by the blood of a bear, the blades were leaf-shaped and longer than any others on the field, and undyed heron feathers dangled from the necks. They pressed hand-prints in white clay on their shoulders and reaffirmed battle oaths to each other in a language that Dubornos, master of eight separate tongues and a dozen dialects in each, had never heard.

Beyond the she-bears, Braint, the young woman of the Brigantes who led the centre of the honour guard in Breaca's absence, bound the skull of a wild cat into the mane of her horse. Closer to the fire, Gwyddhien, who led the right flank, painted the mark of the grey falcon on the left shoulder of her battle-mare above the serpent-spear of the Boudica. It was she whom Dubornos sought. He scuffed down through the tangling heather and stood nearby, waiting.

Of all her people, Gwyddhien was the most striking. Already tall, the war-knot of the Silures tied in her black hair made her taller. Her skin was smoothly brown with few scars and none of them about the face. Her cheekbones were high and set wide, as was the way with some of the western tribes in whom the blood of the ancestors ran clear. One could easily see why another might find her attractive.

The woman finished and looked up; she had known he was there. Dubornos gave the warrior's salute and said, "Airmid sends you her heart and soul for the duration of battle. She walks where you walk and dreams as you dream."

It was the formal greeting between lovers when circumstances forced them apart in times of war. For a moment, Gwyddhien became less the warrior and more the woman. Her eyes were the greyed green of old hazel leaves made brighter by the frost of the dawn. When she smiled, they sparked as if struck by flint and iron.

"Thank you." Her salute was that of a warrior to her dreamer when the latter is of highest rank. It honoured Dubornos intentionally. "Is Breaca well?" she asked.

He would have left but could not; custom demanded that he answer. "She thrives, and the child with her. Her greatest regret is that she cannot join the battle."

"But she sends her other child to take her place and thus deprives you of the chance to fight." Gwyddhien's brows arched enough to make the statement a question without impugning its wisdom.

"Cunomar?" Dubornos grimaced. "No. Breaca would have stopped him from coming, but Caradoc had already said he could accompany us. He felt guilt, I think, at the amount of time he had spent with Breaca and the new babe and then that he had given his mother's swan-hilted blade to Cygfa for the battle. He had to give something to Cunomar of equal worth, and permission to join him today was the only thing that would serve. The boy chafes at the bridle like a yearling that wants to race before its bones are set."

"He thinks the war will be over and he will have won no honour to match his parents'. In his place, I would feel the same."

"Maybe. But I think in his place you would have listened to your elders."

She stared at him, nodding. "As you did at his age. Or older?"

On the eve of battle, the past took root in the present. The breath soured in Dubornos's throat. He would have turned away, but Gwyddhien took hold of his shoulder and held him still, facing her. If he chose, he could read compassion in her gaze, or pity. Very badly, he wanted neither.

Gwyddhien said, "Airmid sent you with the message for me. That should be proof enough that she holds none of your past against you." And then, when he made no reply, "You should talk to her about it some-time."

"As she has talked to you."

Gwyddhien shrugged. "Of course. Did you think she would not? You are the foremost singer of Mona, she one of the strongest dreamers, and yet you speak only when the need is overwhelming. The distance between you has been clear from the day you first came to the island. I asked about it only before the invasion, when it was necessary to know on whom we could truly rely. She named you as one of those whom she trusted most closely, and having seen you in her company, I questioned it. Even know-ing the whole story—particularly knowing the whole story—there was no possibility I would think less of you for it."

"Why not? I do."

"I know. That's why we're speaking of it now. We all make mistakes in our youth of which we are ashamed. The difference is that the rest of us can forgive the ignorance of the child we were and believe in the honour of the adult we have become. You were fifteen years old when Amminios's eagles ambushed Breaca and your people in the Place of the Heron's Foot; you had barely passed your long-nights and had never seen battle. Warriors with more kill-feathers than any died that day. Breaca's father was one of the Eceni's foremost warriors, and they cut him down like a sheep at slaughter. Your father was injured, 'Tagos lost an arm, and Bán was killed and his body taken; Breaca herself was lucky to come out alive. The gods guided you then as they guide all of us always. If you had not feigned death, you might well have died with the others."

"But at least I would have died with honour."

Gwyddhien looked beyond him down into the valley to where the river ran cold and white. She chewed on her lower lip in the way Airmid did when she was thinking.

Presently she said, "It might do you some good to think how many battles you have fought since that day with exceptional honour, how many lives you have saved, how many others have relied on your strength and your presence in the worst of times. You have been central to so much. If the gods had wanted you dead, you would be dead. They do not, and you should care about that if you don't care about yourself. You carry your shame into battle, and it changes who you are. One day it will slow you when the enemy is fast. I would prefer that not to happen. As would Airmid."

Of all she had said, the last words burned deepest. Before the singer could reply, a horn sounded nearby. Bear-claws rattled in rhythm against the hollowness of a skull. A falcon screamed from another fire, a sound to chill the hearts of the enemy. The morning came alive with moving warriors, riding and running in waves down the mountainside. Dubornos felt himself pushed apart from his fellows, a husk with his tongue glued stiff with the shame of the past.

Gwyddhien lifted her sheathed sword from a rock and looped the carry-thong over her head. A spear and shield hung together from her saddle bow. Each bore a frog, painted green, the mark of Airmid's dream. Her hand once again gripped Dubornos's shoulder. He felt the prints for half a day.

"You have chosen the path of greatest courage," she said. "We all honour you for it."

"I do what I must."

"I know. That doesn't make it easy." In her mind, the warrior was already riding the slope down to the river, rehearsing the many varying plans of battle. With a clear effort, she brought herself back, turning to face him. "We will be on the right flank. If you need help to guard the child, get word to me. I will send whoever I can spare. Remember that."

"Thank you. I will."

Cunomar was the only one below fighting age on the mountain. His peers, without exception, had accepted the need to stay at home; in this battle, there were no children carrying water or tending to the horses, no hostages to Rome who might need protection, except this one. He crouched alone on the far side of his father's fire. Hail lay beside him, an unwilling guardian. The great hound's soul remained on Mona with Breaca and the newborn infant. As it had not been with Cunomar, the bonding at Graine's birth had been immediate and complete. The hound mourned her absence visibly, as did the boy, if for different reasons.

Around the pair, warriors finished their last preparations for war, and Cunomar looked on stonily. It was Cygfa whose presence upset him most. His half-sister was nearing her long-nights. For months now her first bleeding had been expected, and it was widely agreed that, once adult, she would be a warrior of a calibre to match their father. She had trained since infancy amongst her mother's people, the Ordovices, and the warriors of the war-hammer were known across the land as the most ferocious of the west. Later Cygfa had joined her father on Mona and trained in the warriors' school, learning sword and spear moves from men and women considered the best of any tribe. When the time of the battle had come and she had not yet gained her spear, the elders had agreed that she could attempt to win it in fair combat, as Breaca had done. Her mother, Cwmfen, fought in Caradoc's honour guard, and Cygfa had been granted permission to ride at her side.

For Cunomar, that alone would have been unbearable, but then Breaca had made a gift to the girl of the shaggy, wide-hoofed war-horse that had carried her as the Boudica through the invasion battle. The beast, known as the bear-horse for the length of his pelt and the shape of his nose, was sire to half of the best young stock on Mona, but his passion was war and he had not seen enough of it. Breaca rode the grey mare for preference, even when the animal was old enough to be turned away to pasture. Granted now to Cygfa, the bear-horse revelled in the smells and portents of war. He stood with his head high and his ears up, and only years of training in the need for silence before battle kept him from screaming his challenge to the morning. His presence, together with the swan-hilted blade that had been Caradoc's gift to her, made Cygfa one of the best mounted, best armed warriors on the field. Cunomar hated her and let it show.

Dubornos skirted the fire towards him. "Good morning."

The child nodded but did not answer. His gaze was fixed on the two warriors on the far side of the fire. Cygfa stood with Braint of the Brigantes, braiding her hair at the sides. In the splendour of the dawn, the pair could have been sisters, or two of the three parts of Briga: the one dark-haired, dark-skinned, and scarred from battle, the other fair of hair and skin and unblemished. All they lacked was the grandmother, grey-haired and lame. Cygfa had not yet killed and had no right to wear the black crow-feather at her temple, but Gwyddhien had given her a falcon's grey-barred tail feather with the quill stained black and red to bring on Briga's luck, and Braint was showing her the proper way to fix it. They laughed together, and the noise rolled down the mountain like the ring of iron on stone. Cunomar scowled, and his mouth moved in a clear, if silent, curse.

Dubornos perched on a rock at his side. Childless, he had never learned the ways of reaching children, and searching his own past for aid had proved little help. He chose, therefore, to address the young as if they were already adult. Often he was successful. With Cunomar he could never tell how it would be.

"Your sister rides for the first time into battle," he said. "It won't help her if you wish her ill. Nor you if she dies and you have no chance to call back your curse."

Amber eyes flicked sideways and away. "She won't die. She's as good as Father, everyone says so. She'll carve the Romans into meat for the hounds."

It was a subtle insult, carefully honed. The legions were rumoured to feed the dead of their enemies to their hounds, one more atrocity in their manifold tally. No warrior of the tribes would ever countenance such a thing.

Dubornos said, "That does not become you. If you dishonour Cygfa, the slur extends also to your father and her mother. Would you wish that on them when they go to fight Scapula and the decurion of the Thracian cavalry who rides the pied horse?"

The mention of the two greatest enemies in one breath had the effect he desired. With his shield hand, Cunomar made the complex gesture that unmade all curses. "They will win," said the child sullenly. "And you and I will have sat here through the day, watching, while others earn their kill-feathers and make the tales that will be told at the fire."

If it was hard for a grown man who was oath-sworn of his own free will to keep back from the front line, how much harder for a child who did so only because he was ordered by his father? Dubornos reached in his pouch for the knuckle-bones he carried as perpetual distraction. He cast them on the scorched turf by the fire and studied the way they lay. "We can only pray so," he said drily. "Meanwhile it will be some time before battle is joined. Would you care to play?"

CHAPTER 16

"Did you know there would be so many of them?"

Longinus Sdapeze sat his chestnut mare, resting his forearms on the front of the saddle. The entire wing of the First Thracian Cavalry stretched out behind him in rows of eight. Julius Valerius, outwardly recovered from his encounter with his god, sat at his side, studying the enemy and the geography of a battle site that was not of his choosing, nor would ever have been. It was the salmon-trap of the Eceni all over again, but then they had known from the start that it would be; the inquisitors had found that for them. Their advantage, such as it was, lay in this forewarning and the other news gathered from spies and fallen warriors. Valerius could only wait and judge its accuracy as the battle progressed.

Meanwhile they had the river to cross. It ran in front of them, in full autumn spate so that the force of the water ate away at the banks, and pools at which in earlier months the deer had drunk were sluicing wells of strong currents. Storm-split branches and other debris from the high mountains spun down heavily enough to sweep horse and rider from their feet and drag them under. At the only sane fording point, the water foamed and spun and crashed through piles of smoothed boulders and jagged rocks, placed days ahead by Caradoc's warriors to make the crossing more treacherous.

On the far bank, warriors in their thousands stood in clusters, or sat their painted horses, waiting. A man who knew what to look for could pick out the bands and sub-bands of the tribes by style of hair and cloak colour and the dyed flanks of the horses. A man searching for one specific enemy could find with ease the yellow hair and multicoloured cloak of Caradoc and the knot of white-cloaked Ordovices about him. That same man could note that the rumours were true and that a second Caradoc rode at his side, white-cloaked and bare-headed and mounted on a horse that had been in every major battle since the invasion but now bore a new rider whose hair was not the red of a fox in autumn.

Caradoc and his daughter did not take part in the posturing that was the usual prelude to battle. From among the rest of their ranks, a warrior would periodically accept a challenge and step forward to hurl insults and spears at the enemy. The tribes had learned since the invasion; the spears they threw were stolen legionary javelins, tipped with soft iron that bent on impact so that they could not be picked up and thrown back at their original senders. On a day like today, with the river so broad, it made little difference; very few had the power to send a spear clean across to the far bank. Their impact was more on the minds and hearts of the waiting legions who must stand and watch what faced them. Twice already, sorely provoked, a century of legionaries had stepped to the river's edge and hurled their own javelins, wasting them likewise in the water.

The morning passed too slowly, with nothing to show for it. Somewhere out of sight a war-band started up a high-pitched, ululating chant that wove through the thunder of the river and soared over it, stretching further the overstretched nerves of the new recruits. In the foremost lines of the legions, men new to battle gripped their short swords and refixed their shields, wasting energy and condensing their fear. On the far right, set back from the river, Scapula's standard cracked in the wind. Twice so far the governor had ridden down to the water and twice backed away again. Valerius watched him and felt the indecision spread south down the line. He felt, also, Longinus waiting for an answer to his question and realized he had answered it only in his mind.

"There are fewer of them than were at the Thames on the first day of the battle," he said. "We should be glad he has gathered only the western tribes. If Cartimandua's Brigantes were not sworn to us, we would be facing twice or three times this number."

He raised himself high in the saddle and looked north. The governor's ewe-necked gelding was still balking at the water. Valerius cleared his throat and spat, a uniquely Thracian habit with uniquely Thracian implications. "We could sit here all day if we're waiting for Scapula to get his bloody horse into the river."

Longinus said, "We may as well. He's only going to make us dismount on the other side. Myself, I'd rather stay on my horse."

"We can if we hold the ford."

"We'd have to take it first."

"I know."

A rider bearing a white armband on his mail waited to one side, designated for the day as a runner, to fight only in extreme need. To him, Valerius said, "Take word to Governor Scapula that the acting prefect of the Ala Prima Thracum believes that his men can make a crossing of the river and hold it so that the legionaries will be able to cross downstream of our horses. If he gives the word, we will attempt it. If he can spare men with javelins to give us cover, that would make the attempt more likely to succeed."

The command was too long in coming. The enemy dreamers had long since marked the men they knew. Valerius had felt them at the beginning, that tickle of meeting minds, of mutual loathing, and the challenge that was of the spirit and the gods and not of battle. Still, it was in battle that the wills of the gods were made manifest, and the delay in Scapula's order gave the dreamers and singers of Mona time to gather on a heathered slope directly opposite the Thracian cavalry and to direct their ire and that of their slingers at one man and the horse he rode. Valerius felt them long before the first sling-stones began to puncture the river in rippling lines ahead of him.

Longinus said, "If you ride in there, you're dead."

"Is that your ill-feeling again?"

"No, it's common sense. You should stay on the bank and give them a target and let the rest of us make the crossing."

"Maybe, but if the god wants me dead, I'll be dead wherever I go. If you think I'm bad luck, I'll stay apart. Otherwise, I'll lead and draw their attention, and the rest of you who follow will be safer."

"Is that meant to be encouraging?"

"No, it's common sense."

"Good. Then have the sense also to remember what Corvus said. The governor wants Caradoc and his family alive to parade before the emperor in Rome. If you're seen to kill him, they'll nail you to a plank and leave you. Others apart from me would think that an awful waste of a life."

"I won't forget."

He had not forgotten, could not forget. Corvus had addressed the officers in a group, but his eyes and his words, and the threat they carried, had been for Valerius. Valerius had smiled at no one in particular and gone away to design his own pennant for the battle. Since the cave, he had begun to understand more deeply the words of his god; there are many more ways to destroy a man than to kill him in battle. He considered those ways and savoured them and prayed that he might bring at least one of them about.

He believed absolutely that the god heard and was with him. All through the morning, the words of the deity whispered in his head. *His death is matched by your death, or the death of one you love.* Caradoc was still very clearly alive. While the corn-gold head remained a beacon amidst the enemy, Valerius believed himself safe. When, belatedly, the order came from the governor to attempt the crossing, he pushed the Crow-horse a pace at a time into the murderous torrent. Thirty-two men of the first troop, First Thracian Cavalry, followed in a line behind.

As they entered the water, Valerius said, "They've seen the red bull pennant. If you were ever planning to pray to Mithras, now would be a good time."

Longinus Sdapeze, who had no intention whatever of praying to the bull-slayer but had been praying all day to his own gods, could have sworn he heard his decurion laugh.

A handful of knuckle-bones lay forgotten on the ash-strewn turf. A man, a boy, and a grizzled three-legged war-hound lay on their bellies on the dreamers' outcrop and looked down on the backs of circling crows. Beneath the birds, a river thundered blackly; on its northern bank, small as field mice, men and women scurried back and forth, fighting for land and life, for honour and fame, for the futures of their born and unborn children. Against them, like so many beetles, fought the legions.

Battle had been a long time coming. For a while, it had seemed to both sides as if the volume of water alone would defeat them and Caradoc's salmon-trap would never be put into effect. Dubornos, watching, feared that Venutios might come too early and his warriors, particularly the small, undisciplined war-bands of the Selgovae, being unable to contain themselves, might hurtle down the mountain at the enemy and betray the plan.

It was only when the Thracian auxiliaries rode in at the rear of the enemy column that he had the first sense of how it might go. From the safety of his god-sworn heights, Dubornos saw first the pied horse, then the rider, and then, impossibly, stunningly, he saw the personal standard fluttering high over his head.

"Briga take him, he's stolen the sign of the bull."

Others around the field had seen it. A string of oaths ran north to south and back again amongst dreamers, singers, and warriors. If Briga listened that day, she was called on more in the first few moments than at any other time throughout the battle. If she looked, she would have seen a man sworn to another god who had taken as his personal emblem the mark of the bull as it was first carved by the ancestors of the tribes at the time when the gods were young.

The gods alone know what the symbol meant for them, but for the tribes the marks of the ancestors were sacred to all, so that no one tribe took them for itself but kept them as a sign of honour for all the gods. The bull particularly was beautiful in its simplicity, bulky and bold, full of pride and unyielding vigour. For the enemy blatantly to take it was ultimate sacrilege. For him to mount it in stolen colours made it more so, and this he had done; the background to the pennant was the iron-grey of Mona, and onto it the rounded flowing shape of the ancestors' bull-form had been etched in a deep, rich red as if painted directly onto the cloth in newly shed blood. Breaca's serpent-spear was painted in exactly that ever-living blood and had been since long before Claudius first sent his legions. The two things together, colour and sign, were an unmistakeable message from a man who had taken part in the invasion battles and had used the time since to learn his enemy's strengths, enough to subvert them for his own use. In language anyone could read, they said, *What was sacred of yours has become mine. I can turn it to my own will. Stand against me if you dare.*

"We dare. Oh, gods, we dare." Barred from battle and close to weeping with frustration, Dubornos smashed the edge of his balled fist against the rock by his head. "Efnís, wherever you are, come to the water's edge and direct the slingers against that one. If we get none of the others, his death alone would make this battle worth the while."

"I'm sorry."

"What?"

The singer's mind and heart were in the battle. He had forgotten the child. Cunomar sat cross-legged beside him, Hail's head on his knee. He was weeping silently but copiously. "I'm sorry," he said again. "It's my fault you're here. If it weren't for me, you would be there in the fight. You could kill the pied decurion yourself."

Dubornos had not meant to speak aloud. It was not part of his oath that others should feel in his debt. He turned on one elbow, dragging his eyes from the gathered armies. "That's not your concern. I am here because I choose to be. There is no fault, no blame."

"But there is, isn't there?" At times Breaca's son displayed a wilful self-ishness that bespoke neither of his parents. At others—now—he was entirely his mother. He pursed his lips, and the straight line carved between his brows, as hers did. His voice was no longer a child's but that of an adult, talking reason.

"Ardacos told me," he said. "You were cowardly in your first battle, and afterwards, out of shame, you forswore the ways of the warrior and became a hunter and maker of harness. Later, when the gods marked you as singer and warrior both, you made an oath to Briga and Nemain to protect my mother's children, your life for theirs, wherever they went. But I would have been safe on Mona, and you could have come here and fought against the decurion on the pied horse, so it's my fault that you can't."

The sun burned from the south-east. In the valley, warriors waded into the water the better to throw their spears. On both sides, the souls of the battle-slain began their journey to the world of the dead. Here, too, they faced a river, wider and faster-flowing than any they had ever met in life. With Briga's aid, they forded it, some more easily than others, leaving only memories in the land of life. On the heights of the mountain, Dubornos mac Sinochos, singer of Mona, once of the Eceni, remembered his father and another day of fighting. It was not a scene he readily forgot; his mornings woke to it, and his days ended with the bitterness of its truth. The child who was the voice of his conscience met his gaze evenly, trading new guilt for old.

The gods demand, and it is given to men to offer their souls. Dubornos searched the depths of his and answered with honesty.

"You may be right," he said. "If you had stayed behind, I might have come here to fight. But I might just as well have stayed on Mona with you, your mother, and the new child, in which case it is because of you that I am here at all to witness what is taking place, and gather deeds to fire the songs of later. My oath was freely given, and the gods know best how to use it. I am here because they willed it as much as you. Would you hold the gods at fault?"

Unexpectedly, the child considered this, frowning. "I might, if they destroyed the things I cared for. Or if they kept from me my heart's wish. Is it true you have loved Airmid since childhood and will take no other lover while she lives?"

The words fell into quiet, as if the howling chants of the warriors giving and taking life in the valley were less than the sigh of a spring breeze. A thrush sang from the rowan, and the high notes pierced Dubornos's head. He stared at the boy, who stared back. Very carefully, because for the first time in as long as he chose to remember, his hold on his temper was not certain, Dubornos said, "Who told you that? Was it Ardacos?"

"No. I heard Braint tell Cygfa. It was while you were talking to Gwyddhien. Anyone could see you were uncomfortable in her company. Cygfa thought you craved Gwyddhien and were sore because she was Airmid's. Braint said it was the other way round. Efnís told her what happened. He knew you all as children in the Eceni homelands before the invasion, she said. It's true, isn't it?"

Dubornos had sworn never again to lie. He had not sworn to expose all of his soul to a child. He said, "If it is, does it matter?"

"It matters to Cygfa. She thinks you don't notice her and grieves for it."

A child may see what a man does not, particularly if the latter's attention is elsewhere. Nevertheless, it was not a conversation Dubornos wished to pursue. "Does she so? That's strange, when she is your father come to life in female form and every other warrior, man and woman, sees it. I think that when your sister is past her long-nights, she will not worry that one man among thousands may not see her in the way that she— What is it?"

Cunomar's eyes were widely black. The whites flared like those of a startled horse. He pointed down into the cauldron of conflict. "The decurion," he said. "The one on the pied horse with the red bull banner. He is swimming his mount across the river. His troop are following him across."

He was right. Some things require a man's undivided attention, and the means by which Scapula's legions forded the River of the Lame Hind in pursuit of Caratacus was one of them. Dubornos lay on his high ledge and watched as a troop of Thracian auxiliaries, led by a man he loathed but whose courage he could not question, swam their horses into the torrent and stood broadside to the flow, stringing a rope between them so that the infantry might wade across and not drown as they did so.

The officer on the pied horse stood midstream, presenting a ready target to the warriors on the far side. Efnís was there, directing spears and slingers alike. He was joined by over half the dreamers of Mona, and the decurion became the target of many warriors. At no time was he hit. Sling-stones and spears carved the white water, legionaries and cavalrymen of other troops died on either side, but the pennant of the red bull remained upright, and the pied horse and his rider beneath it.

Dubornos cursed viciously and knew he was not alone. It was widely believed that, from time to time, Briga sent her emissaries in the shape of enemy warriors to claim the lives of those she had already marked for herself. In those cases, the chosen one could not be killed by normal means but only by a dreamer who was prepared to face Briga's wrath. It was also possible that Mithras, the bull-slayer, was pleased with this man and had the power to protect him on the field of battle in a land that was not his own. Or he may simply have been lucky; it was best to think so, because a man's luck may be made to change by other men who do not require the intervention of the gods. The efforts to kill him were redoubled without effect.

With the rope in place, the legionaries swarmed across the water. One could not fault their discipline, or the order with which they fought. Their clashes with the warriors were fiercest on the north bank of the river. The principle of the salmon-trap depended on the legions' swarming, uncaring, over the rampart into the defile when in all probability the decurion of the Thracians had warned them of the trap. The defending warriors, therefore, must fight as if their lives depended on it, as if the barrier at their backs were a retreat of last resort, as if the war would be won or lost in the rock-cluttered, blood-slick slopes of the mountain. Knowing this, claiming honour and fame with every kill, they fought as savagely as they had ever done.

In the chaos, Caradoc was readily visible, his hair bright beneath the ever-rising sun. Cygfa stayed close to him, both of them blazing beacons in the thickest point of battle. Ardacos's she-bears could be heard howling their war songs, and once in a while a circle of them became visible, surrounding a huddle of doomed legionaries. Gwyddhien's horse-warriors circled the margins, attacking cavalry and infantry alike. Braint held a solid line in the centre, her warriors carving space in the air around them with swords that rose and fell like threshing flails.

On the enemy side, Scapula was surrounded by a century of legionaries and could not be approached. The rest of his men kept to their lines and fought with their shields locked, as they had been trained to do, stepping forward over the bodies of the slain. The officer on the pied horse was visible only because his men held the ground round the water's edge. His standard fell once as the bearer's horse was killed beneath him, but the rider rolled free, and it could be seen that the decurion brought him up on the pied horse and called another man forward to hold the standard until the bearer found another mount. Thereafter, fouled and bloody, the red bull could only rarely be picked out from the others. Dubornos held to his memory of a single moment of hatred and prayed to Briga that the man would die before he could warn his governor of the trap, or simply that he would die.

Horns wailed along the river bank. Slowly, slowly, the legions advanced. The cavalry took the sides, blocking the routes of escape so that the warriors must go backwards or die where they stood. Many died but more of the legionaries died with them. Amidst the clustering souls of the dead, the majority, by two to one, were foreigners lost in a land not their own, seeking absent gods they had not thought would abandon them.

The rearmost warriors had reached the barrier. More were already waiting behind it, providing shelter and thrown spears to keep the legions at bay while their shield-mates scaled the outer surface. Ladders on the inside made an easy descent. In the crowded valley, for a moment, the killing stopped. Both sides paused, taking breath and water and eating handfuls of malted grain or strips of dried meat. On the Roman side, raised and tilted standards sent complex messages along the short, dense ranks. The freshest legionaries came to the fore. At the wings, the auxiliaries dismounted. Everything was as it had been in the lands of the Eceni, but on a larger scale. If the governor recognized the trap, he believed himself its equal. On a rocky outcrop, high above the battle, a warrior and a child looked north, seeking sign of three thousand warriors. In the far distance, on the ridge of a mountain, Dubornos saw a single bare-headed man walking on foot leading a horse. A forewarning of disaster fluttered lightly in his chest.

Go!

The command came in Latin, or Eceni, or simply in thought. The echo of it rattled the heights, sprinted the length of the defile. In the pause was an intaken breath, and in its exhalation, in the roar of the legions, was a single message: *We are the might of Rome, come alive and victorious. None can withstand us!*

In the forest, bears paused in their meanderings, stags halted the battles of the rut. Over the highest peaks, eagles wheeled in flight, facing into a wind not sent by the gods. In the rock-littered valley, legionaries in their thousands beat their blades in thundering cacophony against their shields, and assailed by rocks and spears and sling-stones, the charge to the rampart began.

They made roofs of their shields and huddled beneath them. They clawed at rocks with their bare hands, hacking at oak beams with their blades. Many died but as many replaced them; in Scapula's army, one man was another, each of equal worth and weight. With apparent reluctance, the defenders drew back as the sea of infantry began to spill into their valley, first a trickle, then a flood as the dam cracked and opened. The trap was sprung. All it needed now was a hammer to close it. On the far mountainside, a rider mounted, checked the air for the sounds of dying, and set off at a canter down the track.

Boulders were tilted from their seats into the thickest knots of the enemy. Warriors hurled rocks and spears from the heights, then scrambled down to fight. The legions surged into the valley and made it their own. Their back remained exposed and unchallenged, but no hammer came. No three thousand spears of the Brigantes and the Selgovae. Venutios had not closed the back door to the salmon-trap. Even the scout was lost beyond a mountain's ridge.

If Venutios fails, we will kill as many as we may and then leave them.

Caradoc had said it privately to Breaca and again, frequently, to those who led each of the sections of his force. Every fighting man and woman knew the threefold blast that signalled true retreat, quite different from the wailing horns of the false withdrawals. Dubornos heard it and cursed, his words flapping out over the clashing weapons and the lazy downward spiral of the ravens.

Cunomar said, "They mustn't stop now! The messenger is still coming. I can see the horse. It might not be too late."

"No. A single rider is not a war-host, and it's already too late. Look, the legions are all within the valley. They hold the flat ground and their engineers are already dismantling the rampart, giving them a clear retreat. They are at their strongest when they hold solid ranks, as they do here. We can kill them in handfuls, but we are not enough to overwhelm them. Your father is right. It is time for those who remain to retreat. The forests are safe. Better a thousand living warriors to fight another day than so many dead heroes."

The singer pushed himself to his feet. Despair weighted his chest, adding to old grief. For the first time in three decades' living, he felt stiffness in his shoulders and knees. He clicked his fingers for Hail and felt a damp nose touch his wrist.

"We should leave," he said. "It's not beyond Scapula, or one of his officers, to try to claim the heights. We should meet your father where we agreed, in the woods at the river's head."

Ancient heather knotted the track, slowing their passing. Blueberries stained the ground underfoot, marking the trail of two horses and a hound. Dubornos rode ahead with Cunomar a step or two behind. Hail wove between, as quick on three legs as four. Descending from the dreamers' outcrop, they met a line of dense, hock-deep bracken and turned across it rather than wade through. Shortly after, they met Cygfa and her mother Cwmfen, riding up at an angle from the valley. The girl was stained and filthy, blood oozing from a shallow spear-cut on one thigh. Her own spear and shield were gone, and she bore instead a wide, heavy, man's shield made of bull's-hide stretched tight and stained black; a grey falcon took wing on the boss and again on the leather. If she was in pain or exhausted, neither showed. Life glowed from her, as it did from her father in the moments after battle. A crow-feather fluttered in her hair, braided in haste and not meant to last, but a statement in itself.

Dubornos felt Cunomar stiffen and chose to ignore it. Like first love, the first battle comes only once and should be savoured at its freshest. He gave the salute of one warrior to another and saw it returned joyfully.

"How many?" he asked.

"Eight," said her mother. In her eyes, pride outshone concern for the day and the lack of Venutios. "Eight clean kills that I saw and as many wounded. Beyond doubt she is a warrior. She has outmatched her father. He killed only three in his first battle, and that was considered many."

Cunomar's pony jerked its head against a jabbed mouth. Hail whined, a high keening note out of kilter with the day. Dubornos felt surprised delight and let it show. "She has outmatched all of us," he said, "and all of the champions, going back to Cassivellaunos, who defeated Caesar. If you tell me how it was, I'll make a song of it for the winter fires."

"Later." Cygfa's mother had an eye for Cunomar, who had seen his chance for fame dismantled. Only in a tight space like the valley, and with the legionaries holding their own lives worthless, could kills in such numbers be assured. Such an opportunity came but once in each generation, and he had missed it. Hail keened for him still, giving voice to his pain.

Cwmfen said, "We must find Caradoc first. If we're going to meet him at the head of the river, we should go faster."

Her horse was tired and nodding lame on a foreleg. She pushed it on towards a small rocky crag that bulged out into the path. Her attention was all on her daughter, on the recent past and the future, too little of it on the present, where a leather thong the thickness of a man's thumb lay snake-like across the path and was lifted, expertly, to trip her horse. She did not fall, but the peck and stumble threw her off balance and caused a small flurry of confusion in the horses behind.

Unlike the women, Dubornos was not fatigued from battle. A lifetime's training in combat and the inner prescience of a singer made him throw his horse sideways even as he drew his sword. The movement saved his life, and the club that had aimed for his head struck his left shoulder, numbing his arm. His horse was battle-trained. It completed the full turn to face the danger at his back. An auxiliary stood astride the path, club raised for another strike. Behind him stood a tall, slender man, muddy and blood-streaked from battle but lacking device or helmet plumes that might give ready identification. He wore Roman mail, but that meant nothing; half the tribes wore stolen cavalry armour into battle. In the first moment, seeing only the lean outline of the face and the straight blue-black hair, Dubornos thought it was Luain mac Calma with his hair un-bound, unaccountably stripped of his dreamer's brow-thong, and raised his hand in greeting. Then, in a gesture the singer had seen three times be-fore, that he had spent half a sweating, weeping day bringing to the fore-front of his mind so that his fellow dreamers might know it as intimately, the man he loathed most in the world pursed his lips and touched his thumb to the centre of his chest and, nodding a little as if to an inner voice, said simply, "Now."

Recognition exploded into action. Dubornos hurled his horse at the club-man, intent on murder. He reined back only as a dozen armed Thra-cian auxiliaries rose out of the heather before him.

"Take them," said the decurion. "The governor wants them all alive."

They fought; it was what they lived for. Cunomar was the most vulnera-ble, and all three warriors knew it. They tried to make a circle holding him at the centre but were too few to achieve it, and the boy did nothing to help. From the first, he had counted twenty auxiliaries and seen his chance to win honour greater than his sister's. More than that, he had within his reach the man whom half a battlefield of proven warriors had tried to kill without success. He flung himself at the hated decurion, and the combat, such as it was, lasted exactly as long as it took for a boy on a pony to reach an unmounted man, to be unhorsed with expert precision and held fast with a blade tight at his throat. Cunomar struggled and bit, and the man laughed, and then didn't.

"Stop!"

The command came in Latin, from an officer whose word was law and temper, short. The man opposite Dubornos hesitated and died for it, his head split from temple to nose. The impact shuddered along the singer's arm even as he dragged the blade free and turned on the man's companion.

"No." The decurion's knife flashed. Cunomar screamed aloud. Blood welled from his ear where the lower half of the lobe was suddenly slit. Shouting to be heard, the officer said again, "Stop. Lay down your weapons. The child will die if you don't." He said it twice, the second time in passable Ordovician.

Dubornos raised his blade and turned in toward the enemy. Cwmfen spun her horse broadside in front of him, blocking his attack. "Dubornos! Do as he says. He'll kill Cunomar else."

"He'll kill him anyway. He'll kill all of us." The enemy moved around them. Ducking sideways, Dubornos smashed his shield into a man's face and swung his blade for the retreating head. "You know who this is. Better to die here in battle than be hanged at the fort and fed to their hounds."

"No!" The decurion's voice cut through the clash of iron as Dubornos's blade was turned. "No. I know he is Caradoc's son. No harm will come to him here by our hand if you give up your weapons. I swear it."

For that voice alone, one could kill; for the taunting arrogance of an officer, of victor to vanquished, he should have died a thousand deaths. Cygfa was nearest to him. The battle-rage lived within her, and she could have killed him in a stroke. Her sword-arm was still, held rigidly so by her mother.

Cwmfen flung her shield in Dubornos's face. Anger ran through her as clearly as it did her daughter, but was tempered by reason and a vast, unassailable pride. Here, now, one could so easily see why Caradoc had once loved her.

"You will stop," she said. "Your oath holds you. If you die, Cunomar dies also. Therefore you are oath-bound to live."

It may have been true. All the dreamers of Mona could have taken a month of nights to argue the point in law and constitution. In the moments of decision, it was Cwmfen's unbending will that swayed him. Hating himself, Dubornos reversed his blade and sheathed it. The decurion spoke once in Latin. Around him men lowered their weapons. The chaos of combat resolved. Out of murder grew calm, but for the place just beyond the rock where Hail, who spoke no Latin and had no concept of surrender, hurled himself in tooth-bared silence at the nearest auxiliary.

"Longinus, no!"

It was the decurion who shouted. He spoiled the attention of both hound and man, but not enough. A blade flashed, once. Impossibly, the old hound who had come unscathed through more battles than most living warriors was caught by the full length of its edge. Iron smashed through living flesh. A dozen ribs disintegrated, and the lungs beneath them hissed empty of air. Blood rose like a fountain and rained down, patterning the heather. White-faced, the auxiliary said, "Julius, I'm sorry—" and his words were lost in the noise.

The scream of a dying beast is no different from that of a warrior. It shattered the day, falling to a rasping moan as the great hound collapsed onto the path and lay writhing on his wounded side, fighting to draw air and live. A dozen men, two women, and a boy who had heard the same sound from countless throats throughout the morning heard it now in silence and with appalled regret. The reputation of the Boudica's warhound had spread among the legions no less widely than the name of the woman at whose side he fought, and the men of Rome were not without honour or respect for a valiant enemy.

Dubornos slid from his horse, and no effort was made to stop him. He had lost his own dagger, thrown in the first moments of fighting and lodged still in the chest of an elderly auxiliary. Kneeling, he reached instead for his blade. A hand on his arm stopped him. He looked up, cursing. Protest dried in his throat.

The world inverted. Kneeling opposite him was the decurion of the Thracian cavalry, rider of the pied horse, his face the ugly yellowed white of a man in death-shock. Cunomar, sobbing, had been passed to the auxiliary who had killed Hail. The man looked as if his life had ended. The decurion himself knelt opposite Dubornos without ceremony or protection. On his open hand, reversed to present the hilt, lay his dagger. An arm's length away, beneath smooth brown skin, the beat of his heart pulsed, too fast, through the great vessels of his neck.

In his mind, in the forefront of his being, so that only his will held it other, Dubornos lifted the blade and rammed it home, burying the shining sharpness in flesh and blood and spinal bone, snuffing out for ever the life of an enemy whose mere presence was an insult to the gods and to the memories of those he had killed. His oath stopped him, and the low, grief-heavy voice of the other man, speaking Eceni in a way the singer had not heard since childhood, untarnished by the southern and western dialects of the war. Even Breaca no longer spoke so.

"You'll have to do it. I can't remember the words of the invocation."

It is not given a singer to read the soul in the way of a dreamer. Even if it were, a full life's history cannot be seen in a single meeting of eyes, but enough can pass to know and be known, for the moment of recognition, of appalling, blinding horror, for immutable loathing to garner also pity and a measure of terrible understanding.

Numbly, Dubornos reached for the dagger. The blade was still sticky with Cunomar's blood. The hilt was of bronze, fashioned in the shape of a falcon, with jet beads for the eyes. One had been lost and reset imperfectly. The singer noticed it with the dream-like clarity with which everything came to him in that moment. Testing the blade, he found it as keen as the flaying blades of the dreamers, which are daily honed sharp enough to shave with.

Hail lay stretched on the heather between them, not screaming now, but whimpering his pain. The decurion passed a hand over the old hound's head, speaking words in a language older than Latin, older than the Eceni tongue of his boyhood. The hound whined as he had on the path, recognizing a scent long missed and not understanding its source. He thrust his muzzle into a known and long-sought palm and was held with care. Dubornos found himself weeping and chose not to stem the tears. Through a throat too tight for steady words, he said, "We need to turn his head to the west."

"Help me, then."

They turned him together, taking care for his pain, and the hound sighed at the end. Dubornos found his voice again, and his training of decades. The invocation to Briga may be spoken by any but sung only by those trained on Mona. With his whole being, he sang it, lifting the words high over the mountains so that all those left alive after the battle might hear and know that a great soul passed from this world to the other in the company of the god to whom his life had been given. At the peak, when the song was greatest, Dubornos slid the falcon-blade carefully along the great hound's throat, letting the last bright splash of life-blood spill to the heather. His eyes were on the decurion, who did not see him.

"You are Caradoc's brother."

"You know that's not true."

"I am telling you what I will put in the written reports for the governor, that you are brother to the rebel and that this is his wife and both of his children. It is known he has two."

"No. Cwmfen is no one's wife. Even Scapula must know by now that such a state does not exist. Our women live as they will and love whom they choose. They are not owned by men, nor we by them."

They were speaking Latin, which made it easier to forget what had just passed between them, and they were standing apart, which made it less of a farce than it might have been. The majority of the auxiliaries had been assigned the collecting of rocks, to make a burial cairn for the hound. Cwmfen and Cygfa had been disarmed.

Dubornos had given his weapon personally to the decurion, who had admired the hilt. The officer had recovered his composure. In a knowing parody of the formal introductions of the dreamers, he had said, "I am Julius Valerius Corvus, acting commander of the Ala Prima Thracum. Longinus Sdapeze, duplicarius of the first troop, is the officer who holds the boy. You should be wary of him. His horse was killed beneath him today, and he loved it as a brother. We will introduce the others to you later." And then he had made his statement, which was nonsense.

The moment of shared understanding, of meeting and possible compassion, had passed. Valerius was the officer again. For the purposes of ambush, he had dispensed with his decurion's cloak, but the glamour of leadership shone from him, as it did from Breaca before battle; the certainty of victory that could slide into arrogance were it not tempered in her so clearly by love. In the man who called himself Julius Valerius, there was no love. Dubornos despised him for it.

He said, "I have no brother, as you well know. My sisters are both dead at your hand."

Valerius sighed pointedly. "Warrior, are you tired of life?"

The singer held his enemy's gaze and found, surprisingly, that he did not flinch. "Would you like to return my father's blade and see which of us wishes most to die?"

The decurion smiled. Irony tainted a genuine humour. With studied courtesy, he said, "Thank you, but no. Later, perhaps, but not today. I have particularly precise orders and they do not permit the indulgence of killing Caradoc's relatives."

"I'm not—"

"Dubornos, will you listen and try to understand? I know exactly who and what you are; that is not in question. You should know that if we capture a warrior of the enemy, he or she will be passed to Scapula's inquisitors, who travel with him for just this eventuality. You may not have seen the results of their work, but you should take my word for it that anyone so questioned wishes for death long before the sun sets on the first day— and there are many days. The order extends to every living captive with the sole exception of those who are direct kin of the rebel leaders. These are to be transported unharmed to Rome to await the emperor's pleasure. So I say again that here and now we have taken Caradoc's brother, his wife, and his two children. If you wish to deny this, I won't stop you; your life is yours to prolong as you wish. I would suggest you do not extend the same discourtesy to the women, or to the boy."

It was a day for god-sent choices, none of them easy. Dubornos asked, "What happens in Rome?"

"That depends on the emperor. I couldn't say, but even public crucifixion would be better than what will happen here if you are found to be, say, a dreamer from the rebel isle of Mona."

"Or a singer?"

"The distinction is not one that Scapula will recognize."

Dubornos had trained for years in the ways of the dream. At times and in places, it was given him to hear the voices of the gods or to see their sign. Praying to Nemain, whom he favoured, he looked round at the grey rock and purpled wash of the mountains, at the flesh-greased smoke that rose from the valley, drifting south on a light wind, at the countless crows gathering to feast on the dead. He was considering his death and the means by which it could be brought most swiftly closer when a flicker on a far hillside drew his eye. There, partly hidden by berried rowan and rock, a handful of white cloaks flew in the wind of their owners' riding: the honour guard of Mona. At their head was Caradoc, and at his side, freshly mounted on a new horse and with the gift of a Roman legionary shield, rode the scout of the Brigantes whom Dubornos had last seen cantering down a mountain track towards a lost battle. All rode north, at speed.

It was a small thing on which to hang a life, but it was enough. The decurion had seen the riders with him. His eyes met the singer's, and Dubornos said, "It seems my brother lives to continue the war."

There was a moment before the words and their meaning were clear, then Valerius saluted. On his face was the barest mockery, of whom was impossible to tell. "Thank you. I will enter it so in the reports."

The horses were brought forward. The wrists of the captives were bound. They were helped to mount and were led at a slow walk down the hillside. On the path behind, a cairn of rocks the height of a mounted man marked the last resting place of a battle-hound.

CHAPTER 17

"Breaca? Breaca, wake up."

The night was dark, with no moon. In her dreams, Caradoc slew both Scapula and the pied decurion and rode back to her with their heads wrapped in his cloak as a gift. Delivered to Mona, the head of the decurion had become that of Amminios, Caradoc's older brother, who had sided with Rome. It sang in Latin and mocked her, promising vengeance for a death in which she had taken no part.

"Breaca? Can you hear me?"

She stirred, glad to escape the dream. In the half-world of waking, she knew that her daughter suckled her left breast and should be moved to the right and that cool fingers gripped her wrist firmly. With some thought, she recognized Airmid's touch; it was how they had always woken each other. Sleep-sodden, she opened her eyes.

"Caradoc?" she asked. "Has he won?"

"I don't know." Airmid stood at the bedside, shapeless in her cloak, her hair black to merge with the night. "There's a messenger waiting on the far side of the strait. I've sent Sorcha with the ferry to bring him over. I thought you might want to greet him."

"I thought you might want to . . ." I have seen you force yourself to eat these past three days for your child's sake when your body would have refused food for worry, and I have watched you walk the slopes above the strait from dawn to dusk that you might see a messenger riding down the far mountain and know the message that much sooner.

The promise of news brought her awake, and Graine with her. The child gurned and fell silent, feeding. Airmid fetched a torch and lit it from the fire. Breaca followed her along the path to the jetty where the ferry would put in. Rain, the young hound who was son to Hail, ran ahead, snuffing the night; all day he had been restless and was better out. At the standing-stone on the hillside, they stopped, looking down onto the straits below. The barest outline of the ferry was visible, a sleek shape sliding black on black like a hunting otter. The backwash of the steering oar stirred green light from the water behind, a gift of the sea-god Manannan to fishers and ferrywomen that they might see and be seen. The wind blew briskly from the north, lifting the tidal swell. In the quiet of the night, they heard the sound of retching and the soft consternation that followed from Sorcha, who could not understand that her beloved sea might cause some to feel ill.

The ferry reached them. Wood bumped lightly on wood, and a rope was made fast. Sorcha stepped ashore and turned to offer a hand to her passenger. "This is Lythas," she said. "Venutios has sent him with a message." And then, redundantly, "He's been sick."

Torchlight showed a small, neat young man of Ardacos's build who had indeed been sick, although that was only the latest hardship in his recent past and not the greatest. His tunic was torn at the shoulder and hip as if he had rolled through thorns or slid down a rocky hillside, and his left forearm was bruised along its length, but even these were only markers to the upheavals within. He finished the last bout of sickness and hauled himself ashore. Exhaustion from days and nights on horseback lined his eyes and carved hollows beneath them. Breaca studied them as she might any other warrior returning from a skirmish, but nothing protected her from the shock that rocked him when he looked up and realized who she was. His message, a day old at least, rushed to the front of his mouth, and he would not, or could not, speak it aloud.

"Tell me," said Breaca. "It is best I know quickly. Is he dead?"

"No, lady, not dead. But perhaps better if he were."

Airmid grasped her arm. By the pressure of those fingers, Breaca stayed upright and kept her fear hidden. "He's taken, then? Scapula has him?" *I will kill them all. I will unleash such vengeance as has never been—*

The messenger swallowed. "Not yet." With evident reluctance, he said, "Cartimandua has him and will give him to the governor as a guest-gift. They lured him north by treachery. A messenger was sent—Vellocatus— to meet Caradoc at the River of the Lame Hind. He carried news that Venutios was held captive by the Fourteenth Legion, and that was why he wasn't able to bring the three thousand—"

It was too much and made too little sense. Questions tumbled over themselves. "Vellocatus is loyal to Venutios. How could he—" And then, as the strategies of a summer collapsed at her feet: "The three thousand didn't come? So we lost to Scapula? Or did Caradoc beat him and then take the warriors north to rescue Venutios?"

Airmid's fingers still encircled her wrist, pressing firmly as if waking her from a second sleep. "Breaca, forgive me, but we should move. Lythas has ridden through two nights to reach us. He needs food and water and perhaps some ale. His message will make more sense if he gives it as it was told him, and he'll do that best when he is seated before a fire with a drink inside him and out of sight and smell of the sea."

The man said nothing, but exhaustion and gratitude lit his smile equally. Airmid said, "Come with me. A place is prepared," and they followed her, with the hound behind.

Airmid had been awake awhile, it seemed, and expecting company. The place she had prepared was her own, set on the western edge of the settlement, the place of deepest dreaming. It was built with stone walls and turf on the roof, and a burn ran within an arm's stretch of the doorway, keeping her close to the waters of Nemain. Inside, a fire was already laid and lit, with folded hides placed at three points around it for seating. Lacking other light, the walls were in shadow, and it was impossible to see what else of Airmid's was present, but the scents of rosemary and sage, of pine resin and sea-wrack, mingled faintly with the rising smoke. This was not a usual place in which to greet a messenger, but it was not a usual message, nor a usual time. They were still between midnight and dawn. Hounds stirred, and night hunting beasts, but the dreamers, for the most part, slept on in the greathouse and no apprentices had been woken to serve the messenger with food and ale, as would ordinarily have been the case.

Airmid excused herself briefly and returned with a fresh cloak and a beaker of water for Lythas, but not yet food. She said, "Maroc is preparing meat and oat bannocks. It'll be ready soon, but you should give us the message now, if you will, so we can act without delay."

The man was willing, seeing a day's rest ahead of him. By the light of the fire he seemed less sick, his face less pinched, his eyes less haunted. He sat opposite Breaca on the cushion of hides and relayed his message, word-perfect, as it had been told him.

"The first thing you need to know is that Vellocatus is Cartimandua's man. He has been from the start, from before Venutios ever returned to us from Mona. He has been her eyes and ears in our meetings, her voice in council, saying only what he was given permission to say by her. He told her of the salmon-trap and the plan to raise the two thousand to aid Caradoc. When he suggested that he go north to request aid from the Selgovae, the idea came first from her. It gave him a reason to travel ahead of Venutios without arousing suspicion.

"When the time came to gather the warriors, Venutios found himself betrayed. Two cohorts of the Fourteenth and a wing of Batavian cavalry surrounded him and his sworn companions. They couldn't condemn him—he is father to Cartimandua's child, and they deem him royal for that—but they have hanged all his closest kin and companions from the gateposts of his roundhouse, and he is forced to stay inside while they rot. I was spared because I am no one, neither kin nor sworn spear-chief, not even known as a friend."

He spoke this last as steadily as he had the rest, as if it, too, were part of a message learned by heart. His face, moulded tallow in the firelight, was a mask of death and damaged pride.

Breaca said, "Whom did you lose in the hangings?"

He looked at her sharply. "My father, my sister, two of my cousins and ... a friend. A good friend."

"And you think it would have been better to die with your kin and those you loved rather than to live, to fight, perhaps to avenge their deaths." The Boudica nodded, her gaze lost in the heart of the fire. She spoke thoughtfully, as if to the glowing embers or to herself alone. "It may be that each of them considered the shining honour of it as they choked out their last air on the end of the rope. It may be there would have been another, similarly overlooked, who would have had the courage to ride out of an armed and guarded encampment if you had been considered dangerous and had been honoured with the same death as your kin. But it was not so. The gods chose you to live and to bear the message."

She looked up. A veil of flame separated them. He could not look away. "We are not given the choice of how and when we must serve, only whether we do so with courage and so perhaps succeed, or with fear, in which case we will certainly fail. You have shown courage so far, but if you wish to ride back and give yourself up to the legate of the Fourteenth Legion there is no one here who will stop you. Alternatively, you could continue to act with the courage you have shown so far and pray for the chance to see those you cared for avenged, their families and their land freed from oppression and slavery. These are your choices. If you had to pick one now, which would it be?"

He stared at her. Simply to ask was an insult, and yet she was the Boudica, whose honour could not be impugned. "I will choose to fight," he said. "Always."

"Thank you." She smiled and his world became a lighter place. "Then tell us what you know of the battle in the mountains, how it went for Caradoc and the warriors of the western tribes."

He shrugged. "We don't know very much, and all of that is second-hand from those who captured Caradoc. The rest we must guess." He drank water from the beaker and began again in the rolling lilt of the trained messenger, speaking the words of another as if they were his own.

"It's clear that, without Venutios, the salmon-trap in the mountains failed. Caradoc and the warriors of the tribes fought with outstanding courage and left behind them eight or nine dead of the enemy for each one of their own, but the smashing fist of the trap could not close, and when Caradoc realized they had been betrayed, he ordered the tribes to leave the field. Better to live and fight on than die in a hopeless cause."

"It is always so. He had arranged it beforehand."

"Yes. Venutios knew it, and so Cartimandua knew it, too, through her spy. She alone knew both sides: the setting of the salmon-trap and that it would fail. She sent Vellocatus so that he would come upon Caradoc as if by happy chance just as he was leaving the battlefield to join the warriors of Mona and the spear-leaders of the other guards. He told him . . ." He slowed and drank again, gathering himself. This time his gaze rose to Breaca's face but not her eyes. "He told him that the Boudica was in danger, that Cartimandua had lured you north with a tale of Caradoc's capture, but that you were travelling slowly for the sake of the babe and that if they—Caradoc and Vellocatus—rode swiftly, with little encumbrance and only a few of the honour guard for company, he might overtake you before you reached the strongholds of the north. He went. How could he not?"

Breaca said, "That's madness. I wouldn't go north, and even if I did, I wouldn't take Graine. Why would Caradoc believe it?"

"Because they told him you were in danger and that you had gone believing the same of him. And because the message was given by Vellocatus, whom he trusted, and who had brought with him, as evidence of good faith, the salmon carved in blue stone that is the mark of Venutios."

"Taken by force."

"Of course, but he couldn't know that."

Airmid said, "He wouldn't ask. His only care would be for Breaca and Graine. It is his weakness, and they know it. As Caradoc is ours." The

dreamer sat in the shadows beyond reach of the fire. The stream ran behind her, a liquid song in the night. For nearly twenty years she had lived
and dreamed here, and when she spoke in this place the god spoke with
her, changing the air. Speaking thus, she asked, "Lythas, what symbol do
you bring as proof of your good faith?"

Freed from the burden of the message, the messenger had relaxed.
One could see more clearly the man in him, through the frightened youth.
He was older than he had first seemed. "I have brought no token. There
was none left of any worth beyond Venutios's word and mine that what I
have said is the truth."

He leaned towards Breaca, his face flushed. His smile, and the margin
of hope it offered her, were worth more than any ring or brooch and he
knew it.

"Caradoc is held alone and well guarded," he said. "It would not be
possible to rescue him with an army. The Fourteenth are waiting for just
such an attack. It would be suicide for the warriors, and Caradoc would
die before they ever came close to him. But a small group, perhaps the
Boudica and one or two of Ardacos's bear-warriors, might be able to reach
him. If not that, I believe—and this does not come from Venutios but
from me alone—that there is still time to talk to Cartimandua. She is a
mother, and she has protected Venutios from Rome though she loathes
him and he her. She would understand a plea from the Boudica as a
mother and a lover. For that she might return Caradoc to you alive."

Breaca said, "Rome would never allow it."

Lythas shrugged. "Rome hasn't got the power to stop it. The legions
travel slowly and against resistance—Gwyddhien's falcons and Ardacos's
she-bears harry them as they march, so they must build secure camps at
night and cannot move faster than the slowest legionaries for fear that the
rear of the column will be cut off and destroyed. If we were to ride fast
in a small group, we could still reach Cartimandua days ahead of Scapula."

"But why would she agree to let Caradoc go? She hates him. He refused her a child, and she has never forgiven him. For that alone, she'll see
him crucified and be glad of it."

"Possibly, but she is less influenced by her own petty jealousies than
she was and more aware of the pressures of rulership. She commands
more spears than any other from the east coast to the west, and that has
its cost. If they revolt, she's lost. Moreover, she has to contend with the
northern Brigantes, who are oath-sworn to Venutios. They number thousands and are close to rebellion. To free Caradoc now would raise her

standing with them, possibly enough to prevent an uprising. It would not harm her in the eyes of Rome. She's already saved them once from defeat; they can't reasonably ask more."

In entirely her own voice, Airmid murmured, "And of course, Rome only ever asks what is reasonable."

Reaching into the back of the house, the dreamer brought forward three torches. One by one she lit them from the fire. Dark became light, and the scents of pine resin, herbs, and tallow sharpened and became stronger, clearing the air, banishing the last traces of fear and desperation. Lythas caught Breaca's eye and smiled again, a willing if weary conspirator. Across the fire, an agreement was in the making: he would return to find Caradoc and she with him. It only remained to convince Airmid and the other dreamers of the wisdom of it.

Airmid's shadow fell between them, breaking the moment. She said, "Lythas, you have done all that was asked of you and more. If you are to guide us back to find Caradoc, we should leave you now to eat and rest and find strength for the journey. If you wait, Maroc will bring what is needed."

He smiled gladly. "Thank you."

Breaca stood, raised by relief. Where she had expected argument, there was the beginning of a plan. She would go north, there was no doubt of that; the only question was who could safely accompany her. "We can't take Graine," she said, voicing her first thought. "We'll need to find a wet-nurse, someone who can care for her properly."

Airmid said, "There is Sorcha, the ferrywoman. Her newest son is near weaning, and her milk flows now as freely as it did when he was born. She would have Graine gladly and care for her as her own. Maroc and Luain mac Calma will take care of her other needs and her safety. Neither one would let her come to harm in our absence." *Because our absence may be permanent. If we go, we may never come back. And we will go, both of us together, because we must.* "Will you come outside with me? If we're going to leave by dawn, there are things we must do."

They stepped out of the house of stone and earth into a world filled with dreamers. Luain mac Calma, who could have ruled Hibernia and chose instead the guardianship of Mona, was there. With him was Maroc the Elder, who had once been to Rome to see the enemy close at hand. They stood on either side of the door, naked to the waist as if for the slaughter of bullocks or swine. Each bore a hook-bladed knife with the back edge honed to razor sharpness. Behind them, two of the younger apprentices held ropes of twisted hide. Airmid nodded as the door-skin fell behind her. Maroc pushed it open and entered, smiling.

Breaca spun and was held fast. "Airmid? What is this?"

"He's lying. It's a trap. They mean to take you as they have taken Caradoc." Airmid spoke in the voice not of the god but of absolute certainty.

"How can you be sure?"

"Because that's what I'm here for, to be sure of these things. If you know how to look, it's clear. He's well trained, but not well enough. If I were to guess, I would say Heffydd has had him for a while. He's the only dreamer trained on Mona who would turn our knowledge against us. If you think back to when we first met the ferry, you will remember that Lythas was happy to meet your eye, but he would not meet mine, except right at the beginning when he was still in the boat and did not know who I was. You saw the fear that came straight afterwards but thought it was for you and the pain he brought, as he meant you to. He's a clever man and not lacking in courage, but he is Cartimandua's to the deepest part of his soul. If you go to her and plead for Caradoc's life, she will give both of you to Rome."

"You knew this from the start?"

"Yes. It's why I didn't bring him food. If he had eaten with us, the guest laws would have made it harder to do what we must."

Dawn was near. In the impoverished light, Breaca looked into the eyes of the woman she had known for all her lifetime and did not recognize the dark in the soul who looked back. The bleakness of it shocked her. Such a look belonged on the battlefield, late in the day after the first fire of battle-rage had waned. It is a thing shared by those of both sides who have survived, who have killed and will go on killing, who have maimed and will maim again, who have seen enemy and friends die fast, or slowly, and are resigned to the same end. To Breaca's certain knowledge, Airmid had been in battle only once, and the fact that she had lived through it at all was thanks to good fortune and the protection of the gods, not the dreamer's skill with sword and shield. Combat was not her strength; healing, not death, was her province.

From the hut came the sound of a struggle and a breathless scream.

Breaca tried again to reach the door. "Let me do this," she said. "It's not your work."

Airmid would not let her pass. "More my work than yours. The herb-smoke from the torches does half the job, and you couldn't stay in there for much longer. It was already affecting your judgement. And what we do here is not killing in war. You haven't ever slain a warrior when the battle-heat wasn't on you, and this is not a good time to start. You would carry the guilt, and it would weaken you when we most need you whole for the ride north and whatever comes after. Go to Sorcha and tell her what Graine needs to be safe and happy. Whatever else must be done, we will know by the time you return."

"Then we're still going north?"

"Yes, I believe so. Caradoc has been captured, that much would seem to be true, although I think it may be more recent than Lythas would have us believe. But the message was not sent by Venutios. What we must find is how best to get to him, knowing that Cartimandua expects us."

"And what of Lythas afterwards? What will we do with him?"

Airmid shook her head. "There will be no Lythas afterwards. The carrion beasts will have what remains."

Sorcha was awake in her cabin near the shore, feeding her son. Big and broad-boned, she lived for the sea. Her mother was Belgic, an escaped slave; her father, the Hibernian sea-master who had given the woman both reason and means to abandon the home she had known for two decades. They bore their seven children at sea and six of them sailed it still. Sorcha was the youngest. Her choice to settle on land came late and for much the same reason as her mother had taken to the sea. Her man was a warrior and had died in a skirmish in the early summer. In his absence, she raised their three children in the company of the few others who were born and raised on Mona, and she manned the ferry across the straits as she had done every year since the legions' invasion.

She met Breaca's request to act as Graine's wet-nurse with the same willingness with which she sailed. Motherhood came easily, and she was already regretting the growing-up of her infant. More deeply, she knew what it was to lose the light of her soul to the enemy, what it did to head and heart. She stood with her back to a wall, rocking her child in one arm, studying Breaca in much the same way as she studied the swell of the sea.

"Are you the right one to go for your man?" she asked. "If you see him, you'll not hold back. If it's both of you they want, that's the way they'll get you, using him."

Breaca said, "Airmid will come. She won't be so readily blinded."

"No?" Sorcha's hair was copper, her brows a shade paler, almost lost in the sun-worn freckles of her skin. She raised one of them now. "Unless they take you. Then I'd say she'll be worse."

"Maybe." It was always there, hanging over everything. One took risks, daily, of death, captivity, torture, and prepared in heart and mind as much as one could. One could not do the same for the equal risks to those one loved; no such preparation was possible. Breaca thought of Caradoc and his last words on parting: *I love you, never forget. For your freedom and that of our children, I will do anything and everything, to the ends of the earth.* Her heart lay shattered in the cage of her chest, and words did not mend it.

The cabin was built of green oak, pitted with knots. For a sharp, haunted mind that sought the patterns in everything, the whorls moved and resolved into bears and blades and crucified men. Breaca stared at the shifting shapes, lost in a past that was irretrievable and a future that could not be known.

Sorcha's child fell asleep at the breast. With unhurried competence, the ferrywoman wrapped her son in a lambskin and laid him on the bracken in the high-sided bed with his siblings. A signal bell rang faintly, chiming over the murmur of mother and children; the request from the mainland for the ferry. Sorcha raised a patch of blue-stained calf-hide and looked through the peephole thus uncovered, which gave a direct view of the jetties at both sides of the strait. Pulling on a rope, she raised a signal that could be seen on the far side.

"That's Ardacos. He's there now with his bear-warriors. If he's come this far, Gwyddhien and Braint won't be far behind." She turned back into the room, her jaw set bluntly. "So that's five of you going, and not one whole if another is lost."

"No." Breaca took her turn at the peephole. With her eye to the knot, she said, "Love isn't always a weakness."

She believed it. First and last, more than care of the land or the gods or the desperate need not to see a people made slaves and lackeys to Rome, it was love that bound the inner circle that made her life whole. Ardacos had been her lover in the years before Caradoc, and Airmid had been her first love, long before him. Ardacos was Braint's lover now, as Gwyddhien was Airmid's, and all four were sworn to the Boudica, to protect and to serve until death and beyond. The mesh and weave of given hearts was impossible to unravel, nor would any of them wish to try. Only a stranger would not be pulled into it, and no stranger could ever be trusted with what came ahead.

The ferrywoman reached for her cloak from its peg. Her wide sea-raw fingers pinned it high on the right shoulder. At the door, having thought her words clear, she paused.

"Just remember, while you're away, that there's more lives depend on you living to fight on than that one man. It would be no honour to his memory to lose a land and its people because he is gone."

The land of the Brigantes was grey. In the lowlands, grey mist leaked over barren grey rock. In the high mountains, which were never as high as the startling, snow-bright peaks of the west, thin grey slush rendered hard ground mud and made sodden the lying firewood so that, for the last two nights of a five-night journey, Breaca and those who rode with her ate raw the hares and small fish that Ardacos hunted, and slept in pairs sitting up-right, sharing cloaks and the warmth of their bodies.

They were thirteen, the five whom Sorcha had identified, with two of Gwyddhien's Silures to hold the horses ready within reach of the enemy and five of the bear-warriors, hand-picked for their skill in the hunt. The thirteenth was Tethis, a cousin of Ardacos's just past her long-nights and not yet tested in battle. The reason for her coming had not been apparent when they set out, but Ardacos had brought her, and no one argued. On the fifth day, they learned why she had come.

Through the length of the journey, Breaca and those closest to her had considered the means by which they would locate and free Caradoc. Each of them had believed that he or she alone was capable of penetrat-ing the vast encampment on the northern river where the Brigantes shared fires and food with three cohorts of the Fourteenth Legion. A massed at-tack was impossible; the only possible route was by stealth, but the ques-tion remained as to who should go in and how they would best avoid capture. Breaca could not go. On that everyone was agreed; her height and her colouring were too well known by the enemy, and there was no dis-guise in the world that would effectively conceal her when the Brigantes were expecting her to come. The others did not share her notoriety, but in truth each of them was known to the enemy, and none could plausibly pass as either Roman or Brigante. Tethis had deferred to her elders and those with greater experience of battle, saying nothing until the morning of the fifth day, when the whole group lay on a hillside within sight of the camp and had not yet found a way to do what was needful. Then she showed what she could do.

She had been born and raised in the land of the Caledonii far to the north and had never yet set foot on a battlefield. No one, Roman or Brig-ante, had ever seen her. Better than that, she had the small size and dark colouring of the ancestors so that, with a little planning, she could pass as one of the Brigante girl children, not yet come to adulthood. Dressed in only a thong-belted tunic with her legs streaked with mud and her hair flying free, she became yet another urchin underfoot, to be scolded and sent back to the fields or, if close to the Roman encampments, put to work as a messenger, paid in tarnished copper coins, and later lured into a tent for work that would not be paid.

From warrior to urchin, the transformation took place before them, and it was clear even to Braint, who had been intent on something similar with far less chance of success, that Tethis was their best, if not their only, hope of reaching Caradoc. The arguments had been abandoned, and the girl had left just before dawn, running down over the grey hillside to vanish into the river-mist that concealed the noisome chaos of the fort.

Throughout the long day, they waited, twelve battle-proven warriors, while a girl who had not yet won her spear walked alone among a thousand legionaries and three times that many enemy warriors. Tired, frustrated, and eaten alive by impatience, Breaca lay on her cloak on a ledge of crumbling slate veiled by a swath of dying bracken that lipped over from the hillside above. Straight edges of rock dug into her flesh through the folds of wool, autumn insects crawled from the bracken to explore exposed patches of skin, ants laid a trail a hand's breadth in front of her face. After a while, she began to pray for rain, simply for a change in the attacks on her person.

The rest of the group were no more comfortable. Below and to the right, Braint lay close to Ardacos, each on a similar slate outcrop. Others lay within hailing distance, making hare-nests in the damp bracken or lying out as Breaca did on the rocky outcrops that littered the landscape. One could choose soft lying and be wet, or remain dry but cold and hard. Either way the day stretched each of them to the limits of their endurance.

There were ways to pass the time. Breaca counted the crows that flapped like thrown rags in the wind, tumbling down to the carrion feast of hanged warriors below. In the afternoon, when the wind backed to the east and rolled the stench of those bodies up the hillside to choke the hidden watchers, she began instead to count the dead, to separate and identify men from women, adult from child, blond hair from dark. They were not close and they had hung in the wind for many days so that she counted and re-counted and the numbers were never twice the same, but the effort kept her awake and alert while she waited, always, for the shouted challenge and the clash of weapons that would mean Tethis had failed.

"She's coming."

Ardacos had moved since the morning. He spoke from the bracken to Breaca's left. A moment later he raised his head so she could see him. He was naked but for a belt and a loin-flap of bear-skin, his body lightly greased with goose-fat against the cold. He edged closer, flowing like water over the rock, and for a moment the smell of him covered the stench of putrefaction rising from the valley. His face was lined and creased with four decades' exposure to cold and biting wind. His smile was a rare thing, given as a gift, and she had learned to read it only after years in his closest company. As he gave it now, it was a preparation for disappointment.

"She's halfway up and alone," he said. "See . . . there." He pointed further south than she had been looking. On the hillside, bracken shivered and was still. A hunting fox would have made such a movement, or a badger, caught abroad in daylight. Ardacos chittered like an angry stoat and was answered in kind.

Tethis ran the last few strides. She was alone and looked neither hopeful nor happy.

"I don't care what he says. We will get him out."

"No. He cannot be freed."

"He can. It is only that we have not yet found the means. One of us should go in and look again at night, when the guards are fewer."

It was dusk. They had moved across to the other side of the hill, out of sight of the encampment and away from a wind that had come on suddenly and flung the bracken flat. The bear-warriors and Gwyddhien's Silures stood watch in a full circle. The five and Tethis remained in the centre. The girl had brought dry firewood; its collection had been her reason to leave the camp. Ardacos had dug a fire pit, and they burned the wood for warmth alone. None of them could have stomached food.

An orange glow leaked up from the pit. By its light, they were all too pale, too worn. Breaca ground her knife on her whetstone, a rhythmic scratch and scrape that was lost on the wind. Without that much movement, she would have needed to walk, to squirm through the bracken, to run, to take her blade and attack single-handedly the series of guard posts that stood between her and the distant tent, now identified, where Caradoc was held.

She sat across the fire from Tethis. The girl was small, compact, collected, and deeply moved by what she had seen. She chewed her lip, thinking what to say next. Ardacos asked a question in the northern tongue that none amongst the others understood and was answered cuttingly. Breaca recognized only the name of Cartimandua, spoken twice with heartfelt loathing. In the rest was surprise, vehement assent, and flat certainty, but no hope.

At the end, they fell to a heavy silence until, choosing his words, Ardacos said, "She doesn't want to tell you this because she's afraid it'll only add to your grief, but I think you have to know. The tent in which they hold Caradoc is set over an outcrop of rock. They have him chained to it by neck and ankles. The only way you could free him would be to take a smith along who had time to break the iron. Eight legionaries sleep in there, two awake at all times. They sit with him, talking, or watching him sleep. His every move—every one—is accompanied." His eyes reflected more grief than Breaca had ever seen. He said, "I'm sorry. Tethis is right. There's no way to get him out."

"There must be. She just hasn't found it. Ask her how she knows this."

"I've already asked. She took him his meal. She spoke with him while he ate it." Ardacos paused. His gaze met Airmid's, Gwyddhien's, Braint's, before it would meet hers. Whatever he saw there gave him the strength he needed to continue. Looking finally at her, he said, "Tethis offered him death. It was all she could give. She has a knife and could have used it on him—and then herself—before the legionaries could reach her. For him, and for you, she would have done this."

Cold crushed her, black crawling ice that sucked heat from her body and the fire equally. It took more courage than she had ever known to ask, "Why did she not?"

"He forbade it. The Romans hold hostages. They have taken alive Cunomar and Cygfa, Dubornos and Cwmfen, and hold them in another place away from here. He has seen them, and they have let him speak briefly with Cwmfen, so that he knows she has not yet been harmed, but he doesn't know where they are now, or how Cygfa fares, or Cunomar."

Cunomar. Child of her heart, soft-haired spirit of the gods. She had imagined him safe with Dubornos, even now on Mona, guarding his sister against his mother's eventual return. Her mind protected her; reason rode over the all-engulfing pain. She said, "So if he dies, they will die; but they will die anyway. He should have taken what Tethis offered."

"No." Ardacos shook his head. He tried to speak and stopped and swallowed, and she had nearly reached for him to drag the words out when he said hoarsely, "It's far worse than that. If Caradoc dies, they will live, that's the promise. They will be taken to Rome and held for a lifetime in an underground prison, never seeing the light, nor free water, nor the rising of the moon. It was Cartimandua's idea. She knows that a warrior does not disdain to die, however appalling the circumstances, but that to be made to live in a house such as Rome builds, without sight of the earth, the sky, the stars, for a lifetime is unthinkable. They have promised him this, and he believes it. To buy their deaths, and his, by whatever means, he will stay alive."

Caradoc. Cunomar. Cygfa, who was her father born again as a woman. Numbly Breaca said, "They will crucify him. All of them. They will take them to Rome and make of it a spectacle. Five of them, one after the other, a day apart, with him last."

"Yes. He believes so."

It was too much. Pain rose in her like the bloating of decay. It grew up from her abdomen into her chest, eating the air until she breathed through a reed and barely that. It clamped round her neck, choking her, swelling her tongue and blocking her mouth. It rose up through her cheeks and blocked her tear ducts, depriving her even of the release of tears. Her mouth made the shape to say *Caradoc* and then *Cunomar,* and no sound came out.

Around her was silence. Nobody dared speak or had any idea what to say. Nothing could be said. A whispered voice she recognized later as her own said, "Hail was with them. He was guarding Cunomar."

Hail. Another in the litany of loss and death. Ardacos was weeping. She had never seen him weep. His tears fell where hers could not. Looking round, she saw it in all of them, in Airmid, Gwyddhien, Braint: a brightness of the eyes, running over in the firelight as sap from cut bark. Only Tethis, who had not known him, and whose stillness, whose pallor, was now given reason, did not weep. For her, because no one else would give it voice, Breaca said, "He was my war-hound. Hail. If Cunomar is taken, then he must be dead."

Tight-voiced, the girl said, "He is. I am to tell you he died in battle protecting Cunomar and that Dubornos sang the rites for him. It was his voice we heard in the valleys as we were leaving the battle of the salmon-trap."

I will unleash such vengeance . . . But what use is vengeance when the world is in ashes and all is lost? Her heart stopped. When it started again and she could speak, she said, "Who killed him, is it known?"

"The decurion of the Thracian cavalry. The one who rides the pied horse."

She had never known what it was truly to hate. She knew it then, perfect and pure and alive with its own meaning. She heard it clearly in her own voice saying, "Then he will die, and Scapula with him. They have not won. They will never win."

"Caradoc said you would say that. It was his message to you: never to let them win. And I was to tell you that he loved you, that you were his first thought and his last, for all time."

Section III

AUTUMN–WINTER A.D. 51

CHAPTER 18

"Breaca, you have to understand the dangers. This isn't battle; there is no possibility of an honourable death. If we're caught, Scapula will make examples of us that will rock the tribes from coast to coast, and if we succeed and get past his guards, the danger may be greater. What we are trying hasn't ever been done, and the gods may not condone it. We risk the loss of not only this life but all the ones still to come. You were in my dream, but these things are not fixed. You don't have to join us."

"Yes, I do. If there's a chance to bring Caradoc back, would the gods ask me to stay apart from it? I don't think so."

Breaca sat on a rotting stump on a river bank in the rain. A fire burned on the gravel near the water, the threading smoke lost in the spume from the waterfall behind. The vestiges of the sunset smeared old blood across the western horizon.

The world was full of blood and none of it hers. She had not been killed, or even lightly wounded, however often she threw herself at the enemy. Those fighting on both sides had come to believe her blessed by the gods. Her warriors followed her into ruinous danger, and most came out alive. Legionaries by the dozen had died on her blade, too weakened by fear to fight back properly. Ambushed auxiliary troops had been routed without engagement at the sight of her battle-mare. Assailed without respite, Scapula gathered his legions as a hen gathers her chicks and retreated step by bloodied step towards the safety of the fortress at Camulodunum. He had come to acknowledge the Boudica's existence, and to fear her, but not enough to release Caradoc and send him back to those who mourned his loss.

Scapula might have considered it, but the choice was no longer open to him. Spies from the eastern sea ports reported that Caradoc and his family had been sent by ship to Rome. Legionaries captured alive and questioned had confirmed it. Even if the governor had wanted to restore Caradoc to his people, the warrior and his family were in the emperor's hands and could not be called back.

The fire settled in on itself. Stinging smoke billowed. The waterfall churned in the pool and flowed on into the river. In the echoes of each, Breaca heard Caradoc's name, as she heard it daily in the clash of weapons and the screams of dying legionaries and the call of the crows on the battlefield. With time she did not doubt that it would drive her mad.

Airmid sat opposite on a river rock with her cloak pulled up round her hair. Beads of water stood proud on it, like sweat. Her face was too thin and too grey, but she would have stood out from the rest had it been any different. By night she tended the wounded and cleared a path to the gods for the dead and dying. By day, while the warriors slaughtered the legions in Caradoc's name, she searched the dream for ways to bring him home. Tonight it seemed she might have found one.

To hope was dangerous. The fragile balance of Breaca's mind depended on knowing that all hope was lost, but it was impossible not to clutch at the first thing offered. With her eyes on the fire, she said, "Tell me what you've seen."

Airmid picked a damp log from the pile around the fire and laid it on the flames. Water hissed and became steam. Through its cloud, she said, "Caradoc is in the emperor's hands; that is beyond question. To reach Claudius, we must go through Scapula. Nothing less will touch him; that, too, we have known since the first days outside the Brigante camp. Until now we have not found a means to come near the governor that was not a blatant, and worthless, act of suicide. Tonight we believe he has made a mistake. Ardacos's she-bears have been shadowing his retreat, and they report that his engineers have built their marching camp over the burial site of an ancestor-dreamer. Of us all, Luain mac Calma dreams most closely with the ancestors, and he has confirmed it."

"Whose grave is it?"

"I don't know. Luain can tell us nothing except that her mark is one of the earliest carved on the roof-beams of the greathouse in Mona. There is no standing stone, nor raised mound, but her bones and her dream-marks lie beneath the land at a crossing place of two trackways used by the ancestors. At any other time, it might not be of use to us, but tonight the old moon becomes new and Nemain's powers are at their height. I believe that with the god's aid we can enter the fort and reach Scapula."

"To kill him." Breaca said it flatly, not as a question.

Airmid exhaled slowly, thinking. She rarely took time to think before she spoke in Breaca's presence and only on matters that touched on her relationship with her god. She said, "Ultimately we will kill him, yes, but he must not die by the sword. If you are set on coming, you must swear to me that you will not cut his throat. He must die slowly, over days, or the dream will be broken and Caradoc will die at the emperor's decree in Rome."

Caradoc. Crucified. Cunomar, soft-haired child of the sea . . . Breaca dug her fingers into the rotting log and waited for a wave of nausea to pass. A weak, unwilling part of her grasped at the words and held them. When she could speak, she said, "But if I don't kill him and the dream is not broken, is there a chance that Caradoc and the children might live?"

Airmid nodded. "I believe there may be. Nothing is ever clear and this is more fog-bound than most, but yes, I think that's what the gods are showing me."

It was the barest fragment of a straw in the whirlpool of her drowning, and Breaca held on as if it were dry land. She said, "Then, for that alone, I swear that I will not kill Scapula. But I will come with you. No risk is so great that it's worth breaking the dream to escape it."

"You must become the elder grandmother, or as close to her as you can."

The fire was hotter, fed by dried yew and hawthorn with the berries still on the branch. The pool beneath the waterfall caught the flames and reflected them back, brighter. Between fire and water three dreamers, Airmid, Luain mac Calma, and Efnís of the Eceni, made a triangle and drew the shape of the new-old moon at their feet. Breaca stood in its centre, feeling small as a child and as nervous. Beyond, Ardacos and four of his she-bears waited naked in the dark. They had washed themselves clean of woad and smelled now only of bear-grease and white lime paint.

"The elder grandmother," said Airmid a second time. "*Our* elder grandmother. The first and the best. You have to call her to you and take on as much of herself as she will give."

"I don't remember her." Breaca felt like a child, but her memories were all recent ones of war and loss. Childhood was a world apart, lived by a stranger and reported only in songs. The elder grandmother had died on the day before Breaca returned from her long-nights and became a woman. Then her passing had seemed the worst disaster the world could offer. "I can't even remember what colour her eyes were."

"They were white when you knew her," said Airmid. "She was blind and the central part was wide with white at its core. The rim around it seemed black. She will be different now. You have to call her; you were her last dream. Do you still have the stone spear-head that you used to kill the eagle in your long-nights?"

"Yes." From her belt-pouch Breaca emptied onto her palm the cluttered treasure of her past: Cunobelin's seal ring, given with his oath to protect her; the serpent-spear brooch she had made and whose twin she had given to Caradoc; the hare's-foot from Hail's first kill for her; a lock of Cunomar's hair woven with a strand of mane from the grey battle-mare, made by her son to mark the day when he rode his first war-horse. All of these were from her adult life. From her childhood, she had kept only the flint spear-head made by the ancestors that had been Bán's gift for her long-nights.

She sifted the stone from the rest and held it out. The pale, milky flint subdued the firelight as it had always done. Smoke clung around it thickly, making her cough.

Airmid's voice was quietly insistent. "Look at the stone, Breaca. What does it look like?"

It looked like a flint arrow-head, fashioned by the ancestors. The chipped edges were as sharp as the day it had been made. Against all probability, fibres lingered on the narrowed haft where she had bound it to the grandmother's staff to use as a spear against the war-chief of the eagles. Brown blood-stains marbling the flint became redder, became fresh blood that spread out across the blue-ridged stone. The elder grandmother said, *Welcome home, warrior,* and laughed.

Airmid whispered, "Go to her, Breaca; find her for me," and somewhere mac Calma and Efnís echoed, but their voices came late and were distant whispers from another time; the dream had already claimed her.

The old woman was different, as Airmid had said she would be. The elder grandmother had been blind in the years when Breaca-the-child had been her eyes and limbs, following in Airmid's footsteps. The grandmother now had eyes bright as a hawk's and as sharp. She stood upright, not stooped, and there was no pain in her limbs to prevent her from walking unaided. Her hair was silver-white and did not thin across the crown as it had. Only her face was the same, the skin wrinkled as the hawthorn berries Airmid had laid across the fire. Her eyes, astoundingly, were brown; Breaca had always imagined them grey, like her father's.

The grandmother laughed, a sound to crawl under the skin of a child and make her search her conscience for guilt. "You should eat more," she said. "And stop grieving. He is not dead yet, the one for whom you kill but shed no tears."

That was unfair. Breaca had tried to weep. For nights she had sat with the embers of dying fires, waiting for the explosion of grief that must come, as it had for Macha and her father. All she had found was a cold, limitless anger that drove her to kill and to go on killing and the despair that followed. Neither gave any sense of release.

"You grieve rightly for the dead," said the grandmother. "It is due them and honours their passing. There is no reason to grieve for the living."

I could not be sure he was living, Breaca said in her mind, but it was not true; to the ends of the earth she believed she would know when Caradoc died. Aloud she said, "Is he whole and safe?"

"Who?"

"Caradoc. Who else?"

"Your son, perhaps, or the singer?" The grandmother capered, cackling. Her humour had always been terrifying. Death had not mellowed it. "Dubornos is well. He dreams of Airmid." She grinned and cocked her head to one side, bright as a thrush. "Caradoc has not yet been harmed," she said. "He fears for you and for your son."

"Can we help him?"

"I don't know. Can you? Shall we ask the gods?" Unusually limber, the grandmother crouched on her haunches before the fire. Reaching into the heat, she stirred it with her finger. When the logs fell and resettled, she studied them, reading futures in falling ash. Nodding and mumbling, she rose and walked past a stiffly silent Luain mac Calma to wade into the river. The water was cold—Breaca had washed in it earlier. Unhesitating, the grandmother walked in until the sleek black water lapped at the sag of her breasts. Leaning forward, she breathed on the sleek mirror-surface and polished it with the heel of her hand, the better to admire her reflection.

"I don't know," she said again, more slowly. Raising her head, she looked directly at Breaca. Her eyes shone with the light of fire on water. "Would you rather have him dead and safely in the care of Briga, or alive, knowing that you would never see him again?"

Breaca stared. The words swept through her head and made no sense. She said, "I don't understand."

The old woman nodded. The capering lunacy of earlier was gone. She was serious as she had rarely been in life and then only in the presence of death. She said, "The future is not set, it never is. It may be that Caradoc dies, but there is a chance he may survive. If he dies, you will at least know where he is. If he lives, you may not."

"Is the choice mine?"

"It may not be. But you should know which you prefer in case you are asked."

It was a riddle. The dreamers set them to each other in the dark of a winter's night on Mona, but the promise of life never hung on the answer, nor the gift of death.

Which is worse: to live when life is unbearable, or to die too soon while the heart-flame still burns?

Which is better: to die and escape the threatened pains of gods and men, or to live to see the beauty of another dawn?

Who has the right to make the choice for another?

No one.

The world opened at her feet and gave no answers. With the words dry as bone in her mouth, Breaca said, "I can't choose. It's not my place to decide for him."

Encased up to her neck in freezing water, the elder grandmother shook her head. "Of course not. The gods decide, and those whose souls are held in balance, but still they—and you—must know which you would choose. We cannot go on else."

The night waited. Three dreamers stood around the fire who nightly crossed the boundaries between the worlds. None of them offered help, nor could she ask it.

A lifetime passed and another. She had never thought herself indecisive. *Beloved—what would you ask of me?*

She did not hear his voice; she had not heard it since the day he took Sorcha's ferry and left Mona, but the answer came nonetheless, with the cadence of his speech and the certainty of his memory. She said, "I would want what is best for Caradoc, whether he can be with me or not. If he lives, I will get word of him and he of me. There is no one can deny us that."

The grandmother waded from the water. She smelled strongly of woad. "A good choice," she said. "The pain, then, will be yours as much as his, possibly more so. But it may be that something can be returned to you. Only the gods know that."

"How do we make it happen?"

"Follow me. Do as I do and exactly as I say. Ask no questions and trust those who walk with you, however they seem. They are the men and women you know them to be."

The trackway lay bright in the heather, lit by a moon Breaca could not see. The flint arrow-head was hot, as if recently pulled from the fire. She held it tightly so that the flaked edges bit into her palm. The elder grandmother walked ahead, her head high, her hair alive with the same light as lit the path. Breaca came behind and then Airmid. Efnís and Luain mac Calma had remained at the fire to hold the dreaming and guide them home.

On either side, the men and women of the she-bear shuffled high-kneed through the heather. They wore bear-skins in a way Breaca had never seen before: wrapped round so that man became bear and bear became man. Their eyes were small and dangerous and their breath was fetid. Ardacos had smiled at her and Breaca had believed his teeth long and white. It was the gods' work, clearly. The elder grandmother had grabbed her arm and pulled her away before she could ask him how it had been done.

The she-bears had been forbidden to walk on the trackway. As they came closer to the fort, they dropped onto all fours and ran on ahead towards the timbered stockade and ditch that surrounded Scapula's marching camp.

Each Roman night-camp was the same; built in the evening and removed again the next day, leaving only stake holes, a ditch, and the latrines as evidence of its presence. In their uniformity was their strength. Each man knew his place and his duties; but the enemy, too, after the first few attacks, knew exactly the placement of gates and defences. The she-bears ran for the southern ditch, the one closest to the ancestor's track. The sentries on the inside would have to be blind drunk and stupid not to smell them as they came. Breaca grasped the stone spear-head and regretted again that she had not brought her sword.

"Get down."

"What?"

The elder grandmother hissed her impatience. "Get down, here, while they make the rampart safe. Get down in the heather and crawl."

Breaca felt the old woman's hand in the small of her back, shoving her down until she lay on her belly and squirmed forward like a snake. Heather roots reared up on either side, tall as corn. They scratched at her arms, drawing blood. The earth smelled of old fox-dirt and the mellow,

almost sweet musk of a snake. Something slid past her in the star-lit darkness, dry against the skin of her forearm. She pressed her head into the
dirt, breathing through a wave of panic. Behind her, she felt the elder
grandmother smirk.

A man died on the southern rampart of the fort, and another. Breaca
saw their souls walk ahead of her on the track, lost and alone. She would
have called to them out of pity, but the elder grandmother held her
mouth. Her voice was a rustle of heather. "Quiet, child. Would you have
them know we are here?"

She would not. A legion and a full wing of cavalry camped in that
fort, and she approached it unarmed with a dead grandmother as her
guide. The images of what Scapula did to captured dreamers came vividly
to mind. Crucifixion would be better. She moved more quietly and ignored the mounting number of things that moved with her.

On her left, a she-bear grunted, and she heard Ardacos's reply. He had
been her lover once; she would have known his voice anywhere, even when
he was most fully a bear. Three more legionaries died, not knowing their
assailants. The night became crowded with lost souls.

They crossed the rampart in a line, following the bane-moon track.
Ardacos had placed a log across the ditch and pulled down the three-
pronged stakes that guarded it. Within, bodies of men in full armour lay
scattered to either side, their necks broken and their throats ripped in a
way that did not speak of edged weapons. Through the rest of the camp,
old fires burned dimly before tents pitched in perfect rows and columns;
Rome slept, as it lived, in straight lines that numbed the spirit.

The elder grandmother guided Breaca past sleeping men. Airmid followed. The she-bears were shadows on either side, ahead and behind.
Other things moved in the dark, and it was better not to ask what they
were.

Quietly the grandmother said, "The governor's tent is in the centre,
on the main path. He has pitched it over the grave of the serpent-dreamer.
She is angry and disturbs his sleep. Airmid will disturb it more."

Breaca stopped still on the track. "How do you know she's a serpent-
dreamer?"

"I know everything." The grandmother was scathing. "Why else do
you think you're here?"

"That's it. In the centre, where the other trackway meets ours."

The second track passed from east to west, darker than the surrounding night; amazing that the legion's engineers had not seen it. The governor's tent, placed directly over the crossing point, was twice as large as those close by and many times the size of those that sheltered the sleeping legionaries. Six men guarded it, three facing inward, three out. Two more patrolled the margins. Unlike the sentries on the ditch, none of these were half asleep. To get past them, all must die in the same breath. The she-bears hovered, awaiting orders, but even god-driven they were too few to achieve it without uproar.

The grandmother shook her head. To Ardacos, she said, "Not now. These are not for you. Keep watch for others and stop them if they come. Remember not to step on the trackways."

Breaca asked, "How do we reach Scapula?"

"Airmid knows," said the grandmother.

"She does not."

The words came from behind. Breaca turned. Airmid stood away from the grandmother, her feet lined carefully on the dark moon's track. Her eyes were widely black, staring at the elder grandmother. "You didn't tell me it was the serpent-dreamer," she said. "I've met her before; she guards the oldest of the ancestors' sacred places on Mona. She is not safe."

"Did you ask for safety when you called the dreaming? I never heard it." The grandmother smiled blandly. "Are you afraid, Airmid of Nemain?"

There was a gap, which lengthened. The night became crisp. Airmid said, "Yes."

Impossible. Airmid feared nothing and no one.

The grandmother nodded. "Good. It's time you remembered the humility of that. Even so, you must find a means to make this work, or we return whence we came with nothing achieved but ten dead men."

There were not yet ten men dead. Nobody said so.

It seemed, for a moment, as if they might turn back. Breaca said, "Airmid, if it can be done no other way, the she-bears and I will attack the governor's tent. I have not come this far to turn back."

"You would die."

"I know, but we might kill—"

"No, you would die before you ever reached the tent, and your soul would be held for ever by the ancestor. This is not warrior's work." Airmid spoke to Breaca sharply, but her eyes were on the elder grandmother, engaged in another, deeper dialogue.

Answering it aloud, the elder grandmother said, "Your warrior carries the serpent-woman's spear-head, and she fights under her mark. Is there not something in that you could trust?"

Tonelessly Airmid said, "I didn't know it was the mark of that ancestor." She chewed on her lower lip. Presently she said, "Breaca, with the stone spear-head, do you carry also the brooch in the shape of your serpent-spear, twin to the one you gave Caradoc?"

"Yes."

Once again Breaca sifted through the contents of her pouch. The brooch seemed small on her palm. Years ago she had carved the wood for the mould and cast it herself in silver. Her father had been alive then and had helped her. Two months' work had gone into its making, and she had thought it the best she could ever create. The double-headed serpent coiled back on itself, looking to the future and the past. The war-spear crossed and recrossed, pointing to paths in other worlds. Two threads in scarlet hung from the lower loop, first evidence of Caradoc's love. The light of the old gods' moon washed over it, turning scarlet to black, for death.

"He loved you then and does so still." The elder grandmother said it. She sounded oddly peaceful. "Remember that now. Give it to Airmid with your spear-head, and hold on to the memory of times when the serpent was not looped in black."

It was hard enough for Breaca to relinquish the stone spear-head that had become her talisman and her only weapon. Giving up the brooch also, it was almost impossible to remember a time when the red thread had been new and the love it signalled fresh and unexplored.

"Think." The elder grandmother stood behind Breaca with her hands on her shoulders. "Think of the sea, and a boy washed up in a storm. Think of a river, and another, and another, and another."

Breaca had not thought before that the moments of greatest joy with Caradoc, at least in the early days, had come beside water. With that reminder, it was easier. She was a girl again and dreamed a storm that broke a ship on a headland. In the flotsam lay a corn-haired youth, not quite drowned. His waking smile slipped into her soul.

Storm water had washed them together. In the river of the Eceni, winter meltwater nearly killed them again. Caradoc's face rose above it, laughing. *We can't rescue each other . . . not the point.* He submerged again and came up in the spring, dry and dressed for travel. A cap hid the brightness of his hair, and his cloak was dullest brown. She gave him a serpent-spear brooch cast in silver, the mark of her dreaming. No red thread bound it yet; she had not dared acknowledge the feeling. Still, Caradoc had known it for what it was and had taken it, staring into the river water. Bán had been alive then, and had understood.

In late summer, with Bán long dead, the red threads hung limp as Caradoc's voice said, *I still have the brooch. Whatever happens, it still means what it did.*

Soon after, his daughter was born to another woman and she hated him for it, because hate was safer than love. Autumn brought them close in battle, with love and hate put aside to defend a greater need. In the middle part, with death on all sides, the red threads bound them and they made a child. The river had sung over the sound of their loving.

"We thought we could win then," said Breaca.

Somewhere close the elder grandmother said, "You can still win. Nothing is fixed. The gods do not create their people only to destroy them."

"What must we do?"

"If you can destroy Scapula, that will be a good start."

Airmid said, "Breaca? Can you walk with me? We need to go round behind the governor's pavilion. Here . . . take back the brooch. Use it to hold on to the memories. They are our gift to the ancestor-dreamer. If you can keep them strong, we'll be safe. Come now. I'll guide your steps."

Caradoc was with her, a summer Caradoc, soon after Graine's birth. They walked together, parents and child, in the circle of stones set by the ancestors. Hail ran ahead, hunting. In the Roman camp, Airmid guided her a long way round, past sleeping men, to the rear of the governor's tent. Patrolling sentries passed them, not looking into shadows. The serpent-spear brooch was matte and dull. Only the red thread glowed with its own life, heart bound to heart, bloody in the dark.

They stopped at the back of the pavilion. Airmid counted aloud softly. Breaca said, "What?" The single word slurred.

Airmid said, "The guards walk at the same pace and stop together in front of the tent. They will be away for three hundred heartbeats. If I can go in and come out in that time, we are safe."

The magnitude of the risk came to Breaca. "I should do this," she said.

"No. You swore to me you would not. Just hold the brooch and hold on to the memories of life, not of death. It will be harder than you imagine."

The sentries passed again. The skin of the tent hung loosely pale. Airmid said, "Now," and stepped up to it. The guards heard nothing and did not turn.

It will be harder than you imagine.

The flint spear-head cut the side of the tent as cleanly as any knife, slitting down from knee height to the turf below. The she-bears entered legionary tents in this way, reaching in to cut the throats of the sleeping occupants. Dead men filled Breaca's mind. White flesh and the froth of a last breath choked her. With an effort, she recalled Ardacos's bear-dance on Mona, in the days when she had believed that he or Gwyddhien would be Warrior. Caradoc had been there. She fought to bring the shape of his face to mind, to lay it over the many kills of the she-bears. When that failed, she remembered Graine, who was alive and free, and then created Caradoc around the child, holding her. His smile came last. She tried to rebuild the fire in his eyes as he smiled at her.

Grey. They are grey, the colour of clouds after rain, and the left one droops slightly, from a sword-cut to the brow, where an auxiliary struck down, backhanded, before Gwyddhien killed him. The man had pale red hair, and when he died, he . . . Grey. Caradoc's eyes are grey, the colour of clouds . . .

"Are you sure they were not black? They would be better black, for vengeance." The voice was older than the elder grandmother's could ever be. It offered an opening and a path forward without resistance. "Black," said the ancestor. "Vengeance is black. Is that not what you want?"

"Love is red." That voice was Airmid's, faint. "The threads of the serpent-brooch were red, for love."

The ancestor laughed softly. The sound was a snake, smoothing through grass. "But your warrior has not killed this past month for love. Each man slain has gone to the otherworld with her hate carved on his soul. Even those who wander godless and lost tonight know the name of the one for whom they died. The warrior knows that, if you don't."

The ancestor's voice carried more power than the others. She alone knew the reality by which Breaca lived. "Vengeance," she said, and the word was a gift. "If you want me to kill for you, should the governor, too, not go slowly to his death knowing for whom he dies and why?" An image of Scapula came clear in the dark, racked by endless pain. "Is this not what you crave?"

"Yes."

"Would this not let you rest if it came to pass?"

No. The elder grandmother answered before Breaca could, or it may have been Airmid, or perhaps the two were one. *We want Caradoc alive, and the children, only that.*

It was not true. It could not be made to be true. For two months, Breaca had lived on the need for revenge. It was not possible so suddenly to let it go. She felt the suck of the ancestor and the loosening hold of the elder grandmother.

"Black," said the ancestor. She spoke past Breaca to the elder grandmother, as an adult speaks to a child. "Black is not for vengeance alone, but for all death. It is not wrong to crave the death of another, only to deny what you need. You should know that. Let the warrior give me the black, and I will do what she and you both want."

"Breaca, no." Airmid spoke clearly. "Think of Caradoc without the hate. It is not wrong to hate, but it's wrong to call him back on the strength of it. If he's to live, he must live free of the taint of vengeance, or it will destroy him. Think of him as you would have him live. A lifetime's love should not be overshadowed by a month of hate."

She tried. In the darkness she did her best to build Caradoc, layer by layer, striving to make him brighter, more alluring than the promise of Scapula's dying. A lifetime's love should not be overshadowed by anything, but she had hated Rome for as long as she had loved Caradoc. Love and hate combined were the foundation on which she fought and lived and breathed, and she did not have the power to pull them apart.

Think only of Caradoc, whispered the elder grandmother, and, weeping, Breaca said, "I can't." The darkness drew her in, and the image of Scapula dying, and ten years of certainty wanting him dead as much as ever she wanted Caradoc back, alive. Hate was easier than love, and hurt less, and she could have it here, now, without the terrors and impossibility of hope. The ancestor beckoned, and Breaca, only partly unwilling, followed into a place that was for ever black.

"Bán's eyes were black. You loved him once. Think of him." The new voice was Macha's, mother to Bán. Always, she had the power to command. Now she offered a lifeline and did not allow it not to be taken.

Breaca reached for it, striving to remember. *Bán's eyes were black, resonant, like the hide of a black horse, or a lake in the night, or a crow's wing at the shoulder, where the colour is most dense. They were charcoal and jet, and he did not live for revenge but—* "Bán's dead," she said aloud. "Why would the ancestor want him?"

"He is who he is. He is the red and the black together. Trust me. Remember all of him. Call him." The ancestor spoke with Macha, and the two together were unassailable; no one living could withstand them.

Breaca was not a dreamer; she had no training in the calling back of those who had gone to be with Briga. Knowing nothing else, she drew together the many memories of her brother and breathed them to life.

A small boy sat opposite her in the women's place, grieving over a near-dead hound puppy. His hair was the same colour as his eyes, and both reflected the fire of women's dreaming. "His name is Hail," he said. "I can heal him. Let me try."

In a whelping hut in Cunobelin's dun, an older Bán, and wiser, sat opposite Amminios and challenged him to a game of Warrior's Dance with the slave-boy Iccius as the winner's prize. He had fought the game as he later fought the battle, with the fire of absolute purpose and an intelligence that outplayed a man whose life had been spent in games and hard-fought wagers. Her pride had matched her love for him, both of them overwhelming.

Bán's eyes were black, like the night, and shining. Caradoc had stood beside her. It was easier to remember him now. *Caradoc's eyes are grey, the colour of clouds after rain.*

"Breaca? Breaca, will you come back with me? The sentries are returning; we must be gone."

She did not remember running, although her heaving chest told her that she must have done so. On the far side of the rampart, loping back along the trackway, she said, "You didn't tell me I was calling him."

Airmid was walking behind. She said, "I told you as much as was safe. If you had known, would it have made it any easier to fight the ancestor?"

"I would not let you go into battle unarmed."

"You were not unarmed, and you were not unsupported. You did what you had to do as well as you could do it. It was enough. We're both alive."

"Did it work? Did you kill Scapula?"

"No, but the serpent-dreamer infests his dreams and will continue to haunt him when he wakes. I do not believe a man can survive long under such assault. He will sicken and die, or he will kill himself. He will be dead by the next old moon."

They were alone. The she-bears had left them at the start of the trackway. The elder grandmother had not followed them from the governor's tent. Her absence left a gap that let the wind through.

Airmid said, "I had to leave your brooch on Scapula to bind the dreamer. I'm sorry, but the threads were red when I left it, not black, and they will remain so."

"Then they were red for Bán, not for Caradoc."

"I know. The gods look over these things, in ways we cannot. Macha was there, and she can be trusted to know what is needful. We never found Bán's soul after Amminios took his body. It may be that the serpent-dreamer has access to places we do not and can bring him back into Briga's care. We can pray so."

"To whom do we pray?"

"To Nemain. The other gods will hear it."

There was no moon; there never had been, but the trackway had lit the route to the fort. Returning, the gods withdrew their light and the night deepened to black. Breaca led by feel, slowly, pushing across the moorland where the heather and bracken were least. Night beasts shadowed them, fewer than there had been, but more than other nights; a vixen barked and cubs answered from either side; an owl screamed, the high note that cuts through sleep; far back, near the fort, a bear yammered over a kill.

Breaca stopped. "That's Ardacos."

Airmid said, "Don't turn back," and pushed hard on her shoulder.

Together they walked through the night, blindly.

They reached a small cliff with no way round but to climb down. Lowering herself from an uncertain ledge, Breaca realized she could see her hands in front of her face. On the solid ground beneath, she could see her feet. "Dawn's coming," she said.

"I know." Airmid climbed nimbly. "We have to be at the fire before the first edge of the sun rises over the horizon. Can you walk faster?"

They walked faster, and when they could properly see their feet and the paths winding through the knotted heather, they ran. Mist rose to greet the morning, great blankets drifting over the moor. On the eastern horizon, the morning star rose and sparked fuzzily. Far ahead the light of a dying fire burned red against the paling light. Two figures sat hunched beside it, wrapped against a night's cold. One of them waved urgently.

"Faster," said Airmid.

They ran, careless of the footing, and crossed the river on slippery stones. Luain mac Calma sat on the rotting log before the fire. He did not rise to greet them but lifted his head as they crashed across the rocks. A decade's ageing creased his face and cleared slowly as he looked at them and beyond to the growing light of the dawn. Blinking, he rubbed his face.

"You're back," he said.

He was among the most eloquent of dreamers; when he chose, he could fill a night with rhetoric and have words to spare. He stretched his legs and laid one last branch on the fire. Autumn leaves crisped in the heat but did not burn. Leaning in, he blew until a nascent flame snaked up to catch the lowest leaf.

When it had burned fully to ash, he said, "It would seem there are good reasons why that has never been done. I would suggest we do not attempt it again."

"Did you think us lost to the serpent-dreamer?" asked Airmid.

"You were lost, that was beyond doubt. The question was what parts of you she would give back again." He looked at them, squinting. "Not everything, it seems."

Efnís roused more slowly and walked to the river to wash his arms and face. By the fire again, he spat on his palms and rubbed them together, then reached out and touched a hand each to Airmid and Breaca, reaching up to the brow above the eyes. Feeling heat in his hand, Breaca flinched. Luain mac Calma grasped her shoulders. "Don't move."

It was hard not to move. Efnís's hands scorched her skin. Voices seeped through his fingers. Light flared and was still, and it was not of the rising sun. The elder grandmother laughed, and an older voice joined hers and rang like flint on iron.

Two speaking as one said, "Your time is ours, warrior. When we have need of you, we will call."

Something stung above Breaca's eyes and made her blink. Luain mac Calma stood before her. His knife was of bronze and sharp on both edges. With its tip he had cut where Efnís's hand had been. A bead of blood wept into her left eye and stung a second time. With her own hand, Breaca wiped it away. The day brightened and the mist cleared as if it had never been. The leaking voices died.

From the fire, standing tall with her back to the flaring sun, Airmid said, "Welcome back. If the gods are with us, we will bring Caradoc home as safely."

CHAPTER 19

By order of the emperor, Tiberius Claudius Drusus Nero Germanicus Britannicus, conveyed through his freedman Narcissus, two ocean-going grain cargo vessels sailed from the mouth of the largest eastern river in the north of the province of Britannia. His Imperial Majesty was fully aware of the extreme risk of an ocean crossing, having experienced the wrath of the autumn storms in his single sea voyage during the conquest of Britannia. To minimize this risk, the two ships sailed three days apart, at times considered auspicious by both augurs and seamen. They took the long sea route round the south coast of the island and down the western side of Gaul, to pass east again between the Iberian peninsula and the northern coast of Mauretania on a course straight for Italy. They docked at night and in secrecy at the Roman port of Ostia, recently re-engineered and made safe by the actions of the same emperor.

Each ship was met at the docks by a half-century of the first cohort, the Batavian horse-guards, hand-picked for their unswerving loyalty to their emperor and, importantly, their well-tested ability to keep their counsel while blind drunk. The escort brought a covered grain cart in which the human cargo was transported the eighteen miles to Rome and thence, under cover of darkness, to a secure annexe of the servants' quarters at the imperial palace on the Palatine Hill. They were met by the former slave Narcissus and two other freedmen: Callistus, who had charge of the public treasury, and Polybius, religious secretary and favourite of the Empress Agrippina. On the second occasion, medical help was sought. After due consideration and on Narcissus's express command, the emperor's physician, Xenophon of Cos, was woken and required to attend certain of the emperor's newly arrived prisoners. His subsequent advice was followed to the letter. In the imperial palace, neither the freedmen's nor the doctor's word was law, but both assumed a close approximation.

Dubornos surfaced slowly from dense, unpleasant dreams in which he strove to reach the gods and could not find them. The space they had oc-cupied in his soul was empty, like a house not lately used, and he was alone outside it, calling. He lay still on a pallet of hard wood and brought his mind back to the world around him. For a while, he wondered that the sea had become so still and the taunting gulls so silent. His mind still rocked in nauseating rhythm, but his body failed to follow. His body, instead, no-ticed other things in the stillness: he was in pain, but less than he had been; he was no longer naked, and his wrists, ankles, and neck were un-shackled; the air no longer stank of raw and rotting sewage but of dust and damp plaster and an ointment made from olive oil. Flexing his fin-gers, he found that the pressure on his forearms came from bandages, not iron, and he remembered the hands of the doctor who had applied both ointment and linen. The man had been skilled, had worked with intelli-gent compassion on the ulcerating sores on ankles, wrists, and collarbones where the shackles had chafed. Afterwards there had been hot food, which had been welcome, and wine, which was less so.

In an earlier, easier part of his life, Dubornos had pledged never to drink wine, but then he had pledged also to give his life defending the children of the Boudica from death or captivity and had failed compre-hensively to do so; drinking the gift of the enemy had seemed a small oath-breaking after that. The wine had contained other things besides grapes. He remembered the bitter-spice taint of poppy on the back of his tongue and then the dreams. Swimmingly, they claimed him again.

The lamps had been relit next time he woke, and their steady light made it easier to grasp consciousness and hold it. The dullness had been a blessing; for a fleeting beautiful moment, he was alert and free and could remember who he was, if not where and why. Then the accumulated mem-ories of the past fifteen days returned all at once with terrifying clarity. He lay still, watching the unforgiving black behind his closed lids, and tried to breathe evenly through waves of nauseating fear. A groan rose un-bidden from deep in his chest, and he stifled it against clenched teeth, grimacing afterwards in the gloom, a half-grin of self-congratulation, as if so small an act of defiance were a victory in itself.

He breathed deeply, striving for calm. He was Dubornos mac Sinochos, warrior of the Eceni and of Mona; he would not display fear

in the presence of the enemy. More than that, he was a singer of the first
degree; death was his ally. In his training he had passed the singers' final
test, had lain in an oak casket while Maroc, Airmid, and Luain mac Calma
packed him about with earth and lowered him into the pit he himself had
dug. For three days and nights he had lain still, buried alive in a simula-
tion of death so complete that the boundaries between this world and the
other had blurred to nothing. When, at moonrise on the evening of the
third day, they had exhumed him, he had not wanted to come back. Briga
by then was his friend, the death she offered his closest companion. In the
eternity of darkness, he had walked again and again along the uncounted
paths taken by the souls of the dead in their journey between this world
and the other and had found in the walking a peace he had never encountered in life.

Airmid had worked alone with him for two days to bring him fully
back. The closeness to her and the pain it brought were, he thought, part
of the reason he had not wanted to return. He had wanted Luain mac
Calma or Maroc or Efnís to take her place, but none had done so, and he
had resented all of them for it. Later, in the small moments of profound
joy that gave colour to his life, he had begun to understand the depth of
love she had given him in those two nights and to feel grateful.

In the early part she had made him sit up and talk, endlessly, of their
shared childhood. He had fought that; Briga was less heartless. He had
been shocked to find Airmid's will stronger than his and the god's combined. She had wound him in a thread of remembrance and sage smoke
and refused to let him go. Later they had walked alone together in the low
hills of Mona, and she had made him eat whatever they found that was
yellow, the colour of sun and day and life. It was high summer, and the
wind-coarsened turf had been alive with yellows. He had tasted flowers
and fungi he was sure were poisonous, and yet he had not died. Later still
she had made him bathe in a small craggy pool at the foot of a waterfall
and had joined him in the chill water, holding his naked body to hers, and
his heart had broken and a dam inside him with it, so that he wept tears
that matched the flow of the river until there were no more tears to come.
Afterwards he had slept chaste at her side, fulfilling in part the dream of
a lifetime.

He had woken with his head on her knees, both of them dressed. Her
fingers teased out the tangles in his hair. Her voice had the deep, rever-
berating tones of the god.

"It is not death that you fear, son of Sinochos, whatever your body
may have told you in the terror of your first battle—it is life. To be a true

singer, you must bridge the river and stand evenly on both sides; one foot must be in life to balance the one that stands in death. It is as sacred to sing the newly born into this world as the newly dead into the other. Both must be done with equal heart. Can you do that?"

She was beautiful—he had always thought so—even when they were scrape-kneed children and she with the green frog tattooed on her arm that marked her as mad. In the evening light, she was Nemain, come alive and smiling. He had not believed what she said; he lived daily with the shame that fear of death had brought on him, but he had smiled back and said, "I can try."

He had done his best in the four years since but had not always succeeded. On the mountainside above the Valley of the Lame Hind, he told himself he had chosen life only because he had believed it would help Caradoc to win final victory if he knew his children were alive. Selfishly he had also yearned to see the reaction of the cavalry decurion when Caradoc rode at the head of Venutios's three thousand warriors to crush the tattered remains of Scapula's legions. In the vast, cluttered camp of the Brigantes, faced first with Cartimandua, who had threatened a life that was far worse than death, and then with Caradoc, shackled and bloody, Dubornos had felt his detachment and the strength it gave him begin to waver. In the long spaces of tedium between one humiliation and the next, the singer had begun to recognize the truth in Airmid's words, that death had never been his fear, but that what unmanned him, what left him weak-limbed and sobbing with terror, was the prospect of the last long-drawn moments of life that led up to it.

He was not alone. A warrior can maintain an outward impression of composure, even of humour, in the face of danger, but no one yet living can control his bowels. In the Brigantes' camp, there had been some pretence at privacy, and in theory at least a man could keep the rancid fluctuations of each morning's movements to himself. On the ship, such dignity had been lost. They had been separated from Caradoc; he had been transported on an earlier ship, and for all they knew, he could have been already dead. Without him Dubornos and Cwmfen, Cygfa and Cunomar had lived for uncounted days in the lightless, rat-ridden bilges of a merchant ship, sleeping on fetid planking, feeding and drinking at the whim of the auxiliaries who were their guards, and feeling their way to the slop buckets afterwards.

There had been no need to speak of it, but the two adults, if not the children, had known from the beginning that the aching, mind-numbing terror was not theirs alone and had taken some strength from the knowledge. On the first night, as the ship fell quiet, Dubornos had slept with an ear to the wooden hull listening to Manannan of the oceans whisper and rush less than an arm's length away and had prayed to the god in the silence of his heart that the gift of oblivion might claim them all.

They had nearly lost Cunomar, although not to the sea-god. The boy had begun to vomit as they passed down the Gaulish coast, but when he began to pass bloody, fluid faeces, they realized he was afflicted by more than seasickness. The ship's doctor was an army man, bluntly efficient but with a limited supply of medications. Nevertheless he had done his best. His orders had been unambiguous: he was to deliver his prisoners alive to the emperor's justice. The cost to his own person if he failed was unthinkable.

With this in mind, he had provided the powdered elm bark and poppy to stop the vomiting and diarrhoea and had brought them fresh water with his own hands. At Dubornos's suggestion, he had ordered their slop buckets emptied twice daily and had them moved up to one of the mid-level decks to a holding room with a hatch that could be opened for air and light.

Light and air: gifts beyond imagining that had once been taken for granted. For the first time in days, they had smelled the salt sea in all its dizzying purity. The sharpness had made them sneeze, and sneezing re-woke the shackle-sores on their necks. They wept in silence, hiding their tears from one another, as if such things still mattered. The light, then, was a mixed blessing. The darkness had hidden the suppurating ulcers beneath the irons, the skeletal thinness of the children—so much weight lost in so little time—the depth of care etched on the faces of the adults. Presently they took turns lying with their heads beneath the hatch, staring up at the changing sky because anything was better than looking at what they had become. In the evening, when it could be hidden no longer, Dubornos had learned what Cygfa and Cwmfen had been keeping from him, that the girl had begun her bleeding as they rounded the south-westerly point of the Iberian peninsula and was in transition to becoming a woman.

The news had been devastating. When he thought he could sink no lower, the gods proved him wrong. From the moment of their capture, Cygfa had followed the lead of her parents in displaying an unimpeachable dignity. Only twice had it faltered when, first in the Brigante camp and then again on the boat, a clerk of the legions had asked her outright if she was a virgin. In their presence, she had said nothing, staring over their heads with a frozen disdain that left them silent. Neither had pressed the question, and the girl's reaction afterwards, the pallor and shaking, had gone unseen by the enemy.

The fact of her coming to adulthood was similarly concealed, but its impact was as damaging to her soul as the flux was to her brother's body. Dubornos had offered to do what he could. As a singer, it was in his power to begin the opening rites of the long-nights, the passage from childhood to adulthood, and he was prepared, in the absence of any other, to do his best to achieve the full ceremony. It would not be as it should be, but he had believed that, with Cwmfen's help, he could bring about a true dreaming and the girl could go to sleep as a child and awaken a woman with at least some ghosted whisper from the gods. Cygfa had refused with the same cool restraint with which she had spoken to the legions' clerks, and Dubornos had not pressed his offer twice. Instead he had watched her retreat into herself, building a shell against the outer world. It had seemed effective, and he had admired her fortitude. He did so still, although the unbending fragility of it frightened him more than if she had wept.

The ultimate test had come much later, in a poorly lit sanatorium in the emperor's palace, when Polybius, the religious secretary, had asked Cygfa for a third time if she retained her maidenhood. This man was not a clerk of the legions but one of the half-dozen most powerful men in the land. His orders could be rescinded only by the emperor, who was in bed. When his question was met by the same silence, Polybius had snapped his fingers and ordered the doctor to examine her.

Clearly unwilling, Xenophon, the Greek physician, had done so on a pallet in the presence of armed guards and her mother. Cygfa had not fought him, nor had she wept, even when the physician had pronounced her intact in front of the assembled guards, clerks, and freedmen, but Dubornos, turning back from his fixed study of the depiction of Io on the opposite wall, believed he had seen a small part of the fire in her snuffed out and feared he would never see it lit again. Soon after, the wine had been offered, and he had drunk it, craving forgetfulness.

A singer lives by sound first and all other senses second. Thus even while the memory of Cygfa's blue-white face knotted his bowels, Dubornos was listening, sorting the murmurs of the coming morning from those around him. Without opening his eyes, he established that he was in a small cramped room that was neither the sanatorium in which Cunomar had been treated and Cygfa dishonoured by the doctor, nor the underground holding cell to which they had first been brought. The former had been near the main part of the palace, and the floors had been smoothly marbled, so that sound reflected from them like light. The latter had been tight and airless, and the single lamp had guttered noisily and had clearly done so for years, so that the walls were grey with soot and the air smelled of rancid sheep's fat.

In this new place, the bricks of the wall were so close that the wash of his breath came back to lift his own hair. The muted crackle of burning charcoal to his left and right spoke of at least two braziers alight in the corners. The lamps above were filled with finer oil and had recently been lit with flint and tinder; the sharp smell of it lingered.

The only door was behind him and to the right. Two guards stood there. The one on the left suffered from impacted sinuses and breathed with a whistle, while the other maintained the drifting inhalations of near-sleep. They were horse-guards, the vast Germanic tribesmen who wore their hair tied in a warrior's knot over the left ear. Their reputation had spread to Mona as the men who had carried Claudius to power and ensured that he kept it. The Romans considered them dull-witted but feared them as barely controllable savages. Having watched them through part of the previous evening, Dubornos believed both assessments to be reasonable and accurate.

He was about to turn over when he heard the slow, still breath of a man sitting awake and alert on the opposite side of the room. Two in-breaths later, he knew who it was.

"Caradoc?"

"I'm here."

"Gods . . ." Relief washed him, as the fear had done earlier. "I thought they would hold us apart. Have you seen—" The guards shifted warily. Dubornos bit off the words. Without turning his head, he said, more slowly and still in Eceni, "The larger of the two guards fornicates with pigs. The smaller is his child by a lop-eared sow."

In the hush that followed, the Batavians straightened themselves and became more attentive but did not offer violence.

Caradoc laughed softly. In the same tongue, he said, "Nicely done. They speak Latin and Batavian and, I think, a little Greek, but not Eceni unless they can act better than any paid performer, and they don't have the wit for that. In any case, even if they understood what you said, they have orders not to kill us. If we die, the fate that would have been ours will be theirs. I think it is safe to assume even the horse-guards fear that."

Dubornos opened his eyes. The cell was smaller than he had thought; his pallet took up half the width and two-thirds of the length. The door was oak with iron binding the planks. The walls were poorly plastered, showing the underlying pattern of the bricks beneath; the sanatorium had been done better, the underground holding cell not at all. The ceiling was flat, and unnervingly, it seemed likely to be surmounted not by a roof but by yet another storey of the building. Only aboard the ship had Dubornos experienced life with others walking above his head. He had not found it comfortable then, either.

Three guttering lamps hung from brackets on the wall. In the curling shadows beneath the central one, dressed in a tunic of undyed wool, Caradoc sat up on an identical pallet with his back to the plaster, his knees hugged to his chin, and his arms wrapped loosely round them.

Bandages of unbleached linen cuffed his wrists, the right one crusted a little with dried blood. The contusions on his face from when they took him prisoner were fading, and his hair shone cleanly gold as it had not done since the battle at the Lame Hind, lacking only a single lock, shorn short to the scalp on the right side where Cartimandua had cut away the warrior's braid to keep "as a remembrance." Sometime since his capture they had returned to him the brooch in the shape of the serpent-spear that was the only item of jewellery he ever wore. It needed polishing, but it was clean of blood and the pin whole. Two threads of red-dyed wool hung from the bottom loop, their ends a little frayed. One of them had become stained during the journey and was stiffly black.

Like Dubornos, he was unshackled, and the lack of the irons, or per- haps three days' rest, had set him right again, lifting the haggard weariness of the Brigante camp so that he looked once more the warrior who could lead a nation. Under Dubornos's scrutiny, the cool grey gaze remained level, with a dry spark of irony at its core. If they had not shared a slop bucket for ten days in the sea port before the first ship departed, Dubor- nos could have believed him unafraid.

"You didn't drink the poppy," Dubornos said. They had each taken the same oath against drinking wine; only Dubornos had broken it. Shame was a small thing, a distraction from terror; he welcomed its familiarity.

Caradoc shrugged. "I wasn't offered any. Tonight if they offer us both, you can keep watch, and I'll drink the wine and then sleep."

"Will they do so?" *Will there be a tonight, and will we be in a position to choose to drink or not drink, to sleep or not sleep?*

"I don't know. Narcissus, the freed slave, seems to be in charge. If word on Mona is right, the man is shrewd and intelligent and has no great lust for blood."

"But he answers to an emperor who is neither of those things and who enjoys the spectacle of slow death more even than Caligula, whom he replaced."

Caradoc blinked slowly, exhaling through pursed lips. "Thank you, yes. In which case, we should be grateful that Claudius is said to be weak and ruled by his wives and freedmen. If he had Caligula's instincts and the same lack of restraint, the dying would already have begun. That one once made a father sit and drink wine while his son's skin was flayed from his body before him. I don't recall what happened to the father." The grey eyes flickered. "Is that what you wanted to hear?"

Dubornos's skin prickled beneath his tunic, as if the nerves were already exposed. He said, "Sooner started is sooner ended," and knew as the words left his mouth that he was not alone in thinking it but should not have spoken it aloud.

"They have the children," said Caradoc flatly. "Xenophon the physician has been tending them. He came here this morning to make sure that you were still asleep. He believes that Cygfa and Cunomar may be allowed to live, if only in slavery. If there is anything—anything at all—that we can do to keep them alive, we must do it. It's all there is left." He looked up sharply. "And don't say what you were about to say. Xenophon knows it but has told no one else as yet."

Cygfa is no longer a child.

Dubornos sucked in air and made himself unsay the words that had so nearly rolled off his tongue. They hung in the clotted air, a sentence of death unspoken.

Caradoc's smile was a brief baring of teeth. "Thank you. If this is over in less than a month, it may be they will never find out. Meanwhile you could tell me your entire stock of heroes' tales, or we could find some other way to pass the time." He eased himself down on the pallet until he lay on one elbow, Roman style. "I don't suppose you still have your knuckle-bones with you?"

Dubornos's knuckle-bones had been taken from him soon after his capture, and he had not made any more, but they fashioned gaming pieces from fragments of plaster with crosses or lines scored on them with a fingernail and played with them a primitive version of Warrior's Dance. Through the passing afternoon, with the autumn sun baking the southern wall of the cell so that the place became a roasting oven and sweat ran freely from guards and prisoners alike, they played a game that neither had taken the time to practise since before the invasion. From that they relaxed slowly into talk and the sharing of such news as they had garnered since their capture.

Moving a piece idly forward, Caradoc said, "Do you remember Corvus? The Roman who was shipwrecked at the same time the *Greylag* went down?"

Dubornos looked up. "How could I not? He beat me in the river race, knocked me into the water, and then helped pull me out before I fell into the gods' pool. He was the hero and I the fool. I hated him for it."

"And now he is prefect of a Gaulish cavalry wing, and we could both hate him if we chose."

"Do we choose?"

"I think not. He had integrity then, and he does so still. He was here on other business, but he found I was here and came last night to see that I was being treated well. He left our land only four days ago and sailed direct to Ostia."

"So he has recent news." Dubornos tried not to make it sound like a question. From the moment of his capture, the thing he had wanted most was word of Mona and those he loved.

Caradoc could have been no different. He nodded a little tightly. "He does indeed. If he's telling the truth, the western tribes are buzzing like bees round a kicked skep. They wiped out two troops of cavalry in as many days, leaving only one survivor, and he lived only because he convincingly feigned death. If he is right, the attacks were led by Breaca, which means she—"

He stopped abruptly.

Breaca.

The name rattled in the stifling dark, a reminder of all that was lost. It was the first time any of them had spoken her name in Dubornos's hearing since their capture. Even now he thought the word had leaked out accidentally, sprung under pressure from a mind that knew no rest.

Very quietly Caradoc said, "Which means she knows what has happened and is, predictably, angry about it."

He strove for irony, or a measure of humour, and failed. The saying of the name had broken something in both of them. Without either asking the other, they abandoned the game. Dubornos gathered the pieces and slid them under his pallet, for later perhaps. Caradoc pushed himself back until his shoulders were against the wall. He covered his eyes with one hand, hiding them and whatever anguish they might betray. The fingers of the other ran over and over the serpent-spear brooch pinned to the front of his tunic.

The central lamp above his head had run out of oil and not been relit. The poor light carved hollows beneath his cheeks, made plainer the tensions in his face, which had not gone but been hidden by an effort of will, or by a deliberate act of leadership, even in this place where there was only one other man to lead. He looked now as Dubornos felt, a soul adrift in a limitless space, shouting aloud for his gods and hearing not even the echo of his own voice. His breathing, which had been deliberately slow, became progressively more ragged.

Dubornos waited, holding his breath. He was reaching for air when Caradoc's fist smacked on the wall, lifting a scallop of badly laid plaster. His voice cracked with hard-contained passion. "I wish to all the gods I knew how she was."

It was the first move either prisoner had made that could be considered violent. The guards, clearly, had been awaiting some such. Grinning, they moved their hands to their weapons. They could not kill but were permitted a measure of entertainment. Menace, which had been distant, came closer. The smaller guard clutched a fodder of lead. Through the whole afternoon, he had toyed with it, folding and refolding, moulding it to his hand like fine bees-wax. It fitted perfectly now in a strip across the outer ridge of his knuckles. Experimentally, he flexed his fingers. Dull metal rippled across them. Stepping in to face Caradoc, he drew back his arm.

A horn sounded in the distance, a rising wail. Mid-stride, both guards fell to attention, rigidly, carved statues of disappointment. A second detail marched the length of the corridor and halted somewhere behind the door. A password was requested and given, both in guttural Latin. A single man stepped forward.

Dubornos found a knot on the bare wood of the pallet and rubbed around the edge of it with the ball of his thumb. Counting the rhythm slowed the screaming panic in his mind. On the other pallet, Caradoc made a peak of his fingers and rested his chin on the point. His hands were still, but the rims of his nostrils flared white, and one who knew him well could see that he fought to steady his breathing. In the sweating gloom, the only sound was the rush of blood in the ears and the nasal whistle of the taller guard's impacted sinuses, faster than it had been.

The approaching feet stamped to a halt. The door opened. A centurion of the Praetorian Guard, resplendent in precious metal, said, "The emperor commands your presence." When Dubornos rose, stretching the stiffness from his calves, he met a sword's point at eye-height. "Not you. The leader only. Caratacus, who defied him for nine years. Claudius will see him now and judge him."

Dubornos said, "Then you take me with him."

"Not unless you wish your head to go as a gift to the emperor."

"If it's necessary, yes."

"Dubornos, no. One of us has to stay. For the children." Caradoc rose smoothly, saluting the guard as one officer to another. They shackled him again at the wrists, crushing the bandages. Before they were done, blood was leaking onto the rusting metal. Raising both hands together, he made something close to the warrior's salute to Dubornos. "The children," he said in Eceni. "Do whatever it takes to keep them alive."

"I will."

Afterwards, when the sound of footsteps had gone, Dubornos used the slop bucket and did not care that the guards were watching.

CHAPTER 20

The children. Do whatever it takes to keep them alive.

Caradoc walked to the beat of the words. The wrist chains chimed it, brisk as armour. He had no idea how he could do anything to protect anyone. It was enough to walk steadily, ignoring the old and the new pain, and to close his mind to what might yet come that was greater than either, to acknowledge with courtesy the guards on either side of the door to the audience room, to enter into the presence of an emperor he despised and display the demeanour and bearing proper to a warrior and leader of warriors.

He passed from a poorly lit corridor floored in black-and-white mosaic into an open sunlit audience room laid with vast slabs of finest red porphyry, crimson as aged wine, unevenly spattered with snowy flecks. The walls were of marble-smooth plaster, painted crimson and decorated on the far side with a frieze of the monster Polyphemus, arraigned in unhealthy love before the sea-nymph Galatea.

On Mona the singers told the myths and fables of Greece and Rome alongside their own. Travelling bards of other lands had given them colour and performed them as plays in the greathouse. As a youth taking ship to the sea ports of Gaul to escape the long reach of his father, Caradoc had seen attempts to bring them to life on walls or ceilings, cluttered frenzies of paint created by minor unskilled craftsmen. He had never seen them executed with such quality of purpose as he saw in the imperial audience chamber, or with such wild abandon.

An exhausted, pain-racked mind, seeking distraction, could readily become lost in that frieze, falling into the flowing colours and the relief they gave from the concussive red of the walls and the naked passions so readily displayed, but Claudius was there, somewhere, in the sunlight flooding in from the garden, or more likely in the shadows it threw, so bright after days in half-darkness, so bright—

"Father!"

In all the blood-red was a child: Cunomar, thin and hollow-cheeked, his hair roughly cut, a great scab on one earlobe. He was running, his arms wide open. Free. Six guards blocked the doorway, all armed. Who can tell their orders if a headstrong boy skids on polished marble and runs into them? . . . *Do whatever it takes.* . . .

"Does a warrior run in the presence of an emperor?"

The child faltered, his face crumpling. Caradoc made the salute of one warrior to another and saw its hesitant return and the indecision that followed it. *My son, we did not train you for this. I am so sorry.* Stepping forward, he scooped his son into a shackled embrace, holding the tousled head close to his shoulder. *You weigh nothing; if you live, your growth will be lessened.* "My warrior-to-be, have the Romans treated you well?"

Safe, in his father's arms, the child chattered boldly. "I had the flux, but it got better. I'm well now, and the Greek physician with the long nose let me eat proper food today, not the milk porridge they gave me on the ship." The small face darkened, showing his mother's anger in miniature, a thing to be cherished for itself alone. "But he defiled Cygfa. He should die for it. And the one who gave the orders." Blessedly he spoke Eceni, but Claudius was famed for his mastery of foreign languages and was still there, watching and listening, invisibly.

Caradoc said, "I heard what he did. He, too, follows orders. The gods will take care of it. We may not do so here. Have you spoken with the emperor?"

"The old man with the palsy? He dribbles. He touched my hair. I hate him."

"But a warrior behaves always with courtesy to his enemies, in victory and defeat." *We should have told you this long ago, spoken it daily from birth and before. Why did we not?* "Do you know where the emperor is?"

"There, by the columns into the garden." The child pointed, but not usefully. His attention wandered and, with it, his arm. "There are statues and fountains all the way along. Even the flowers are planted in rows, the way the legions fight. They leave nothing to the gods here."

He had been right, then, to think the brooding presence sat in the denser shadows. Still with Cunomar in the crook of his arm, Caradoc turned.

A row of columns broke the way through to the garden. A thin voice from the shade of one said thoughtfully, "He is very clearly yours. Your hair is his, and the stamp of you stands clear on his face. None would doubt you his sire."

Cunomar frowned up at his father, confused. The words made no sense. No one had ever doubted that Caradoc was sire to Cunomar. Half a battlefield had been present at his conception; he had been told so often enough. Caradoc saw his son draw a breath to ask the obvious question and made a sign for silence. He was relieved beyond measure to see it understood and obeyed.

The shadow-voice said, "The child does not understand Latin?"

The child had been taught Latin and Greek by the best of Mona's dreamers, but the emperor's Latin was archaic even by the standards of those for whom Latin was a child amongst languages, too new to be fully formed. One could not say this. Caradoc inclined his head. "He understands, but only if the words are spoken clearly."

"Then we will speak them so. Come here, boy."

If you harm him, you will die for it, if it kills all of us, I swear it.

Smiling, Caradoc shoved his son gently in the small of the back. The child stepped warily into the late evening sunlight, his straggled hair melted to a pool of tarnished silver. The shadow-movement came from the third column from the left, and this time Caradoc could see its origin: a man in his sixties, showing his age, stooped at the shoulders, with untidy grey hair and a weak chin and bat-wing ears. He walked lame on his right foot, and his right arm was withered, shaking out of time with the rest of his body. As not with other men, one looked at his head last, after the withered limb. The skin of his face was an unhealthy grey, blushing overmuch at the cheekbones. His eyes were bloodshot, with dark rings beneath from lack of sleep. In the first moments of meeting, they shied away from direct contact; one would not care to buy goods from this man, or follow him into battle.

An unsteady hand reached forward to caress Cunomar's hair. The boy stood rigid, his skin flickering like that of a horse bothered by flies. Caradoc stepped up behind him, granting the comfort of a father's presence. The sunlight scoured his prison-darkened eyes. The air smelled too heavily of fruit and sweet autumn flowers. With a little time, it became clear that Claudius was the source of the strongest smell, of concentrated roses, and that it covered imperfectly other scents of rosemary and pungent garlic and underneath of old age and dried spittle.

"So clearly yours," said the emperor wistfully, and this time his eyes held contact a fraction longer, so that soul, fleetingly, could meet warped and pensive soul, could plumb the depths of a fierce, thwarted intellect locked in a marred body. Caradoc felt ice track down his spine and fought not to shudder.

Claudius smiled. "They say your family has been your first priority since their capture," he said. "And that their concern has been first for you and then for each other. This is, of course, a truly Roman virtue and most commendable. My wife has expressed a desire to meet you, and I have allowed it. In fact, I have commanded all of my family to meet you and your son. Together you are an instruction in what binds a family close in love and in adversity."

A brass bell decorated with geometric symbols lay on a table close at hand. The emperor rang a trilling peal. Echoing bells rattled on down a corridor and were answered presently by the scuff of footsteps. A youth only a little older than Cunomar ran in with little ceremony, although the guards saluted as he passed between them.

Father greeted son stiffly but gladly. Claudius said, "This is my son, Britannicus. He is named for the conquest of your country. Your presence here means he will be able to visit your province in safety long before he becomes emperor."

He cocked his head, the better to judge the impact of his words. Caradoc smiled and let his eyes take in the full length of the child. The boy was flat-footed and small. His wavy mouse-brown hair was not his father's; nor did his features carry Claudius's stamp, a fact for which he may well have been grateful. When he grinned at Cunomar, he radiated an innocence and charm his father lacked. He could have been any man's son. There was nothing to mark him as Claudius's get.

"A fine child," said Caradoc. "I trust he will make as fine an emperor." *If his stepmother does not have him slaughtered to put her own son on the throne.* On Mona it was not Claudius's son who was considered most likely to be the next emperor, but his stepson.

Claudius laid his good hand on the child's arm. There was a pattern to his tremors: they were worse when he was making decisions and stilled afterwards. Reaching for the bell, he rang it again. The violent shaking of his hand steadied as the peals fell to silence. "You must meet the remainder of my family," he said.

Caradoc, smiling steadily, retrieved his son and brought him to a safe distance.

The stepson came first: Lucius Domitius Ahenobarbus, known as Nero. He had been a beautiful child and was growing into a beautiful man, and knew it. The curled red-gold hair, hanging longer than true Roman sobriety allowed, fell lightly on his alabaster brow. He walked with the careful tread of a dancer and the head-tilt of a Greek actor of the old school, giving life again to the young Achilles, but his skin was pure as a girl's, and his eyes were a girl's eyes, craving love. For a breath's pause, balanced in the doorway, facing his stepfather, he could have been Helen, confronting the maddened Menelaus. A question was poised on his lips, a request, a boon, which might have been answered, but a cacophony behind him drowned it unspoken, and his entrance, careful as it was, vanished beneath the waves of his mother's arrival.

In Rome, where women were given no power, the Empress Agrippina, niece and wife to the emperor, mother to Nero, had taken it with both hands and held it tight to her breast. Like everything else in her life, her entrance into the audience chamber was a choreographed affair. The sound preceded her, reaching those waiting while she was still beyond the turn in the corridor: the measured tread of her bodyguard, the murmurings of Polybius, Claudius's religious secretary who had become her man in all but name, the muted chiming of gold on gold, and the delicate counterpoint rattling of pearls.

Clad in the totality of her wealth, a sum greater than the entire tax revenue of Britannia in the nine years since the invasion, Agrippina needed no retinue to proclaim herself regal. The bodyguard still did their best, and the shine in their eyes proclaimed a devotion that was not felt by those serving Claudius or either son. She emerged between them, a vision in red and gold. The audience room was her chamber, clearly; no one else would have required the red of the walls so exactly to match the colour of her lips and the rubies at her neck. The soft dyed doeskin of her shoes blended perfectly with the blood-wine porphyry of the floor, the pearl buttons sitting proud as pale flecks in stone. Her hair, parted severely in the middle and pulled back to the nape of her neck, set about with hairpieces of jewel-studded gold, could have been sculpted from marble. Her stola was a whisper of red silk, bordered in imperial purple, and the skin of her arms, emerging from its folds, was as flawlessly white as sand on a northern beach. In every respect, she was the archetypal woman of Rome, a thing of plucked and painted beauty, brought to power through her husband and the violence of her intrigue. She was as far from Breaca as the trained and pruned flowers in the garden were from the oaks and hawthorns of an uncut forest. It was impossible to imagine them cast of the same flesh and blood. Caradoc, bowing, did not try.

Her eyes were aquatic green, and they held a man's gaze for as long as the earth turned and beyond. Caradoc bowed again that he might avert his own gaze without causing offence. Faced daily with this, he, too, would have developed the shifting half-glances of the emperor. Nero, whose eyes were a pale imitation but who nevertheless should have been acknowledged, was forced to shuffle sideways, to avoid the bodyguard.

The procession came to a halt, a spear's length from the doorway. The empress stared, unblinking, taking in Cunomar before Caradoc. "The barbarian who cares so much for his children. How wonderful."

The lady smiled, a practised flexing of painted lips. Claudius grinned with her in perfect, vacuous mimicry, and it might have been a reflex, the true expression of the inner fool caught in the radiance of his superior, but that his eyes, swaying sideways, locked, shockingly, with Caradoc's. In that look was all the proof one could want that the rumours on Mona were true, that the emperor would deny his wife nothing, not the least whim, until such time as she stepped over some final invisible mark—and then he would kill her as he had done her predecessor. Perhaps the assassination of his only son would be that mark. Perhaps she knew it. Caradoc looked at the boy Britannicus and saw the rictus grin of fear stretch his mouth far more palpably than it did his father's. He knew where the danger lay.

"Is it necessary to shackle him so? We hold his wife and daughter, after all. He will not harm us, surely?"

Agrippina said it winsomely, tilting her head on one side. Her eyes blazed with guileless charm. The heavily painted lids blinked once, daring the prisoner to prove her wrong, to prove himself the better of the guards and of Claudius.

Still grinning, the emperor nodded. The nearest of the horse-guards reached for Caradoc, who stepped back a pace and held himself out of reach, taking Cunomar with him.

"I think not," he said. "It is better they stay in place, my lady. In so beguiling company, I might else forget too soon how I came to be here."

The guard hovered, awaiting orders. The empress's smile became brittle a moment, then plastic again, a source of sympathy and amusement, solace and the offer of freedom. The emperor ceased to smile and looked on thoughtfully.

"It need not have been so," said Agrippina at length. "Had you not set arms against us, you would be welcome here as one of our subjects. We would be discussing trade and the collection of taxes, not the manner of your death and the fates of your family."

Caradoc inclined his head. With perfect civility, he said, "And I would be imposing an unwanted slavery on an entire people, instead of simply those of my blood."

"But you would be free and rich from the collection of taxes."

"I was free before, and rich beyond measure, without the imposition of taxes to keep others in ancient gold." His eyes swept the antique gold of her neck chain, the Macedonian staters fixed in her earrings. Rome had grown to power in the three centuries since they were first minted.

The green eyes flashed. Agrippina, who had spent her early adulthood in exile off Mauretania, diving for sponges by order of Caligula, unhooked a trail of pearls from one ear. Holding them high, she said, "I dived for these, and others like them, twice a day, bursting my lungs to find them amid the grasping weeds and the dark places beneath the sea. They are the product of no man's taxes. I believe I have earned the right to wear them."

They were small seed pearls, not very even, hanging together like grapes on a vine, the only imperfect items in the whole of her ensemble. She rolled her fingers that they might catch the light from the garden, then flung them high out over the marble.

Caradoc lifted his hands against the weight of the chains and caught them. Blood leaked from his wrists to make small liquid pools on the porphyry. Cunomar shuddered, biting his lip to hold silence. On the far side of the room, Nero winced.

Ignoring them both, Caradoc held the pearls high in the light, as she had. "They are beautiful, my lady. I do not question your right to wear them."

"But you do question my right to my gold."

She was angry but not yet vengeful. It was said of her that she admired courage above all other traits and despised sycophancy. Offering prayers to silent gods that the rumours be true, Caradoc said, "Among my people, gold is considered the province of the gods. It cannot be eaten or ridden, it provides no warmth against winter's chill. We give it first to the gods as evidence of our gratitude, and what is left we wear in their honour, not our own."

She was quick; she understood the words he left unsaid. One painted brow peaked. "And so the gods should not be robbed so that men can pay their gold in taxes?"

"I believe not. It is not only the gods that suffer, but the people. Our land was our own; by the grace of the gods we farmed it, we reared our horses, we hunted, we bred our hounds, mined our lead and tin, silver and gold, and we lived as a free people. Why, because we have lost one battle, should we submit ourselves to slavery that others may grow rich on our labours?"

"That is the penalty for losing a war."

"But we have not yet lost the war."

Agrippina's lips parted fiercely. "You will not think that as you die."

"But the governor, Scapula, as he dies, may do so."

He had spoken beyond himself, unthinking, with words not his own. In the cracked silence that followed, Caradoc felt the withdrawal of the gods as a man feels a blade pulled out of flesh in which it has just now been embedded. He had not thought himself so ready a mouthpiece, nor that his gods desired his death so urgently. He lifted his gaze to that of the empress, expecting to see the work of a morning, the careful weaving of care and courtesy, destroyed. The lives of his two children hung on this woman's care and her courtesy. Very badly, he did not want to see either destroyed.

"My lady, forgive me, I—" *My lady, forgive me, I spoke out of turn. The last time I saw Scapula, he was riding his horse across a battlefield he had just taken. If he is dead, the gods know it, but I do not.*

He did not say it because he was no longer given heed. The hard green gaze was focused beyond him and was quite unreadable. Claudius, too, appeared to have forgotten his presence; he was turned toward the doorway, his face searching, like a blind man in winter who feels the heat of the sun.

"Your excellency—"

Caradoc turned. Between the guards stood aged Callon, father to Narcissus, the elegant, tutored freedman who ran the empire for his master. Agrippina's perfect painted lips twitched in open disgust. In Claudius's court, the enmity between the empress and those secretaries whose loyalty remained solely with their emperor was legendary.

Ignoring her, Callon signalled again to his master and was invited to enter. Stooping, he murmured in his emperor's ear. Claudius stopped smiling. For a long moment, it seemed he might faint; then he turned to his empress and her son.

"You will leave us."

She glared at him, snake-eyed and venomous. Silence stretched between them. At length the empress nodded. "Whatever my lord commands." With consummate dignity, she gathered her son and departed.

Unsmiling, Claudius turned back to the garden; his treasure and his escape.

"You will walk with me," he ordered. The sweep of his arm included all those who were left.

CHAPTER 21

"Scapula is dead."

Narcissus, son of Callon and emperor's freedman, was hysterical, or close to it. He stood in the doorway to the prison cell, flanked by the horse-guards and two Praetorians. The evening before he had seemed to Dubornos urbane and all-powerful. A man of middle height and middle weight with dark well-barbered hair and heavy brows, he had commanded the guards and the doctor, had procured the bandages and clothing, food and wine, had spoken Latin and Greek with equal fluency, and had displayed a working understanding of Gaulish. His reputation had preceded him as Claudius's most trusted adviser and the man who had persuaded the mutineering legions to embark on the ships that took them to Britannia in the long-delayed invasion. Word on Mona, brought months after the event, said that the invasion itself was Narcissus's plan, his means to consolidate his master's power and thereby his own.

Daylight, leaking along the corridor from some distant window, treated him unkindly. His skin was yellowed with age and strain. Threads of silver showed in his hair. His tunic, which had appeared in the previous evening's lamplight to be a model of restrained good taste, sparked at the hems with silver and gold bullion in vulgar quantities. He took a step forward into the room, not quite close enough for Dubornos to strike a hand across his neck and kill him. The guards hovered protectively.

"Scapula is dead," Narcissus said again. He ran a pale tongue round paler lips. "The governor of Britannia has died in his bed. In Camulodunum they say it is the dreamers' work, in revenge for our capture of Caratacus. Is this true?"

Dubornos said, "It may be." Horns sounded in his skull, a great fanfare of victory. Joy made him light-headed. His fingers sought the wall and pressed against the plaster for balance. The danger to his own life seemed, at that moment, irrelevant.

"How would they do it? They have not come near him—they couldn't. He is guarded day and night. Can they kill at a distance?"

Warnings clattered in Dubornos's mind. He said, "I don't know. I'm not a dreamer."

"No." The freedman snorted, horse-like, high in his nose. "You have only lived these past nine years on their cursed island. Of course you don't know their ways." He pursed his lips explosively. Violence and the threat of it clung to him. Caradoc had said, *The man is shrewd, intelligent, and has no great lust for blood.* He had chosen to forget that Claudius routinely tortured to death those who conspired against him; or that his ministers did so in his name.

Narcissus's agitation brought him a further stride into the room, well within reach. In his head, Dubornos heard Caradoc's voice: *They have the children . . . If there is anything we can do to keep them alive, we must do it. It's all there is left.* To kill the emperor's favourite adviser would destroy any chance of Cunomar and Cygfa's survival. Dubornos watched the man's arms and the space above his eyes, and his heart rocked in his chest as it did before battle. An image of Scapula dead floated before him, as real as the room. He thought, *Airmid will have done this, for Breaca,* and was sorry only that Caradoc was not there to hear the news with him. Aloud, he said, "Men die all the time, from war-wounds, pestilence, ill-prepared food. Why should the governor's death be considered dreamers' work?"

From the passageway behind the guards, a second foreign voice said, "The tribes believe it to be so, and the legions with them. Word has spread through the ranks that they used Scapula for practise and will come now for his master, that Claudius's life can be counted in days, not months. The legate of the Second has flogged a dozen men for sedition, but the rumour still spreads like fire through the harvest. If it reaches Rome, he is as good as dead."

Callistus, secretary to the Privy Purse, stepped past the guards and squeezed into the room. He was slightly built with a narrow face and lips artificially red. His hair was entirely white, whether by birth or age or accident was not clear. His eyes were bloodshot, and if they had colour, it could not be seen beyond the wide void of the pupil. Like Narcissus, Callistus was panicked, and panicking men are as dangerous as fire-blind horses. He said, "Claudius must not die now, he must not. You will tell us how your barbarian soothsayers could reach Scapula and then how we might stop them from similarly assailing the person of the emperor. You will tell us of your own free will or under harshest duress, but you *will* tell us."

And so the waiting was over, so easily, with so little forewarning. Relief and the apex of terror made Dubornos dizzy. He laughed. They stared at him: a lunatic, or a witless fool. His skin prickled with the promise of pain. He rolled his shoulders, feeling afresh the coarse scratch of the tunic as it touched his back, his waist, his arms. The crush of the shackle-wounds on his wrists felt warm and comfortable, a known and measurable sensation. Blood pulsed from his head to his feet, and he knew every part of himself. For the first time in thirty-two years, he felt at home in the body he was about to lose. As Airmid had said he should, he stood on the dividing line between the worlds, a foot on each bank of the gods' river, evenly. His thoughts flowed freely, released from all constraints.

"If you believe they are seeking revenge for Caradoc's capture," he said, "you have one easy recourse. Release him, return him to his family and his homeland. Withdraw the legions from our land. The emperor will live to old age, and you will be hailed as heroes for having achieved it."

Narcissus stared at him, a man who sees his life's work threatened and counts its preservation worth a hundred thousand other lives. "We cannot withdraw now from Britannia—we will not. The emperor's standing with the people depends on it."

Callistus's priority was finance. He said, "We have invested too much to withdraw now. The loans to the eastern tribes alone are worth forty million sesterces; they cannot be recalled in time. There will be another way. You will give it us."

Dubornos shook his head sorrowfully. "There may be another way," he said, "but I doubt it, and even if there were, I couldn't tell you. It's true that I have lived for some time on Mona, but I am not a dreamer; I was not privy to their rites. I would have died for it had I ever tried to find out what they were, and that death would have been worse than anything you could do here."

Narcissus smiled, lips tight against his skull. "I very much doubt that."

"I don't. If I had defiled the dreamers' ceremonies, I would have brought on myself everlasting shame. Here the shame is all yours."

Narcissus stared at him a moment. Across the gulf of cultures, there might have been some meeting had Callistus not already snapped his fingers. The guards came forward to take Dubornos's arms. In the last moments, because he no longer had anything left to lose, he fought them.

The knife was very sharp. It pressed into the skin below Cunomar's eye, drawing fine beads of blood. By looking down, he could see the blue-grey iron and the thousand faint cross-hatchings scored on the metal where it had been ground back and forth on the whetstone. They vibrated under his gaze, but the knife was steady. It was his own body that shook.

He looked past the knife to where his father knelt on the cold marble, held still by two of the horse-guards. The guards were alive only because of Cunomar, that much was clear to them all. If his son had not been there, were not being threatened before him, the man who had slain a thousand Romans would have slain a dozen more, up to and including the emperor and his family, or would have died trying.

Because of Cunomar, Caradoc did nothing but instead knelt where they held him with his gold hair twisted tight in the grip of a guard's hand, with blood sliding down from the newly opened cut on his left cheek, scarlet against bone-white skin. His lips were greyed, from anger or pain or the vast, superhuman effort he was making not to fight, and he spoke to Claudius as if His Imperial Majesty were a slow-witted apprentice goat-herd, which was as bad, really, as if he had truly fought.

There was nothing a child could do. Cunomar stood very still so that the knife did not cut him and watched an elegant bronze fountain splatter water on the emperor's elegant garden. The water came from pipes played by a naked goat-footed boy-child. It spewed out musically, to spray a thousand rippling teardrops into the green marble basin below. It was not good to think of tears. Cunomar stared at the serpent-spear brooch that had not yet been ripped from his father's tunic and prayed to be returned to the company of his mother, whose symbol it was, to the Boudica, Bringer of Victory, who should have been able to save them. He had long ago resolved that, whatever happened, he would not weep. It was the only thing he could do for his father, and even this much was hard. Over his head the adults conducted a conversation, the implications of which were too appalling to contemplate.

"Dubornos knows nothing. Whatever you do to him, he can tell you nothing. There is nothing to tell. If Scapula is dead, it is not the dreamers' work. If they could kill at a distance, if they could threaten a governor and the person of an emperor, do you not think they would have done it long ago? How many of them did Tiberius crucify? How many did Gaius? How many have you? Tens? Hundreds? If it were possible for any or all to exact revenge, do you not think one of them would have attempted it in the days and nights of her dying? To believe otherwise is superstition, and it ill becomes a civilized nation."

Caradoc spoke in the short clipped tone that made clear what he thought of the drivelling imbecile standing before him. The sound of it made Cunomar wince. The horse-guards not directly involved stood still as carved marble, staring rigidly ahead. In their very stance was their terror. If a man could lose his life for speaking thus to an emperor—and quite certainly he could—then so, too, could those who had witnessed it.

Claudius was renowned for his secret trials and summary executions. Callon, who had brought the news of the governor's passing, had withdrawn to a distance, as if half the length of the garden were enough to render them deaf and thus safe. Closer, a yellow cage-bird trilled. Liquid notes poured into discord and were lost. Ignored, it fell soon to silence.

Cunomar could sense the emperor's uncertainty. The man had not known that his governor was dead; the news brought by the freedman was as unexpected as it was unwelcome. Given the facts, his first thought had been for the spectacle of his planned victory celebrations, his first emotion anger at the thoughtlessness of his subordinate in so untimely a death. Pressing his hand to his temples as if his head pained him, he had said, "He can't be dead. We need him for the procession. Who will take his place?"

Callon had long dealt with his master's priorities. With practised tact, he had said, "We will find another governor to replace Scapula, your excellency, or we can excuse his absence and substitute a representative. I believe it might be best if his death were not widely known for some time, perhaps until spring. But before that we must ensure your excellency's safety. The brother knows nothing. He is unconscious; he fought, and the guards were overzealous. They have been disciplined, but he will be some time returning to us. We may not have time. Answers must be found by other means."

"What?"

Thus had the unnatural peace of the emperor's ghastly, oppressive, flower-scented garden been breached. Claudius and his freedman had been speaking Greek, thinking themselves in some measure secret, and certainly the horse-guards had not understood, but Caradoc had been schooled on Mona, where Greek had been written and spoken for five centuries and Latin was the upstart youth in a world of wise and ancient languages. Even Cunomar had understood enough to foretell his father's abrupt intervention.

"What *exactly* have you done to Dubornos?"

Caradoc had not attacked anyone, only stepped forward a pace towards Claudius, his shackled arms rising, but the guards had not been of a mind to give a man room to make himself plain. They had treated it as an attack on the emperor's person and responded as they thought fit. Horse-guards were not employed for their subtlety, nor for their respect for an enemy leader.

After that the freedman had withdrawn, and now there was only his father, catastrophically angry, facing a madman who had the power to kill them all, or worse.

The children. Do whatever it takes to keep them alive.

My son. Cunomar stood in the grip of the guard, his skin tinged blue at the mouth, his eyes round as river pebbles. Tears trembled on the brinks of his lids, and the effort he made to keep them from falling was plain. *My warrior-to-be. You will die now, because of me. Cunomar, please forgive me.*

The guards' fingers goaded, twisting Caradoc's hair. The shackles bit into his wrists. In the first moments, they had been unlocked and locked again behind him. They were drawn now high up his back so that his joints cracked under the strain. He had expected pain, had been steeling himself against it daily since his capture, until the reality was almost welcome. He could breathe and he could think and he could see that his son stood unhurt and only threatened by a knife; that much was bearable. What hurt far more was the loss of his self-control and the descent into anger and pointless violence, the unexpectedness of it, the futility, the wasted opportunity. If the bridges to Agrippina had been fragile before, they were broken now, and those to Claudius were shattered beyond repair. Agrippina had been humiliated in his presence, and her pride would never let her forget or forgive. Claudius was afraid and angry, but more than either, he was suspicious. The man had remained alive through fifty years of tyranny while those around him died like rats in a fire. His intellect, steeped in subterfuge, had allowed him to do so.

The emperor had regained control of himself after the first high-pitched squeal and the scurry for safety. The twitching arm was still, as was the head with its jug ears. His gaze was oil-smooth with turbulent currents beneath. His soft voice, rasping, said, "You will apologize."

"For what?"

"For attacking the person of your emperor."

"You are not my emperor." It should not have been said. In the jagged cave of Caradoc's mind, no room was left for diplomacy.

The emperor stood as still as any normal man. He pursed dry lips thoughtfully and smiled. To the guards, he said, "He will apologize."

It had always been rumoured of Claudius that he enjoyed the spectacle of inflicted pain. The guards were practised at accommodating him. The wrist-shackles twisted tighter and higher by slow degrees. Iron cut through healing ulcers on both wrists to grind the raw flesh beneath. Pain came in nauseating waves so that, for a while, it was no longer possible to speak or to think or even to breathe.

For his son, if for no one else, he would say nothing. In the locked space of his skull, Caradoc of the Three Tribes reproduced for himself every syllable of unspeakable invective he had ever learned through three decades of seamanship and the leading of armies. He cursed in Eceni, in Greek, in Latin, in Gaulish, none of it aloud. If he were lucky, if he kept the image of Cunomar in the front of his mind, he believed unconsciousness might claim him before any sound passed his lips. He closed his eyes and built a picture of his son behind his closed lids, but it was Breaca who came when the strings of his right shoulder tore apart and the darkness claimed him.

They pushed his head into the fountain to bring him back, then drew it out again before he could take the necessary breath that would kill him. He emerged, gasping. The rasping voice was closer, too close. Again it said, "Apologize."

"For what? Stating the truth? Is that lost now in Caesar's court? I thought Polybius valued truth and integrity above all other qualities in a leader." The gods gave Caradoc the words. He had neither the strength nor the wit to find them.

Silence; and the falling water of the fountain. In Rome even water must be controlled.

Claudius's mouth was set hard. Only a small smear of saliva betrayed him. It was said that he held the old values dear above all else, but there was no way to know if that was true. He nodded weightily, a practised act designed for the Senate, where rhetoric was valued above even valour in war.

"Polybius was not dealing with barbarian soothsayers who strove to kill him from afar," he said. "Truth and integrity are marks of civilization. Barbarians apologize to their emperor."

The shackles were lifted, and the twisting began again in the opposite direction, more slowly than before. They had no wish to lose him to unconsciousness again. To think clearly, to speak distinctly over the pain, was a warrior's challenge set by the gods. On Mona, Maroc the Elder had talked of Rome and what drove the fledgling empire to war. Fragments of memory floated up through the rising agony. Each was given such breath as it needed to be heard while there was still time. He spoke to the scholar now, not the tyrant.

"The dreamers were civilized before Polybius was a squalling babe . . . before ever Romulus and Remus suckled the she-wolf. If they kill now . . . in defence of their land and their civilization, does that make them uncivilized? Rome kills and she is not under threat."

"But her emperor is."

"Her emperor . . . need not be."

A finger was raised. The shackles were released. Relief, briefly, was as debilitating as the pain had been. The guards stepped back, and they were alone, Caradoc and Claudius: two men who led their people, who could order death or its suspension. The emperor blinked. The tremor returned to his head. Indecision curdled the shiftless gaze. Fear and the offer of safety fought with power and the need to use it. The tremor acquired a rhythm and became a nod. "You knew the governor had died. Did you order it before you left?"

"No. I have no power to order the dreamers."

"But they have chosen you to lead their cause in war. If they have killed Scapula, it is because of your capture. I believe they will listen if you order them to recall their curse, or never to cast it."

Airmid! Whatever you have done, I thank you. He had been powerless and yet was given a measure of power. He fixed his eyes on the fountain, not certain he could keep the understanding from his eyes. Without raising them, he said, "You ask a great deal of one who has little left to lose. Why would I so order the dreamers?"

"Because you value the life of your son."

A straight bargain, like bartering iron for horses. An emperor's life is worth more than a single child. Caradoc said, "And my wife and daughter."

"No. Both of these raised a sword against Rome. Your wife was seen to kill many legionaries in the battle. Your daughter killed one of the auxiliaries who took her captive and wounded another beyond repair. It cannot be allowed that women bear arms in war."

Caradoc dared to laugh. "You would expect a daughter of Caradoc willingly to submit to slavery and rape? Would that make of your victory celebration a thing of value? Would we remember your ancestor, the deified Julius, for his victory over Vercingetorix if that warrior had surrendered his blade at the first hint of attack? Does not the valour of the conquered give honour to the conqueror?"

Thoughtfully Claudius said, "We honour every victory gained by our ancestors, those of the deified Julius most of all."

"And yet your conquest of Britannia is held in such high esteem because Julius attempted it and failed. By his actions are your own measured. If it is time to strike when wrong demands the blow, then surely it must be time also to show mercy when right argues as strongly for it."

The emperor stared. The grey straggled eyebrows rocked to the limits of his brow. "You would quote Homer to *me*?"

"I would quote your own words to you. How often have you said exactly that to the Praetorian tribune before an execution? Even on Mona you are famed for it. When a man becomes so readily predictable that his enemies can put words in his mouth, it may be time for him to consider a change of rhetoric. You have a choice, by which history will judge you. You can match your ancestor, or you can exceed him. Gaius Julius Caesar was renowned as a warrior but not loved for his magnanimity in victory. Scipio, who pardoned the defeated Syphax, was both loved and respected. The one may be valued more highly by posterity than the other, or both together."

The guards became restless. Rhetoric had no place in their world. The emperor signed them to stillness. Slowly he said, "Let me understand you correctly. In return for your order to the dreamers revoking their curse on me, you wish me to spare the lives of your women and your son? You do not beg for your own life?"

"I do not ask the impossible, but only what may be freely given. In my place, would you not also argue for the life of your family?"

Uniquely, Claudius's smile carried a flash of true humour. "My son Britannicus perhaps, but only him. In this we differ. Your family, it seems, fights only the enemy." The smile faded. The emperor's eyes fixed on a thing unseen, his gaze clouded. Distantly he said, "You argue well. I concede your point. Your wife and children, then, will become hostages for my life. If I die, they die. While I live, they will live. They cannot be free, but they will not be enslaved. A place will be allocated them from among the imperial holdings. Well? Can you do this? Will the dreamers retract the curse at your command?"

Caradoc nodded. "I will do my best. They may still listen to me, but I will need an intermediary, someone to take the message who will be heard. Dubornos would be one such, if he lives."

"He lives. They would not kill him without my consent. But he will die with you. I will not send a warrior back to his country to continue this rebellion. The prefect Corvus will take your written message to Britannia. He is due to travel with the evening tide. Between now and then, you and he will find a way to convey your letter whither it must go. I am told the dreamers can read and write in Greek. They will return, in writing, their confirmation that their curse is lifted. If it is received, your wife and children will live. If not, they will die as you die. Knowing this, you will exert every pressure on those who threaten us."

The emperor clapped his hands once. The guards advanced. Claudius smiled. "Pen and ink will be brought to your cell. Prepare your words well. You are dismissed."

CHAPTER 22

The sun rose more slowly than it had ever done. Dubornos had lived through countless mornings before battle when time had slowed to tripping heartbeats, but never before had it seemed entirely to stop. He sat with his back to the wall, tight-shouldered to Caradoc, sharing with him the space of one man that each might see what he could of the creeping light through the high, barred window of their new cell. They had asked to see the dawn, and this was the closest that could be found commensurate with the emperor's order that they be kept in close confinement.

The horse-guards had withdrawn as a courtesy. They were no longer necessary for security. Cwmfen and the children were hostages not only for Claudius's life, but for Caradoc's death. Such was the nature of the warrior's agreement he had made with Claudius: for the price of a letter written in Greek to Maroc of Mona pleading for the emperor's life, and for Caradoc's oath that he would do nothing to impede his own prolonged and very public death, a woman and two children would be allowed to live.

Dubornos had no illusions as to his place in the arrangements. He was an accessory, his death an adornment to the main event, which was almost upon them. He existed in a place beyond fear, hollow and light, like a shell emptied of its snail that becomes later an echo of the wind. On this last morning, it was not the poppy that had achieved this, but time. For the past fifteen days, judicious use of the drug had dulled the stabbing aches of the broken collarbone and the splintered fingers of his left hand achieved by Narcissus's questioners, but it had not, at any time, dulled his fear or emptied his mind.

The awakening dawn had achieved what nothing else could. The closer they had come to the day appointed for the emperor's procession and the death of his two most notorious captives, the greater Dubornos's fear had been, until this last morning, when he had crested a wave of a terror so overwhelming he had thought that, like a shrew teased by a hound whelp, he might die of sheer fright—and had emerged beyond it, unafraid.

Time nudged onwards. The window was set too high to see the horizon or any part of the blazing dawn, but the small square of black that had been night faded slowly to grey and then to a hazed blue threaded across with whispers of flesh-coloured cloud. A dovecote woke nearby. Squabs and adults roused with the light, warbling.

This time tomorrow, or perhaps the day after, it will be over. The doves will call as they have called each morning, and we will be gone.

Dubornos could think this now without the words running dry in his head. It was a fact to be weighed with all the others, and it counted for little against the greater fact of his soul's loss, for his failure, on this last dawn as on all those before it, to connect with his gods. He leaned his head back against the wall and, closing his eyes, searched again in his heart for Briga, who was mother of life and death, and for her daughter Nemain, the moon, whose light had slid past the window in the night, casting the iron bars in muted silver. When these failed to respond, he cried in his echoing mind for Belin the sun and Manannan of the waves; being male they might find Rome more acceptable. Neither of them came to him.

He remembered the spirits of the slain Roman legionaries, wandering lost on the battlefield of the Lame Hind, searching for foreign gods in a country not their own and finding themselves abandoned. He had imagined them weak, deficient in prayer, lacking the true connection that comes from a life lived under the eyes of the gods. Thus was hubris added to his inner list of failings.

A grey-winged dove fluttered on the window ledge, pecked at the ridged mortar surrounding the bars, and flitted away. Dubornos felt Caradoc stir and dared to interrupt his silence.

"Do you feel the gods?" he asked.

For a while he thought he had not been heard. Caradoc sat as he had all night, with the elbow of his uninjured arm perched on his raised knees and his chin resting on the heel of his hand. The slow lift and fall of his breathing passed through his body to Dubornos's but gave no indication of his state of mind.

The patch of light on the wall grew brighter. Outside, at the front gates to the palace, one guard replaced another. Armour chinked, and the night's watchword was exchanged: *Britannicus,* name of the emperor and of the emperor's only true son, final proof of conquest.

More distantly the earliest of Rome's risers, or the latest of her retiring drunkards, called to one another across the streets. A handful of men shouted obscenities, their target silent and unknowable. Presently a woman laughed and was answered by a single man. A dog barked and set off half a dozen more, all higher pitched than any hound of the tribes. The single lamp with which the cell was lit cast fewer shadows of its own.

Caradoc was not asleep after all. Releasing his fingers, he stretched carefully, taking care for his ruined shoulder, with a rattle of cracking joints at the end. He turned sideways on the pallet, the better to see and be seen. The new light was harsh on his face, highlighting the greyed pallor of hunger and exhaustion. Night had been kinder. His eyes alone burned clearly, as they had always done. It was impossible to imagine them lifeless.

Dubornos caught his breath painfully. He said, "Breaca will continue the war. She has the weight of Mona's dreamers behind her, and the gods behind them. It's all that matters." He could say her name now, at the end, without its damaging either of them.

Caradoc smiled at the sound of it. "I know. But we are not abandoned." He turned his face to the window. The colourless light bleached his hair to the white of old age. In profile he was austere, not worn. The rents in his tunic had been mended, and the serpent-spear brooch glistened on his shoulder, a statement of defiance that would continue beyond death. He said, "Do you fear the coming day?"

"No. Not anymore."

"Then we have all we could possibly ask for. The opportunity to face death knowingly, to see ourselves tested in the way we face it. The rest is ours alone. Afterwards, when it's over, the gods will come."

"Are you sure? The Roman dead wander lost in our land. Is there a reason why we should not do the same in theirs?"

From the doorway, a dry voice said, "They did not have anyone waiting who could restore their souls to the care of their gods. Your dreamers will know how to do it and when. It is a skill that has largely been lost in Rome; the gods here are worshipped for their ability to generate money and power for the living, not their care of the dead."

"Xenophon!" Caradoc, delighted, rose in greeting, as he might have done had Maroc entered, or Airmid. "I had not expected to see you again.

Your work here is done, is it not? We are alive. We have not died of foul blood or broken bones. We will remain in fair health until the emperor chooses otherwise, at which point your intervention would not be politically wise or, I fear, effective, however famed the teachers of Cos."

It was said lightly, but not taken so. The emperor's physician was not a man to deal in trivia. He drew bony fingers down his long bony nose. "Many things are taught on Cos," he said. "Not all of them are to do with preserving life."

He stepped over the threshold into the room, making the cramped space tighter still. They had come to know the man well this last half-month. Since the audience with the emperor, they had been his main charge, after Claudius, Britannicus, and the Empress Agrippina. He had dosed them with poppy and infusions of leaf and bark until, if the broken bones and torn joints had not mended completely, at least the bruising around them had lessened and the skin healed. They had come to welcome the sight of his lean stooped frame in the doorway, as much for his company and the sharpness of his conversation as for the medications he brought and the orders he gave that they be permitted use of the baths and provided with clean clothing. When a junior officer of the horse-guards had objected to this last, he had turned on him the weight of twenty years' study and said starkly, "You can't crucify a man if he's died of blood poisoning beforehand. Did you want to take his place in the procession?" There had been no further objections.

The frequency of his visits had long ago numbed the horse-guards to his presence. If they had searched him at all this morning, they had done so with their eyes closed. He bore two small flasks, one in either hand, and a full pouch hung from his belt. Leaning the flasks against the edge of the pallet, he sat down.

"Healing is not always about saving life. Every physician knows that there are times when it is better that the soul be allowed to depart cleanly. To learn the rites of that passage, we of Cos travel to Mona if we can, or listen to those who have learned there. I have sat at the feet of dreamers older than any now alive and learned only enough to be certain that it would take me another lifetime to learn those things they know and I do not." He pressed the bridge of his nose. "My memory is not what it was and much of the teaching is lost, but I remember enough to send you freely to the river when the time is come. Before that we have those things I have learned from Rome. What will happen today is not an uncommon event. There are as many ways to die as there are men to hammer nails into flesh. Some are faster than others."

He looked up at the window, frowning. Footsteps trod the paving out-side; a heavy, masculine step, lame in one leg. When they had passed be-yond earshot, he said, "I have spoken to the centurion of the Praetorians who has charge of . . . the necessary details. He fought against you in the invasion battle and served at Camulodunum after that. He is a soldier and respects his enemies. He cannot go against Claudius's orders, but he has some discretion as to their implementation. You will not be stripped but left in full barbarian battle dress, at least as Rome perceives it. I would ad-vise you not to refuse. It may not in any way resemble what you would ac-tually wear in battle, but I doubt they'll agree to hang you wearing a shirt of stolen cavalry mail. Whatever, it is the weight that counts. The heavier you are, the faster the death."

He was a doctor and could say such things without rancour or af-fected delicacy; in his presence, two days of drawn-out dying were reduced to a problem of engineering.

In this spirit, Dubornos said, "If we're that heavy, the nails will tear out."

"If they do, it will be the first time. The Praetorians have had more practise in this than any of us would care to imagine. They use squares of pinewood as washers to spread the weight and drive the nails between the bones of the forearm. You can trust that they will be secure."

"If death comes faster, then the pain will be greater."

"No. That is, potentially yes, which is why I have also brought you this . . ."

The pouch he freed from his belt was of old weathered doeskin with a drawstring of plaited linen, dyed a deep blood-red. Stilted side-on fig-ures painted in blue and yellow ink processed across it. Some were rec-ognizably human, most were not. "Alexandrian," said Xenophon. He prised the neck open as he might the mouth of a patient. "The pharaohs, too, knew what it was to lose their way home and have to find it again in the dark." He drew out two twists of vine leaf, each tied with the same red linen thread as formed the drawstring. Opened, they con-tained a fine-ground powder, as much as would fit in the hollow of a cupped palm.

He held one out with great care, away from the draughts of his breathing. "Each of these contains a mix of belladonna, poppy, and aconitum. The one weakens the heart, the second, as you know, numbs mind and body to pain, and the third brings slow paralysis to the legs. If you cannot take weight on your legs, the pressure on the arms, and so the heart, is greater, and with the belladonna, death comes more swiftly. The poppy, if dosed right, befuddles the soul, carrying it out of the body. There is not enough of any to cause outright death—I cannot do that unless I wish to join you in death, and my admiration for your minds and hearts does not extend that far—but it is the closest I can reach. The poppy will take effect soon. The others will be slower, but you will be in the company of your gods by nightfall, I swear it."

It was a gift beyond price—and not one they could accept in good conscience. Dubornos felt his mouth grow dry. "Xenophon, this is too much. We're in your debt for your care of us this past half-month. You must not put yourself in this danger."

The old man laid his treasures on the pallet and leaned back on a wall, his arms folded across his chest.

"The danger is in my being here. If you take this before they come for you and the vine leaves are secreted under the pallets, away from searching eyes, it will not be any greater. Take it with my blessing. The flasks contain Batavian ale, which I am assured is to barbarian taste. If you mix the one with the other, the taste will not be any worse than the ale alone."

His lips were pressed tight, and his eyes had narrowed to slits, as if staring into the sun. A lesser man might have been thought to weep.

Dubornos took the offered flask. "Thank you," he said. "In that case, we accept." He turned, his heart light, offering peace and oblivion to a man he had come to admire above all others. "Caradoc?"

Caradoc sat again on the pallet. The deepening light from the window made spun gold of his hair. His features were still, carved in marble and very white. He stared at the open vine leaf as a man might stare at a poised snake, awaiting the strike. His breathing was shallow, an afterthought to the struggle within. Presently, lifting his gaze from the fistful of powder, he said to Xenophen, "Can the poppy be taken out of the mix?"

"Hardly. I ground them together myself. Even the monkey-servants of Anubis who can discriminate the sands of the desert couldn't separate them now."

"Then no. Thank you, but no. Dubornos should take it—must take it—but I can't."

"Really?" Xenophon studied this new phenomenon. His tears, if they had been real, were gone. "You have a need to experience such extremes of pain? I had not thought you afflicted with Roman vices."

Caradoc laughed, a quick bark drawn from somewhere beyond himself. "No, assuredly not. It would take longer than a month, I think, to acquire that one."

"Then why not the poppy?"

"Because this is not over yet. I need, at the very least, to have a clear mind and to be seen to do so. If I take poppy, I will fail in that."

"Oh, my dear man." Xenophon folded his long limbs and sat, all straight lines and angles, like a cricket, on the pallet that had been Dubornos's. In the days they had known him, he had been brisk and dry, and they had thought him a rationalist to the core. Here and now, in the tone of his voice and the unashamed, undeniable tears that did indeed fill the corners of his eyes, they saw the depth of his care.

Leaning over, he took one of Caradoc's hands in both of his own. "My friend, you have more courage than any man I have ever met, but you have to learn, even this late, when to accept that you have lost."

With his chin, he gestured to the wall above where sunlight slashed citron across the plaster. "They will come for you before the sun reaches the far edge of your window. You have that much time to drink and no longer. I cannot reach the Praetorian centurion in time now to change his plan. He will carry out his side of our agreement, and that is not something I would wish on any man. Please, I urge you, for your own sake and that of your friends, take what is offered."

"No." It was easier to say it a second time. They could both see that. "Why?"

"Because even this late, when I have lost—and I do know that—the children and Cwmfen are still my responsibility. We have not yet received word from Mona guaranteeing the emperor's life. Until we do, their lives depend on my keeping my bargain with Claudius, clearly and openly. I have sworn that I will do nothing to impede his plans for today. What you are suggesting steps beyond my oath, in spirit if not in word."

"You think Claudius will keep his side of any pact with such exactitude?"

"I don't know, but if he believes he has been deprived of his just vengeance, he certainly won't. I will not give him that excuse."

On battlefields, in the preparation for war, in nine years of constant armed resistance, Dubornos had watched the breadth and scope of Caradoc's will. Never before had he seen the sheer immovable strength of it so plainly displayed. He stared at the twin flasks and the mouthful of powder that would have changed the manner of his dying.

By this time tomorrow, or maybe the next day, it will be over.

More likely tomorrow, without the powder, unless the centurion was less than Xenophon believed him to be, but the space between would be worse than he had ever imagined. With a regret as profound as any he had known, Dubornos pinched the vine leaves together again, tying the linen thread at their necks, and set them on the old man's knees.

The physician's gaze stitched through his own. Xenophon said, "Claudius has no pact with you."

"No. Mine is with myself alone. And Caradoc."

Caradoc flinched. Colour flooded his cheeks. "Dubornos, you don't—"

"Yes, I do. And you have no power to stop me. Don't try."

The strength of his own conviction surprised him. All the dishonours of his life, small and large, linked together to point him to this: one final act of true worth. He smiled broadly, and it was not a sham. "I, too, have pledged my life to the care of the children," he said.

Xenophon rose, his nostrils pinched tight. "You're both mad—and that is a professional opinion as well as a personal one. I have no gods, but I will pray to yours for a swift passing."

Caradoc offered his hand to be shaken, Roman fashion. "We thank you sincerely for all you have done. The risk you have taken today is no less because we can't accept. If we had a way to repay you, we would do it."

The old man hesitated. "Then for my sake, would you accept a visitor?"

Dubornos felt the hairs rise on his neck. The gods may have abandoned him, but he had not lost his ability to read a man's intent. In panic, he said, "Xenophon, no! Not now. Have you lost all humanity?"

"Not at all," said a voice he had heard only in dreams for half his lifetime. "He thinks we will make a tearful reconciliation. He knows us all that poorly. It's a failing of Greek physicians; they believe they can alter the fates of other men and that they have the right to attempt it."

The morning paused in its progress. In the free world beyond the window, a dove bathed in a fountain. Water sputtered finely on the outer wall of the cell.

Caradoc turned with exceptional slowness. The cell was not built for four. Julius Valerius, decurion of the first troop, First Thracian Cavalry and, next to Scapula, the most reviled officer of the invading army, stood just beyond the threshold. He wore full dress armour, his mail polished to silver fish-scales, his cloak the black of the Thracians. His sword and belt were of cavalry style, embossed with images of the empire's heroes. No man, seeing him thus, would have deemed him other than Roman. Only the small insignia of the bull at his shoulder, drawn in the way of the ancestors in ox-blood red on a grey background, marked him as something apart, that and the searching black eyes, which mirrored ones they had seen daily for nine years on Mona.

The room lacked air, or there was too much and the pressure of it crowded the lungs; either way, it was hard to breathe and harder still to think. Forewarned, Dubornos pressed a hand to the wall for support and did not try to speak. Caradoc, who had had no such warning, stared and went on staring. The will that had commanded armies kept his hands from reaching out to touch the man who faced him. That will could not keep the shock from his voice.

"Bán?"

"Bán of the Eceni, half-brother to the Boudica?" The officer shook his head. "Absolutely not. I am Julius Valerius, decurion of the First Thracian Cavalry. Bán died a long time ago at the hands of Amminios, brother to Caradoc. I am not he."

In denial he made it fact. Stripped of the armour, he was his mother's son; his hair was hers, the high cheekbones and lean contours of his face, the length and beauty of his fingers, the smile that began in mischief and had once ended in joy. All these combined made him the child they had known, and all were soured beyond imagining the shape a man they could not begin to know. Still, he was Bán.

If the guards had slain Cunomar and Cygfa and thrown their heads at his feet, Caradoc might have managed himself better; that at least was within the realms of his imagining. The dignity, the wrappings of self-control so carefully nurtured to sustain him through the coming day, fell away raggedly. His gaze switched from the figure lounging in the doorway to Xenophon and back again. On the third pass, his eyes settled instead on Dubornos. A glimmer of intellect returned to light the wreckage of his mind. "You *knew*," he said. "How long have you known?"

"Since the mountainside when we were taken. I wasn't certain at first, but then he gave me his knife to release Hail from life because he couldn't remember the words of the invocation to Briga. Who else in the world would have done that?"

From the doorway, the too-familiar voice said acidly, "You knew before that. At the salmon-trap in the Eceni lands five years ago, you knew me as well I knew you."

Dubornos shook his head. "No. I knew only that you hated me, not who you were or why you felt so. I had spent too many nights warding the dreamers as they strove to recover your lost soul and return it to Briga's care. In the chaos of battle, one does not expect to see that same soul living and fighting for the enemy." For nearly two months he had lived with the knowledge of this and had chosen to forget it. Faced with the living reality, the enormity of it left him dry-mouthed. "Do you think, if I had known you, I would have rested until you were dead? We loathed you, believing you fully Roman. How much more so, had we known the depth of your betrayal?"

"How much indeed." The black eyes mocked him. "I'm disappointed. I really thought you knew who I was. All those years of vengeance, wasted."

Dubornos hissed air through his teeth, unable to speak. Distractedly Caradoc said to him, "Why did you not tell me?"

"What point was there? Would you go to your death better knowing that Breaca's lost brother had lived beyond Amminios's attack and had returned to slaughter his own people? Would Cunomar live better afterwards knowing that his own uncle was the one who had enslaved him? The boy has worshipped the memory of Bán Hare-Hunter, saviour of Hail, since he was old enough to hear the tales at the fire. It would do him no good to know the great deeds of the past are wiped out by the calumny of the present."

He had spoken with intent to wound and saw his effort wasted. Valerius lounged, smiling, in the doorway, untouched and untouchable.

Caradoc was more direct. Until then they had been speaking Latin, as a courtesy to Xenophon. He changed now to Eceni and, speaking as an elder, giving due weight to his words, said, "Bán, son of Macha, half-brother to Breaca. For the boy you were, for your own sake and your sister's, I would gladly have given my life. For the evil you have become, if your emperor did not hold the lives of my children as hostage, I would kill you where you stand."

"I have no doubt you would try." The man who was Bán and yet not Bán replied in Latin, pointedly. "Which is precisely why your children did not die on the hillside above the river that marks the site of the governor's last resounding military victory. There are more ways to defeat a man than simply to kill him in battle."

It was a practised taunt, the edge dulled with inner repetition. Baldly Caradoc said, "Scapula is dead."

"I know. I brought the news to Narcissus. Doubtless I will follow him. The dreamers have their mark now; it won't take them long to find those of us they hate most." Valerius smiled, wolf-like. "It is good to think you will have made the journey ahead of me. I would have hated to die with Amminios's favourite brother still living."

Dubornos laughed. "Are you insane? No one could believe that Caradoc had ever lived in Amminios's favour. They loathed each other, and everyone knew it. Amminios betrayed all of us to Rome. Caradoc and your sister were each sworn to kill him on sight. If he had ever had the courage to return to his father's dun, he would have died within the day."

"Bán believes otherwise, does he not?" Caradoc had control of himself again. He settled back on the pallet. His eyes searched the other man's face, absorbing those things that had changed and those that had not. "The last time we met," he said carefully, "you defeated my brother in a game of Warrior's Dance as long and hard-fought as any battle. Afterwards I swore to attend your long-nights and speak for you before the elders. I learned the details of your death—we really did believe you dead, I will swear that by any god in whom we can both trust—only when I returned to Eceni lands in fulfilment of my oath. In none of that would you have had reason to believe I held any love for Amminios. You knew the depth of hatred between us."

"But still you betrayed my sister, my father—all of us—to him before you left to take ship for Gaul." He was a child again; they all heard it. Almost, Valerius was the boy they had known, but his eyes were adult and would not yield.

"No." Caradoc was standing now, his head high, his anger no longer restrained. With quiet force, he said, "Whatever Amminios told you, whatever you choose to accept, you cannot believe that I would have damaged Breaca. I won't allow it. Your half-sister is my heart and soul, the rising of my sun in the morning. She has been from the first meeting and will be until I die and beyond. I would no more betray her than I would cut the throat of our newborn daughter. If Amminios told you otherwise, he was lying to hurt you."

"Or he was telling the truth to achieve the same end?" Valerius's lip curled. "The sons of Cunobelin were ever famed for their quick ways with words. You may squirm now to save your dignity, but I overheard your brother speaking of it to his factor at a time when he had no idea I was listening. He had no reason to lie; you have too many to count. In this I choose to believe the dead before the almost-dead."

"You would believe *Amminios* over me?"

"Yes."

It was said with perfect certainty. Only his eyes, at last, betrayed the first edge of doubt.

Dubornos took a step towards him. "Bán, you don't believe—"

Caradoc said, "But he does, he needs to. His life has turned on this, hasn't it, Valerius?" He spoke in Eceni, the single Latin name harsh in the flow of rounded syllables. "What other lies did Amminios tell you? Did he say that your family were all dead and there was nothing to come home to? That you would be blamed, perhaps, for the defeat at the Place of the Heron's Foot? He could lie so well, my brother. I know; I grew up in the shadow of his tongue. I took to the sea at twelve to escape it. But you had no escape, did you? Amminios had closed all the routes. What would you have done if you had known at the time that Breaca was still alive after the battle? Would you have come home to find her, to fight at her side in the invasion? Even to die for her?"

He spoke to a ghost. Bán stood in the doorway, bone-white, his eyes black holes in his skull. He swallowed and opened his mouth and no sound came out.

Caradoc said, "If you had the chance now, would you still—"

Dubornos laid a hand on his shoulder. "Enough. Stop now. He knows. There is nothing to be gained by making it worse."

Bán—Valerius—found voice enough to laugh. "Worse? There is nothing you can say that will make anything worse. You are lying—every word confirms it, and it counts for nothing. It would be amusing to talk more, but the emperor orders otherwise. The crowds must be entertained, and they find the death of others most engaging. Very soon your dying will begin. Eventually it will end. Afterwards I will continue to serve my emperor and my god to the best of my ability until your cursed dreamers—"

"Stop." Caradoc could still lead effortlessly. The once-Eceni stopped in mid-sentence, his mouth agape. A flash of anger gathered and fell away as Caradoc said, "Listen . . ."

Dubornos listened and, unwilling, heard. Time had moved on. The citron sun had passed beyond the limits of their window. Outside a half-century of men marched at parade pace up the hill towards the palace. A cart wheel squealed, wanting oil, and halted outside at the end of the corridor.

The fear, so long held at bay, rushed to return. Dubornos swayed, light-headed. Bán stared at him for a lingering moment and then spoke past him to the physician standing at the back of the cell.

"Xenophon, you should not be here."

"And you should?"

"Yes, of course. Forgive me; I became diverted by the amusements of our captives. I am to lead the prisoners in the procession and escort them to the tribunal. Claudius commands it. He requires a man who speaks both Latin and Eceni to translate the final speeches."

They had been speaking Latin for over half their conversation, faultlessly. Caradoc said, "We need no translation. Claudius knows that."

"Nevertheless, it will be done. The emperor wishes his defeated barbarian savages to be truly barbarian. It goes against the grain to execute a man who speaks Latin better than half the Senate."

CHAPTER 23

I am Julius Valerius, decurion. I am sworn to the Infinite Sun. Mithras, Father, help me.

The words ran in Valerius's head, marking time with the beat of the small drum by which each part of the procession was driven. They gave him little solace. No part of the emperor's triumphal parade was going to plan. At the most mundane level, the white, blue-eyed mare he had been loaned was afraid of mules, and riding her close to the prisoner's mule-drawn carts took more than half his attention. Beyond that he was assailed on all sides, and it was not only the prisoners who were the enemy.

From the procession's first creaking progress, the crowd lining the parade route had been difficult. The vast majority of Rome's population had already gathered under awnings on the plains in front of the Praetorian camp, where the culmination of the parade was scheduled to take place in the third hour before noon. The thousands who lined the Via Tiburtina were the dregs of the city, those lacking either the influence or the money to gain a worthwhile stance on the plains.

They had been enough to hamper the procession's progress. In the beginning, it was the quantity and quality of the precious metals on the carts that had caught the crowd's attention. Every item of gold and part-gold taken from the tribes of Britannia and presented to the emperor, his wife, his sons, and his freedmen had been loaded onto eight long, low-sided platforms, the better to be seen by the people. The morning sun had made of them a lake of flocculent butter, each item lost in the dazzle. Torcs of twisted gold wire hooked through others of hollow metal sheet embossed with wild animals and scenes of battle; enamelled armbands a hand's breadth wide gleamed near delicate, intricate necklaces of gold and silver, amber and pink coral; silver mirrors thrown in at random made moons in the shining day.

It was an impressive display. Inspired by it to holiday mood, slaves, lesser merchants, and their filthy, snot-nosed children had run alongside the procession or, easily outrunning the mules, had taken short-cuts through back streets to come out ahead and watch the carts pass again.

Captives had followed the spoils, providing even greater entertainment. First had come four carts of women and children destined for slavery. Those bearing the scars of battle had been placed on the inside, that the people might not readily see the evidence that barbarian women fought alongside their men.

Nearly two hundred men followed, all acknowledged warriors. Already some wore gladiatorial armour, if not yet their weapons. Their public combat, in pairs or groups, had been scheduled for the following day. A hundred tall Numidians had been hand-picked to fight against them. Thus would the two barbarian ends of the empire be brought together, each demonstrating their inferiority to Rome.

Last in the procession came the family of the rebel king, Caratacus; his wife and two children had been granted a cart to themselves. The two women were dressed in modest white linen, moderately clean. They stood upright with commendable dignity and had not been chained. The boy Cunomar swayed between them. A beautiful, almost feminine child, he bore the marks of recent bruising about his face, and his hands were bound behind him with cord; an afterthought, or an emergency measure against a child's instinct to fight his captors. Women in the crowd cooed as he passed, and some of the younger men blew noisy kisses. His face became paler and more fey as the cart ascended the hill.

The family was followed at the last by Caratacus himself, the barbarian king who for so long had spurned the rule of Roman law and would pay the price. For a while, the crowd had been impressed by him.

Bigger than the others, his cart was drawn by two grey geldings with black trappings and black feathers in their brow-bands. The horses were pale, almost white, and someone with more imagination than experience had painted swirling whorls on their quarters and flanks with deep grey-black river clay to represent barbarian woad. Later a legionary who had served in the invasion forces and knew more of what he was about had added the sinuous lines of the serpent-spear in ox-blood red on their outer shoulders.

The man himself stood tall in his chains, his eyes straight ahead, as befitted his rank. His dress was pure barbarian: his tunic, breeches, and cloak were of rough wool in loud Gaulish check; his only armour was a leather corselet stitched about with the crudest of metal plates, some so poorly polished they could have been lead and not iron. His brother, standing alongside, was a poorer imitation, the lesser in all respects, including his inability or unwillingness to maintain a dignified silence. He spoke constantly to the officer at his side, ignoring his status as prisoner.

From Valerius's perspective, the trouble had started in earnest when Dubornos began to pass comment on the things around him. They had been crossing an intersection. Sunlight leaked between tall buildings, the houses piled on houses that kept the populace of Rome concentrated within an easy walk of the Forum. Here costs had been cut and margins creamed; the windows were placed so close together that a whore could lean out of one and offer her services to a man at the other, and he, if he were daring and chose to believe the building might remain upright for the duration of the transaction, could clasp her hand and accept. Along the length of the street, mortar flaked from the lintels, and gaps with streaks of green slime below showed where roof tiles had slipped and gutters failed.

Dubornos had said, "I have seen two grandmothers walking the streets, both lame, neither supported by a youth to be their eyes and ears, as would happen even now in the tribes."

The soft, rolling Eceni fell into the crowd and was not welcome; those for whom his death was the day's entertainment resented being excluded from his pleadings. Someone hissed. Others began the low, pulsing groan that greeted the loser of gladiatorial combat.

Ignoring them, Dubornos said, "Were you not the eyes and ears to the elder grandmother after your sister sat her long-nights? Does it not shame you to be part of this? Does your god look on and feel his people well cared for?"

"My god is not your—" It had been a mistake to answer. Silence had been Valerius's best—his only—defence. The mare jerked her head, and a small cheer rose from a different part of the crowd, congratulating the captive on his strike; not all of the city's population favoured the legions.

Whatever their allegiance, the masses wanted most an excuse for a riot and were close to finding it. A hand's length of firewood bounced on the edge of the cart near the mare's eye. She skittered sideways, her hooves sliding on the metalled road. Her hindquarters knocked up against a doorway and hit something soft. A woman screamed from low down underfoot.

Caradoc, who had been silent since the cart had left the prison, said distinctly, "Watch yourself, fool." The tone of it stung.

Valerius hauled on the reins, swearing in Thracian. The mare backed out of the doorway, lifting her feet too high. Beneath them, bleeding freely but still living, the drunken, par-blind beggar-woman who had chosen it for her night's rest lay on her back with her legs splayed, yammering incoherencies. Her left leg was withered from the thigh down. Her left wrist, which had been whole when she lay down to rest, was broken.

"Help her, god damn you!"

It was said in Eceni, but the meaning was clear to the entire crowd. Somewhere a man laughed coarsely. "Go on, decurion, get her up. Look what she's offering. How can you resist?"

A small group of youths near to the old woman began to cat-call, as they would a prostitute out alone too late.

"Bán, for god's sake—"

I am not Bán. I am Julius Valerius. Your gods are not my gods.

In the time it took to think this, to repeat it, seeking certainty, Valerius lost control of the crowd. Caradoc's voice had cracked like a whip above the tumult, losing him what small sympathy his position might have garnered. The crowd booed. From the rear ranks, someone made the sound of a horn blowing the legionary order to advance.

The driver of the captives' cart, who had been chosen for his youth and beauty before any ability to deal with complex matters of imperial decorum, let the grey horses idle to a halt. Caught by the noise, the teamsters driving the mule carts did likewise; their orders had been to keep the procession intact. The cat-calls, trumpet-noises, and whistles grew to a common jeering, gathering rhythm with volume.

Valerius cursed, looking round for help. He had dealt with crowds often enough to know their patterns. Soon they would begin the slow, taunting hand-clap of the circus, and soon after that there would be blood; the century of Urban Guard escorting them was not enough to prevent it. A movement on the cart caught his attention. Swearing passionately, he wrenched the mare back.

Caradoc was contained, but only barely so. A Praetorian legionary was at the cart's side; his drawn sword was all that prevented the prisoner from jumping down.

Dressed in the ludicrous lead-stitched armour, with clay swirls flaking from his cheeks, Caradoc radiated anger. His eyes locked with Valerius's. If ever the one god lived in a man, he did so now. The blazing gold hair was the newly risen sun, the fury fuelled by centuries of imperfect worship. In perfection was beauty and astonishing nobility. That it should come here and now, in this man, was unthinkable sacrilege. Valerius felt his diaphragm clench and fought not to vomit.

The grey gaze could not be broken. The immeasurable voice of the god said, *"See to her. Now."*

The part of himself that dismounted and knelt by the old woman was not one that Valerius remembered with any certainty. When he spoke, it was at first in a language he had neither heard nor spoken in nearly twenty years. With considerable effort, he set aside the tongue of his ancestors and repeated his question in Eceni, Gaulish, and finally Latin, working his way from distant youth to adulthood. Only at the last did the old woman understand him: "Grandmother, where are you hurt?"

She tilted her head, searching the blind, noise-filled horizon for his voice. "My arm," she said querulously. "My arm hurts."

He took her left arm firmly, above the break. Her skin was greasy and fragile at once, not at all like the elder grandmother of his past. She stank of rancid wine and urine and neglect. Inwardly he heard the voice of his own childhood, *I swear to be your eyes and ears, until time or the gods relieve me of it.*

From the same place, an old woman in a badger-skin robe said, *You abandoned me. I had no one. Could you not have come home for me?*

Shaking his head, he leaned closer. "Your wrist is broken," he said. "It was my horse who trampled you. You will be recompensed and a bone-setter found. Is there anywhere else that hurts?"

"My chest," she said. Awareness of it made her cough, liquidly. Blood threaded her spittle.

Valerius sat back on his heels and forced himself to think coherently. *I am Julius Valerius, decurion, Lion of Mithras.* He was in the suburbs of Rome, in a hostile crowd, in a procession whose timing had been arranged with utmost precision. Already the delay was such that he faced possible death. If it lasted longer, he would be lucky not to join his foes on the nearest free cross. Whatever Caradoc might say, however he might be supported by the returning ghosts, Valerius had neither the means nor the time to aid a crippled grandmother.

He propped her up in the doorway. "Stay well. If I am alive when this is over, I will come back for you, I swear it."

The guards had surrounded the cart, standing face out with their swords drawn, keeping the mob at bay. The centurion, who was named Severus, had served on the Rhine in the time of Caligula. Valerius caught his eye. "Get the cart moving. Clear the way. If any of us is to live, we need to be at the edge of the plain in front of the camp before Claudius reaches it."

The officer grimaced. "Do you think the muleteers can get their beasts to run up the rest of the hill?"

"They can if they understand their lives depend on it."

I am Julius Valerius, decurion of the first troop, the Ala Prima Thracum....

By the beat of the drum, Valerius knew where he was. His orders were etched in acid on his liver; he could have carried them out blindfolded, with his ears stopped with wool, which was as well when the ground before him was so uncertain and the words he heard most clearly were in Eceni and all from the past. What had been merely unpleasant was descending unchecked into nightmare. Ghosts of all his ages crowded on him, clamouring. They had not come at him so vividly in daylight since his time in slavery to Amminios. They were not yet close enough to hear the words precisely, but that made no difference; Caradoc's voice replaced theirs, echoing from the prison. *What would you have done if you had known at the time that Breaca was still alive after the battle?*

The god had asked the same question, and forced by the presence of deity, Valerius had answered honestly. Here on the emperor's plain in the emperor's procession, he would not—could not—do the same.

I am Valerius, decurion, sworn Lion of the god. I serve my emperor with my body and my god with my heart and soul....

If he spoke aloud in the vault of his head, he could hold on to his sanity. He dared not close his eyes. The officer in charge of the procession was Marullus, centurion of the second cohort of the Praetorian Guard, the one who had branded Valerius in a cellar in another lifetime, his true Father for ever under Mithras's care. His presence burned as the sun, keeping the god in focus, but did not dispel the voice or the memory of a man who had reached divinity and did not know it.

Caradoc is not the god. He never has been. If it seemed otherwise, it was the ghosts' doing.

Out on the plains, nine cohorts of Praetorians and three of the Urban Guard—less the one century that was detailed to march with the prisoners—lined in perfect ranks before their camp: nearly six thousand men, armed and trained to the highest level the empire could achieve. From a distance, all that could be seen was the blinding reflection of polished helms.

Closer, the wavering sway of the officers' plumes stood proud like reeds fanning a lake of silver. Bán's mother—*Valerius's* mother—walked between them as if they were trees, a wren flying high above. He had found her charred body lying on a pyre after the invasion battle and had watched her soul begin the journey to the other world. He had not seen her since. His father, too, had been absent since the final day of the invasion battle. He stood squarely ahead of Valerius now, his shield face-on and his spear readied so that it would be impossible to ride forward except through him. It was best not to think of that.

The ghosts were fewer to the left, where the crowd waited. Looking over his shoulder, he could see them, a great massed array standing facing the militia, separated by a space of a mere ninety feet. They were less tangibly ordered, but the layerings of rank and influence were no less distinct. Between these two, the paired tribunals of the Emperor Claudius and his empress, Agrippina, occupied a position of utmost visibility and dignity. Fifty senators, picked for their seniority, were seated on benches a short distance away, conspicuous both by their position and by their separation from the person of the emperor. In the open ground between them waited the shade of Iccius, the Belgic slave-boy who had seen the last days of Bán as he was and whose death had triggered his birth as Julius Valerius, officer in the emperor's auxiliary cavalry.

I have stood in the presence of the Bull. Dear god, I have touched the Bull. Why will you not take this away?

The timing of the procession did not allow for incapacity on the part of one of its leading figures. At precisely the appointed moment, to a briefly deafening fanfare from the cohorts, forty-eight sweating, heaving mules dragged their laden wagons forward into view. Slaves in sombre dress carried choice items alongside: shields of carefully worked bronze, the best of the mirrors, neck chains in solid gold set about with amber, jet and blue enamel. Through the jabber of his mind-noise, Valerius heard a blanket of silence fall on the humming conversation of Rome's populace. This, at least, was predictable. No crowd in the world is so jaded that gold by the wagonload does not inspire the hush of avarice, however short-lived.

After, the tide of conversation rose again to a muted roar, louder than it had been. Goldsmiths and jewellers strained forward to see the intricacies of individual pieces. Others, who might perhaps commission an imitation, took note of the weight of the pieces and the more distinctive styles. In the other world that clashed with this one, a hanged Eceni girl-child, three years old, skipped beside a cart, swapping the frayed rope at her neck for a necklace that had been her mother's. Valerius did close his eyes then. When he opened them sometime later, the child, at least, had gone.

The wagons were spaced apart so that the first had passed halfway across the parade area and the dust of its passing had begun to settle before the second fully started. They moved in a crescent, beginning near the Praetorians, curving in towards the crowd and coming back to a station just behind the imperial tribunal where they were covered, temporarily, with hides. When all eight had completed their procession and were lined up together, the coverings were pulled back in unison, allowing the sun once again to meet the gold. The sudden blaze of reflected light made a fulgent halo around the emperor, blessing him. As one, the crowd vented a long-drawn sigh. In the world between the worlds, the ghosts pretended awe that, having lived amongst the gods, they could not possibly feel.

Only the prisoners remained unmoved. From the wagon at Valerius's side, Dubornos said, "Luain mac Calma did it better for Cunobelin." It was not clear from his speech or demeanour whether he, too, saw the ghosts. Valerius hoped not.

Caradoc said more thoughtfully, "The Trinovantes said that your emperor considers himself a god. Until now I had not believed it true."

Valerius stared into the blistering light until his eyes hurt. The gods of his past and his present hovered on the edge of imagining. Claudius was not amongst them. He would not allow Caradoc to be. *What would you have done if you had known . . . ?*

"You will believe it as you die," he said. "Better men than you have called on Claudius to release them from life, naming him first amongst their gods. You will be no different."

He wanted them to disagree. Caradoc nodded. "Our saying it will not make it true." The ghost of Eburovic, father to Bán, agreed with him sorrowfully.

A whistle blew from beneath the scorpion-standard of the Guard. The carts bearing women and children rolled forward onto the plain. The gossiping crowds fell silent, not in appreciation but in mannered boredom. The slave auctions would draw their interest again; until then, this was a necessary part of the spectacle but not one to speak of later at dinner. In the hush, the murmurings of business associates could be heard, using the time to deal with other matters. Valerius, sensitized as he had not expected to be, noticed that the warriors amongst the women had moved to the outside and made a ring about the mothers with children. Their dignity was wasted on an inattentive crowd. A multitude of ghosts wept for them bitterly.

The wagons of men came next, outstanding for their height and the barbarity of their dress, or their shameless nakedness and the outlandish markings on their skins. In the last cart were three dreamers who were also warriors. They saw what their countrymen did not: all three acknowledged Macha as they passed. Amongst the Romans, none save Valerius saw the gestures. The greater mass of people craned their necks to see the two rearmost carts: the family and the rebel king himself. Of the rest, Dubornos, who was more than halfway to a dreamer, saw and began to understand. Watching him, Valerius saw the moment when his vision changed and the ghosts became part of his present. He acknowledged them, smiling with unfeigned joy.

"If it is Mithras who holds the souls of the dead, as your myths teach, one could find it strange that he calls on the soul of an Eceni dreamer to stand watch over her son. Do you think perhaps instead that—"

"I think nothing. And we are moving. If you speak while the carts process before the people, the guards have orders to tear out your tongue. The ghosts of your past will not stop them."

He was not certain of that, but he spoke with the certainty and authority of an officer, and it seemed he was believed. Dubornos fell to arch-browed silence. At a hidden signal, the cart that carried Cwmfen, Cygfa, and Cunomar rolled forward. The child's hands had been untied; Caradoc had bound his son instead with an unbreakable oath not to bring disgrace on his family, and it had been accepted by the Praetorian centurion who had charge of the proceedings. Thus the three of the family stood upright, pale in their linen shifts, their uncut hair lifting slightly in the wind of their passing. They had the height and colouring of Gauls but were less clearly cowed. The women particularly held themselves as queens, fixedly dignified. Word had passed that they were perhaps to be spared execution but not that they might also be spared slavery. In the foremost rows of the crowd, the wealthier and more daring of the senators' wives began privately to bid for their services.

On the flat ground in front of Valerius, the shade of Eburovic raised his shield to battle-readiness. On the plain, the cart containing Caradoc's family reached the mid-point of the marked track. At the plain's edge, the Praetorian centurion raised a discreet hand. Valerius felt his heart lurch, as at the start of battle. He hissed at the driver of the grey horses, "Get ready. When Marullus drops his hand, move at a walk. Follow the tracks of the others. If you value your life, don't let the horses stop."

The man nodded, his face a mask of fervent concentration. In this place, death hung close, like flies on a still day. A mistake in the emperor's procession would meet with only one outcome; the only question would be the manner of their dying.

The drumbeat matched the cadence of the horses as they moved forward into a walk. The cartwheels turned, whispering greasily on their shafts. The white mare was parade-trained, and she stepped out like a war-horse—and on through the shade of a man she had never known. Bán felt the cold judgement of his father wash through him, a man he had respected above all others. Frost sheathed his heart. Only the willing warmth of his horse stopped him from toppling out of the saddle. As Valerius, he swore in Gaulish, Thracian, and Latin. None of these helped.

Dubornos said, "He loved you," and there were no guards close enough to tear out his tongue.

The crowd held its breath. The cart carrying the defeated rebel leader moved at a pace far slower than any that had gone before it. Drowning in the appreciative lingering silence, Julius Valerius, decurion of the First Thracian Cavalry, rode by instinct, blindly.

"You've worked a long time for this; you should enjoy it more." Dubornos was ebullient. One would not have thought him a man whose death would begin a few short speeches away and end with another dawn.

In Eceni, Valerius said, "I will remind you of that, come dusk."

Ahead, the wagon bearing the rebel leader's family reached its appointed place and turned. The boy, Cunomar, raised his head and asked a question of Cygfa; across the field Valerius saw it and cursed the fact that the child had not been given poppy to keep him pliable and silent. Caradoc's cart reached the mid-point of the processing pathway and curved back towards the emperor. The sun-gold glare was blinding, Claudius a hazed silhouette in its nucleus. Agrippina was more easily seen, being less the focus of the light. She had dressed all in white, perfect as pearls, with her hair chastely hidden and no jewellery but small clutches of seed pearls at her throat and ears.

Sweating, Valerius counted the paces in to the tribunals.

Twenty. Ten. *What would you have done if . . .* A hushed mutter from the crowd surged to a soft peak and subsided into silence. Five paces. A single horn blew, devastatingly loud. Blessedly, the horses ignored it. Two paces. Begin the halt. . . . *you had known that Breaca . . .*

Mithras. Father of Light. I need you.

The precision of their arrival shocked Valerius into momentary clarity. Whoever had organized this knew exactly what they were doing. The shadows of the waiting crosses met in a tripartite linkage of straight lines and bold blacks, and the centre point fell with mathematical exactitude between the horses as the prisoners' cart slowed for the line. Caradoc, who had been gold in the sun, became muted in shadow.

Narcissus stood in the herald's place to the right of the tribunal. He had the voice for it; when he chose, he could project to the back of the waiting silence as well as any actor.

"Halt before the person of your emperor! His Excellency Tiberius Claudius Drusus Nero Germanicus Britannicus commands it!"

As the words fell away, they halted. Legionary horns sounded a deafening fanfare. Julius Valerius, floundering officer of Rome, found himself eye to eye with his emperor.

This close, Claudius's tremors were apparent. He stood, his toga luminescent in the radiant light. The palms embroidered on the tunic beneath waved as if alive. He might have been their sole focus of attention, but Agrippina leaned forward. Even seated, she was regal. No sane man could imagine her earning her living diving as a slave-girl. She studied the two prisoners on the cart as a cook might study fresh fish at market. In a long while, her gaze transferred, equally searching, to Valerius.

"One is fair of hair, one red, one black," she said at length. "They do not look of one tribe."

In Latin, Caradoc said, "My lady, we are not."

The empress's exquisite brow rose to the height of her hair line. Narcissus twitched. The crowd could not hear them now. Fifty senators, straining forward, were their only audience. They had better breeding than the masses: they did not sigh their surprise but swayed as if they had.

Valerius was not so lost to reality that he could no longer sense danger from his superiors. In Eceni he said, "You might wish to consider the future of your children before you speak again in Latin. In this place, at this time, you do not know it."

Caradoc inclined his head. He was no longer the god, but neither was he a cowed and beaten prisoner. His face was a mask of restrained, intelligent dignity from which his eyes laughed. Agrippina smiled into them beautifully.

In the breathless silence that followed, Narcissus, reading from a scroll, began to announce the long list of the emperor's victories over the rebellious tribes of Britannia. Under cover of the noise, Claudius said, "We have received word from your dreamers. They do not agree to our proposal. They will not lift their curse in exchange for the lives of your wife and children."

The ghosts already knew this: Macha, Eburovic, the slave-boy Iccius. Surprisingly, each greeted the news with gladness. Cwmfen and Cygfa, standing within earshot in their wagon, quite clearly neither knew nor were glad. It was possible they had not known of the bargain at all. Valerius saw a sudden movement and turned in time to see Cwmfen, who had been silent, clamp a restraining hand on her daughter's arm. A single harsh word in a foreign tongue slid out across the plain, unnoticed by most. It took Valerius some time to identify it as Ordovician, straight from the battlefield, a command to give ground immediately in the face of the enemy. It could as easily have been meant for Caradoc as Cygfa, or for both.

If Caradoc heard, he gave no sign. White-faced, he opened his mouth to speak and snapped it shut again while Valerius, remembering late his role, made the fiction of translating the emperor's Latin into the language of his childhood. He struggled over one or two of the words, finding poor representations, but then he could have spoken the words of an infant's sleeping song and it would not have mattered. All those within hearing understood what had been said.

The time it took gave Caradoc a chance to recover. He no longer smiled. In Eceni, in absolute earnest, he said, "I did the best I could. I have kept my side of our oath."

Translated, Claudius said, "Indeed. Your friends in the rebel territories, however, do not hold your family's life as dearly as your own. They would sacrifice them for you."

"What?"

That needed no translation. Behind them Narcissus reached a small climax in his descriptions of martial valour: the triumphant entry of the emperor into Camulodunum, borne on the backs of elephants. The emperor smiled and raised a hand to the grateful crowd.

When he could be heard again over the tumult, Claudius said, "If you die, I die. That is their exact declaration. Not only do I die, but my death will mirror yours exactly. I ask you now, and you should know that your family's well-being hangs on the truth of your answer, can they do this?"

Worlds stopped while Caradoc considered his answer. They could have been alone, two men facing death in different ways. On the rostrum, Claudius the fool was replaced entirely by Claudius the survivor, the excellent scholarly mind tuned always—above the need to witness pain in others or to dominate—to the absolute, unconditional need to preserve his own life.

Opposite him Caradoc, too, had shed the armours of pretence.

Stripped to the bone, he stared at Claudius, the inner workings of his mind laid bare. If he had laughed at the emperor, he did so no longer. If he had disdained his failures as a man and a leader of men, he did not disdain his mind, nor the manifest reach of his power. More clearly even than in the prison, the core of him blazed for all those close enough to see it.

On the wagon behind, Cwmfen and Cygfa stood still as marble, and as white. At the emperor's side, Agrippina tilted her head and ran a single perfect nail down the side of her cheek. Among the Senate, several men sat more upright. The ghosts crowded close, supporting the warrior in ways he would never know. Valerius, striving wholly to be the instrument of his god, set his teeth and prayed that he not be sick and that the nightmare be taken from him.

"Can they do it?" asked Claudius again. "I asked you once before, and you refused to answer. You will tell me now. You have lived among them; you must know it."

Valerius translated woodenly. The silence afterward stretched the limits of endurance. If Caradoc could have gone to his death without answering, he would have done so, that much was clear. His family's life depended on his answer, but he had no indication as to which way Claudius would lean. Eventually, in Ordovician, the language of his own childhood, he said, "They will say that they can. I do not believe it."

The words drifted out into the golden air and left their own echo. The emperor, the empress, and fifty men of the Senate, to whom they meant nothing, turned to the decurion of the cavalry for his translation. The dreamers of the Eceni signed for Valerius, who had once been Bán, to interpret accurately, using wards of binding that would have stopped him dead as a child and forced him to compliance. They bound him no longer. On the contrary, they gave him the first indication of what he could do, what his god required of him; whatever the ghosts of his enemies so badly wanted, he would do its opposite.

In a glorious moment of freedom and perfect clarity, guided by his god and with the promise of vengeance hot his heart, Valerius translated the two sentences as, "The Governor Scapula took ten days dying, each one in pain. In that may be your answer."

Caradoc's gaze was grounded in stone. Dubornos grunted as if punched in the chest and clamped his teeth on his tongue. Cygfa, standing beside her mother on the wagon, hissed a stream of invective in withering Ordovician. The ghosts fled, chittering.

Claudius turned to his decurion. "You brought us the news of our governor's death and yet did not tell us this. Is it true?"

Valerius bowed, light-headed as if with wine or the promise of combat. He balanced on the edge of a precipice, and a step the wrong way would see him slowly dead. He said, "Excellency, it is. Those of my command who travelled with me can confirm it. The legate of the Twentieth Legion sent a written report, and my orders were not to speak beyond that unless directly asked by yourself or another in high command. I have not been so asked. I believe the legate saw no point in disturbing your excellency with unnecessary detail."

"I see. We will consider this at a later date." Returning to Caradoc, the emperor said, "You knew before word reached me of Scapula's death, and now you know the detail before it is openly told. How can you do this?"

"The gods may speak to any man in a time of need." It was Dubornos who said it, in Latin, out of turn, in the presence of the emperor and interrupting the man who was ostensibly his king. Caradoc stared at him fixedly but said nothing.

The emperor nodded. More was at stake now than protocol, and he could not further condemn one already sentenced to die. Valerius heard a man he despised take risks to protect him and regretted it. The ghosts addressed Dubornos in whispers, and he listened, nodding.

Speaking to Caradoc, Claudius said, "Our life is threatened. This cannot be allowed. Your family will pay the price for your failure. You alone will live as Vercingetorix did, held in confinement in perpetuity as hostage for my life. The rest will die over the coming days."

Caradoc had recovered himself. In Latin he cast his voice beyond the emperor to reach the listening Senate.

"And so Imperial Claudius is brought down by the might of barbarian soothsayers and bards? I had thought better of you than that. And that an oath between kings was binding."

It was a naked incitement to murder, the act of a man who preferred any death to life. Valerius, listening, heard his efforts unravel and saw for the first time that the ghosts, perhaps, had known him better than he had believed.

His mother was staring at him, her lips pursed in thought. In his mind he said, *I am not your instrument, now or ever. If Caradoc wishes to die, I will not be his saviour.* She raised her brows and smiled, and the skin crawled on his spine.

On the podium of the tribunal, Caradoc's words were absorbed with due regard by the emperor and the men of the Senate, but it was Agrip-pina who responded first, waving amused dismissal. She no longer smiled for Caradoc but for Claudius, whose death would put her sixteen-year-old son on the throne. No one doubted who would rule in truth if that came to pass. Several in the Senate saw the possibility stepping closer.

"The barbarian is bold," she said. "I have rarely heard a man plead so eloquently for his own death. Clearly he seeks to persuade you to its op-posite. The strength of his plea is proof of his true desires. I say, instead, you should let him have what he purports to crave. Kill him as you have decreed. We will sacrifice to Mars Ultor and again to Jupiter and see if his soothsayers are a match for our gods."

"And yet we may regret at leisure what we have committed in haste." Seated, with his chin on his hands and the crown of laurels on his brow, Claudius was another Augustus, epitome of wisdom and arbiter of rea-soned justice. "This man is a warrior and king of his people. It is long known that among the barbarians, the king will sacrifice himself for the greater good. It may be that he knows the dreamers' power and believes his death will aid them. For such a reason, he would seek his own death."

Narcissus, freedman and minister of state, completed his announce-ments to the crowd. Entering the conversation as if by right, he said, "If there is any such risk, it must not be taken. The man may be spared with-out harm to your self or standing."

The freedman set himself in opposition, once again, to the empress. Those amongst the Senate, tuned to the internecine warfare of the court, saw a parting of ways and a need to take sides. Nods of agreement began slowly and were taken up, or not, by those with most or least to lose.

Agrippina frowned decorously. One would have had to be watching very closely to know if she noted those who supported Narcissus amongst the Senate. "We have a victory procession," she said. "Triumphal distinc-tions have been voted for Ostorius Scapula. We do him and ourselves no honour if we do not demonstrate the magnitude of our victory. The crosses must not remain empty."

Claudius nodded pleasantly. "The brother will die, and the men who fought against us. The people's desire to see blood will be assuaged, and yet at the same time, they will be reminded that their emperor is not with-out mercy. It is a good combination. Thus did Scipio win the favour of the people by his release of Syphax. Narcissus can provide a speech for Caratacus in which he throws himself on our mercy, and we—"

"No."

It was not said forcefully, but still the Senate jerked back as if struck. Two of the Urban Guard stepped forward, their hands on their weapons.

Claudius directed his attention at Caradoc. "Your life will be spared. You are not in a position to argue."

"Am I not?" The grey eyes scoured him. Valerius knew that look. "You have killed countless hundreds of your enemies, but have you ever yet tried to keep a man alive against his will? To make him eat and drink as much as a body requires to live into long life? I promise you, our death, yours and mine, will be as lengthy as flesh can make it."

The emperor said, "Once, in my audience room, you implied doubt that your dreamers could reach me. Did you then lie?"

"Yes. I believed it would protect my family. I retract it. The governor's death is proof of their powers. If they can reach him, guarded by the legions, what is there to keep them from you?"

"I see." The emperor spent full days in the law courts, acting as judge. It showed in him now, as he weighed actions, motives, and consequences towards judgement. "You would go lying to your own death but resort to truth only when your family is threatened. Am I then to believe that you value your brother's life above your own?"

"And those of the warriors, yes. I will not live to see another man die in my stead."

"How very noble," the empress sneered. The expression, if not the sound, was repeated here and there amongst the ranks of the Senate. "Let them all die," she said again. "Xenophon and the horse-guards together will see you come to no harm from it. You are the emperor. You have no need to be cowed by a barbarian."

She spoke as a mother to a recalcitrant child, demanding obedience. Breaths were drawn among the Senate, audibly.

With excruciating slowness, Claudius turned. He leaned a long moment on his elbow, the better to look to his left. Fifty men of good birth and high standing stared rigidly ahead for all the aching time it took their emperor fully to face the woman who was his niece and yet professed to love him. When he spoke, his words were widely spaced and each one a weapon.

"Nor by my wife," he said distinctly.

The words fell one by one into dead air. Narcissus smiled in triumph. Agrippina's eyes blazed. She opened her mouth to speak and closed it again, finding discretion at last. The men of the Senate discovered new places to look that were away from their emperor and his wife. Valerius swayed and had to hold himself upright. His heart hung lifeless in his chest. His mother smiled at him, and he turned away, tasting ashes on his tongue. Caradoc and Dubornos, thinking themselves unseen, each made with the fingers of his left hand the sign of thanks to the gods. Cwmfen wept silently in her wagon. Cygfa, smiling her hate, bent to Cunomar and kissed him.

Fringed around them all, the gathered ghosts of the Eceni dead raised a cacophony of silent celebration. A wren spiralled high in the clear sky, singing.

SECTION IV

AUTUMN A.D. 54

CHAPTER 24

Julius Valerius, decurion, disembarked from the merchant ship *Isis* at the harbour of Ostia, eighteen miles west of Rome. He arrived after nightfall on the twenty-fifth day of September in the 14th year of the reign of the Emperor Claudius. That he did not fall to his knees and kiss the sea-stained wood of the dock in thanks for a safe landing was a testament both to the benevolence of the one god and to the presence of Severus, centurion of the Urban Guard, who had come to escort him to the palace. Mithras had never required the obsequities demanded by other deities, and the centurion had made it plain from the moment of first greeting that time was short and not to be wasted. Nevertheless, Valerius stood for a moment holding the mooring rope and let the land support him while the swimming nausea of the sea receded.

He had never been good on water, and an ocean crossing made so soon after the equinoctial gales was an invitation to hell for the duration of the voyage, if not some considerable time thereafter. Valerius had known as much when he first received the message to take ship and travel to Rome, but the seal had been imperial, and no decurion who cared for his career would use poor weather and the risk of shipwreck as an excuse to refuse his emperor's summons. It might have been more reasonable to claim that no master in his right mind would set sail at such a time, save that the *Isis* rode at anchor on the Thames and the decurion had been given three turnings of the tide to set his affairs in order, find a fast horse, and reach her. Because he cared more for his career than for anything in his life except his god, Valerius had been aboard before the second tide was fully out, carrying a flagon of wine but no food in order that the nightmare might pass quickly, or seem to.

Standing on the solid planking of the dock with his guts lurching to the rhythm of the sea, he was grateful for the wine. More than the nausea, it clouded his memory of Rome, so that he could greet Severus with equanimity, recalling their time served as part of Caligula's army on the Rhine while avoiding any memory of the day they had together shepherded a blighted victory procession up the Via Tiburtina or of the fiasco that came afterwards on the broad plain in front of the Praetorian camp.

Valerius had put over two years of dedicated effort, prayer, hard work, and the judicious use of wine, into banishing the ghosts that had plagued him that day. He did not intend to let them return simply because the emperor had need of him in Rome.

Presently his guts began to settle and his mind to clear. Small details that he had missed on first landing became plain. Severus was darkly cloaked, and he waited in that concealed part of the harbour where both the quayside lamps and the lighthouse failed to cast light. His horse bore no marks that would identify it as a mount of the Guard. The spare gelding whose rein he held was outstanding in its ordinariness: a solid brown with no splash of white on face or legs. Valerius had ridden a horse like this once before in his early days on the Rhine, when it had been important to blend in with the background and not be noticed. Then it had been the emperor who was dangerous. Now it seemed less likely to be so.

His legs had begun to trust the land. He stepped away from the circle of light. The dark held an honesty that the orange blaze of the lighthouse had not. Severus watched him carefully. The man had been a solid soldier on the Rhine, hard enough to be a good leader without crushing the spirits of those who served under him. Age had granted him dignity and white hair but no fresh scars. None of this suggested he was a man who might break his first and strongest oath to serve his emperor in all things or die in the attempt. Still, he was not branded for Mithras and so lacked the added certainty of brotherhood, and the word in Britannia was that Agrippina owned the Praetorians in their entirety. It was not safe to assume that she did not own the Urban Guard as well, or a substantial portion of it.

Valerius's orders had stated that he should come unarmed. His dagger and his cavalry sword were safely bound in his pack. On impulse, as he left the ship, he had picked up a filleting knife owned by the cabin boy, and he held it now in the curved palm of his right hand. Scale-slime slipped between his fingers as he moved his grip to the mid-point of the haft, ready to throw or to stab. With a prayer to the god, he asked, "Whom do you serve?"

"The emperor," said Severus. "To the grave and beyond." He did not say whose grave, but it was not the centurion's death that was daily rumoured in Camulodunum, nor his wife who was said to rule the palace and the empire from her boudoir.

"Good. And I also." Valerius reached down to adjust his boot and let the knife slide unseen through a gap between the planks of the dock. The small splash of its falling was lost in the wash of the tide. "The sea is out of me," he said. "I am safe to ride. Perhaps we should go?"

Severus nodded. "With all speed," he said. His eyes marked the space through which the knife had dropped.

They rode fast and hard and kept to the Via Ostiensis until they reached the main gate into Rome, where two men of the Guard let them through as if expected. In the city, they took the quieter streets, avoiding the main thoroughfares with their parties of drunken youths and too many wakeful eyes who might know a centurion by name and ask questions concerning the identity of the man he escorted.

Valerius had spent half a month in Rome on his last, ill-fated visit and believed he had come to know it. Riding through, he found it little changed and was surprised. The rumours in Britannia had been of a city slumping to ruin along with its emperor. It had been easy to imagine the insidious beginnings of decay overlaying the memories of slave-crowded streets and bright sun and constant noise. He had forgotten the quieter Rome of night, away from the taverns and whorehouses, where citizens retired at dusk and rose at dawn and slept at peace in between. Riding behind Severus, he came to remember the reassuring calm of streets lit by starlight where the only sound was the soft hoofbeats of two horses and the smells were of night and old buildings and not at all unpleasant after the racking salt and sick of the voyage.

He did not recognize the palace until Severus halted near a door in yet another long, high wall. Coming to it in the dark and from the west, the palace looked smaller and less imposing than he remembered from his last visit. The gilded roof shone no more than glazed tiles under the starlight, and the outer walls could have been yet another anonymous villa. Valerius dismounted, feeling the stiffness of the voyage cramp thighs that had been three days without a horse. His pack weighed more than he remembered. He unhitched it from the saddle and hooked it over his shoulder.

Severus took his reins. "Go to the door in the wall on your right and knock twice. Wait until someone comes. It may be a while."

Valerius thought himself dismissed and was turning away when the centurion gripped his elbow, drawing him back. Up close the officer's eyes were bloodshot, like those of a man who has slept too little. "If he needs you so badly that he has called you across the ocean, do as he asks," he said. "He has few enough who will."

"I took the oath as you did," said Valerius. "His will is mine."

"Good." Severus grinned as a man grins before battle who does not expect to survive it. "Long may it remain so." He led the horses back into the dark, and Valerius was alone.

The door was a slaves' entrance, lacking adornment. Standing before it in the quiet of the night, Valerius felt currents of fear that were not his alone. The place reeked of uncertainty and betrayal, and ghosts pressed close that had nothing to do with the tribes of a foreign land and everything to do with the desperation of a dying emperor. No sane man would remain in it for long.

Ghosts were no longer Valerius's concern, and fear had long ago ceased to be an enemy; wine and the memory of the god had allowed him to conquer both. Setting his mind to blankness, he raised a hand to tap twice on the door and found it already a hand's breadth open with a wide-eyed boy peering through the gap. Valerius felt the hairs of his scalp prickle a fresh warning; in the old days, the palace doors had not opened so silently.

The watch-boy lifted a small soapstone lamp and, by its light, stared at the decurion's face as if matching the features to a description: straight black hair cut to military length, fine lean features, and eyes that would strip the skin from a slave-boy who dared to stare too long. The boy jerked back, leaving the door only just ajar so that Valerius had to put his shoulder against it if he wanted to follow. Inside, the lad had not waited but was already leading the way down an unlit corridor. It was not the behaviour expected of a slave, but this was a place where freed slaves ruled, or had been; nothing was done in the normal way. Raising his pack, Valerius followed warily.

The palace was overly warm. The slave-boy was silent and scared and led Valerius into emptiness, but the walls thrilled to distant activity. For a man who had spent the past decade at war, the place reeked of ambush. Valerius hitched his pack round and knew he could reach neither his dagger nor his sword in time for either to be of use in an emergency. He thought of the filleting knife he had dropped through the dock and cursed himself for a short-sighted fool.

They stopped at a chamber far from the main palace and large enough only to house a bed and a small clothes chest. The walls were of plaster, painted simply in pale aquatic green with sinuous fish near the ceiling and a floor of sand-grey tiles so that he could have been standing twenty feet beneath the surface of the ocean, staring up into the world of air and light. The effect would have been better in daylight. At night, with a single brazier and a rack of hanging lamps pushing a poor glow into the dark, it was more like the river just north of Camulodunum: muddily damp and smelling of mould. The boy nodded and left. This door, like the one before it, was well oiled.

The room was empty and remained so for some considerable time. Valerius was hungry and alone. Neither of these was unusual, and the latter was, perhaps, better than any of the alternatives. He propped his pack in a corner, opened it, and moved his dagger to a place where he could reach it at need; then, leaning back against the furthest wall from the lamps, he set his mind blankly to wait. Half a lifetime in the legions had taught him this skill above all others; when he put his mind to it, Julius Valerius could outwait the Sphinx.

He had expected the freed slave Narcissus to come, or Callistus, the paymaster; both were reputedly still loyal to Claudius. He got Xenophon, the Greek physician, which disturbed him more than he would have chosen to admit. The man brought ghosts with him simply by his presence. Valerius stood in the semi-dark and strengthened the walls around his mind, concentrating on the details of the physician's features, excluding the possibility that others might have joined them in the shadows.

There was much to see in Xenophon. Even allowing for the uncertain light, the physician had aged greatly in the years since their last meeting. The man who had engineered the confrontation between Valerius and his former compatriots had been of vigorous middle-age, exuding vibrancy and intelligent humour. The man who stood in the doorway to the underwater room was tired to the point of exhaustion. His hair had thinned back from the crown of his head, and the little left at the margins, which had been a distinguished silver, was a lank, translucent white. His skin was mottled with age-spots and creased with care. His nose was hooked like a hawk's over a face too thin for its size.

"Have you eaten?" He spoke from the gloom beyond the reach of the lamps. His voice had the same cadences as that of Theophilus, who was still field physician in the fortress at Camulodunum and with whom he had undoubtedly enjoyed a brisk exchange of letters these past two years.

"I haven't eaten since the ship." Valerius roused himself from his corner. He had not drunk since then, either, which was bothering him more, although he chose not to say so. "Is it safe to eat in this place?"

The physician gazed at him a moment and then nodded as if confirming a quite different question. "For you, it probably is," he said. "Safer than Britannia, from what I hear."

That could only have come from Theophilus. Valerius shrugged. "Britannia is safe as long as you don't venture into the western mountains in units of less than a cohort's strength. And keep clear of the Twentieth Legion for the time being. They have all the bad luck." He grinned sourly, daring the physician to challenge him. When he did not, Valerius said, "You mentioned food?"

"Of course. My apologies." Xenophon leaned out of the door and signalled. An ill-fed lad with lank brown hair and shy eyes entered, bringing a tray of cold meats, cheeses, and—blessed boy—a full jug of wine with two goblets. He bowed to Xenophon, regarded the decurion with a disquieting, professional curiosity, and loitered for an extra moment when dismissed.

"Philonikos, my apprentice," said Xenophon, when the lad had gone. "I always swore I would never take one, but I have allowed myself to be persuaded to make an exception."

"And you regret having done so?" Valerius sat on the clothes chest, balancing the tray of food on his knees.

"No. He may do so, in time, but I will not. I have discovered that it is good, in one's old age, to believe that a lifetime's knowledge will not die with its progenitor."

"Indeed." The wine, newly poured, was heavy with age and good vintage. Valerius breathed in the smell of it as a man breathes fresh air after staying too long indoors. The first taste fortified the walls of his mind as the solid certainty of the harbour at Ostia had steadied his legs and his gut; the second washed him clear of the need to talk nonsense. Settling his shoulders against an expanse of green-blue plaster, he said, "So now, perhaps, you might tell me why I'm here?"

"Why do you think?"

"Not to play guessing games with you."

"No. That would be unfair to us both."

"And to Theophilus?" It was the soldier's way, learned long ago, always to expose the enemy's weapons to clear view.

"Perhaps." The old man was tired, and his guest had just taken the only seat in the room. Surprisingly, given his evident care for his dignity,

Xenophon sat on the floor. "How is life in Britannia really?" he asked. "I heard the new governor has stopped the hangings amongst the eastern tribes. That must ease the tension somewhat?"

He had not been summoned to discuss politics, either, but there was some refuge in doing so, and Valerius took it. "Markedly. The Trinovantes and their allies are delighted. In the west he has sent cohort after cohort of the Second and the Twentieth to their destruction, which nicely bolsters the morale of the Silures and their allies among the Ordovices and the warriors of Mona, while in the north he lets Venutios raise the spears of the northern Brigantes and threaten Cartimandua's hold on those who remain. If our governor believes the emperor requires him to keep the tribes happy, to give them succour and support their belief that they will drive us ultimately from the province, then yes, he is succeeding beyond his wildest dreams."

"You would prefer it if he returned to the constant hatred that existed under Scapula? You know what the tribes think of you and how many dreamers have sworn to see you dead?"

"Of course." In that one short sentence, they moved to a new, more personal level. It was not unexpected, simply poorly timed; before the wine arrived, it might have been more damaging. Valerius drank deeply and, smiling, met the physician's eye. "Who cares if they hate, as long as they fear?"

Xenophon blanched. "Caligula used to say that."

"I know." The cheeses were made of goat's milk, whitely crumbling. They matched well with the wine. Valerius broke one in half and ate it delicately. "In this, as in many things, he was right."

There was no possible answer to that. Xenophon knew as well as any man exactly the disdain in which Valerius had once held Caligula. They sat for a while in silence, each reviewing his weapons.

Xenophon pursed his lips and pressed the tips of his fingers to the bridge of his nose, thinking. Valerius watched him make a decision and reject it twice before he lowered his hands and drew a strained breath to speak.

"Theophilus tells me you were a changed man when you returned from Rome two years ago; that you drank to excess, of wine and not ale; that in the gap between Scapula's death and the appointment of the new governor, you slaughtered the natives unchecked, hanging men, women, and children for 'crimes against the emperor'—real or imagined—until, even more than before, your name became a curse in tribes from the east coast to the west; that you ran riot through your own ranks, killing an actuary of another wing so that the men threatened mutiny and only the intervention of their prefect kept you safe. Is it true?"

Valerius sat very still. Even after his return from Rome, he had believed Theophilus an ally. The physician had nursed him through the bull-dreaming and knew the measure of his encounter with the god. He had seen the ghosts after the decurion's return, too, having raised them once with an excessive dose of poppy given to dull the pain while he stitched a spear-wound in Valerius's thigh. The consequent ravings had not been dignified, but they were at least contained within the private room of the hospital at Camulodunum. It was not something of which they spoke, but Valerius had refused the drug ever after and Theophilus had not pressed it on him, even when cauterizing an infected sword-cut. There had been nights later when he had offered the same private room and the company of his presence to a man who had urgent need of both. At the time, Valerius had been grateful to have someone with whom he could share the long nights when neither wine nor hard work had kept the walls between the worlds intact. Now, listening to Xenophon speaking in ways designed explicitly to raise the dead, he wondered if the overdose of poppy had not been so accidental, if all of this had been planned.

Valerius drained his beaker of wine and poured another. He would have liked the succour of divine instruction, but Mithras came to him only patchily these days and hardly ever when he was in company. He had taken part in initiations of more than a hundred acolytes since his first branding; at different times, he had cut the wrist-cords, lit the lamps, and led the chanting. He had seen countless men come to the god and had seen the change in them, not just in the cellar but on the battlefield and the training grounds. They shone with the touch of the deity, and each of them believed that Valerius shared that. Theophilus knew the truth, and so he must assume Xenophon knew it, too; that the visit of the god was a rare thing, sustained through the barren years by hope and faith and a mess of incoherent dreams.

The knowledge of this had never yet stopped him from striving to reach the Sun and all that it stood for. Doing so now, he was surprised before he was grateful when his view of Xenophon wavered and the other worlds pressed in. The red-roan bull came first, as it had done ever since he had seen it in the flesh. Valerius met it as an old friend—his only true friend—and with its strength, he built the square-blocked altar to the god, adding the incense and the memory of brand smoke to make it real. On the sea-green plaster behind Xenophon's head, he painted an image of the capped youth who committed slaughter at the behest of older, angrier gods. The roan bull died, forced to kneeling, and the god wept. Tears mixed with the blood and leaked onto the sandstone floor. The gathered ghosts claimed them for their own.

Valerius stared at his god, and his god stared back. The ancient and recent dead filled the space between them, howling. Xenophon waited in silence. At some time when the distraction was greatest, he moved across the floor to sit at Valerius's side. The decurion felt a lean, withered hand test his forehead for heat and another lift his wrist for a pulse. A voice from outside time asked, "What do you see?"

"Nothing." He would not speak of it again to anyone.

"Are you blind, then?"

"No." Valerius cupped his palms over his eyes. Sometimes the blackness worked, sometimes it made things worse. This time it gave him space to gather the words he had half-prepared, expecting such an attack as this. When he could speak with a steady voice, he said, "Theophilus is a physician. He views the world through different eyes from those of us who are required to maintain discipline amongst fighting men. Umbricius attacked me openly; I killed him in self-defence. It was witnessed by my troop and his. No one disputes it."

"And the rest? The slaughter of the natives? The hangings? The villages razed and their children burned?"

It was too much and too deliberate. Blessedly the anger came; not the surging, vicious fury that had killed Umbricius, but enough. It worked as nothing else ever did to lessen the haunting. In the consuming cold of his rage, the screaming dead screamed less. Macha, mother to Bán, faded from sight as if she had never been.

A single cold, clear voice remained, of a man still alive who had once echoed the voice and features of the god. *What would you have done if ...?* Only with extremes of wine could that voice be made to stop, but Valerius had learned, over time, to think past it. He dropped his hands from his eyes and was gratified to see Xenophon flinch from what could be read in his face. He remembered the knife in his pack and saw the possibility of death strike the physician. He smiled and knew what it did to the other man's fear.

With deliberate clarity, Valerius said, "Killing is what war is about. If you don't like it, you have the ear of the only man who can change it. Tell

Claudius to pull his legions out of Britannia, and the killing will end. Until then we have to win, or we die. I do not intend to die, but if I was brought here to face the executioner, you should know that my death will not end the war."

"I have never believed it would."

Xenophon was not truly afraid of him, which was a mistake. In the renewed emptiness of the room, the possibility of murder hung between them. Valerius set his goblet down and rested back against the wall, his fingers laced behind his head. He was pleased with the steadiness of his hands; it was not always so. "You still haven't told me why I'm here," he said. "I don't believe it was to quibble over the death of a Gaulish actuary."

In that single sentence, a thousand deaths were reduced to a minor point of law, and Roman order was restored. With evident regret, Xenophon moved back to sit at his place against the opposite wall. When he spoke, it was of other things.

"You're right, of course. The emperor would not pay what he did to bring you here to discuss the death of a Gaul, although your reasons for killing him may have a bearing on the outcome of your task. Military discipline matters more to some than others, particularly here and now . . ."

The physician drifted to silence, staring into the reflective surface of his own wine, choosing his phrases for best effect. "If we leave aside the bull-slayer and remain in the temporal world, to whom do you, as an officer of the cavalry, owe your ultimate loyalty?" he asked. "Whose order will you obey without question, to its fulfilment or your own death, whichever comes first?"

Valerius said, "The emperor's. That is, Claudius." It mattered now to state a name.

"And if that emperor is slain, then are you loyal to his successor, or to the one to whom you gave your oath?"

Thus did they quietly enter the realms of treason. Men had died over days for far less. Valerius dropped his eyes. He, too, studied his own floating reflection for the answer. It was not something to which he had given serious thought, although perhaps he should have done. *I serve my emperor, in life and to death.*

"The emperor commands the armies, whomsoever he may be," he said presently. "The loyalty is to the position, not the man. In absolute terms, my allegiance is to my prefect, through him to my governor, and so to the emperor. But Britannia is not close to Rome and the winter is almost upon us. If an order failed to reach the governor before spring, he would act on

Claudius's last command and amend it as his powers and the situation required. I would take my orders from him."

"What if, hypothetically speaking, the emperor—Claudius—were to give you a direct order in person, and you were not to return to Britannia before spring? There would be no chain of command to cushion your choices."

"No. I could see that." Valerius set the tray of food carefully on the floor. Always before, action and the promise of action had brought him back to himself. It did so now. Thinking aloud, he said, "May I take it that the order I might be given would be contradicted by the next emperor, were he to find out what it was?"

"You may. If you are careful, he will never find out, and you can return to your unit a far richer man. If you are careless—"

"—then I will die. That is always the case. The god knows I have been careful so far." Danger sparked lightly along Valerius's spine, welcome as a lover's touch. "Is it fair to assume that you are empowered to give me this order?"

"Yes. I have it here, written by Claudius in his own hand and sealed before witnesses." The scroll the physician drew from his sleeve was a small one, sealed with the imprint of an elephant, the emperor's personal and private seal, used only in relation to Britannia. The order recalling Valerius to Rome had borne exactly that image.

Xenophon held it loosely, as he might a captured finch, soon to be released. With unusual gravity, he said, "I can give you the scroll, but may not do so unless you swear beforehand on your god and your soldier's oath that you will accept in its fullness the order contained herein, that you will carry it out to the last breath of your life or die in the attempt. This is for your own protection. Without that stipulation, if you refused, you would have to die."

"Obviously. In a matter of this secrecy, you could not risk that I might speak of it beyond here. Do you know the nature of the command that I am given?"

"I do."

Valerius was standing now, his hands damp. His heart careened in his chest, rebounding off the bars of his ribs. The room had emptied, utterly. In place of the multitudes, he felt the distant presence of the god, drifting like old incense, promising victory. "In my place, would you accept this?" he asked. "Would you give your oath to carry it out?"

"Willingly and without question."

"Thank you." Valerius drank the last of the wine. The decision was no decision, as Xenophon must have known it would be. The lure of danger was too great, and greater than that, the god was with him in a way he had not been these last two years.

Savouring the sweetness of it, he said, "In that case, in Mithras's name, on his honour and my own, by my pledge on his altar and by my oath to the emperor, I accept in its fullness Claudius's order, whatever it may be. His will is mine, to death and beyond."

CHAPTER 25

Cwmfen of the Ordovices, prisoner-under-amnesty to the Emperor Claudius, gave birth at dusk five days after the autumn equinox in the third year of her captivity, that being also the fourteenth year of the reign of the man by whose whim and under whose protection she lived. The child was a boy, son to Caradoc, full brother to Cygfa, and half-brother to Cunomar, who was no longer his father's only son.

The delivery was prolonged and painful. Outwardly the warrior of the Ordovices had changed little since her capture, but each passing month of the emperor's hospitality had softened the trained iron of her muscle until, when her time came, she was no more fit for the bearing of children than any other of Rome's women.

It was the first childbirth Cunomar had ever seen; when his mother had given birth to Graine, she had done so with only the dreamers to attend her, and he had seen the infant only afterwards, when the blood and the screaming were done. He did not believe his mother had screamed. He was sure he would have heard her, however far away she went. Since coming to Rome, he had heard the sounds of birthing often enough to know it was different here. The walls of the second-floor apartment in which they lived were so thin that he might have been in the same room as their neighbours on either side, above, and below, and what noise did not come in from them radiated across from the opposite side of the street and those behind. The fat Latin woman whose apartment shared their stairway had, as far as he could tell, a child every year and shot them out as a hen lays eggs, but the freed slave-woman downstairs and the silversmith's woman and the sullen, silent one who lived alone and who the Latin woman said was a whore had each passed through long, painful births in the last two years, all of them noisily.

Cwmfen screamed and was ashamed of it, Cunomar could see that. In order that he would not shame her further by witnessing it, he spent the day fetching water. In the early morning, he took the half-dozen buckets they owned and filled them one at a time from the sunken cistern on the ground floor that served their apartment and four others near it. Carrying water was always his job, and on most days he resented it, as he resented all things Roman. In his world, the one the gods had made, water was a gift from Nemain, flowing in streams and rivers, or from Manannan when he made the endless sea. One gave thanks to the god and used it with care, but it never ran dry. In Rome water came in aqueducts or underground pipes and was delivered directly to the houses of the rich and the public bath. For those, like Cunomar's family, who lived in penury and not near a bath, there were wells and cisterns, but they were privately owned, and if one did not have to pay for the water one had to carry it. Either way it became another symbol of drudgery and separation from the gods.

On this day, uniquely, the slow walk up the stairs with water slopping onto his legs was a blessed relief, and Cunomar repeated it frequently, even when the water was not truly needed. In the afternoon, when the buckets were all still full, he borrowed a pair of sewn goat-skins from the fat Latin woman and carried them down the long hill to the public baths and the cracked fountain that served the houses and market stalls that surrounded them. He craved sunlight by then and had the excuse that he had three newly made belts to deliver to the merchant who sold them for him. The money he made scarcely paid for the leather, but his tool-work was improving and he could make three or four belts in a day and, from those, earn enough to buy bread and ale or a jointed hare or, better, a sea-fish freshly caught and brought in from Ostia.

It had taken some time for the family to find ways to survive. In the early days after their release, they had been novelties, and Caradoc especially had been in demand to appear at supper with senators and consuls and those who hoped to become such, who needed to demonstrate their support of Claudius and saw in the pardoned captive a means subtly to do so.

The serpent-spear brooch that he wore had been borrowed—for a fee—and replicated and became, for a while, the symbol of support for the emperor before the fad passed and something less barbaric replaced it.

The brooch had been returned by the silversmith who copied it, who had stayed for the afternoon to discuss its making and the creation of other pieces, similar but not the same. It had seemed that something might come of that to earn an income, but the silversmith had died of eating bad pork and no others had come in his stead.

Caradoc's appearances had not been paid, but each time a fresh set of clothes had been provided, each outdoing the last in ostentation and poor taste, and these had been sold later to feed the family for a while and perhaps pay for firewood as well. Later, as the invitations dwindled, they had found that Dubornos's skills were most marketable. There was little call for a trained warrior, particularly not one damaged for life by the attentions of the emperor's horse-guard, but a storyteller with a quaint barbarian accent was welcome, particularly if he was a healer. Xenophon had helped, supplying herbs and bland bases for ointments and salves, and they had lived from these through the first winter.

In spring inactivity had driven the others to action as a way to keep from going mad. After several false starts, they had found that Ordovician leatherwork was valued, even if those buying it could not decipher the symbols burned and worked into the hides. Cygfa had come out of herself a little and made a belt, spending days on the tooling. It had sold quickly, and the rest had learned from her. It was not warriors' work but was better than the alternatives. They made belts and pouches and scabbards for the weapons they themselves were forbidden to wear and, once, a consignment of boots that they found out later, appallingly, was destined for the cavalry fighting in Britannia.

Standing in the raw September sunshine, Cunomar weighed the copper coins he had been given for the belts and decided that, today of all days, his father needed ale more than anything, and that Cwmfen would probably appreciate it when the babe was out. He bought a flagon and set it in the water of the fountain to chill for a while before he carried it back, hoping the whole mess might be over by the time he returned.

It was half over, which was better than nothing. When he had left, Dubornos had said he could feel the first arc of the crown against his searching fingers. When Cunomar slipped into the room and took his place sitting in the far corner, he had almost the whole head.

Experience of foalings and lambings in the time before Rome told Cunomar that the worse part was the shoulders and that a head alone was not enough, but this babe had a narrow chest, and the shoulders came as the last of the sun tipped over the edge of the rooftops to the west so that the infant emerged soon after into lamplight and the arms of his father. He was bald and wrinkled and red and ugly, but Cunomar had learned that that was to be expected and did not remark on it.

For Roman propriety, they named him Gaius Caratacus. Amongst the family, he was to be Math of the Ordovices, a name his father had used in his youth and that, for his parents if not for Cunomar, sang of freedom. In accordance with what little of his heritage it was possible to recreate, Dubornos spoke the words of Briga's welcome while Caradoc carried the child two flights downstairs to the small plot of their vegetable garden and, with Cygfa and Cunomar as witnesses, showed him to the night sky, to the earth, and to water, then returned him to his mother, who was already asleep. The child had wide pale eyes and, after the first squalls of birth, viewed them all in shocked silence, as if he had come expecting a roundhouse and a world at war and had prepared no response for the sight of four walls and a city that pretended peace.

Afterwards the ale was as welcome as Cunomar had hoped it might be. They built a small fire, although it was not truly cold, and sat with it for a while in silence, enjoying the warmth of the flames and the bite of the drink and the quiet of the evening before retiring to sleep.

Cunomar worried constantly about his father, who worried constantly about all of them. Each did his best not to let it show. The crowded living of the apartment had demonstrated early that none of them could afford to give way to petty resentments if all were to keep their souls and sanities intact. Cunomar lay awake most nights reminding himself that Rome was the enemy, not Cygfa or Dubornos or Cwmfen or, gods forbid, his father. If it was hard for him not to descend into petty squabbles, how much harder for Caradoc, who shouldered the burden of care for the family while still the subject of talk wherever he went? If Cunomar found that the limitations of life in the apartment drove him to distraction, how could he show it when his father bore for life the stigma of the pardoned captive and the damage of his imprisonment?

The physical scars were most obvious, if not necessarily the most damaging. Despite Xenophon's best efforts, neither Caradoc's ruined shoulder nor the shackle-sores on both Dubornos and Caradoc had healed fully. The sores festered, and neither man had recovered full use of his wrists and hands afterwards. Caradoc's wounds were worse, Cunomar thought, because he had been bound more tightly and because he had fought against the shackles that day in the blood-red room when the emperor had used Cunomar as a lever in an effort to extract the words he wanted from his enemy. It was then, too, that the strings of his shoulder had been ripped apart, and Xenophon had said at the outset that the warrior would never recover full use of that arm.

Knowing that, Cunomar went to lengths both to support Caradoc and to hide that he was doing so. In little ways, he did what he could to save him from having to use his hands for delicate tasks. He worked the finest tooling on the leather. He chopped wood for kindling, because it was hard for Caradoc to wield an axe left-handed and his right arm did not have the power to split logs into splinters. He learned to fillet fish and never brought one home but its guts were already gone. Caradoc had spent a large part of his life aboard ship in his youth, in the days when he was Math and the few years after, when he abandoned the pretence and was known clearly as Caradoc, renegade son of the Sun Hound. He had acquired a taste for sea-fish then and never lost it. Possibly he might have preferred fish even to ale as a treat for the evening.

Cunomar was lying awake, his mind drifting from ale to fish to the memory of how carefully his father had grasped the new child, as if afraid he might damage it, when Cygfa appeared in the doorway.

Stiffly, unwillingly, she said, "Dubornos, can you come? Cwmfen's bleeding. I can't make it stop."

It was too dark to see. Cygfa had always had the eyes of a cat. Cunomar heard Dubornos's muffled answer and the sound of his feet on the floor; the singer must have been awake already to respond so quickly. Rising, Cunomar found the doorway by habit and then saw his way to the front room by the poor light of the lamps still lit within. By those, also, he saw how still Cwmfen was lying on the bed and the spread of dark blood on the floor. Ahead of him, Dubornos grasped Cygfa's arm.

"We need help with this. Go to Xenophon at the palace. Ask for his ergot with my sincere apologies for not accepting it when he first offered." His eyes shifted past her to the doorway, and he said, "Take Cunomar. It's not safe for you to be out at night on your own."

Cygfa opened her mouth and closed it again. Of them all, she was the one who had adjusted least well to life in Rome. She had no visible scars and had not, besides the examination by Xenophon in the emperor's quarters, been physically assaulted in any way. Nevertheless, that examination, and the fact that she had passed to womanhood and not yet taken her long-nights, had been enough to cut her off from the world, and her family with it. For the whole of the first year, she had spoken to no one but her mother and then only at times of absolute necessity. The making of the belts had been a turning point, and she had begun after that to speak to her father and brother, seeming at times almost recovered. With

Cunomar particularly, she had begun to develop a true friendship so that he had begun to understand at last what it meant to have a sister and to rejoice in it.

Dubornos was different. Cygfa loathed Xenophon with a cold, consuming passion, and Dubornos was his friend. Caradoc was his friend, too, but he was her father and could not be held at fault. In any case, he had not been present in the audience room on the night of their arrival. Dubornos, who had been present, had not been forgiven, nor perhaps ever could be.

Cunomar had been sure that his sister had loved the singer once. Certainly she had yearned for him, and her withdrawal from him in the messy, tangled winter after their reprieve had the brittle feeling of one whose offer of love has been rejected, or honour besmirched. His closeness to Xenophon, Cunomar thought, gave her an excuse to behave the way she did, but it was not the first reason.

Whatever the cause, Dubornos had felt it and been hurt. Over the past two years, he had made every effort to show her respect, to treat her exactly as he treated her mother, as a warrior and an adult. Faced with her unyielding resistance, he had, in the end, become as formal with her as she was with him until they barely spoke from one month's end to the next.

Only now, with Cwmfen's life in danger, had Dubornos's careful formality slipped, and then badly. To imply that the streets of Rome were more dangerous for her than they were for Cunomar was tactless at best. Cygfa was a proven warrior with eight kills to her credit. Moreover, for the past two years, she had worked to keep herself as fit as she had ever been in the days when they were free. The streets were safer by far for her than for Cunomar, who had killed no one, and to suggest otherwise was an insult. She stood in the hallway, and it was quite clear to all of them that the only reason she had not struck Dubornos was her mother's need for him.

In the lamplight, Cunomar sought her eyes and, meeting them, sent a silent plea that she let go of the insult and do as she was asked. If Dubornos wanted them gone, it was for a reason, and there was nothing to be gained by pulling holes in his logic. The new friendship between them worked. Before, she would have ignored him. Now, delighted, he saw her waver and change her mind. Nodding, she said, "What are you going to do?"

Dubornos was already halfway into the room. "Pray," he said. "And see if I can find where she's bleeding and stop it."

"It's deep inside. She can feel it. Ask her; she's still with us." The girl turned and squeezed Cunomar's arm. "I'll get my cloak. You should bring yours. It's not cold now, but it will be later when we've walked to the palace."

It could take half the night to get there, they both knew that, and they might not be able to find someone who would wake Xenophon for them. Needing not to leave yet, Cunomar said, "Can you get it for me? It's on the bed. I was using it as an extra blanket." His voice was breaking. It came out low and gruff, deeper than his father's. He coughed and felt the heat rise in his face. Cygfa squeezed his arm again and walked away into the dark.

Left alone, Cunomar turned his full attention on Caradoc. Cwmfen was not his mother, and whereas he would be sad if she died, a lot of that sadness would be because he knew what she meant to his father. Caradoc had not yet left the birthing room. He was naked to the waist. Old battle scars coursed in tired rivulets along his chest, back, and arms. He held his newest son to his good shoulder, his lips pressed to the infant's head. The hands that held him were cramped, with the fingers half shut as they always were at night when Caradoc was tired, but they still held him with the care they had done at his birth, and would do for the rest of his life, Cunomar was sure of it. The child had fed and was quiet, his breath a soft measure of life in a room that so obviously harboured death.

Dubornos was already kneeling by the bed. Cwmfen opened her eyes but could not hold them so. The singer felt her pulse and her forehead. From the doorway, Cunomar could see the latter was clammily wet.

"She has a fever," said Caradoc woodenly.

Dubornos said, "It's not as bad as it looks. Half of this is the exhaustion of childbirth." It may have been true. A bucket of water sat by the bed with a cloth over the rim. The singer laid a damp compress across Cwmfen's brow. Water leaked into her hair, diluting the sweat. Caradoc stood still as stone at the bedside. Dubornos looked up. "This is not your fault."

"No? I think I could be held at least half to blame." It was said without humour where once irony would have lightened it. Cunomar heard the change, and his heart ached at the sound of it.

Dubornos moved to the foot of the bed. The concealing sheets, brought in after the birth, had long since been stained and cast aside. He knelt, seeking the source of the steady trickle of blood. It was not yet a flood; that much was good. Somewhere outside a detail of armed men marched through the claustrophobic streets. The stamp of two dozen feet rocked the walls of the apartment. That, too, was something to which

Cunomar had not and would not become accustomed: the nightly arrests of the innocent and their disappearance thereafter. They had grown more frequent of late. Perhaps with good reason, Claudius was becoming increasingly paranoid, and more men were required to die for his safety. An officer called the halt, his voice so close, he could have been in the room.

Dubornos shuddered. He, too, hated the legionaries. "Rome is to blame," he said. "Or Claudius, or Breaca's godforsaken brother, but not us. Or if you are to blame, I am equally so. She was in my care when we were taken."

"Ha." Cwmfen twitched under his probing fingers. The husk of her voice said, "You are become Roman, Dubornos. I am a warrior. I live under no one's care."

Caradoc knelt and took her hand loosely in his own. "You are the finest of warriors. You will pass this test as you passed all the others."

"Of course." From the doorway, Cunomar could see the love as she smiled into his eyes and felt, as he always did, the odd mix of grief and displaced envy that twisted his gut whenever he saw Cwmfen taking the place that was rightfully his mother's.

Ashamed, he turned away that he might not be seen. Cygfa appeared at his side and draped his cloak over his shoulders. "Here," she said. "It was under the bed, and I couldn't find it." Outside in the streets, men of the Guard were running at the order of their officer.

Cunomar drew his cloak up round his shoulders and stopped, feeling the coarse weave and the old musty smell that marked it as his old cloak, the one he had cast aside at mid-summer when the leather-trader had given him an extra coin for his work and he had bought a new cloak with it. Cygfa had been there to help him pick it. She had stitched the care-marks of the Ordovices along the hem as protection; she should have remembered it.

A day's worth of resentments spilled over in Cunomar. Throwing the cloak on the floor, he said, "This is old, and it smells. The new one's on the bed under the blanket where I—"

He stopped, frozen. From a street full of armed men, someone had entered the apartment block. Light feet ran up two flights of stairs and stopped at their door. Cygfa, who had more courage than he could begin to imagine, stepped past him to open it.

"Good evening." Philonikos, apprentice to Xenophon, hesitated on the landing. Dubornos had always said the lad was Hermes come to earth, inadequately fed. His hair was a dusky brown, heading to gold and too straight to be truly beautiful, and his features were pinched and hollow-cheeked, as if his mother had starved him in childhood and the habit had continued beyond her care. His long artist's fingers were already swollen round the joints, the product of hours spent grinding pastes in a pestle.

Xenophon had found the boy in the library reading medical texts written by Largus, the emperor's former physician, an act at once of calumny and astonishing precocity. They had made an agreement soon after: Philonikos would cease to study texts by those whose writing Xenophon deemed unworthy, and in return he would be considered for an apprenticeship. The consideration period was a fiction; there had never been any doubt as to the youth's application or ability. He was obsessive in his care of the sick and gifted in his diagnoses and healing. For the past eighteen months, Cunomar had watched with something close to envy as the other youth trailed after Xenophon in the way a stray cur follows the one who feeds it, listening always, speaking rarely, and learning a trade that would keep him rich and healthy long into old age, as it had done Xenophon. Then that same youth was here, in the doorway, and that could only be on his master's orders.

The boy was a wraith, unable to cross thresholds uninvited. His eyes were widely pale, like a monkey's. His shadow fell like a handful of twigs across the floor slats, cast by half a dozen lamps. Of all the adults, Dubornos had had the most dealings with him. The singer stood up, squeezing blood from his hands. He spoke in the old-fashioned Greek with which the lad was most comfortable and that all of them now understood.

"Philonikos, be welcome and enter, please. Xenophon told me he was not a dreamer. It appears he was being unnecessarily modest."

The physician's apprentice hovered yet in the doorway, his gaze switching from Cwmfen on the bed to the sleeping, silent infant at Caradoc's shoulder. "Is she sick?" he asked. "Did the babe come out badly?"

Cunomar slid past him into the room. "I haven't asked him for the ergot," he said. "Should I?"

Ergot, it seemed, had only one use in the post-partum woman. Philonikos was transformed. "She's bleeding?" In two steps, he had crossed the room and knelt where Dubornos had lately been, squinting in the inadequate light.

"It's not too bad. She will live if she doesn't get milk fever, but we should pack her to be sure the bleeding doesn't start again," he said. "I can't go back to the palace. They've sealed it off. Largus will have ergot, but he's across in the Aventine; we won't get to him in time. We need cold water and linen, torn into strips. This will do."

He picked up a clean sheet, saved for the first day after birth and not yet befouled, and threw it to Cunomar, who caught it without thinking and began to tear, his mind unwillingly dragged to the world outside. "Why is the palace sealed off?" he asked. And then, because the adults all stood in silence and he realized he did not want to know the answer, he asked, "Why did Xenophon send you here now if not to tend Cwmfen?"

Philonikos looked at Caradoc for permission to speak and, after a moment, received it. He knew his message by heart and delivered it without emotion. "Claudius is under siege," he said. "He may already be dying—poisoned by Agrippina—but if not, it will come within the next half-month. They will blame Xenophon, although he has done his best to prevent it. Agrippina has control of the palace. She will put it about that the emperor is ill and we should pray for him. Her astrologers will wait until their stars are more fair, and then, when the time is right, she will set Nero on the throne and rule through him. From that moment, you are not safe here. She hates you. In the wave of deaths, of Narcissus and Callon and all those others who have opposed her, or angered her, or witnessed her humiliation at the hands of Claudius, yours will be one of the many that no one notes."

The speech had Xenophon's cadence, if not his warmth and passion. Cunomar watched Cygfa step to her mother's side. For a long time, she had simply ignored Philonikos, staring through him as if he did not exist. Then he had not been a physician with the skills that might save her mother's life. There was defiance and guilt and a more basic need to erase the past when she said, "The people love Claudius as much as they despise Agrippina. If we let out that the emperor is threatened by her, they'll storm the palace, surely?"

If Philonikos understood the change in Cygfa, he did not let it show. He was absorbed in his care for her mother. Already Cwmfen's bleeding had lessened. He reached for her wrist, his head bent over, the better to feel the pulse. "You can't," he said absently. "The guards won't let you."

Sharply, Caradoc said, "What guards? The ones outside?"

There had been silence after the marching and the shouted orders and the short burst of men running to station. Sniffing the air, Cunomar smelled burning pitch, which meant torches, which meant, in turn, there would be fire. It should not have surprised him; too many of the recent executions had been covered by convenient fires. He watched realization take shape on the faces of his father and Dubornos, even on Cwmfen on the bed, and saw them all turn to him and try to disguise it.

An old familiar nausea returned. "They've come for us," he said. He had always known it would happen.

"Yes, but not to arrest you, to help. They come on Claudius's orders and are still loyal to him. That doesn't mean they'll let you raise a riot in Rome on their watch, though." Philonikos looked up. "The bleeding will stop soon. It was not as bad as it looked. Can someone get Cwmfen some clean water, perhaps with a little honey in it? She will be better if she drinks."

That much Cunomar could easily do. He ran for water and returned. Cwmfen drank and lay back. Her breathing was easier than it had been. The apprentice boy stood. He was fastidious in his personal hygiene. Cunomar watched him tear a fine strip of linen from one of their best sheets and use it to wipe the blood from his hands. Clean and with the sick woman settled, he returned his attention to his message.

"You have to leave," he said. "The guards will arrange that your absence is not noted, at least in the first instance, possibly ever. Ostia is watched by men loyal to Agrippina. You cannot go there, so you will be escorted instead to the northern Gaulish coast. If you ride hard and fast, you should reach it before the middle of October. If you do so, a vessel will be waiting. It is not yet too late for a ship to sail across the ocean to Britannia, provided you do not delay. The emperor has given his consent to this. The officer of the escort has a signed order for one family to leave Rome and travel to the port of Gesoriacum, there to take ship. Your descriptions are accurate; only the names are different."

Philonikos could have been a singer as good as Dubornos. He had the memory for the lengthy tales and lineages, learned back down the ages, if not the capacity to think through what he had said. Or perhaps his attention was still elsewhere. He hovered uncertainly by the bed, watching Cwmfen take her infant son to her breast to feed. His gaze was clinical, assessing the flow of milk and the evident strength of the infant. Cunomar watched his father melt at the unspeakable beauty of it.

"Philonikos?" Dubornos shook the boy's arm. "Why should Claudius do this? He has no love for any of us, no wish to see Britannia rise against him again."

"He knows he's dying." It was Caradoc who answered. Rousing himself, he sat down by the bed and slid a scarred and cramped hand beneath his child, supporting the infant's weight to spare Cwmfen's arms. "Britannia was his conquest, his passion, and his claim to immortality. He has no reason to bequeath it in peace to Agrippina. This is his revenge."

The physician's apprentice nodded, his owl-eyes serious. "And he may repent past acts. It is not unknown in one who feels the cold wind of death; he wishes to make amends in life that he may not be called to account by the souls of the dead when he meets them. Certainly Xenophon believes this. You are not the only ones tonight for whom messengers bear signed warrants of release. But there is need for haste. These few apart, Agrippina has control of the Guard. If she hears . . ." He faltered. The two parts of him, messenger and physician, came together for the first time. "But you can't," he said. "Cwmfen and the babe—they can't ride yet."

It had been obvious from the start. Cunomar had known it and seen the weight of it in Caradoc's gaze. He had not counted on Dubornos's seeing it, too. The singer said, "I'll stay with Cwmfen. Caradoc will take his children home to their birthright."

"No." From the far side of the bed, his father's stone-grey eyes met the singer's quiet brown, both resolute.

Cunomar felt a fault crack along the foundations of his world. For more than two years, living so close as to step on each other's toes, these two men had striven to hold a family together, had laid aside their differences, such as they may have been, and had worked together more closely than brothers. Now most of all, it mattered that they not come into conflict.

Desperately willing it otherwise, he heard Dubornos say, "You are needed on Mona, by the tribes as much as the dreamers. The governor is weak; the western tribes have set the boundaries, and the legions dare not cross. With you back, the warriors of all the tribes will be united as never before. East will join with west to drive the legions back all the way to Rome. They'll see it as a gift from the gods, a demonstration of their unqualified support for our cause—and fairly so. You have no choice but to return. The gods and the people need you. Mona needs you." At the end, unsaid, because no one ever spoke the name aloud or needed to: *Breaca needs you.*

They were weapons Dubornos had no right to use, and he did so shamelessly. Caradoc stared down at his feeding son. From the bed, Cwmfen said, "He's right. You have to go. You and the children." She was a warrior; her voice never wavered. That Agrippina would kill both her and the infant was obvious to them all.

The babe squirmed and was changed to the other breast. In the streets outside, a hound barked and was kicked to silence. A legionary coughed and his armour rattled. Caradoc knelt by the bed, staring at a world none of them could see. Cunomar set his fingers to his brow, as he had seen his mother do before battle, and prayed to Briga and Nemain and the great, vast god of the ocean that his father might, this one last time, set aside his pride and let Dubornos have his way.

The ringed scar left by the shackles at Caradoc's neck wavered in the fey light, pulsing to the slow and steady rhythm of his heart. Without doubt Cygfa got her courage from her father. Cunomar kept his gaze on his father's face, offering silent support. He brought his mother to mind as he had not done in two years and sent the essence of her into the room to call him.

When Caradoc raised his eyes, they fell first on his new son and then on Cunomar, who saw the full measure of pain and unbearable burdens. The voice he heard was the one his father used in council but only rarely, announcing the dishonourable death of a warrior. "I rode away from battle once, leaving others to die in my place," Caradoc said. "I do not believe the gods would ask it of me again. We go together or not at all."

Cunomar choked and did his best to keep it silent.

After a space that lasted for ever, Dubornos said, "Then we stay. Cwmfen can't ride."

"But she might travel if we find her a litter. Is that not so?" Caradoc turned aside to Philonikos, who was standing apart, doing his best not to be included. Pressed into a response, the lad gave a half-hearted nod.

"Good." Caradoc stood. He had more certainty then than Cunomar had seen at any time since the day on the plain under the burning sun when he had faced down the emperor. Cunomar thought he might break with pride until he heard the words his father said.

"Dubornos will ride ahead with Cygfa and catch the ship. They can carry the news that we're coming. The rest of us will travel slowly, at whatever pace Philonikos allows, and if we reach the coast late, we'll find another ship, or wait until spring. The fighting season is over. Mona will live without us another half year, and if the dreamers know we are coming, that will be enough."

Dubornos and Cygfa, the two warriors, who could ride and fight. Cunomar heard the names, and his breath clogged his throat. His mind screamed, an incoherent welter of pain without words behind it.

Dubornos, friend for ever, heard him and shook his head, saying, "The ship can carry the message, but not us. You said it: we go together or not at all. I will not sail to Mona without you."

So then, whether it was safe or not, the mettle of each man was tested and found equal by the other. The hush of the room held them long enough for this last confrontation, for the seeking of weaknesses and the acknowledgement, at last, that they did not exist.

Caradoc broke away first. Rising, he turned to Cwmfen and kissed her. To Cunomar and Cygfa, he said, "Start packing. You will need travelling clothes, gold, and a knife each, nothing else." To the physician's apprentice, who stared as if his ears had lied, he said, "Philonikos, bring what you need to care for Cwmfen on the journey. If Xenophon sent you now, he meant you to come with us at least to Gaul. He values your life and safety as much as ours. If he is in danger, he would want to know you were safe."

It was not a request but a command, given by one with long experience of leadership. Philonikos opened his mouth and shut it again. In eighteen months of service in the palace, he had learned when not to argue.

The fire began as they packed. Smoke leaked through the floorboards, giving form to the lamplight. In the next apartment, the fat Latin woman howled in alarm and was echoed by others on either side and across the street. The legionaries posted outside were already helping to evacuate the building. A detachment crashed upstairs, passing in single file up the narrow space. They came burdened, their footfalls weightily unbalanced as if by firewood or weapons or both. It would not be the first time; everyone knew someone who had died at Claudius's command and others who had succumbed to fires in the ill-protected tenements.

Cunomar was carrying his father's pack to the front room when the soldiers reached the door.

"Cunomar—" His father's voice was unusually soft. "Put the pack down and come here."

Doing as he was bid, he ran across the room, panic pushing at his guts. His father's arms enfolded him. Strong hands that had once led armies ruffled his hair in a way they had not done since childhood. His father's lips rasped dryly on his forehead and the deep voice of council said, "My son, can you stay with Cwmfen? She needs someone to help her."

Cunomar went, not asking what a warrior who had just given birth might need help with in the face of the enemy. Cygfa was already there, alert and watchful. She smiled wryly at Dubornos as she had not done these past two years, and the singer met it with relief. If he had had any time for regret, Cunomar would have mourned the fact that it had taken the certainty of death to begin to heal that rift.

The door crashed open. Cunomar saw Caradoc meet Dubornos's eye and step round to stand with him, shoulders pressed together in front of the bed. Neither was armed; their amnesty had expressly forbidden the keeping of weapons. There were knives for cooking but none within reach. Dubornos began to sing the song of soul passing, quietly.

Caradoc said, "And so we argued for nothing. The gods, it seems, would prefer us to stay." It was said wryly, with humour at last, another brought to wholeness by the promise of escape from life.

A helmetless dark-haired man poked his head round the door. Smoke framed him. He scanned the room, taking in its occupants, and jerked his head, speaking over his shoulder. In harsh parade-ground Latin, he said, "Here. Three adults, two children, and the doctor's boy." He turned back. "And a babe." He was puzzled. "We don't have a babe."

"We don't need one," said a voice that stopped the world. "The fire will be good. No one will be looking for an infant."

It was a nightmare, a dream without substance. Relief crushed the air from Cunomar's throat; however bad they might seem at the time, such things were escapable. On Mona every apprentice had been taught the techniques to ensure safe waking from a dangerous dream. For the dreamers, it was life-saving; for the children, an escape from unpleasantness that made the nights safe. Airmid had taught Cunomar the way to do it long ago, when he had dreamed three nights in a row that Ardacos made the protection wards wrongly and the enemy found them. All he needed was to find something that should be solid and prove that it was not; then he would know he was dreaming and his mind would wake him up.

Focusing on the upright of a corner between two walls, he began to do as Airmid had taught him and was surprised to see Dubornos do the same; he had not expected to be sharing his nightmare. It might have been comic were it not so desperate. In an effort to prove that nothing was real, Dubornos did his best to pass his hand smartly through the wall to his left. His knuckles barked on rough plaster, and he scraped skin off his palm when he tried the other way. Cunomar, watching in astonishment, tried the same and was equally hurt.

"Hitting walls won't stop the fire, singer." The voice mocked from the doorway, in Eceni. "You can roast if you like, but I would consider it churlish myself, as would the shade of the emperor, I have no doubt. And it would leave those who remain behind to explain why the bodies of two identical red-headed singers were found in the ashes of the fire, which would be damnably inconvenient."

Cunomar lifted his eyes slowly, still locked in the nightmare. The man he had been told was his mother's brother, the most revered of all Eceni warriors, stood before him in the uniform of an Urban Guard, grinning. It had been so once before, on the arid plain where Caradoc had faced the emperor. There the man had been an interpreter and had tried to have them killed. In horror Cunomar looked up into his father's eyes and knew he was not dreaming: the pain and loathing etched on his face were too real for a dream.

Sharply, Dubornos asked, "Why are you here?"

"To escort you to freedom." The officer smiled like a hunting snake. "I made an oath in ignorance, possibly in arrogance, and this is the penalty. I suspect we can blame Xenophon for it, but he's beyond our reach. Whoever is at fault, your safety is my responsibility up to the boarding of a ship on the northern coast. On my own honour and that of my god, I am sworn to protect you or die in the attempt." His tone took any honour out of the words. "Because I prefer to live, we will do what we can to ensure that your escape is not suspected by those who might wish to follow." He turned to the doorway. In Latin, quite differently, he said, "In here. Quickly."

Half a dozen men entered, laden. Their burdens, when dropped to the floor and rolled from their sackcloth bindings, were recognizably human and dead, if not freshly so. Their hair was most striking, being the most un-Roman. The tallest pair of adults were blond, as were the two youths. The single, slightly smaller man was a redhead, balding on top. On his chest, beneath the torn stuff of his tunic, a knife-wound showed in the corpse-grey skin.

Cunomar felt tides of nausea wash over him. His father's hand gripped his shoulder, keeping him steady. Caradoc was as close to losing control as Cunomar had ever seen him. His voice sliced through the smoke. "You killed them?" he asked. "These people died in our place because you took an oath?"

"Of course." The traitor stared him down. Cunomar remembered those eyes sometimes, on the worst of nights when the noise of the city and the cold and the smell of mouldy plaster all conspired to keep him awake. Then the black eyes of a falcon laughed at him from a man's face. He had never thought to see them again in life. They flickered over him now and barely noticed his existence. The voice, full of scorn, said, "This is war, Caratacus. If you want to live, others have to die. When you return to Britannia, you will find it the same. Unless you want to die here, and your children with you? You should choose quickly. Fire has even less patience than I do, and I have little enough."

They were already risking their lives. Orange flames raged outside the southern window. Patches of soot feathered up on the heat. Caradoc glanced there once, and Cunomar saw the decision made. "We are packed. We can leave now, but we cannot press the pace faster than Cwmfen and the babe can manage."

"Clearly not. Xenophon thought as much after his apprentice boy left. She will be escorted in a litter to the city walls and thence on a wagon until she is fit to ride. If we are lucky, we will still make coast at Gesoriacum before the ship leaves. If not . . ."

"We will spend six months as fugitives on Roman soil?"

The decurion shook his head. His smile was poisonous. "Not Roman, no. I had rather thought we might find somewhere quiet in Gaul. But I think we should all pray it doesn't come to that. Half a year in one another's company might be too much for any of us to bear."

CHAPTER 26

At dawn, in a riverside clearing half a day's ride south of the sea port of Gesoriacum, beside the glowing ashes of a night's fire, Valerius, oath-bound decurion, lay awake as he had done for most of the night, counting the fading stars in an unsuccessful effort to forget where he was and whom he was with and how he had come to be both.

He wanted wine badly, and there was none to be had. He had brought three flagons with him from Rome, thinking them more than enough to last the journey. Night and morning he had measured the doses, using as much as he needed to keep the ghosts at bay and the voices quiet and his smile sharp against the constant loathing of Caradoc and his family.

The longer they travelled and the closer they came to Gesoriacum with its memories of Caligula and Corvus, of Amminios and Iccius, of hate and love and vengeance and death, the more wine it had taken to re-tain a semblance of stability. The last flask had run dry three days since, leaving Valerius afraid for his sanity. Surprisingly, Philonikos had helped him, supplying from his medical stocks a fierce, honeyed liquor of a strength to burn the throat and send numbness streaking down the limbs. In the face of spirit that strong, the whispers of the past had withdrawn and even the present pressed less closely so that, for two nights, Valerius had slept. Only in this last evening, with their destination close at hand, had the physician's apprentice inexplicably withdrawn his gift, and Valerius felt the lack.

The stars faded too fast. Unlike Britannia, where he prayed each night for the god's light to rise and banish the dreams, here, in this place and this company, the decurion had no wish for day to begin. He would have welcomed dreams if they could displace the memories of his first visit to

Gesoriacum, of who he had been before he arrived, and who before that, and before that; or if they could have erased for one moment the presence of Caradoc and the accusations the man carried with him.

The monumental irony of the oath Xenophon had wrested from Valerius had been its own shield in the apartment and for the first days out of Rome, but it had not survived long on the road north. The decurion was used to being feared—even Longinus was afraid of him now—but he was still respected, even by the Gauls who had supported Umbricius. Until this journey, he had not known how his spirit fed on that respect, or how its opposite drained him. Because he must, he believed that, with the god's promise of success to lead him on, he could survive this final day without any outward sign of what it cost. More deeply, he knew that one day was the most he had left.

The stars were gone. The sun cracked open on the eastern horizon, and the god's light spilled through the trees, smothering the dim glow of the fire. The fire had never given smoke—Valerius had built it with care using wood dried the previous night—but a rising ruffle of hot air tilted mildly to the left, showing a southerly swing in the breeze. The music of the river changed note as the wind backed round, and somewhere, a long way distant, a cock crowed.

Valerius pushed off his cloak and rolled to his feet. It was a matter of pride that he rose first, as it was to find the fires of those who hunted them. They were hunted, there was no doubt of that, and in this the decurion had the better of the warriors he led; he knew intimately the exact danger posed by the hunter, his strengths, his weaknesses, and, he believed, his intent.

There was relief in movement. Soundlessly he crossed the clearing and took a path through the sparse woodland. Behind him he heard the soft padding of the warriors as they, too, rose and took other routes through the woodland. Soon all he could hear were the noisier strides of the child, Cunomar, who had been too long in Rome and had not yet learned to walk silently.

The river was high after ten days of rain and ran turgid with mud. He found a leaf-stirred eddy at the side in which to relieve himself and then moved upstream to check the horses and splash his face in cleaner water. He felt better for that, the wine-deprived thickness in his head and tongue less than they had been. The bank led south and west to a place where the river widened and the torrent slowed. He crossed on greasy, treacherous stepping-stones, taking each one slowly and testing the footing. On the southern bank, a deer path led through thorn scrub and round a sunken grassy dell that rose on its far side in a steeply wooded slope. He climbed up, using the angled trunks of the scrub thorn as handholds. Shed beech leaves, shiny as beaten bronze, crisped beneath his feet. On the thorns, the berries were crinkled for winter, holding the damp in heavy drops that drizzled his thighs and wept coldly onto his cheeks.

Reaching the crest of the slope, he squirmed forward under low branches until he had a clear view out over a broad stretch of water meadow to a cluster of oak and beech beyond. Smoke rose faintly over the canopy. Marullus, centurion of the second cohort of the Praetorian Guard, had never learned the art of smokeless burning, or perhaps he was intent on signalling his presence, a warning sent by a Father to one of his many sons, one under the blessed cloak of Mithras, set on opposing sides by ill-fortune and an oath carelessly taken. They were not yet in conflict and might never be. The god, one hoped, would prevent it.

Valerius lay still under the thorns for a while, letting brisk air and the relief of solitude work a measure of healing. Presently, as the inner and outer mists thinned, he saw what he was looking for: a handful of men moving jerkily amongst the trees, readying horses for travel, and the one who lay in the deep cover opposite, watching.

"They're playing with us. They know we're here."

Valerius jumped. The speed of it bludgeoned the delicate parts of his brain as he turned. A bubble of pure, easy rage rose to his head and burst. Almost, he struck out. A decade's training as an officer stopped him, and the oath to his god.

If the girl Cygfa saw the danger and its passing, she showed no fear. She had come up behind him silently and sat, as silently, watching. More than Caradoc with his frigid scorn, or the child Cunomar with his all-consuming loathing, Cygfa unnerved Valerius. She spoke little and never willingly to him, and yet he had never once moved apart from the others but she was there on cat's feet, following. She crouched now in a hidden space between the thorns, staring at him with her father's eyes.

Sometime in the journey, she had begun to braid her hair in the way of the warrior—an act forbidden in Rome—and overnight she had found three crow-feathers and woven them into the left side. They hung damply in the mist, and her face, thus framed, was that of sexless, androgynous youth so that Valerius, biting his lower lip, had to repeat aloud in his mind the single fact that this was a woman, not a man, and that the god would never return Caradoc to him cleared of age and all betrayal, or those who had been lost to his treachery. *Amminios was lying . . . What would you have done if you had known Breaca was still alive . . . ?*

Enough. Stop now. He knows.

The decurion held himself still and believed he showed nothing.

Cygfa raised a familiar mocking brow. "Do you not intend to slay these men as you did their tracker?"

She asked it to goad him, not because she was interested in his answer. Early in their flight, two days out of Rome, he had left his charges for half an evening to hunt down and cut the throat of the single Dacian tribesman who had followed their trail. He had said nothing to the others, but Cygfa, following, had witnessed it, and word had spread amongst the others of the man's death and, perhaps, of the needlessness of it; the tracker had lost their trail when he died. If he had been confronted, Valerius could have countered with his argument that the group would travel faster without the need for secrecy and that one dead tracker was one fewer enemy wielding a blade against them later, but the question had never come, and he had not chosen to raise it himself.

All this he read in Cygfa's eyes as she watched him watch the watchers. On any other day, Valerius would have walked away, but her choice to braid the kill-feathers had made of her presence a greater challenge, and on this last day, he was tired of challenges. Answering the words, if not their intent, he said, "We can't attack now. We are too few against their many."

"And yet they still don't attack us. We were vulnerable when Cwmfen was lying ill in the wagon, less so now that she is better and can ride," she said. "Why do they stay back?"

She thought like her father, or like Longinus. It was not good to think of him. Longinus had charge of the wing while his decurion was away. Their parting had not been easy, but nothing between them had been easy since Valerius had come back from Rome with the need for wine increased.

Valerius eased back to a place where he could sit up without being seen. It might not have been necessary, but there was an integrity in the fiction of concealment. "They are waiting for a signal," he said. "When they have it, they will attack."

"Or they wait until Claudius is dead."

"The two are the same." Her Latin was stilted, not as fluent as her parents'. Easing himself down the bank to the shallow dip of the dell, Valerius found himself matching the cadence of it. "When Claudius dies and Nero is made emperor, the signal will come. Then they will be safely under Agrippina's command and can act without the dishonour of treason."

Cygfa sneered. "So in Roman eyes, it is honourable to kill an infant of fourteen days if the command comes from the woman who is the emperor's mother, but not if it comes when she is only his wife and his niece?"

The dell was crowded with the debris of the forest. The hollow carcass of a beech trunk lay across it, speckled with bright, toxic droplets of red and orange fungi, and old rodent droppings. Valerius jumped onto the top, rocking it rottenly beneath his feet. The action matched the rhythm of the throbbing in his head and soothed it. He thought the girl might walk on alone, but she waited, her eyes still asking the same fatuous question about Roman honour, as if anything other than that same honour had kept her alive these past fourteen days.

Bluntly, he asked, "Have you ever slain a man in battle?"

The grey eyes scorned him. She raised a finger to the topmost of her feathers. "You have seen me do so."

"And they were men, who were once fourteen-day-old infants, yet you killed them without hesitation, am I right?"

"That's different."

"Is it so? Is life less precious to the grown man who loves life and understands exactly what he has to lose, than to the infant who knows only the comfort of the womb and the muzzling warmth of his mother's breast? I think not." A dog-fox had used the log as a marking post. The musk of its scent rose with his rocking, metallic as horse-sweat and the tears of the dead. Breathing it in, Valerius said, "This is the reality of war. Thirty years spent living and growing make little difference if the soul you set free is that of an enemy. A child slain today will not grow to be the warrior who drives a blade into your back twenty years hence, and that is what may keep you alive. You are a warrior; you should know that."

She said, "We would never kill the children of our enemies."

"I know. That is why you will lose the war and we will win it."

He jumped down from the log and began to force a way through the scrub beyond. Cygfa's voice sought him out. "If you despise us so much," she asked, "why do we yet live?"

In half a month of travel, not one of them had yet suggested he might betray them. Valerius stopped still. Her gaze speared his back. He spun slowly on one heel. "I told you in Rome," he said. "I took an oath. Before my god, such things are binding."

"And why was this oath asked of you?"

"I have no idea." He pushed on away from her, raising his hands to protect his face from the thorns. He lied, of course; he had a very good idea why it had been asked, the crux of which involved Theophilus and Xenophon, two Greek physicians who took their care of the soul as seriously as they did the healing of the body that clothed it. He did not share his thought.

Cygfa followed him along a path that was no path, stretching under the dragging brambles, kicking through thorns and nettle beds. Emerging, Valerius ran across the mud-greased stepping-stones: a warriors' challenge to reach the far bank without falling. Long ago he had watched three other men run a rain-wet log across a river. Only one of them had fallen, and he the one who mattered least.

Valerius reached the far bank with dry feet. Success rallied him. He said, "To find why the oath was asked, you would have to ask the emperor, who may be dead. Perhaps Dubornos can ask him for you. He seems to have friends amongst those who have already joined the gods. I do not."

"No. In the realms of the dead, there are those who merely hate you and those who will wait for eternity to greet your death and avenge their own. Anyone can see it."

"Indeed?" He heard his own voice brittle. "Are you a dreamer that you can see the souls of the dead?"

"Hardly. I don't need to be. Any child can see those that circle you."

He walked away, leaving her on the far bank with the stones ahead of her, and did not wait to see how she fared.

He came to the clearing alone. The rest of the group were ready and waiting. Cwmfen had Math bundled against her chest, ready to ride. The child was growing hair, fuzzily, and his eyes were less vacant. His mother had made good progress under Philonikos's care; for the past three days, she had begun to take an active part in the journey, where before she had lain in a wagon and all her strength had been taken simply to live.

Today she had spread the fire and doused it, covering the ash with turf cut the previous night and scattering old leaves over that. The centurion and his party might find their campsite, but only by diligent searching, and the very act of looking for it would lose them time. It might not matter when their destination was so obvious, but again, there was a warrior's integrity in concealment, and none would willingly break it.

The men had been similarly busy: at the margins of the clearing, the horses were gathered and unhobbled. The wagon mules had been abandoned long since and a mare bought for Cwmfen so that all of them rode horses of good blood, but for Cunomar who had been given a small cobby gelding. The child was there now, standing by his mount, breaking his fast with his father on the cold roasted saddle of a hare that Dubornos had caught the night before. The singer claimed to have sung it into his hand, a conceit Valerius did not believe. The man looked up and waved in ready friendship. Valerius stopped, staring, and then heard Cygfa's soft tread behind him and the sibilant Ordovician greeting.

She would have walked past, but he intercepted her and, so that the others might hear, said, "We will reach Gesoriacum this afternoon. You will have to either unbraid your hair or cover it if you do not wish to be arrested for sedition. I suggest you take that seriously. Tomorrow is the Ides of October and the last chance for a ship to sail. If Claudius can live two more days, you will be safe and I can return to my unit. When I am free of this oath, we will see which side is stronger."

Caradoc's daughter grinned at him, baring her teeth as uncounted others had done on uncounted battlefields, and spoke the words that every man and woman who had opposed him had said, in one form or another: "I will greet the day with delight. Your head will look good mounted on a spear at the roundhouse on Mona."

Of all the things she had said that morning, Valerius considered that last most often in the long day's ride towards the coast. In the days when he had been Bán of the Eceni, his people would not have kept the heads of their enemies as trophies. The bodies of even the most reviled foes had been given intact to the carrion eaters and the gods of the forest.

Gesoriacum, port and civic centre, had changed little in the sixteen years since the youthful Caligula had ordered the great pinnacle of the lighthouse built and sailed his flagship *Euridyke* out onto the ocean to accept Amminios's surrender, claiming as he did so victory over both Neptune and Britannia.

For Valerius, return flayed to the white bone a mind already laid open by the journey. In Britannia new memories overlaid the old, and it was possible to forget what had been. Here too much was too familiar. The land around the town was quieter than he had known it, lacking two legions camped on its margins, but the brisk, sharp smell of the sea made his eyes water as it had always done and brought on the vague nausea that had dogged his every voyage. The wind tore the words from his mouth, and the circling sea-birds cried with the voices of the dead, and he was glad then that Cygfa could hear them as well as he could.

They reached the walls in the late afternoon, dipping down into the valley of a small stream and walking the horses up a meandering path to the southern gate. On the far side of the town, a fishing boat had put into

the harbour, drawing its blizzard of screaming gulls behind. The noise of
them was crippling. Valerius's morning headache, lacking the medication
of wine or Philonikos's spirits, had increased with the passing miles so
that, as they approached the town, he rode forward blindly, letting his
mare pick her own route. His helmet bound tight along his brow, as if the
metal had shrunk or his head had swollen, and the pressure of it crushed
his mind.

The sky was too bright. He looked down, focusing with pained clarity on the crushed grasses and small withered autumn flowers that pricked
the turf in pink and white. His mare had a white pastern on her left fore,
and the hoof beneath it was striped brown against amber. He was counting the stripes in his mind, repeating the numbers over and over in Gaulish, Thracian, and Latin, trying not to be sick, when Caradoc, riding
behind him, said, "They've kindled the lighthouse fires. Is that normal in
daytime?"

What would you have done if—

"What? Where?"

"Behind and to the right."

The nausea vanished. The pressure of his helmet became a necessary
protection. Valerius looked up. From the platform of the lighthouse north
and east of their position, buckets of pitch poured oiled black smoke up
into the daytime sky, poisonous against high drifting clouds.

"It's the end of a signal chain." He knew it in his gut. "They'll be re-
sponding to another." He looked around, cursing the sea and the gulls and
his wine-deprived inattention, and saw what he should have seen before.
He thrust out an arm, pointing.

"There."

Behind them, far back in the hills, a column of grey smoke slanted on
an unfelt breeze. The canopy of the woodland nearly concealed it; had
they been a mile further down in the valley, they would have been as blind
to its presence as were the nine armoured men who rode out of the woodland on the far side of the stream and, as one, halted their horses and
looked up to the column of smoke rising above the town.

Valerius felt ice ball in his chest. "Claudius is dead," he said, and, with
the same certainty, "Agrippina rules. We're dead, too, if we stay in the
open." Cwmfen rode just behind him, the infant Math strapped to her
chest. Her face was lined with pain and fatigue, but he had seen it worse.

He asked, "Can you ride at the gallop?"

"If I have to."

"You do." He spun his horse and swept out his arm, taking them all in. "Ride for the south gate and follow me through the town. Anyone who lags behind will be left to Agrippina's men. I wouldn't expect them to be kind."

Gesoriacum was crowded. It was not likely that the entire population had actually emptied onto the streets to impede their passage, it simply felt like it. The roads were narrower than Rome's so that the litters of matrons paying afternoon visits to the villas of friends took the whole width from house-front to house-front and held up the men on foot, dawdling, and the fisherfolk streaming to and from the harbour and the merchants and the stationary wagons—because Rome's daytime ban on wheeled vehicles did not extend to the provinces—and the dogs and the children who ran for their mothers as the strangers on horseback passed through, uncivilly fast. They still cleared the way, tardily but enough. On this last day, Valerius had taken time in mid-morning to shake out the uniform of the Urban Guard from his pack and don it over his travelling tunic. Even those who might have understood the meaning of the lighthouse fire would not risk offending an officer from Rome.

The town's harbour was a small one, for all that it had seen half an invasion fleet depart a decade before. Warehouses, merchants' stalls and fishers' cottages crowded close up to the quayside, with only a cobbled path to keep them from toppling forward into the water. A low stone wall projected out into the sea, studded with oak mooring posts. Three green-painted fishing boats ranged prow to stern along the left-hand side of it, each tilted to seaward, their flaking keels resting on mud, straining against taut mooring ropes. On the right, a barnacled merchant ship lay similarly grounded. Valerius stared at it, cursing floridly in Thracian.

"The tide's out. We can't sail." Caradoc was the seaman amongst them, but even Cunomar could have told that the ship was not going to sail this side of high tide. The child's father dismounted and knelt on the rimed stone of the jetty, leaning down to study the clusters of bubbled weed and the wavering lines of molluscs. The sea rolled up and down at its leisure, in no hurry to rise or to fall.

Caradoc sat back on his heels. "It's on the turn," he said. "But the ships won't be afloat before nightfall. No master in his right mind would sail before dawn. Agrippina's men will be here long before then."

They were here already. Far back on the southern edge of town, litter-bound matrons and dawdling men clucked and flustered a second time as another group of armed horsemen carved their way towards the harbour.

Valerius cursed viciously in three additional languages, then said, "You need to get out of sight. When you're safe, I'll find the ship's master. He'll sail tonight if I have to hold a knife to his throat as he does it."

Cwmfen said, "You'd see us all drown?"

"I'd see you half a mile offshore and out of reach of Marullus and his men. That much my oath requires. What happens to you after is not my concern. Come on."

His horse's feet skidded on mud as he turned. Momentarily, the slanting sun blinded him. He accepted with gratitude the god's reminder of his promised success, so close now he could reach out and touch it. He did not doubt that Marullus would concede defeat as soon as the ship was safely offshore. A father did not hold a grudge against a son when he had lost a challenge in fair combat. In the meantime, action kept the ghosts at bay almost as well as wine.

He blinked, and the sun was gone. On the quayside, a small crowd had gathered. Mucky-nosed children gawped openly at his armour. Valerius moved his hand to cover the mark of the red bull on his left shoulder and jerked his head at Caradoc, who was staring into the crowd. "Mount, now, before you attract more attention. The Praetorians will pay for information. We should see there's little to be had."

He led them west, then east, then doubled back west again, threading his way into the poorest quarter, dismounting and leading the horses when the streets became too narrow to ride. They left the horses eventually in a cattle pen at a butcher's, with the man paid enough to buy the promise of silence and scared into its certainty by the threat of the emperor's displeasure and the more tangible danger of the decurion's knife. Some men can threaten death with absolute authenticity; Valerius had found these last ten years that he was one of them.

The tavern to which he brought them was in an alleyway so narrow that the churned, dog-soiled mud of its floor never saw sunlight. Wedged in the gap between a tannery and a laundry, the inn made no effort to avoid the stench of either, or to pretend, as others might have done, that the fabric of the walls was anything but a fire trap, or that the beds had ever been free of lice.

The proprietor was a man of uncertain ancestry who called himself, with due irony, Fortunatus. Over the years, he had acquired the art of hazy recall in the identification of his clients. Rarely did a face stick in his mind, and then only if the circumstances were unique. In his years of service, Fortunatus had only once before played host to a junior officer of the cavalry and then it had seemed accidental, the meanderings of a young man lost in search of himself, brought to wine for solace and, perhaps, repentance and to this place above all others for its guaranteed anonymity. That man was older now, of higher rank, and if the hair was as black and the lean delicacy of his features as striking as they had been, the fires that fed his soul burned manifestly more harshly. Seeing him in the doorway, the proprietor breathed in danger much as his clients breathed the stench of stale urine and rotting skins and hated it with the same fervour.

"We need a room from now until dusk."

The decurion's voice was quiet and did not allow the possibility that he might be refused. The coins that spilled from his palm onto the noisome straw of the floor were worth more than the inn and its half-dozen boy-whores combined. His right hand, resting lightly on the hilt of his dagger, made the alternatives clear. Fortunatus was grossly obese, partly as a defence against clients' knives—only the longest would reach any vital organ shielded by the layers of fat. He was considering his possible courses of action when the decurion raised one fine black brow and shifted his hand to his cavalry sword, which looked easily long enough to run through a horse and still spit the man behind it. The proprietor jerked his chin towards a curtained opening. At this time of day, his one room was always free.

The officer's smile was charming and entirely unpleasant. "We are not here. You have neither seen us nor heard of us. If you value your life, you will remember that, as will the rest of your ... staff. You will find us cheese, bread, and olives that are fit to eat and a flagon of watered wine that a child can drink safely."

The man had no sense of humour, clearly; no one else could have said that last and kept a straight face. Fortunatus's nod became a palsied bobbing of the head. Only after the curtain had dropped behind the woman bearing the infant did he find his girth was such that he could not stoop to fetch the coins on the floor and had to ask one of his "staff" to find them for him.

He had not counted them as they fell. The urchin he had picked was one of the few with any intelligence, which may have been a mistake; the lad handed up a handful of copper and silver but no gold. Fortunatus had seen gold. He was reaching behind the bar for his whipping rod when a knife blade came from nowhere and hung horizontally in the air beneath his chin, cutting like a razor into the first row of jowls. He found himself frozen, too shocked even to sweat.

"How much for the boy?"

Fortunatus knew the decurion by the unnatural quiet of his voice.

The man was just behind his shoulder, where either or both of the knife and the cavalry sword could skewer him. If the curtain had moved, the tavern-master had not seen it, but clearly the officer was here and asking a question that any other client might ask. The boy had been beautiful once. His hair, although matted, was still so blond as to be almost white and his lowered brows failed to hide the strange blue gaze of the Belgae. He raised them now; he, too, had seen the colour of the officer's money and was doing what he could to make himself presentable. In poor light, he might still be considered attractive. Fortunatus thought of a price and doubled it.

"Ten denarii?" A value greater than half a month's legionary pay but less than he had seen dropped to the straw. He tried hard not to make it sound like a question, but his voice betrayed him.

The decurion hissed nastily. The sharp edge of the knife shaved the skin over Fortunatus's larynx. The humourless voice said, "Not for the afternoon. To keep. For life. How much?"

Fortunatus was sweating now. A river of scalding saltiness ran into his left eye, stinging it so that he could not think. The knife-tip moved up to rest below that same eye. A single gold piece appeared in the air beside it, twin to the one that had been dropped on the floor. Or perhaps it was the same one and had never dropped. "I will give this to you, and you will give me the boy. He is mine, now and for always. Is that clear?"

At last a question Fortunatus could answer, which was good, because it took all his presence of mind not to nod. It mattered not to nod; the knife was too close to his eye to allow him to move unless he wanted to lose it.

"It's clear," he said.

"Thank you." The knife was removed. Fortunatus allowed himself to breathe. The lethal voice said, "Every one of the adults in that room is armed. If they are disturbed, they are sworn to leave you dying, whatever else befalls them, and if they fail, I will find you and take vengeance. You will not enjoy that. Do we understand each other?"

"Yes."

"Good." The decurion turned to his new purchase. "You have a name?"

The lad was bright enough to understand that his entire life had just been altered for ever by a man who wielded a knife as if killing came without a second thought. He shook his head. His mouth flapped, but no sound came out.

"But you understand Latin. Good." The man smiled coldly. "Then you are Amminios. Remember that; it's a name with a history, and there are others who will know and admire it. Come with me. We have work to do."

Fortunatus waited until the two shadows, man and boy, had passed beyond the exit to the alley before he sank down onto both knees and felt through the mouldering straw for the remaining coins. He found no gold piece.

The tavern was full when Valerius returned. He had bought a cloak and pulled it close to his uniform, hiding all but the shape of his cavalry sword, which ensured his safety. The Belgic urchin, who had not spoken in the entire afternoon, waited at the alley's mouth. He might have been voiceless, but he had eaten and drunk at the quayside, both with the hunger of the half-starved. Valerius had thought the lad might run then, but fear of the consequences and lack of anywhere else to go kept him at heel like a beaten hound all the way back to the mouth of the passageway leading to the inn, through which nothing short of extreme violence would have made him pass.

"Stay then," Valerius had said. "Keep watch. Look, you can wait in the doorway to the tanner's. Here, take this." He had given him a denarius, flashily silver. The boy had clutched it as if it were more food. "If anyone in a uniform comes asking questions, get word to me."

The lad had scuttled into the tannery doorway. He might leave, he might stay. Valerius had no way to predict; nor particularly did he care; he had bought the boy on impulse and was putting some effort into not dissecting his motives for having done so. It would be a blessing in many ways not to have to make any further decisions regarding his future.

In the front room of the tavern, amongst drinking, fornicating men, Fortunatus was waiting, wringing fat hands. "The room...I have clients...they need privacy."

"Really? I hadn't noticed." The tavern-keeper stank worse than the boy had done, of stale sweat and unwashed man-meat. The urge to kill him, as an act of mercy and a cleansing of the world, was overwhelming. Valerius kept both hands by his sides. "You've been paid enough. We'll be gone before dark."

"Good. Will you? Thank you. Good." Fortunatus nodded. Flesh-bound eyes glinted piggily, seeing greater fortunes. Valerius pushed past, taking care not to touch either the man or his nearest client, and slid into the back room.

In the other world beyond the curtain, lamps had been lit and food shared. The claustrophobic space had been tidied to warrior neatness with fresh straw on the floor and the foul bedding rolled away in a corner. Bread, cheese, and olives had been eaten and the remains stored for later. In a corner, seated on clean straw, the physician's apprentice was tending Cwmfen, who bore his ministrations with the fortitude of a mother who humours a child. At her side, Cunomar played knuckle-bones with Cygfa. The girl had braided the crow-feathers back into her hair in a clear act of defiance. Valerius saw it distantly, noting it with that part of his mind that could still function, the same part that saw the flask of wine and judged it almost full. The rest faced the three men sitting round the table, each one armed with a sword of Gaulish making, each of whom laid a hand on his weapon as the door-skin fell and was still.

Three men.

Valerius had left two.

Nothing had prepared him. Nothing could have prepared him. He stopped, his legs at once ice and water, too stiff and too weak to move. On the far side of the room, a bare spear's length away, Luain mac Calma, heron-dreamer of Hibernia, elder of the council of Mona, once-lover of Macha, who was dead, rose smoothly on long, angled legs. After a moment's appraisal, he extended his arm in the traditional salute of dreamer to warrior.

"Bán mac Eburovic. Welcome. They told me you had changed. I would not have believed how much."

Valerius felt his jaw slacken and shut it tightly. *Bán mac Eburovic. His name means "white" in the language of the Hibernians, Excellency, the place where he was conceived.* He had heard that long ago, and believed it; the one who had spoken had no reason to lie and every reason to know the truth. Unlike the man opposite with his lean face and straight black hair and high brow, who held a hand out to Valerius and named him son of Eburovic, the man who must have known that Eburovic, master-smith of the Eceni, had never been to Hibernia and could not have sired a son there with Macha or any other woman.

I am Valerius, decurion, child of the one god and of my Father under the Sun. The name and nature of the one who sired me matters not. The words beat on the inside of his temples, awakening the headache, which had all but gone. Without his directing it, the heel of his hand passed over his sternum, pressing squarely on the raven brand, and then touched briefly to the bull on his shoulder. In his mind, he spoke the name of the god.

Aloud he asked, "What are you doing here?"

Mac Calma sheathed his sword. "We were awaiting your return. You need a ship. By now, you will have found that the master of the *Gesoriaca* will not sail before dawn. There is a second ship, anchored offshore a short distance westward along the coast. She sails under a master of greater courage. I will take you to him."

"Really? How thoughtful. I'm sure Caratacus is grateful that his dreamer knows the minds of other men. Sadly I have other plans." Valerius's voice was softer than it had been—a Gaulish actuary had died hearing just such a voice. "Perhaps I did not frame the question correctly. How do you come to be in this room in this town, when our flight was known only to the emperor and to Xenophon?"

"And to the Empress Agrippina. You know Marullus is searching the town from south to north seeking word of you?"

"And you, presumably, know the fate of any dreamer caught alive on Gaulish soil. Neither point answers my question. How did you know of our flight, and how exactly did you know we were here?"

Images of Fortunatus, skewered for treachery, etched themselves across Valerius's mind. He cleared them temporarily, awaiting an answer.

"I have friends in the port. They tell me things that may be useful." Luain was smiling. His eyes were the those of a heron, stalker of still waters. Gulls cried in the harbour. *I have heard they can send their spirits as white birds on the wind . . .*

The dreamer said, "You and the Belgic boy can hide out in the harbour-master's whorehouse if you choose, but I will not let you take Caradoc or his family to a place where they will be caught like cornered rats. The gods have other need of them. They come with me. If you value the oath you made in the name of your foreign god, you can come with us west to the Sound of Manannan and see them safely aboard the ship that will sail with the moonrise tide. Alternatively, if you surrender now to the centurion who hunts you, you may be able to persuade him that you are as loyal to the new emperor as you were to the old, and perhaps he will lift the charge of treachery that is laid against you."

Treachery. The god had promised success. Whatever the dreamer said, Marullus was only a centurion; he did not have the power to lift a charge of treason, or the penalty of death that accompanied it. Only the new emperor could do that: Nero, whose mother ruled for him. Agrippina was not known for the breadth of her mercy.

Valerius did not waste his breath asking how the dreamer knew of the harbour-master's whorehouse; the mere fact that he did was enough to render it unsafe. He weighed the risks and his options. The charge should not have come as such a surprise. Xenophon had been explicit, and the risks had always been clear: if Valerius was careless, he would die. He did not believe he had been careless so far. He tried to build the image of the god on the dirty plaster of the far wall as he had done in the emperor's palace and could not do so. Striving for distance, he said, "An enticing choice. Which did your dream tell you I would do?"

Luain mac Calma stared at the same patch of peeling paint and shook his head, as if the effort and its failure were clear to him. "My dreams tell me nothing," he said. "What you will do is not yet known. At any given time, the gods offer different paths to the future. They never force our choice of which to take."

Valerius was losing composure. His smile stretched too tight over his teeth. His skin had shrunk, or his skull grown, and his joints had stiffened. The Infinite Sun, in whose name he had given his oath, was silent, and yet the oath remained. He said, "They must at least laugh at our indecision."

The dreamer shook his head, his hunter's eyes wide as the moon. "I doubt that."

The pressure in the air was enough to crack open a walnut. Valerius squeezed his eyes closed. Orange shapes flared out into the blackness of his mind. His mother, Macha, appeared before him, speaking Eceni, and he ignored her. Iccius followed her, the Belgic slave-boy who had died in a hypocaust and was not, absolutely not, come back to life in a slave-boy newly bought. If Iccius had lived, the world would have been a different place.

Valerius had long ago learned to shut out both of these two voices. In their presence, and in the absence of the god, he could resort only to the oath that bound him. He forced his eyes open. "You should leave here," he said. "Fortunatus has already sold your presence to the town guard. They wait only for dusk so that they may seem to find us by accident and he will not die for it."

"And you?" asked mac Calma. "What will you do?"

"Me? I will watch your backs as you leave and take the time to remind Fortunatus that treachery is unacceptable. When he is chastened, and I am sure you are not being followed, the boy and I will join you."

He forgot, in the end, that he had named the child Amminios.

CHAPTER 27

Luain mac Calma led them. Valerius brought up the rear. They rode in single file along the margins of the sea-turf. The smell of it rose in the still air, sharply sweet and spiked with the sorrel freshness of shoreline herbs crushed underfoot. The light was failing fast. Out on the ocean, the ship that promised freedom was a ghost barely seen in the grey dusk, the sail a billow of white, still too far away for safety. The sea was restless, white manes cresting the waves as Manannan rode to greet them, or to kill. Along the shingle, the hush of each receding wave brushed the stones, a little closer each time as the tide came in. Cunomar watched it, marking in his mind where the next biggest wave would reach and counting a tally for when he was right. It was a child's game, but it kept his mind free of fear, and he would die before he showed fear in the presence of the traitor who claimed to be his mother's brother and yet wore Roman uniform.

The horses walked like hounds, their hide-bound feet falling softly on the turf. Cunomar rode third from last in the line. Cygfa rode behind him, keeping him safe both from the pursuing Romans and from Valerius. She had become more protective since the morning when she had spent time in Valerius's company, and her disdain of the man had become more apparent.

The decurion had joined them late, as they were collecting the horses, and Cunomar had seen him sheathe a bloody knife, then draw his sword and slide the length of it into the mud and ordure of the butcher's holding pens. Sensing himself watched, the man had raised his eyes and smiled his cold snake's smile and said, "The moon is up and the sky clear. It will help us see the way to the ship but will also show us to Marullus and his men. I would advise that you cover your brooches and bridle bits and if you would not have your weapons give you away. You, too, will drag them through the mud. I apologize if it offends your warriors' instincts."

This last had been directed with heavy irony at Cygfa, who had ignored it but nevertheless had done as the man suggested. Cunomar, disgusted, had watched as his father, Dubornos, and Cwmfen all drew the blades given them by the dreamer mac Calma and similarly sullied them. At the last, he had done the same with the blade they gave him, but only when ordered to do it by his father. It was not a way for true warriors to ride into battle.

Riding in the dusk, Cunomar's ears ached with the effort of listening for the sounds of attack. The solid weight of the sword tapped against his thigh with each stride of his horse. It should have been reassuring but was not. All his life he had wanted to be a warrior, and now that the chance had come he knew himself unfit. Cygfa had practised daily with the seasoned men and women of Mona before her first battle. Cunomar had lived more than two years in Rome, where the carrying of weapons was forbidden him and practise impossible on pain of death for the entire family, but even had he practised, the blade he had been given was a man's and too heavy for a boy. Testing it in the small back room of the inn before the decurion returned, he had found that if he held it with both hands, he could perhaps swing it once with credible force before the enemy closed on him. He had read the disappointment in his father's eyes and been ashamed, the more so when mac Calma had gone out again and returned with two small sharp-pointed daggers, one each for Cunomar and Philonikos. The physician's apprentice was tall enough and old enough to bear a blade but had no skill to use it and was thus treated as a child; it hurt to be considered in the same thought.

In the time before Valerius walked in, Caradoc had shown both youths how to use the knives if there were any danger that they might be captured alive, drilling his finger over and again into the place between the fourth and fifth ribs on the left side where they should stab, angling the blade in towards the breastbone so that the heart and great vessels would be split. Dubornos had repeated it later when they reached the horses, and then Cygfa had shown them again after they had mounted, to make sure they understood. In the eyes of each warrior could clearly be read the absolute certainty that it was better to die early than to face the new emperor's executioners.

Cunomar knew it was better to die in battle than on his own knife, but he had listened and repeated their instructions until the act was so real in his mind, it was astonishing that he was still alive. Imagining it as they rode the shoreline, he knew both that he could do such a thing for himself and that the Greek youth did not have such courage. When the counting of waves could not take his mind off what was coming, he thought through the hundred ways in which Cunomar, son of Caradoc, outliving all of the adults, would kill two Romans and end Philonikos's life before turning the small cheating blade on himself. With constant repetition, he could feel the bite of the blade through skin and muscle and on into his heart. He could see the disappointment on the faces of the enemy as they were deprived of their prize and feel the blackness draw in and the face of Briga grow more clear as he died. Even such thoughts of defeat were better than the other, greater fear that nagged at the borders of his awareness: the cold, clinging question of how his father was going to wield a blade in battle when his prison-wrecked body could not properly wield an axe.

The ship remained at a distance. For each hundred strides forward, it seemed a hundred further away. The shoreline changed. Scattered boulders more frequently littered the margins, the same grey as the dusk so that the horses slowed, picking their way. In time rocky outcrops stretching for a hundred paces or more forced them inland and hid the ship from view. At one such, the path angled so sharply that for a few strides Cunomar had a clear view of the decurion riding behind. What he saw did not cheer him. Valerius was drinking openly. He held his naked sword in one hand, laying it across the neck of his mare, and with the other he poured tavern wine into his mouth.

The slave-boy rode double behind, clinging in terror to his tunic. He was not a born rider, that much was clear, but he had witnessed whatever chastisement Valerius had visited on the obese tavern-keeper, and his fear of the man was far greater than his fear of the horse. Cunomar watched as Valerius reached back, offering the boy a taste of his wine, and saw the urchin, terrified, shake his head. Undeterred, the officer waved the flask to the sides, offering it to invisible passers-by. His face was blandly still, beaded with sweat that gathered in the dewdrop above his upper lip and ran in runnels at his temples. It had been the same each morning and evening as he drank steadily beside the fire, causing deliberate offence to those who rode with him. In the fourteen days of their journey, Cunomar had learned to gauge the progress of this man's inebriation. He judged him barely conscious now.

"Do you think to escape the pain of battle, or to find the courage to fight your own kind?"

His voice betrayed him. It broke in mid-sentence so that while the beginning was deep and resonant, the end piped high and shrill and far too loud. On the ship they could have heard him, or inland, where the Roman guards were seeking their path. Cunomar felt his father turn sharply and saw Dubornos lay a calming hand on his arm and was grateful.

Valerius slewed sideways in his saddle to face him. His gaze came eventually to rest on Cunomar's face.

"If I did, there would be no escaping now, so you had better hope I have found the courage as you say. Or perhaps the god will stay Marullus's hand long enough for words to do battle instead of blades. You could pray for that."

Valerius spoke quietly, his words barely carrying over the waves. He did not sound drunk, but then Cunomar had seen him finish an entire flagon before this and not yet heard him slur a single word.

The path widened between one outcrop and the next. Cygfa rode forward to Cunomar's side, as restraint perhaps, or protection. Perversely, Valerius rode up at his other side, coming so close that the legs of the slave-boy riding behind him brushed Cunomar's thigh. The tremor of fear passed from one to the other, destroying the calm of the sea.

From the left, Cygfa said, "Do your ghosts warn you now of your death, Roman?"

Valerius rolled his eyes in mock horror. "Why don't you ask them?"

"They don't speak to me."

"No, of course not." The decurion focused elsewhere on the night around them. "They warn of nothing yet. And my god promises success."

"Is continued life all you need to judge success?"

Valerius laughed aloud. The wine in him made the sound less than controlled. Gathering himself with some difficulty, he said, "You have spent too long on Mona, warrior, listening to the rhetoric of your elders. Yes, at any other time than this, life would be success enough. Only tonight your life and that of your family must also be preserved for one to judge it victory."

"And you think to do that through wine?"

"I will do it by whatever means are to hand." The man raised the flask, smiling. Behind it his eyes burned black with anger and unfathomable pain. Cunomar, seeing it, understood then that Valerius could have drunk any amount of wine in this company and never been less than sober.

Dusk progressed towards night. The sun carved indigo cracks in the cloud and lined them with fire. Slowly the refugees came closer to the ship. At a certain point on the headland, Luain mac Calma cupped his hands to his mouth and made the sound of the hunting owl. It was well done, but he might as easily have shouted; only a man born and bred in the city would believe that an owl might hunt over the sea, and Cunomar did not believe that Marullus, the centurion who tracked them, was a soft city man.

On the ship, the signal was heard and answered, and all semblance of secrecy was gone. Lamps flared to light in the half-dusk, casting a chain of wavering fires onto the sea. One, burning more brightly than the rest, began a slow, disjointed progress up the rigging, carried by someone who climbed one-handed and took good care in doing so. When it was halfway up, it began to swing rhythmically from side to side. At this signal, a skiff set out from the ship's side. It did not look big enough to carry five adults, two youths, and a babe, but Cunomar had no doubt it would seem bigger as he approached it. At any rate, it answered the question of how any or all of them might reach a ship standing eight spear-casts offshore.

The skiff speared the water. The oars left foaming trails of pale green light, showing its progress like tracks in sand. It aimed straight for a projecting spur of the headland that one could see was well within reach. Cunomar, watching it, felt a surge of hope such as he had not felt in two years of captivity. He turned to Cygfa, saying, "The traitor's god may have given him—"

He stopped. The Romans hunting them, having no need for secrecy, had not dragged their blades in the mud. Far back inland, the dying sun drew fire from the length of a *gladius* and showed up the mass of moving shadows around it. Cunomar choked.

Seeing his face, Cygfa spun her horse. Valerius was faster. The wine flask dropped from his hand and rolled on the turf. He spoke in Belgic, very briefly, then in Eceni. "Mac Calma, take the slave-boy. Ride for the skiff. I'll hold them."

Caradoc answered. "One man against nine? I think not. The rocks here curve well and will guard our backs and flanks. We will stand and fight them as warriors. If we are to die, they will remember us for it."

He had led thousands in war. His voice could contain them all, and protect them. Cunomar felt the certainty of it, the courage and honour that were his birthright, and knew hope for a second time, and a heady pride. The boy drew the blade mac Calma had given him and felt the weight of it drag at his arm. His hope faltered. Now it came to it, he was not certain he could manage even a single swing. He held the blade one-handed and felt for his knife and knew that if the horse jigged beneath him he would lose both and be taken alive and if that happened his father, at least, would stop fighting. It had happened before in the imperial audience room and had cost his father the use of his shoulder. Cunomar would not see it happen again. He shifted both hands to the hilt of the sword and rested the blade on the neck of his horse as the decurion had done. Something inside him melted, messily, and he feared for control of his guts. The bound-leather sword-grip slipped in the sweat of his hands, and it was all he could do to keep it from falling.

Cygfa tapped his thigh. "Get behind me. If I am killed or the horse dies beneath me, stay close to mac Calma instead. If there is a chance, ride for the skiff."

Cygfa was fully alive now, so that Cunomar remembered truly who she had been on the morning before the last battle, when he had watched her braid the barred feather into her hair with Braint. He remembered, too, how he had felt and the curses he had spoken. He felt something similar now, but then envy had been a simple, unsullied thing, and now it was tainted by her clear care for him and whatever he felt for her that he could not name. The crow-feathers in her hair flew and spun as she turned her head, catching his eye, the marks of a warrior, which she had earned and he had not. She did not mean to flaunt them, at least not at him, but still a kernel of resentment glowed in his chest, firing his resolve.

"No. I will fight at your left, as your shield." He smiled as he had seen his father smile before battle. "Trust me."

For a long moment, she stared at him, her eyes strange, then said, "Good. It's time you made your kill, and if we are to cross to the other world in Briga's care, it would be good if you came to her a warrior." She grinned as she had once done for Braint, and for the first time, Cunomar understood the comradeship of battle; he loved her and she loved him, and they would fight the enemy as equals, each protecting the other. A blossoming joy merged with the fear so that he could not tell which it was that choked him.

Cygfa said, "If we're going to be shield-mates, you must do as I say without question. Will you swear to me now you will do so?"

He remembered an oath from long ago, sworn on the head of his infant sister. He repeated it word perfect and was pleased to see her eyes widen. "Very good." He thought she looked impressed. "Then keep your horse's back to the rock, and don't dismount unless you have to. And stay on my right, not my left. That place is yours today." She glanced past him and raised her arm. "Philonikos! Bring your horse in here behind us."

The youth came. He looked ill with fear. Belatedly, at Cygfa's prompting, he drew his knife. It shook in his hand. Cunomar smiled for him, as he had for Cygfa. "Their armour is weakest under the arms," he said, having heard it from his mother. "Stab for them there if you can. Or go for the eyes."

The boy nodded sickly. Cunomar marked again in his mind the spot on the youth's chest where he would have to stab to end his life cleanly when they were overwhelmed.

The remaining warriors had brought their horses in at his right hand with the rock to their backs, each protecting the exposed flank of the other except at the ends, to Cygfa's left and Caradoc's right, where the rock curved round to keep them safe. At the end of the line, Caradoc swung his blade, testing the limit of his right shoulder. When it was clear he would not be able to fight that way, he moved his shield to the right and swung his sword with the left. They learned such things in the warriors' school on Mona, but Cunomar did not think his father had learned it well, and even if he had the scars on his left wrist made it weaker. Caradoc said something inaudible to Cwmfen, and she changed sides, coming to his right. Like her daughter, she was whole and supple, but the babe Math was strapped to her back and hampered her movements.

Along the rest of the line, mac Calma and Dubornos, dreamer and singer, stood together on Caradoc's left. Dubornos asked, "Will they have archers?"

Valerius shook his head. "Not unless they have brought them from the town guard."

Mac Calma said, "There are no archers in Gesoriacum."

"But I can count more than nine in their line. Your centurion has called on reinforcements from somewhere." Cygfa said this last and was right. The enemy had slowed now, knowing themselves seen. More than a dozen men strung out in a line in the darkness, marked by star-lit glimmers of bronze and unsheathed iron.

Cunomar tried to count the exact number of enemy blades and could not. The hilt of his own sword still slipped in the running sweat of his palms. He gripped it with both hands and repeated to himself the oath he had sworn to Cygfa. All warriors felt fear, his father had told him so; the test of true courage was to fight in spite of it, not in its absence. The thrill of absolute terror vibrated in his chest, and he swore to himself in Briga's name that he would die a warrior, true to his heritage

The advancing line was close enough to see the detail of the enemy armour, if not their insignia. Dubornos, squinting, said, "I can count eight more besides the nine that have followed us. The new ones are Gaulish cavalrymen." He glanced sideways at Valerius. "You were with the

Gauls when you forced the salmon-trap, were you not? Maybe they've sent your old troop against you."

Valerius was stiffly white. The thought, apparently, was not new to him. "Maybe they have," he said.

He was not part of their group but had placed himself in front and to the left. In the tribes, only one resolved to stand and fight in single combat—or to die—would do so. As if remembering late these two alternatives, he spoke sharply in Belgic to the slave-boy riding behind him, who shook his head, clutching the back of the man's tunic more tightly. Valerius lifted his arm as if to hit him and stopped suddenly, staring out into the night. He let the arm fall.

"Stay if you will," he said, and then, "That's the Cockerel on the standard, not the Pegasus. These are not the Quinta Gallorum. He's brought a detail of the town guard." The relief was audible to them all, and the spare, unvaunted courage as Valerius pushed his horse forward. "Now would be a good time to pray that Marullus truly has brought no archers."

He stopped in full view of the enemy, raised his hand in a cavalry salute, and shouted.

"Marullus!"

The strength of his voice was astonishing. It was clear that he had fought on battlefields where an officer might need to be heard at a distance, shouting to his own men or, as here, calling the name of the man who led his enemies.

"Marullus!" He shouted a second time, and the name hung clear as beaten bronze in the silence.

The enemy halted, granting him the honour of a hearing. No arrows fell from the night to punish his impudence.

As if speaking from a memorized text, Valerius said, "Father! Greetings in the name of the slain bull and the raven. A Son should not oppose his Father, nor be opposed. I wish you no ill, but I am under oath to god and emperor. Let their will be done."

Marullus's voice was deeper, and it, too, had known war. It shook the chests of all those who heard it, as Neptune's might. It was not unkind. "The god's will is unknowable, but the emperor has named you traitor. His will is law. You will die now or later. Better for you that it be now."

Traitor. Mac Calma had said it already, but it had more certainty now. The word drifted like snow in the night, coming down again and again on those who stood waiting with their backs to the sea and the last taste of freedom. One could imagine the death that Rome offered a traitor, and fear it.

Valerius's voice was steady. "Who is emperor?"

"Nero, sworn successor to Claudius. You know that. You saw the black smoke of the lighthouse fire."

They had all seen it. Even Cunomar had known it signalled their certain doom. The decurion had been alone in believing otherwise.

Still casting his voice to the dark, Valerius shouted, "My orders were taken in good faith from a living man. If his successor wished to countermand them, he had only to send word."

"He tried. You cut the throat of the bearer who had tracked you for two days to deliver exactly those orders to you in person."

Valerius fell silent. In his lack of words was Cygfa's unvoiced accusation. *See? You killed without need. No true warrior does so.*

Mac Calma knew nothing of the slain messenger. Breaking the silence, he said quietly, "Thank you. They will not turn back now, but you have done your best and we are grateful. There is still time for you to leave. The track to the west is clear and leads to villages where there are those who do not support Rome. I think they will not follow you when they have us penned here."

Valerius laughed harshly. "And where would I go? If I am named traitor in Rome and Gaul, then as much so in Britannia. The Prima Thracum has no use for an officer who has committed treason against his emperor. It seems the god has spoken and no longer promises success. Perhaps in the after-world, he will explain why."

He looked out into the night. He ran his sword along the crook of his elbow, wiping the blade free of mud so that the rising moon and the stars raised a glimmer on the surface. Raising it, he shouted a final time, "Your choice, Marullus! We will test the Son against the Father."

More quietly to those around him, as if ordering his cavalry troop, he said, "Be ready. The rock prevents them from attacking the flanks, so they will send half the Gaulish auxiliaries as a spear-head to force a breach in the centre, then come at us in line abreast. If the spear-head works and you are split into two groups, form circles with your backs to the centre and the weakest inside. Keep as close as you can to the rock; it will act as a shield."

He raised his blade in salute, and his face held the same dry, wine-fuelled mockery he had maintained for their two weeks of journey. To any and all he said, "Good luck. If your gods still listen, pray to them now for a clean death in battle. We are outnumbered by more than three to one. It should not take long."

However much they loathed him, they could not call him a coward. In the moments before the two lines closed, Cunomar heard him speaking aloud in a tongue that was neither Eceni nor Latin nor Gaulish. To untrained ears, it sounded like a litany of names, spoken in defiance. At the end he heard three spoken hard in Eceni, as a summoning. The last of them was the hound's name, Hail.

With bitter vehemence, Valerius cursed the many names of his god in the tongue of the eastern magi who had first brought him to men. He did not want to die. He did not want to face the ghosts without Mithras's protection. He did not want to fight against Marullus, whom he respected as much as any officer of the legions and more than most. He particularly did not want to fight and die in the company of Caradoc of the Three Tribes, who may or may not have betrayed him, and of Luain mac Calma, who may or may not have sired him. If he had to do all these things, then he wanted a shield, badly, and the company of Longinus Sdapeze, who alone of all men could still settle him before battle, could make him laugh and set impossible wagers that made the business of war seem less brutal and more of a game.

Mithras did not answer the curses any more than he had answered the day's prayers. He sent seventeen trained men against five adults and two children, and it was not a game. Valerius was grateful only for the mare; he had picked her himself from the emperor's stables before he left Rome, and she was battle-trained to a standard even Longinus would have appreciated. In the stretch of time before the first clash of iron, Julius Valerius, who had once been Bán of the Eceni, called in the ghosts that judged him most harshly, challenging them to stay with him until he died.

The Gauls came in a spear-head to break the centre, as he had said they would. Valerius held the mare back until the first had crossed blades with Caradoc and then launched in from the side, acting as his own one-man wedge to break their group. It was not an orthodox manoeuvre, but it was what an officer would do. He would not have it said later by Marullus that he had acted either rashly or without courage. As the mare plunged forward, he heard the Belgic boy squeal in terror and offered a quite different prayer to the god, of regret for a child's needless dying.

He killed the first of the enemy on a reflex, striking the unprotected throat of a man who would kill a weaponless slave-boy simply because he was an easy kill, and only afterwards, as the body fell away from him, did he see that it was a Roman, not a Gaul, whose life he had ended and that he knew the man. It was too late by then for regret; regret led to death, and his body would not allow it.

Wrenching his horse away from another slicing blade, Valerius passed Cygfa, who killed as one born to it, keeping Cunomar safe at her side and Philonikos behind her. Breaking the sword arm of a Gaul for her, he heard her shout to Cunomar, "That one is yours!" and turned back in time to see the man use his shield to batter aside the boy's powerless stroke and thrust the boss on through for his face. It was a killing blow, aimed to crush skull and vertebrae to the marrow. Valerius's sword moved in a line of its own making, slicing up beneath the tilt of the man's helmet into the only unarmoured space that would ensure a kill.

The shield dropped from nerveless fingers, missing the boy's face by less than a hand's breadth. The Gaul toppled from the saddle. Valerius saw Cunomar's mouth contort in a scream that may equally have been despair and hatred—or less probably, thanks—but heard nothing. The noise of battle was already too great to hear one voice above many. Other Gauls attacked from the sides, and a boy's missed chance of glory mattered not at all.

The defenders killed and took wounds, but none died. The rocks protected their backs and sides so that the enemy could only come from the front. In that much, Marullus had misjudged them, or had not thought to send scouts ahead to check the terrain. Valerius knew a blossoming hope until, in a moment of quiet, he heard the clatter of scattering shingle, like rain on a roof, and, looking to his right, saw a fresh body of horsemen riding hard from the west, the side away from the town. They blocked all chance that any of the defenders might slip back from the battle line and run for the skiff, which was doubtless why they were there.

The officer in him admired Marullus's tactics afresh even while he sought to counter them. The mare spun back of her own accord. Two men came at him, one on either side, and Valerius pulled on her soft mouth, hurting her, taking her up and out of reach. He felt a sudden draught on the small of his back and knew the slave-boy had fallen away and was sorry. He killed the first man and found that Luain mac Calma had taken the second. The dreamer should not have been there; he was needed elsewhere. In the knot of warriors that held both Caradoc and Dubornos, Valerius could hear the false ring of iron on at least one weak blade. When he took time to look, he could see that Cwmfen had moved her horse closer to Caradoc's right, shielding him, and that the warrior was visibly tiring. He had no love for any of those who fought with him, but if their deaths were to be entwined, he did not want it sooner than he could help.

Marullus's second line of men moved in. Breaking a thrust spear—the Gauls had spears!—Valerius shouted to mac Calma, "See to Caradoc. I am well."

"Then get the boy back and ride for the skiffs. It is you they are trying to kill, not us."

It was true. The brunt of the Roman attack was aimed against him. Only the dangerous shifting shingle of the beach and the warriors on either side stopped them from overwhelming him. In the mayhem, the dreamer shouted again. "Get the boy!" His blade danced right and left, making space about them. His hair and his cloak flagged in the wake of his turns. "Ride for the skiffs, man!"

"Can't...new troop of Gauls in the way...death to move from here."

"No. They're our Gauls...friends..." A blade cut the flank of mac Calma's horse, and the beast reared, flailing, spoiling the killing stroke. The dreamer slashed back in his own right. Iron belled on iron. There was a chance he might live, which was more than could be said for the others.

Caradoc was wounded. Valerius could see from the way his horse moved that his right hand no longer controlled the reins. He pulled away from mac Calma. *Our Gauls?* Impossible. All Gauls were sworn to the emperor and Rome. A blade streaked across at eye height, and the impossibility of Gaulish allies would have killed him if he had thought about it more.

Thinking kills. Unthinking, he knocked his attacker from his horse and then reached low from the saddle to slice the man's leg below the chain mail, leaving the great vessel spewing blood and his enemy clutching his last moments of life. *Is life less precious to the grown man who understands what he has to lose...? I think not.* He was becoming detached so that a part of him floated above the battle, watching and judging. As always at such times, the ghosts had gone, which was unfair; if Valerius was going to die, he wanted them there to witness it. Savagely, he called them back, and his heart rejoiced when they came.

Instinct pulled him to the right-hand end of the line, to where Caradoc had slid from his horse and was fighting side by side with Cwmfen, using his body to guard Math, who was strapped to her back. Dubornos was wounded but still used his sword to good effect. He knelt at Cwmfen's side, lacking the use of one leg. Weakened and without shields and proper armour, none of the three could live long.

Valerius was about to dismount and join them when a shield grazed the knuckles of his left hand, the grip pressing into his palm. He had swung his blade halfway to the side before he understood and slowed its arc. He took his eyes off the enemy long enough to look down and found the Belgic boy, who had neither ridden nor sailed but who might, once, have seen battle, or heard of it around a fire in the winter in the days when he was free. The boy smiled and was indeed Iccius, who had died in a hypocaust. The pain in Valerius's chest might have been enough to kill him, had not a ringing, many-voiced battle-cry from the west jerked his mind away from the past.

Our Gauls. A dozen horsemen charged at a full gallop into the chaos. They bore spears and long swords and good shields, and screaming to their gods, they carved into the Roman auxiliaries as blades into meat. In a single pass, five of the enemy died. *Our Gauls.* Warriors still loyal to Mona and the old gods, who would risk their lives in defence of a dreamer who travelled often to Gaul and those who rode with him.

Our Gauls. *Mithras! I thank you.*

The slave-boy was standing in frozen stillness among the plunging horses. In Belgic, Valerius shouted, "Give me your arm. Come up on my horse. They must know you are one of us."

The boy clutched at his sleeve and was hauled up. He weighed less than Iccius had ever done, even after Amminios had gelded him.

A loose horse passed, foaming white at the mouth, its eyes wide with fear. Valerius grabbed the reins and tore it round, bracing his weight against it. Dragging it beside his mare, he forced a way forward. Behind him the slave-boy whimpered once and was silent.

On the ground, Caradoc was holding his blade two-handed, carving air, but not cleanly. Valerius used the free mount bodily to block a Roman attacker. Thrusting the reins forward, he shouted, "For you! There's a chance now. Mount if you want to live."

The warrior's reply broke apart in the chaos. "No . . . Dubornos has . . . greater need."

The second wave of the incomers was on them, attacking at random. Valerius ducked and slashed and realized late that he had not forgone his decurion's armour and was beset by those who were ostensibly his allies. Mac Calma shouted violently in Gaulish, and the strikes against him lessened. In the cramped space in front of the rocks, Gauls fought other Gauls, and only by the blue-stained heron-feathers flying in handfuls from the hair of the newcomers could friends be told from foe. Marullus's Romans were pushed to the margins and, not knowing what to look for, did not see the distinction and so could not kill.

"Get to the boat!" It was mac Calma, singing his single litany.

Light-headed with fatigue, Valerius laughed. "You need a new chant, dreamer."

He swung round. Dubornos mounted the gelding he had caught. His leg was bleeding but not broken. Two horses were brought, one each for Caradoc and Cwmfen. Cygfa joined them, white-faced and cursing, shepherding a raging Cunomar, who wanted to kill even if he died trying to achieve it. A pack of howling, blue-feathered Gauls surrounded them and escape seemed possible, but for the sudden crash of the falling sky as Marullus, who had kept clear of the fray to give orders and had now, at the last, committed himself, came crashing through.

"Go!" Valerius screamed it in his battle-voice, in Eceni, as he had never screamed before. "Go for the ship. Marullus is mine. To get me, he will let you go."

There was no time to see if he was obeyed. The centurion was a bull, inward and outward, and he swatted Gauls as a bull crushes summer flies and with as little care. Men fell before him and around him as he ploughed his horse through the battle lines to get to the man he had called son, whose life he had chosen not to take these past fourteen days.

The stolen shield saved Valerius. The first blow of the centurion's blade cracked it but did not break through. The power of the strike numbed his arm. The second swiped sideways for his head, and he might have died, but the mare slipped on the blood-slick shingle, going down on one knee, and the sweep of the blade missed them both. She was a good mare. Valerius heard her grunt as she rose and knew the bone broken in her forelimb, or the tendons split. One last time he dragged hard on her mouth, and she gave him what he needed, rising high on her hind legs. The Belgic boy slipped backward to safety. The mare caught the backswing of Marullus's blade, taking it full in the side of the head, splitting bone and muscle down to the teeth. She screamed hoarsely and toppled. Crimson blood spumed from her nose. The sword wedged in her, held fast in the bone, and the centurion, loath to let go, was pulled off balance. Valerius was already clear, dropping the shield, rolling on the shingle, bruising the entirety of his back, rising with his blade still in his hand. Longinus would have liked that. Longinus would never hear of it. Marullus was above him, still in his saddle, still off balance, bellowing.

Knowing himself lost for all time to the god and the legions, Julius

Valerius Corvus, first decurion of the Prima Thracum, struck into the un-guarded face of the man who had branded him, who had taught him the litanies, who had given him a reason to live when there was none. Marul-lus died, despising him, and was added to the ghosts. A shout in Latin recorded it, and the Romans on the margins of the chaos, seeing him die, abandoned their discretion. No longer attempting to discern friend from foe, they began instead to attack every Gaul within reach. On the pebbles of the shoreline, the mare died, thrashing.

"Come!"

It was shouted in Gaulish and repeated in Eceni. A hand dragged on Valerius's sword arm, pulling him along beside a running horse. Other hands caught him under the armpit, and he was raised up and thrown bodily onto the back of a mount. The battle fell behind and behind, and he dragged himself upright and took control of the reins and saw the Bel-gic boy held safe by Dubornos and was glad it was not Caradoc, and then they were on the spit of land with the rocks and the seaweed and the pin-point barnacles lit fire-bright by the oarsmen's lamps. Only because he could ride no further, Valerius braced himself against the saddle, ready to dismount. His mind would not allow him to consider where he might go when his feet met the beach.

"You're not coming!"

Surprised, he looked up. His new horse was footsore and had trouble on the wet rock and turned only slowly. Before it was fully round, he re-alized that it was Cygfa who had spoken and that she was weeping. She would never weep for him.

From over his right shoulder, he heard Caradoc's voice, held unnatu-rally steady, say, "I can't come. I'm sorry, truly. I can't, not like this." The warrior's right arm hung at his side. It might still have movement, but it would never again raise a shield.

"You must. The warriors of Mona, of the Ordovices, of all the united tribes, will accept you, whole or not. You can still come. You must. With-out you we are nothing." She was whispering, to get the words out past her grief. They hushed into the sea.

"No. They may accept, but they will not respect." Caradoc spread his left hand. The fingers crooked inwards on both, and they shook as one with palsy. "Cygfa, I don't do this to hurt you, I swear it. If we were not at war, I would return without hesitation, but I can't lead a battle as I am. Better that they know I am free and in Gaul and that they believe me whole. It will be said I stayed to fight while you escaped. Word will be spread later that I am alive, and it will give heart where my presence will not. I'm sorry." It was a prepared speech, as Valerius's to Marullus had been. One could not tell how long ago he had prepared it.

The dreamers, evidently, expected this. Dubornos showed no surprise. Luain mac Calma took no part in the exchange taking place an arm's length away and instead watched the skiff on one side and the battle beyond, where a line of Gauls was slaughtering the remnants of Marullus's men.

Cygfa said, "Mother? Will you not return to your people?"

Cwmfen was behind Caradoc. Enemy blood stained her face and arms, but no tears. She shook her head. "I stay with your father. Math must grow knowing his father as well as his mother. He needs both of us to teach him who he is and what lines he has come from. It is better like this. We will hear word of you and you of us."

"Then I'll stay with you. I'll guard you, and my brother will grow knowing his full family." She did not suggest that Cunomar should stay.

"No." Caradoc reached for her arm. "You must sit your long-nights. Mac Calma says it's not too late, but that it can't be done in Gaul. The gods no longer live here as they do on Mona."

Valerius watched the change in her, the sudden swamping wave of a hope that had been buried so deeply for so long that she had forgotten it was there. Her father had not forgotten, nor her mother, and nor perhaps Luain mac Calma, who could see what she might have been and might yet be. The understanding of that filled her visibly.

She glanced sideways at the dreamer, who nodded. Caradoc smiled, at what cost was not clear. "See? It is better this way. Go now. You must sail, and we must ride."

He reached for her other arm, no longer the clasp of a warrior but the full embrace of father for daughter. The careful mask of his composure broke open. Tears made clean tracks on his cheeks. His hand went to his shoulder to the serpent-spear brooch that was all that remained of Britannia. He unhooked it and pinned it to Cygfa's tunic. The red threads on the lower loop were entirely blackened with his blood. Kissing her, he said, "I have no blade to give you—mac Calma will see one is made for you that is fit. Take this, and take heart. While you live, my soul and your mother's fight the enemy through you."

"Father . . ." Cygfa lifted his hand to her cheek. Through streaming tears, she said, "We will drive them from the land, every one. Then you can come home again."

Caradoc smiled brokenly. When he could speak, he said, "We will wait daily for that news."

His gaze moved back beyond Cygfa to where Cunomar watched, forlorn, abandoned, unspeakably angry and lost. He had entered the battle a boy and emerged the same, lacking a single kill. Until Caradoc spoke, all of his attention had been on the fighting behind them. Valerius, watching, saw that Dubornos was holding the boy's horse and that three of the blue-feathered Gauls had been ordered expressly to watch over the lad and keep him safe.

"Cunomar, you fought well." Caradoc was more controlled now, enough to pass off a lie with some credibility. He drew the knife from his belt and held it, hilt out. "I have no sword to give you, but take this, as if it were one. Mac Calma will see it made real." He stopped, searching for words. Those that came were not prepared. "Your mother . . . your mother will know this is right. Stand at her side in my stead. Protect her for me."

He knew his son well. The boy's face had collapsed at the sight of the knife and the hollow praise for his actions. In the name of his mother, he pulled himself together and sat straighter in the saddle. For the first time, he took his eyes and his attention completely from the fading battle at the rocks. He had been born on Mona and grown amongst its ceremony. He made the salute of a warrior to a member of the elder council, perfectly.

"While I live, she will not take harm," he said. "In Briga's name, I swear it."

The gathered adults witnessed the oath with due solemnity.

Their parting was swift after that. The Gauls took the horses. The oarsmen, who were for the best part also Gauls, helped the warriors to board the skiff. Philonikos chose to accompany Caradoc and was wished well by Dubornos, who had been closest to him. The Belgic boy, wretchedly confused, was given the same choice and, perhaps not understanding, said in his fractured Gaulish that he wished to remain with Valerius, wherever he went. Where Valerius was going was not clear to any of them, least of all the man himself.

Mac Calma made the decision for him. "If you stay, our Gauls will kill you. They don't believe me that you are not of Rome."

"They're right. I'm as much of Rome as any man they killed tonight."

The dreamer smiled crookedly. "Then if you wish to die, you may stay on this beach. If you wish to live, you can at least board the boat. We have five days' journey, perhaps more. Decisions can be made and broken a dozen times in each day, and if you really want to die Manannan will take you." When Valerius did not reply, mac Calma said, "If you stay, the boy Iccius will die with you. I do not have the power to make them let him live."

It was the name that made the difference, although later Valerius railed against so flagrant an abuse of his past. At the time, he knew only that he could not see the child die again whose ghost he still carried with him, and so the decision was made.

"Stop." Valerius had turned to board the skiff when Caradoc grasped his arm. It was easy now to see the man in him; the god had never looked so broken. The cloud-grey eyes were bloodshot and held a world of pain. The courage it took to keep them level could not be measured. Caradoc held out his hand. "Give me your knife," he said.

"What?"

"Your knife. The one with the falcon-head. Give it to me."

Waves brushed the shingle. A night gull cried. An oarsman grated his blade on the sand. Slowly Valerius drew his knife from his belt and held it out on the flat of his palm.

Caradoc touched the shaking fingers of his left hand to the weapon but did not lift it. He said, "There is a challenge amongst my mother's people, the Ordovices, to test the truth between warriors. Two hands clasp the knife-hilt. Each strives to strike the other in the throat. Only one walks away alive."

Valerius barked a laugh. "The Ordovices were always known for their savagery."

"Perhaps, but it has its place. I swear to you now, on the hilt of your blade, that I did not betray you to Amminios, that I never at any time in your childhood wished you ill, that I took joy in your joy and heart in your love, that I respected the power of the dreamer you were and the warrior you could become. I would have spoken willingly before the elders at your long-nights and felt myself honoured to be asked. I still would." Caradoc was neither a dreamer nor a singer, but his words carried their power. His eyes burned. They were not the god's eyes. In a different voice, he said, "If you doubt me, we will take the challenge. Mac Calma is not empowered by our elders to oversee it, but Cwmfen is."

"You think she wishes to oversee your slaughter?" The mere suggestion was ludicrous. Valerius was weary from the battle but not incapacitated. Caradoc was on his feet only because his will would not let him fall; he was in no condition to hold a knife. Valerius said, "You have the chance of life in Gaul. Do you wish to leave Cwmfen to rear a child without its father? That is not what you just told your daughter."

"I would not have my son grow to adulthood with his father accused of treachery."

"Worse things have been said of men."

"Not of me."

They stood apart on the shingle, with a knife-blade between them. Behind, the battle ended. Valerius heard a man die, and then the silence of spent warriors who will stand awhile when the danger is over, until they can find the strength to walk. He had seen it on both sides, sometimes in the same day, when the battle has gone beyond the endurance of everyone left on the field and no one can win.

Caradoc said gently, "Bán? You have to choose. You can't go back to Breaca believing that I betrayed you."

Your sister is my heart and soul, the rising of my sun in the morning. She has been from the first meeting and will be until I die and beyond.

The child who had been Bán had not seen that. The man who was Valerius had spent fifteen years denying it.

Valerius closed his hand around the knife's hilt. Slowly he removed it from Caradoc's grip. "You think I could go within reach of my sister if I had killed you? She must have changed a great deal."

"She hasn't." Caradoc smiled. "Then you believe me?"

You would believe Amminios over me?

Yes.

He could lie so well, my brother . . .

"I won't kill you to prove a point."

Fingers stronger than he imagined closed on his wrist, crushing skin onto bone. Cloud-grey eyes burned with a fire he had thought long spent. With quiet intensity, Caradoc said, *"But do you believe me?"*

The ghosts were gone. His god did not watch over him. Alone in a crowd of strangers with no one left to help him, Julius Valerius abandoned the certainty that had sustained him since before he joined the legions.

"Yes," he said, "I believe you."

CHAPTER 28

"It's a ship!"

The gale whipped the words out over the sea. It caught the unbraided parts of Breaca's hair and spread them like sea-wrack about her face. It lifted spray from the waves and dashed it onto the rocks at her feet, and over the fire, and her cloak, and her face, and she raised her arms and let it cover all of her, saltily sweet. Laughing like a child, she shouted to Airmid over the noise of the wind and the water, "Look! Near where the sun hits the sea. It's a ship. Graine was right. It's Luain's ship!"

She had not believed the dream; no one had. It had come early one morning, halfway through the first of the autumn's storms. Graine had told it to Sorcha, who had waited almost to noon before, at the child's insistence, she had walked through the rain to the greathouse and told whoever would listen. The first few had smiled and laid more wood on the fire and done nothing; a young child's dreams are too unfocused to be true, and no sane man would sail in the face of an autumn storm. Airmid alone had believed her and had persuaded Ardacos to take the ferry across to the mainland to search for Breaca and bring her home.

The small warrior had taken three days to find the Boudica, and another half-day passed before she was persuaded to abandon her stalking of foraging legionaries on the strength of a dream told by the daughter she had barely seen these last two years. The promise of a ship had swayed her, and Airmid's word that the dream was true.

Airmid had been waiting on the jetty for their return, carrying lit torches, with the horses saddled behind. Graine waited with her, standing on her own, no longer needing to hold an adult hand for support. Breaca could not remember when that had happened; sometime in the summer perhaps.

Graine was wearing a grey cloak and a small dreamer's thong at the brow. That, too, was new. Her ox-blood hair hung in sodden rats' tails around her shoulders, darkened to oak in the rain. Seeing Sorcha, she had run forward to be lifted and swung in the air, squealing. Set down on the ground again, she took a step towards her mother, then, faltering, looked back to Airmid for help.

"Go on." The dreamer had smiled quiet encouragement. "Say what you dreamed."

The child took a breath. Slowly, measuring the words, she said, "Luain-the-heron is on the boat that's coming. He brings our brothers with him."

It was an easy mistake. Graine was less than a quarter year past her third birthday. Her words were good, better than they had been in the summer, but they were no more precise than her dreaming. The difference between a brother and a father was not great either in dreaming or in language.

Airmid, standing behind, had shrugged. "She's been saying that since she first dreamed it," she said. "I promised I'd let her tell you."

"It's a kind dream, thank you." Smiling, Breaca had knelt and opened her arms. Graine came into them shyly, as if to a stranger, and they hugged, a mess of wet wool and rain-blackened hair. Manannan, god of the sea, sent a wave to wash over the jetty and their feet. Breaca stood, lifting her daughter in her arms, and kissed the top of her head. "Thank you for coming out in the rain. If you stay here with Ardacos now, he'll give you dry clothes and keep you warm, and Airmid and Sorcha and I will ride west to the coast and see who's on the boat. If Cunomar's there, we'll bring him back to you. He'll be glad to be home, and your father with him."

The child's great green-grey eyes had been solemnly wide, like an owl's. "You're not to be angry with him," she said. "The grandmother said so."

Breaca could not imagine being angry. It was enough to stand on the brink of hope, like a child on the edge of a winter torrent, not daring to step forward. For nearly three years she had known that Caradoc, Cwmfen, and the children were alive in Rome, but nothing more, until Luain mac Calma had read something in the flight of a heron and heard something else from a passing Greek trader and had taken a late ship for Gaul. Breaca stood now, braced against the wind, with the spray from the sea fierce on her face and hands, and felt her heart swell to bursting in her chest as the same vessel fought the swell of the waves to bring him home.

Sorcha stood with her, and Airmid. Both of them saw the ship now, and watched its progress. Sorcha alone knew how well it fared. The ferrywoman was their link with the sea and all that sailed on it.

"That's the *Sun Horse*," she said, "Segoventos's ship. He knows this coastline as well as I do, but the wind's too strong for him to come inshore. We should take the small boat out and meet them."

Breaca said, "Is that safe?"

Sorcha grinned. "I don't know. It's safer than if mac Calma tries to row the ship's boat in to shore, but that doesn't mean we won't drown. It's your choice. We could wait here for the wind to die down, but it could be next spring before that happens. I didn't think you'd want to wait that long."

It was good to hear someone who could still laugh. Airmid was silent, as she had been since they left the forests and came within sight of the sea. Her gaze rested on the western horizon far beyond the ship where the sun lowered itself to rest on the low mountains of Hibernia. Breaca laid a hand on her shoulder. When it was acknowledged, she asked, "Did you dream with Graine? Is that how you knew it was true?"

"No. Your daughter dreams alone now. But the ancestor-dreamer visited while we were riding; we passed over one of her resting places. She is bound to us now and we to her, whatever happens. She would have us both know that the threads of the serpent-brooch are weaving in the way that we asked for."

The wind did not lessen, but it seemed as if it did. In a bubble of quiet, Breaca said, "Sorcha, thank you for your offer. We'll take the small boat. You're right; I don't think I could wait until spring."

Waves swamped them, and the wind pushed their boat hard to the north. They rowed against both and moved at less speed than the sun in the sky. In time, sodden and shaking and sick from the swell, they came alongside the ship. Airmid jumped to catch the rope that was thrown them. Luain mac Calma raised them up, with help from Segoventos, ship's master, merchant seaman, and spy.

Airmid went first, and then Sorcha. Breaca, who had faced death in battle more times than it was possible to count, struggled to find the courage to join them; there had been a pain in not knowing, but it was bearable. Graine's words rushed at her, carried on the wind and the waves:

You're not to be angry with him. Only now, when it was too late for answers, did she think to ask with whom she might be angry and why. Feeling a nausea that had nothing to do with the sea, she wound the rope round her waist, lifted the free end, and held on.

The ship's sides were steep and slick with weed. The first pull of the rope stripped the skin from her hands and wrenched her arms. Mac Calma looped the rope on a roundel and used it to winch her ever higher. She came over the edge of the deck and was hauled in by sea-strong hands. A gaggle of strangers waited to greet her, with Airmid on their margin. Gold hair, made wet by the waves, stood out amongst darker reds and browns. Scanning them too fast, Breaca searched for known faces, and slowly they emerged: the haggard features of the children who were no longer children and had just survived four days at sea in a storm. In that first look, she saw no one adult and only one child whom she recognized.

"Cunomar?" She crouched, finding her balance on the deck, and held open her arms. As Graine had done, her son came forward stiffly, a stranger to her as she was to him. He kissed her cheek formally and held out a dagger, balancing the blade across his palms. "Father sent me with this," he said. "If you make it into a sword, I can go into battle. When we have killed all the Romans, he can come home again."

There was quiet, and a tension as if too many of those around her had held their breath for too long. Breaca searched the faces of the strangers again, fighting panic.

A tall young woman with corn-gold hair pushed forward from the group. "Father's injured. He couldn't come; the warriors wouldn't have followed him. He sent you this, with his love—" The words spilled out, like barley poured from the hand. She held out a brooch, dulled by the sea. The two-headed serpent coiled back on itself, looking to past and to future. The spear made an angled path across it, showing the many ways to go. At its base, looped in the coils of the snake, two threads hung blackly.

Breaca stood, staring and not seeing, her mind frozen on the point of knowing. Someone—Dubornos, perhaps, if Dubornos could be so thin, and so lame—said, "Breaca? He couldn't come. It was the right choice. He's alive, and he'll return when he can. He'll get word to you in the meantime. For now there is someone else you should meet."

The world descended into madness. The storm made black the afternoon sky, and the dying sun flared beneath. Westerly winds slammed ship and sea together, so that the deck heaved and bucked and simply to stand was hard enough. To stand and to understand and to believe and not to break was impossible. Airmid was holding her, one hand firm on her wrist. Luain mac Calma stood on her other side, leaning into her shoulder to keep her upright. The man who had spoken—it was Dubornos, scarred almost beyond recognition—stepped to one side so that what he had been hiding might be exposed to the sulphurous sunlight and to Breaca's sight.

She thought she was dreaming truly then, and that Luain mac Calma both stood at her side and lay on the deck-bed, greenly pale with sickness. Then she looked again, and it was Macha, grown leaner and harder and eaten alive with an anger that soured her soul. Then she looked a third time, and it was neither of these, but the eyes that stared into hers, alight with rage and fear and a desperate, aching wish to die, were quite black, resonantly so, the colour of charcoal, or a crow's wing at the shoulder, where the colour is most dense—

"Bán?"

A wave slammed at the ship, rocking it. Salt water sprayed her hair and her face, scouring the skin. Further out towards Hibernia, a single gull cried, a sound like a child or a lost soul, wandering. On the deck, nobody moved. Friends and strangers waited, watching the sea. In other worlds, a grandmother sighed, or laughed, or wept; they were all the same and all lost in the storm.

The man lying sheltered on the deck-bed smiled, wryly, as if at a private joke. Slowly, taking care for unseen injuries, he pushed himself onto one elbow. The move was consciously Roman; no man of the tribes would lean so. "Caradoc said the same, just like that." He spoke in Latin, and that, too, was deliberate. His eyes sought hers for the first time and held them. A dark irony, and pity, sparked in their depths. "You are very alike. Did you want to know that?"

She was alone, deserted by everything that made the world safe. "Are you Bán?" she asked again.

"Not any longer." The smile hung on his face, forgotten. He looked down and studied his hands. "I may have been once. More recently, I have been Julius Valerius, decurion of the first troop, First Thracian Cavalry. Now I am no one. If you need answers, ask mac Calma. This is his doing. I have no doubt he understands it better than you or I will ever do."

He brings our brothers. Graine had said so, one quarter year past her third birthday, and Breaca had dared to presume that a child's uncertain dreaming could not distinguish between one love and the other. *You are not to be angry with him.*

Think of Bán. He is the red and the black. Trust me.

She was sick. It had been a long time coming, and she had ignored it. Airmid held her, guiding her to the stern so she could lean out over the ocean and not soil the deck. Cygfa, recognizable now through the changes of age and battle and hardship, brought her rainwater and a sponge to clean her face. Breaca drank some of the water and spat it out, washing the salt and sick from her teeth. Standing, she took the bowl and emptied it over her head. The sudden deluge did not make her any wetter, that would have been impossible, but the shock brought her back to herself, cold and vividly angry.

There was no hope. There never had been; at heart she had known it. Instead, there was a world of care and killing and the refuge of anger and a man who lay on a deck-bed wearing the uniform of a Roman cavalry of-ficer. Not two days since, she had killed a decurion who wore its twin, but the dead man had not worn at his shoulder the badge of the red bull, mark of the Eceni ancestors, painted in living blood on grey.

When she let go of the face and the eyes of the enemy lying on the deck-bed, the red bull claimed all her attention. A pattern wove through other patterns and rose above them.

I have been Julius Valerius, decurion of the first troop, First Thracian Cavalry.

Hail is dead. The decurion of the Thracian cavalry killed him, the one who rides the pied horse.

I will unleash such vengeance . . .

Tightly, Breaca said, "You killed Hail."

The vestige of her brother said, "Not exactly. But it is my fault that he died."

Breaca had brought no sword, but her sling was knotted at her belt and the handful of stones rolled in her pouch. The moves to draw one and the other and join them grew from more than two years' practise and a summer of certain kills.

"No."

Luain mac Calma stopped her. The decurion—the obscene travesty of what Bán had been—would not have done. He lay still, his eyes moving from Breaca's to the space a little to her left. When mac Calma closed his fingers on Breaca's arm and the sling-stone fell to the deck, the not-Bán smiled weakly. "Your elder has an unhealthy regard for my welfare. You shouldn't let him stop you."

It was the track of his eyes that warned her, and Airmid, standing too pale and too still, just beside. Breaca had heard Macha's voice on the night of the ancestor-dreamer, but she had not seen her since she left the lands of the living. Turning, she saw her now, and the others gathered around:

the elder grandmother and, more distantly, her father. Luain mac Calma stepped carefully past them, coming to stand between Breaca and the deck-bed. The ghosts milled around him, as dogs to a hunter. Macha was foremost.

You're not to be angry. The grandmother said so.

Trust me.

Macha had been a grandmother, if only for a day, but always Bán had been her first love.

How does one display fury to a ghost? As if she were alive, Breaca said, "Did you speak to my daughter? Did you send Graine the dream?"

The ghost nodded, saying nothing. Moving slowly, she sat on the end of the deck-bed. Bán, her son, watched her, frozen, as a shrew watches a hunting snake. If he had loved her in life, he did so no longer. With visible effort, he drew his eyes back to the living, to Breaca. "They want me on Mona," he said. "Neither you nor I can live with that. You should use your sling." For the first time, he spoke in Eceni. His smile was as she remembered. Her heart was too broken for pity. She hated him no less.

Her fingers closed on another stone. Luain mac Calma did not reach for her hand, but said only, "Breaca, don't. The gods need him alive."

She shook her head. "Not on Mona. Not in my lifetime."

"But he must not die. You have to believe me in this. He must live beyond today."

"Then where? He cannot return to Rome; he has turned his back on the legions."

"I know. If you will not have him on Mona, you must say where else."

Sister and brother reached the answer together, or the ghosts guided them to it. The sun spread light on the western deck. Macha stepped into it, lost in the cold amber. Luain mac Calma joined her, a tall heron from another land. A day's sail to the west, the mountains of Hibernia rose to meet the evening.

Breaca stared at them and, turning, found her brother had seen the same. His eyes sought hers, black without end. If they carried a message, she could not read it. His lips framed the word before she spoke it so that, in the end, it seemed as if two voices sounded together.

"Hibernia," she said. "Segoventos can take him to Hibernia. If he is ever to find peace, it will be there."

AUTHOR'S NOTE

For details of this period in the Roman occupation of Britain, we are indebted almost entirely to Tacitus. Without his précis of Scapula's disarming of the eastern tribes and of the events surrounding the betrayal, capture, and pardon of Caradoc/Caratacus, this period of history would be a white fog, obscured further by random archaeological finds. Tacitus, of course, was not writing for a modern audience but for a Rome barely fifty years beyond the events he was describing. Among his primary sources were his father-in-law, Agricola, who was not present in Britannia within the period of Scapula's governorship. Others may have given personal accounts, but it is likely that a great deal of his information came from military reports from the field. As recent experience of empires at war teaches us, battlefield reports are written with their own heavily accented spin, designed to display the invader in the best light possible and the opposition in the worst. When a general reports that the enemy fought with a ferocity exceeding everything previously encountered, even now in the twenty-first century it would be fair to assume that this is an excuse for significant losses on the side of the one writing the report, very possibly compounded by some serious tactical errors. It seems to me likely that the same imputations can be read into just such a report written in the first century for an emperor not renowned for his magnanimity, where the penalty for failure was rather more permanent than a barracking by a hostile press.

Even without the inherent bias of his primary sources, it would be naïve to believe that Tacitus himself did not add his own spin; regarding the western frontier, he admits to telescoping the events of several years into a single brief narrative to make them more comprehensible, and in Rome he grants to Caradoc a monologue of commendable literacy and brevity, loaded with implications for an audience not yet born. The challenge for the modern writer of fiction is to sift through the ancient fiction for those kernels of plausible truth and then to find from them the motivations of all those involved.

In this respect, other authors are constructive. Suetonius gives us an insight into the temperaments of the various Caesars and is certainly our most authoritative ancient source who may have had an understanding of Claudius. That emperor has benefited in recent years from the rather pleasant whitewash promulgated by Robert Graves and Derek Jacobi, in which Gaius/Caligula's successor emerges as a well-meaning idiot surrounded by scheming madmen. Suetonius's account is less flattering; his Claudius is an efficient bean-counter with a heavy leaning to sadism, balanced only by an overwhelming instinct for self-preservation and a very healthy (and justified) paranoia. He was not as clearly unhinged as Caligula, but his reign lasted longer and far more of his subjects, slaves, and conquered enemies died in the palace and in the Circus than in the reign of any emperor before him. There seems to be some evidence that Nero, for all his pretensions, went some way to curb the excesses of public sadism instigated by his step-uncle.

If we believe Tacitus that Claudius did, in fact, pardon Caradoc, then the question remains as to why a man who so clearly enjoyed the slow death of his enemies chose to do so. It is possible that Caradoc simply presented one wholesome speech and so won the life of himself and his family—but not likely. The answer, I feel, lies in Claudius's overwhelming need to survive, and for this there must have been some threat, real or imagined, by which Caradoc bought his life. It may not be as I have written it, but it makes sense within the context of this fiction.

It should be remembered, above all, that this is fiction. The skeleton of known fact is very thin and disjointed, and the fantasy woven around it is designed to fill in those gaps in as compelling a way as possible. Don't take any of it as sworn fact. It won't be.

NAMES AND
THEIR PRONUNCIATION

This is a complex field, not least because we are dealing by and large with a language that no longer exists. Clearly the inhabitants of tribal Britain in the first century A.D. did not speak English in any form—that came later, with the Anglo-Saxon invasions of the Dark Ages. Instead, two forms of early Gaelic were spoken: In the early fourth century B.C., "q-Celtic" spread from Ireland to the Isle of Man and Scotland, evolving into the Gaelic of today. The other form, "p-Celtic," was spoken in the south and east and gave rise over time to the Brythonic languages of Welsh, Cornish, and Breton.

Some characters of Boudica's time had names already in place and it was simply a question of choosing which form to use. As for the fictional characters, there are records of Gaulish names and it is therefore possible to choose those consistent with the period. However, for ease of reading in the modern world, I have incorporated some contemporary Welsh and Irish names as well.

The names below are spelled phonetically, the sound correspondences for the vowel sounds followed by an approximation of how to pronounce each name. In each case, there is equal stress on all syllables.

TRIBAL CHARACTERS

Breaca: \brā-a-kə\. \brā\ = the *a* of "prey"; \a\ = the *a* of "mat"; \kə\ = the *u* of "cut." Bray-a-ku.

Bán: \bän\. \bän\ = the *a* of "farther." Ban.

Macha: \ma-kə\. \ma\ = the *a* of "mat"; \kə\ = the *u* of "cut." Maku.

Eburovic: \i-bŭr-ə-vik\. \i\ = the *i* of "tip"; \bŭr\ = the *oo* of "wood"; \ə\ = the *u* of "cut"; \vik\ = the *i* of "victim." I-boor-u-vik.

Dubornos: \düb-ər-nəs\. \düb\ = the *u* of "flu"; \ər\ = the *u* of "cut"; \nəs\ = the *u* of "cut." Doo-bur-nus.

Cunobelin: \kün-ô-bel-in\. \kün\ = the *u* of "flu"; \ô\ = the *aw* of "law"; \bəl\ = the *u* of "cut"; \in\ = the *i* of "tip." Koon-aw-bul-in.

Togodubnos: \tō-gə-dəb-nəs\. \tō\ = the *o* of "toga"; \gə\ = the *u* of "cut"; \dəb\ = the *u* of "cut"; \nəs\ = the *u* of "cut." Toe-gu-dub-nus.

Amminios: \a-min-ē-əs\. \a\ = the *a* of "mat"; \min\ = the *i* of "tip"; \ē\ = the *e* of "me"; \əs\ = the *u* of "cut." A-min-ee-us.

Efnís: \ef-nēsh\. \ef\ = the *ef* of "effervescent"; \nēsh\ = the *e* of "me" and the \sh\ of "shy." Ef-neesh.

Iccius: \i-kē-əs\. \i\ = the *i* of "tip"; \kē\ = the *e* of "me"; \əs\ = the *u* of "cut." I-kee-us.

Ardacos: \ar-dak-əs\. \ar\ = the *a* of "mat"; \dak\ = the *a* of "mat"; \əs\ = the *u* of "us." Ar-dack-us.

Gwyddhien: \gwith-ē-ən\. \gwith\ = the *gw* of "Gwynneth"; \i\ = the *i* of "pith"; \th\ = the *th* of "thin"; \ē\ = the *e* of "me"; \ən\ = the *u* of "cut." Gwith-ee-un

Cunomar: \kün-ô-mär\. \kün\ = the *u* of "flu"; \ô\ = the *aw* of "law"; \mär\ = the *a* of "farther." Koon-aw-mar.

Cwmfen: \küm-vən\. \küm\ = the *u* of "flu"; \vən\ = the *e* of "kitten." Koom-ven.

Cygfa: \sig-və\. \sig\ = the *i* of "tip"; \və\ = the *u* of "cut." Sig-va.

Luain mac Calma: \ləw-ān mak kälmə\. \ləw\ = the *u* of "cut"; \ān\ = the *a* of "fade"; \mak\ = the *a* of "mat"; \käl\ = the *a* of "farther"; \mə\ = the *u* of "cut." Luw-ain mak kalma.

ROMAN CHARACTERS

Latin is rather closer to our language, although we would pronounce the letter "J" as equivalent to the current "Y," "V" would be "W," and "C" would be a hard "K" in all cases. However, this is so rarely used that it is simpler to retain the standard modern pronunciation of these letters.

BIBLIOGRAPHY

In addition to those books mentioned in the first volume, the following were particularly useful:

Claus, M., *The Roman Cult of Mithras*, trans. Richard Gordon (Edinburgh University Press, 2000).

Cunliffe, Barry, ed., *Rome* (Oxford Archaeological Guides, Oxford University Press, 1998).

Farvo, D., *The Urban Image of Augustan Rome* (Cambridge University Press, 1996).

Holder, P. A., *The Roman Army in Britain* (B. T. Batsford, 1982).

Holland, R., *Nero, The Man Behind the Myth* (Sutton Publishing, 2000).

Linderman, Frank B., *Pretty-Shield, The Story of a Crow Medicine Woman* (University of Nebraska Press, 1932).

Paolis, U. E., *Rome, Its People, Life and Customs* (Longman Group, 1958).

Suetonius, *The Lives of the Twelve Caesars*, ed. Tom Griffith (Wordsworth Editions Ltd, 1977).

Tacitus, *The Complete Works* (Modern Library College Editions, Random House, 1942).

White, M. A., *SPQR, The History and Social Life of Ancient Rome* (Macmillan, 1965).

ABOUT THE AUTHOR

MANDA SCOTT is a veterinary surgeon, writer, and climber, not necessarily in that order. Born and educated in Scotland, she now lives in Suffolk with two lurchers and too many cats. She is known primarily as a crime writer, and her first novel, *Hen's Teeth*, was shortlisted for the Orange Prize. Her subsequent crime novels are *Night Mares, Stronger than Death*, and *No Good Deed*, which was nominated for an Edgar Award for Best Novel. Her acclaimed first novel in the Boudica quartet, *Boudica: Dreaming the Eagle*, is available in paperback from Dell, and she is currently at work on the third novel in the Boudica saga, *Boudica: Dreaming the Hound*.

If you were swept into Manda Scott's world in
BOUDICA: DREAMING THE BULL, you won't
want to miss the first mesmerizing novel in the
Boudica quartet: BOUDICA: DREAMING THE
EAGLE. Look for it at your favorite bookseller's.

And read on for a tantalizing early look at the
third book in the series, BOUDICA: DREAMING
THE HOUND, coming soon from Dell.

BOUDICA:
DREAMING
THE
HOUND

Manda Scott

Boudica: Dreaming the Hound
Coming soon from Dell

Listen to me, I am Luain mac Calma, heron-dreamer, once of Hibernia, now Elder of Mona, adviser and friend of Breaca, who is the Boudica, Bringer of Victory. We are in a time of great peril; if you do not understand the past, you cannot come to understand the present and without it, the tribes of Britannia have no future. Here, tonight, by the fire, you will learn what has come before. This is who we were; if we win now, this is who we could be again.

It is fourteen years since the Emperor Claudius sent his legions to invade our land. Then, we were a diverse peoples, of many tribes and many gods, united only in our care of our dreamers; the men and women who came here, to the gods' island of Mona, to study for a dozen years in the great-house under the elders. Warriors, too, came to learn the arts of honour and courage that might lead later to acts of heroism in battle. We fought against each other, for show, and thought each skirmish a mighty battle.

Then Rome came, with its legions and cavalry. The men of Rome do not fight for honour or to hear their names sung in the hero-tales at winter. They fight for victory, and when they have made a land their own, they do not leave it.

The tales of how we fought have been told in other places; the battle of the invasion lasted two days and will be told forever round the fires. A thousand heroes lost their lives and those few who emerged alive did so through the sacrifices of others. It was then that Breaca, once of the Eceni, then Warrior of Mona, led the charge to rescue Caradoc and earned the name by which we know her: Boudica, Bringer of Victory.

Breaca and Caradoc were amongst those who, on the orders of their elders, left the battle-field. They did so with reluctance, fleeing only to continue the war against Rome, and to protect the children, who are precious above all else. They brought them here, to the gods' isle of Mona, where warriors and water hold safe all that is most sacred; where dreamers, singers and warriors of many tribes come to know themselves in the full gaze of the gods, that they may take that knowledge, and the wisdom it brings, back to their people.

From here, they fought for ten years, preventing the Roman legions from gaining any foothold in the west. Thus the Romans built their first fortress in the east at Camulodunum, which had been the stronghold of Caradoc's people.

In the early years of the occupation, thousands of warriors and dreamers died in the east; whole villages were slaughtered in reprisals for rebellions, real or imagined, and it was declared illegal for any man, woman or child to bear a weapon.

The legionaries who broke the swords of our warriors were led by an officer, Julius Valerius, who rode a pied horse. More than anyone else he was hated, for he had been Eceni once, and had sold his soul to Rome and its gods. He fought for Mithras and for the Emperor and both thrived on Eceni blood.

Breaca and Caradoc had a son, Cunomar, and then a daughter, Graine. Shortly after her birth, Caradoc was taken captive by treachery and made prisoner in Rome. Captured with him were his son, Cunomar, and his elder daughter, Cygfa, a warrior of high renown.

The family were taken to Rome, to die at the whim of the Emperor Claudius, only that Airmid, the dreamer who is the other half of Breaca's soul, found a way to bargain with the oldest and most dangerous of the ancestors and was able to prevent their death and, much later, to bring about their freedom.

Caradoc was tortured and maimed beyond repair. He was well enough to bring his family to the coast of Gaul, but not to go beyond it. He could not have returned as a warrior to Mona—his injuries were too great for him to wield a weapon as he had done with such success before his capture and he would not inflict on his warriors the pain of seeing him brought low by Rome. Thus he stayed in Gaul and word was sent that he gave his life to save his children as they boarded the ship that would bring them back to Mona.

That was three years ago. Breaca mourns Caradoc, but inwardly. Outwardly, she has given herself heart and soul to the battle against Rome. In summer, she leads the warriors of Mona to keep the legions from reaching our island, and to push them back as far as she can from the mountains of the west. Through winter, she hunts alone, taking men singly or in pairs and they have come to fear her, as if she were a spirit of the mountains who feeds on their souls.

One other returned on the ship from Gaul, who was not expected; Julius Valerius, the once-Eceni cavalry officer who had led the oppression of his people. By the will of the gods, he was called back to Rome by the ailing Claudius to undertake a final duty; to escort Caradoc's family to the Gaulish coast and thence to a ship that might take them to freedom.

Claudius died before the family could reach freedom and Nero, his successor, required that they be returned. Valerius could not go against an oath sworn in the name of his god, and thus was named traitor, and forced to flee.

I would have brought him to Mona, for reasons that are not only my own, but Breaca forbade it and she is not only the Boudica, whose word holds sway with the warriors, she is also Breaca of the Eceni, sister to the man who was once Bán and became Valerius, an officer of the legions.

These, then, are the ones who have fashioned our pasts: Breaca, who hunts legionaries in the mountains of western Britannia, and her brother Valerius, who is in exile in Hibernia, where he drags out a living as a smith. Neither can continue at this forever. The world changes and they must change with it, or die.

Meanwhile, the children, and the dreamers, wait on Mona, watching a world that grows more brutal by the year. Rome seeks revenue from its provinces, and Britannia is not the rich vein of silver and gold that Claudius believed it to be. Nero was made Emperor in his place and Nero is ruled in turn by his advisers. These are men without pity, for whom a land and its people mean nothing, unless they have gold or can be made to yield it.

This is the future we fear and against which we fight. Mona is safe now, under the care of the gods, but if it is the gods' will that it be no longer safe, then all that is sacred will continue in the hearts and minds of those who hold the lineage of the ancestors. We are those people, you and I. Dream now, and know that in the dreaming is your future and all that we believe to be true.

Autumn AD 57

Prologue

Marcus Publius Vindex, standard bearer of the second century, third cohort of the Twentieth legion, stationed on the far western frontier of Britannia, drank wine sparingly when on winter foraging duties and never took
unnecessary risks. When the late-night need to urinate became overpowering, he stepped away from the watch fire only for a moment and told his
armourer where he was going and why. Passing between the tents, he whistled the tune of the ninth invocation of Jupiter as evidence that he was still
alive.

At the margins of the firelight, where the rain became silver and the
sound of it hammering on the tent hides was too loud for his tune to be
heard, Vindex called out to the armourer and was answered. The stream of
his urine cascading on rocks made a good counterpoint to the rain. There
was a cold satisfaction in pissing on the base of the mountain; for as long
as the sound of it lasted, he was solid in his victory over the weather, the
sucking mud, the lack of game and of corn and, best, over the native warriors who grew out of the dark and left the unwary dead to be found in
daylight. He shouted as much to his armourer, slurring only slightly.

The last word had barely crossed to the fires when a hand caught his
chin and dragged his head back and up. He did not feel the slice of the
knife across his throat, the blade was too sharp to create pain, but it cut
down to the bones of his spine, severing the soft tissues in its path. The
tidal wave of his life surged out to earth.

The standard bearer died surprised, and his ghost, surprised, did not
know itself dead, only that the night grew suddenly bright, as if noon had
come, and that, impossibly, where once had been fire-warped shadows, now
one of the native warriors knelt in plain view by the fallen body of a man
carving a curse mark on the forehead.

Vindex had lived through too many battles to waste time in questioning the impossible. His sword had already stabbed at the exposed neck of the enemy before he had thought to question the identity of the corpse lying so close to his feet. As his body lunged after, he gave all his breath to a shout that would rouse the entire camp.

His sword, his arm, and the full weight of his weightless body passed through the crouching warrior. His shout, which could cross a battlefield, raised no armoured men to his aid although a decurion of the cavalry, drinking wine by the fire, pulled his cloak tighter and stamped his feet, cursing the sudden cold.

Vindex opened his mouth to shout again and then stopped as the part of him that reasoned noticed at last that the men of his watch had not noticed him at all.

"They can't hear you. Your people choose not to hear the cries of the slain. It's your strength and your greatest weakness. You'll never live safely until you learn to listen to your ancestors and your newly dead."

The voice that filled Vindex' head had a different quality to those of the men he had left at the fire; it spoke to his soul, not his ears. The enemy warrior finished carving the curse mark and, rising, turned round.

Thus, for the first time, in the darkest part of the night, with no sun and rain clouds covering the moon, the standard bearer of the Twentieth saw the face of his enemy. He saw rain-damp hair the colour of a fox in winter with the warrior's braids left loose in mourning and the single crow's pinion woven in at the left with the quill dyed entirely black, for one who has severed all connections to family and tribe to hunt alone; and thereby perhaps to die alone. He saw the blood-wet knife, recently used, saw the sling hanging at the belt beside the pouch of river pebbles and knew with a soul-knowing beyond vision that each stone was painted black, that they might more surely kill those against whom they were sent. He saw the sign of the serpent-spear carved on the brow of the body—his body—and, because he had seen the same mark on the brows of other men eight times in the last three days, its meaning was already carved on his liver.

By the cumulation of these, finally, Marcus Publius Vindex, son of Gaius Publius Vindex, knew the identity of the woman who had killed him and thus came to understand that he was dead.

Feeling foolish, he lowered his sword. From the fireside, the armourer shouted a new question with an edge of concern in his voice. The silence which, living, the standard bearer should have filled, stretched too long.

The Boudica rose slowly, sheathing her belt-knife. "Whom do you worship?" she asked. Her mouth did not move but the words became part of the night.

In the same way, Vindex answered, "Jupiter, god of the legions, and Mars Ultor, for victory." Then, appraising, "You should leave. They'll come soon to look for me. You cannot stand against so many and live." The quality of his care surprised him. Dead, he discovered that he harboured neither the hatred nor the terror he had in life.

"Thank you. I'll go when I have to. Your men have not yet lit a torch and I have never yet met a Roman who could see well in the rain."

She grinned and Vindex read no fear in her eyes, only the exhilaration of battle, beginning to wane. He had known that feeling, and the boundless peace that followed it, and knew that it was for these he had fought, far more than the silver he had been paid, and that he was not alone.

Moved by his new compassion, he said, "You will never win, fighting as one against many."

Amused, the Boudica raised a brow. "I have heard that before. Not everyone who says it is Roman, but most have been, and all of those were dead."

"Then you should listen to us. We bear you no ill, but can see some things more clearly." It was true; the concerns of his life were melting away, leaving behind a clarity Vindex had sought throughout his life and never found. "I offer you this as a gift, from death to life: if you do not rouse the east of the province to battle, the legions will win and Rome will bleed your people dry."

The Boudica finished wiping her hands on the turf. She nodded, thoughtfully. "Thank you. I will consider your gift in the morning, if I am alive to do so." She was no longer smiling, but she did not hate him, either. "You should go home," she said. "Your gods will know you in Rome. They cannot reach you here."

The armourer shouted a second time, and was not answered. A legionary emerged from the safety of the tent-lines and his terror at the sight of the body was far greater than Vindex' had been. His cry brought the armourer and he, finally, called for torches. Men ran as they had been trained and if the space behind the tents did not blaze for them as light as noon, it was enough for the fox-haired warrior to be seen.

She did run then, fluidly and with no great urgency, like a deer that has not yet heard the hounds. The armourer of the second century was a clear-thinking man who abstained entirely from wine. He had also, for three years, been his cohort's champion spear thrower; honoured for the speed and accuracy of his casts. He called afresh and five men ran to bring him spears, passing each one new to his palm as the last took flight. Ten were thrown in the space of a dozen strides. The foremost of the torch-bearers saw the eighth one strike and shouted to the armourer and to Mars Ultor, claiming a kill. Vindex, seeing with different eyes, knew that the Boudica was wounded, but had not joined him in death.

From beyond the margins of the camp, her voice filled his head. She sounded breathless and disjointed and he was unable to tell if it was pain that afflicted her, or an overwhelming need to laugh.

"Go home," she said again. "The journey to Rome is faster in death, I promise you, and the land is warmer. Why stay here in the rain, where you're not welcome? The legion no longer owns you when you're dead. You can go where you want."

The thought had occurred to Vindex more than once in life. In death, joyfully, he understood himself free. Passing through the walls of the officers' tent and the insubstantial matter of his centurion, he began the not-so-long journey back to Rome.

At the place where he had been, three more men of his watch died in a hail of black-painted river pebbles. The armourer was the last of them.

Chapter One

The water was cold and made brown by peat and recent rain.

Breaca of Mona, known to all but her family and closest friends as the Boudica, leader of armies and bringer of victory, knelt alone at the side of a mountain stream and washed her face, hands and the bleeding wound on her upper arm in the torrent. The water ran briefly pink where she had been. She cupped clean water in both palms, rinsed her mouth and spat out the iron after-taste of blood.

A blue roan mare dozed in the shelter of a nearby beech thicket, the end result of a lifetime's breeding and better than anything Rome could offer. She was haltered, but not tethered and came to call, her feet bound in soft leather to soften the sound of her progress. Mounted, Breaca travelled north and a little east, moving up into the mountains, keeping to rocky trails where Coritani trackers, paid by Rome, would be least likely to find signs of her passing.

If she had scaled the peaks, she could have looked west past further mountains and across the straits to Mona, but did not. The standard bearer's warning echoed, disturbingly, with the muted footfalls of her mare and would not be made silent. *You will never win, fighting as one against many.* Vindex was not the first to have warned her of the dangers and futility of fighting alone, or even the second, but he was the enemy and she did not have to trust his opinion.

It was harder to ignore the warnings of those who cared for her; the elders and dreamers of Mona, who watched over her children through her long winter absences, and could not tell them where their mother was or if she had died yet, at the hand of a standard bearer who was not quite as drunk as he might have looked.

Luain mac Calma, the Elder of Mona, had been first, quietly, to say that the Boudica's life was worth more, and vengeance for one man's life worth less, and he had been followed by a succession of others who claimed to love her and hold her best interests at heart.

Only Airmid, dreamer and soul-friend, had always understood why Breaca needed to hunt alone as she did and had never spoken out, openly or in private, against the black feather braided into the Boudica's hair and the winter killings that it foreshadowed.

Airmid was on Mona and Mona was another world and Breaca chose not to look at it and thereby not to think about it, or its people.

She passed upwards, and the track became rockier. Grey stone lined either side of the tracks, marbled by swirling lichens. She dismounted after a while and unbound the mare's feet, that it might grip better on the wet stones. The rain became less; it had belonged to the night. Clouds on the eastern horizon parted to show the first knife lines of light. Lacking any binding, the wound in her arm slowly ceased to bleed and ached only a little. The officer whose spear had caught her had kept his weapons scrupulously clean, for which she was grateful.

Half a day's ride to the south, at the overnight campsite where a standard bearer, an armourer and two junior officers of the Twentieth legion had died, a wisp of greased smoke rose at an angle to the sky. Crows roused and called and began to drift towards the scent of burning men.

The thick-set grey-haired man stooped over the neck of his horse with his attention fixed on the trail did not appear to notice either of the two sling stones that cracked on the rocks near his head. His horse, noticing both, shied a little, throwing him off balance, and he clutched ineffectually at the saddle. The care of his gods kept his head from cracking on the stones of the path as he fell, and a cushion of heather gave him safe landing but he did not rise afterwards, even as Breaca knelt at his side.

"Where are you hurt?"

He flicked dry, cracked lips. "I have the flux. You shouldn't touch me, you'll be tainted."

"Maybe, but the harm is done now." Breaca pushed her good arm under his shoulders and levered him to his feet. She would have given him water but carried none. In its absence, she used the sick man's horse for support, wedging his shoulder against the saddle. He swayed and made himself stand.

His accent, his horse and the weave on his tunic were all of the northern Eceni. A mark worked in ink in the skin below his collarbone showed the falcon and running horse linked. Breaca ran her forefinger along from horse to falcon and felt the small nodule of amber buried under the skin beyond the falcon's wingtip that verified its authenticity.

"Are you from Efnís?" she asked, and when he nodded, "Why were you following me?"

"I wasn't. The mountains are alive with Romans and I would deliver my message from a living mouth to living ears if the flux does not kill me first. I was seeking shelter in the forests near the coast."

Breaca shook her head. "You won't reach them in time. The men of the fifth cohort are stationed near the coast. The third cohort lost four men last night; the signal fires have been lit since dawn, waking every other legionary into action; they will have ringed the forests long since. I know of somewhere closer that may be safe if we are permitted to enter. Can you ride another two dozen spear throws?"

"If there's shelter at the end of it, yes."

The cave mouth was a vertical crease in the cliff face set by the gods at such an angle that it was invisible unless approached exactly from the southeast. The hound-sized rock placed by the ancestors to guard the entrance was patched with damp moss and hidden by the grasses that had grown up around it. In years past, it would have been scoured clean when the ancestors were honoured at each old moon and the carved marks swirling on its surface would have been made bold again with red ochre and white lime and ash. In the bleak new world of Roman occupation, those who should have done so were either dead or had taken refuge on Mona and the rock and the cave mouth behind it were blurred with neglect.

Breaca had passed the cave only once, and that the previous winter, but had seen then what others might not, committing its location to memory without any real intention to use it. She probably would not have attempted it now, had her need not driven her to it; the risks of entering such a place without a dreamer were far greater than the risks of death or capture by Rome.

Standing alone before the hound stone, Breaca said, "I offer greetings to the oldest and greatest of the ancestor-dreamers. I will clear your dwelling place as I leave, I swear it. For now, the weeds are my protection as they have been yours. Will you permit me to enter and to bring one other with me?"

A voice beyond the range of hearing said, *"Who asks?"*

Formally, she said, "I ask, Breaca nic Graine mac Eburovic, once of the Eceni, once Warrior of Mona, hunting now under the black feather of no tribe. My mark is the serpent spear which was yours before me and will be yours again when I have gone."

The ancestor dreamer said, *"So. I endure and you may not. It is good you remember that. Have you come to ask my aid in your vengeance, as you did before?"*

"No."

She was the Boudica, who led thousands into battle and her palms were sweating. She wiped them now on her tunic. It was far easier to face the legions in the rain and the dark armed with nothing more than a knife and a pouch of river pebbles than to speak to an empty cave mouth in daylight. She remembered Airmid, and the fear in her voice when she had last faced the ancestor dreamer: Airmid, who feared nothing and no-one.

Breaca looked back down the path to where the dying messenger waited out of earshot. He had dismounted when she did and stood leaning against his horse. As she watched, he slid slowly to his knees, and then toppled sideways to lie curled like a child, breathing harshly.

If she had been alone, she would have taken her chances dodging the legions and stayed out in the open. If she waited, she would be alone before too long, but the dying man was Eceni and from Efnís and he had given his life to bring a message to Mona. She could not with any honour leave him to die on a mountain path within reach of the legions when there was shelter at hand.

Touching the hound-stone as much for courage as luck, Breaca said, "We are two, one wounded, one assailed by flux. We ask only to enter into your protection, bringing our horses, nothing more. The Romans who seek our lives are close behind; I saw them enter the valley as we climbed the mountain. It is my belief that their trackers will have no knowledge of your dwelling place, and that if they did, the legionaries would not dare to cross the threshold. Even they recognise the sacred when they meet it."

"*Or if not the sacred, then the simply dangerous.*" The ancestor's laughter was the slide of snake over winter leaves, a sound to erase all peace and the hope of peace. "*They know I will pierce their dreams, waking and sleeping and they will die as did their governor, slowly and in madness. They may not fear you enough to abandon the land, Breaca once-Eceni, but they fear me enough to make offerings in secret to quell my wrath.*"

Breaca had seen the twists of corn and broken wine flasks and once, the rotting head of a doe as she led the horses up the trail. She had not known them as offerings to the serpent-dreamer and even now could not confirm it. She said nothing. A lifebeat of waiting passed. Then, "*Yes, you may enter. I, who may yet destroy you, give you leave.*"

The cave was not as fully dark as Breaca had expected. The horses walked willingly into the entrance and were made safe in a chamber open to the sky, three spear-lengths inside. Here, bird lime streaked the walls in layers of white and caked the floor, cushioning the sound of hooves. Hollows in the rock held water and the recent rain had made them clean.

Further in, the sky could not be so clearly seen, but grey light leaked for a while from the towered heights of the roof. On the floor, the skeletons of small beasts cracked underfoot where they had fallen, unwilling sacrifices to the ancestor and the gods. The walls pressed inwards so that the pathway became a tunnel and rock snagged Breaca's tunic at both shoulders.

"We should stop." The Eceni messenger could barely walk. He tugged on Breaca's sleeve.

"Not yet. There's a turn ahead and then the floor opens into a chamber with a river running through. We can rest there and you can drink the water. You need it."

He held on to her, staring. In the failing light, she could see the widening whites of his eyes. "Have you been here before?" he asked.

"No, but I know of it." She did not tell him that the serpent voice of the ancestor-dreamer drew her on, whispering, nor that it had spelled out the time and manner of his death.

The chamber they entered last was too broad for Breaca easily to map the margins, and entirely without light. Working by feel, she laid and lit a small fire. Orange shadows drew monsters from the dark, casting ghost-flames on the small river flowing through the northern corner of the cave. Echoes of water thickened the silence. The sound was pleasanter by far than the sibilant hiss of the ancestor.

At the river's edge, Breaca tended the dying messenger. She folded her cloak and his and laid him on both on a bed of flat rock. He had brought his own water skin, long empty, and she filled it and let him drink and then washed his face, neck and hands with what was left.

"You should not," he said, less certainly than before. "We were three; two brothers and a sister, each charged with the same message. We had ridden only two nights when the flux took us. It passes from one to the other faster than a cough in a winter's roundhouse."

Breaca said, "If I am to die, this place is as good as any; the legion's inquisitors won't find us here to wrench what we know from the last breath of our lungs. If I am to live, then you can rest tended in safety. What happened to your brother and sister?"

"I don't know. We took separate roads when we met the legions. Each of us was to ride for Mona. With three, there was hope one would live to reach the ferry and deliver our words."

"Ask him his message." The ancestor's voice cracked off the walls. In her own place, she sounded far louder than the dying man.

"When he has peace." Breaca spoke aloud and the messenger was too near death to notice.

She had tended the dying times without number on the battlefield, but only rarely with other sickness, so that it took some time to do what was needful. She bent over him, trying to see past the tallow-grey skin to the life and the mind beneath. His face shrank onto the bones of his skull. His eyes had fallen deep into the folding flesh of his face and his hair was slick with sweat and the water with which he had just been washed.

Ask!

Touching her palm to his forehead, she said carefully, "This is your resting place. Briga will take you from here and the ancestor will guide you safely to the lands beyond life. I will return to Mona when it's safe to travel. Is it your wish that I carry your message with me?"

"It would be, but I can't give it while not yet on Mona." The man grimaced, trying to rise, and failed. "I'm sorry. It would kill both of us if I tried. Efnís laid a geas on all three messengers. If I tried to speak, my tongue would swell in my mouth and block my breathing before the words were out. More, the one to whom I spoke would die, if not as suddenly, then as surely. If caught, we were permitted to say that much to whoever tried to press the question."

Breaca smoothed the hair from his brow and poured on a little water to cool it. "Efnís is wise. If you had been captured, it would have been good to die swiftly, knowing your message safe and Rome's interrogators condemned to a slow end."

The man struggled with that, frowning. "But not so good now when I am dying in the company of a warrior and friend. I will take my message safely into death and Efnís will never know of my failure."

"He will. No-one passes to the other worlds but the dreamers know of it. Even so, I may have an answer. Would I be right to believe that your message was to be given to the Elder of Mona, Luain mac Calma, or, failing him, to Airmid of Nemain, and that it concerned the Boudica?"

It was a risk. Neither of them knew the margins of the curse. The messenger smiled faintly and tested his answer silently twice before, nodding, he said, "You would be correct."

They both waited. In the moments that followed, his breathing was not impaired, nor did his tongue swell any more than the flux had already swollen it.

Breaca let out a breath. "So then if I were to tell you that my daughter, second child of my heart, soul and flesh, is called Graine after my mother and that my father was Eburovic, smith and warrior of the Eceni, would your mouth remain unblocked and your tongue unswollen as you delivered to me your message?"

His eyes had fallen shut and did not open when she finished. Waiting, Breaca did not know if he slept, or if the shock of her identity, however obliquely revealed, had carried him beyond speech.

The relief when he reached out and gripped her hand left her without words. He opened his eyes and tears wavered on rims, cast in copper by the firelight. His voice was a fine thread, drawn tight by pain and effort. "You are the Boudica? The Warrior of Mona?"

She nodded, smiling. "Yes."

He shoved himself upright, wheezing. "Why then are you here, unbraided, wearing the black feather of no-tribe and hunting alone in lands held by Rome?"

She had not expected his anger, nor the sudden energy it gave him; he knew nothing of the soul-stripping meetings between the Boudica and the dreamers she served, of the battles fought amongst friends with words the only weapons. He did not choose to hide the accusation in his voice or the hurt in his eyes. He laid himself down again, but his gaze, stripping hers, could have been mac Calma's, or Dubornos', or Ardacos', or any one of her children.

Rising, Breaca laid a fistful of heather roots on the fire. Fresh flames sparked green and a violent blue where the earth burned before wood. Staring at the colours and not the man, she said, "I have been killing Romans, as you saw. The four dead of the third cohort were my kills, and two the night before last."

The messenger was an intelligent man. Watching her, he said, "So you hunt alone because the risk is too great to expose others to the danger and Briga will take you into death when she feels the killing is enough. Do the elder dreamers of Mona consider that a good risk?"

"Not at all." Breaca smiled, surprising them both. "But it is not for them to forbid it. My life is my own and I believe it is a good risk. It's nearly winter; the time for fighting is over but the legions must still forage far beyond their forts for food and firewood. There's more damage done to their minds with four men dead in the night than forty dead on the battlefield in open warfare. Each death leads to desertions and those left behind dream of a time when they can leave and sail for Rome. An army that comes to the field without heart fights to lose, you know that."

"I do. And a people lacking the leadership of the gods does not fight at all." An old anger flickered, and a more recent fear. Each died away, leaving only the fatal weariness that had cloaked the messenger when he first fell from his horse.

Carefully, Breaca said, "The Eceni do not lack leadership."

"They do now."

He was dying fast, both of them could feel it. Words unspoken weighed on them, sucking breath from the air. Choosing the path that offered least damage, Breaca asked, "Can you tell me in what way your people and mine are leaderless?"

"I don't know if I can tell you this without killing us both."

He gathered himself and then, against her protests, pushed himself to sitting. His gaze devoured her face and then moved down to the reddening wound on her arm. The spear's head had not, after all, been so clean. Blood seeped a little from the gash, but the arm around was angry and hot and had begun to throb alarmingly. He reached out to touch it and they both felt the flesh twitch under his fingers.

He said, "Perhaps Efnís was wiser than either of us knew and you are dying anyway."

Breaca sluiced water over the wound. "Perhaps. I have felt closer to death than this, but they say Briga often comes when least expected."

"Not for me." He smiled and the shape stayed on his lips long after his mind had gone elsewhere. In a while, he said, "Efnís' crafted his words for Airmid, dreamer of Nemain, but the tales have always said that she holds one half of your soul and Caradoc the other. If that is true, then it may be that, in the gods' eyes, I am speaking as if to Airmid and I can speak to you safely. I am willing to try, but my death is certain, I have nothing to lose. You could have many more winters of hunting Romans alone. Will you risk the loss of that, to hear my message?"

Breaca closed her left fist, feeling the brush of pain in her palm that was the memory of a sword cut. It did not ache to warn her of danger. The spear wound in her upper arm throbbed alarmingly, but other wounds had been as deep and gone as bad and she had not died of them.

She looked across the fire into the darkness of the cave but found no help there; the ancestor-dreamer was uncharacteristically silent. As at all the most important decisions in her life, Breaca was alone. There was a freedom in being so.

She said, "There is not so much pleasure in killing Romans that I would want to miss a message from Efnís that has cost the lives of three warriors. Yes, I will share your risk."